SHADOW AT EVENING

Further Titles by Max Marlow

ARCTIC PERIL
GROWTH
HER NAME WILL BE FAITH
MELTDOWN
THE RED DEATH
WHERE THE RIVER RISES

SHADOW AT EVENING

Max Marlow

This first world edition published in Great Britain 1994 by
SEVERN HOUSE PUBLISHERS LTD of
9–15 High Street, Sutton, Surrey SM1 1DF.
First published in the USA 1995 by
SEVERN HOUSE PUBLISHERS INC., of
425 Park Avenue, New York, NY 10022.

Copyright © Max Marlow 1994

All rights reserved.
The moral rights of the author have been asserted.

British Library Cataloguing in Publication Data
Marlow, Max
 Shadow at Evening
 I. Title
 823.914 [F]

ISBN 0-7278-4699-X

This is a novel. The events and characters are invented and
are not intended to portray actual persons, nor has the
incident described yet taken place.

All situations in this publication are fictitious and
any resemblance to living persons is purely coincidental.

Typeset by Hewer Text Composition Services, Edinburgh.
Printed and bound in Great Britain by
Hartnolls Ltd, Bodmin, Cornwall.

". . . I will show you something different from either
Your shadow at morning striding behind you,
Or your shadow at evening rising to meet you:
I will show you fear in a handful of dust."

The Waste Land,
The Burial of the Dead.
TS Eliot.

CONTENTS

PROLOGUE	1
THE FOLLOWING YEAR	23
Chapter 1 Tuesday, 6th July	25
Chapter 2 Wednesday, 7th July	37
Chapter 3 Friday, 8th July	49
Chapter 4 Saturday, 9th July	52
Chapter 5 Sunday, 10th July	57
Chapter 6 Monday, 11th July	63
Chapter 7 Tuesday, 12th July	69
Chapter 8 Wednesday, 13th July	77
Chapter 9 Thursday, 14th July	81
Chapter 10 Thursday, 14th July (continued)	85
Chapter 11 Friday, 15th July	108
Chapter 12 Thursday, 21st July	121
Chapter 13 Friday, 22nd July	124
Chapter 14 Friday, 22nd July–Midnight	140
Chapter 15 Saturday, 23rd July–pre-dawn	146
Chapter 16 Saturday, 23rd July–morning	160
Chapter 17 Saturday, 23rd July–morning (continued)	172
Chapter 18 Saturday, 23rd July–noon	180
Chapter 19 Saturday, 23rd July–afternoon	191
Chapter 20 Sunday, 24th July–pre-dawn	206
Chapter 21 Sunday, 24th July–morning	208
Chapter 22 Sunday, 24th July–noon	239
Chapter 23 Sunday, 24th July–evening	262
Chapter 24 Monday, 25th July–pre-dawn	278
Chapter 25 Monday, 25th July–dawn	289
Chapter 26 Monday, 25th July–morning	307
Chapter 27 Monday, 25th July–mid-morning	326
Chapter 28 Aftermath	332
EPILOGUE	343

PROLOGUE

A white Volvo Estate bounced over the rough track into the car-park, two excited dogs dancing in the back eager to leap out at the familiar scenting spots. As Liz Cobb released the catch the driving door was almost torn off its hinges by the Force Eight wind. As she opened the tailgate for the dogs, her anorak was flattened against her body and her hair and scarf ends whipped against her face, stinging. Torn, puffy clouds hurtled across an intensely blue sky and L'Ancresse Bay, at the north end of the Channel Island of Guernsey, was full of huge breakers which burst against the rocks sending tons of white water cascading over the distant Pembroke headland. Spume-topped rollers rushed towards her to pound the rocky outcrops beneath the old Buttes, and to hurl themselves up the shore below the car-park before drawing, dragging, rolling thousands of pebbles, each weighing several kilos, down to the seabed. Liz grinned to herself, exhilarated, stimulated by the boisterous Equinoctial gale, and by the comfortable familiarity of it all. She was on home territory; born here in Guernsey, she and her brother, Pierre, had grown up at L'Ancresse, on the common and the beach. They knew every rocky outcrop, the most interesting remains of German World War II fortifications – when the Channel Islands had been the only part of the British Isles to be occupied by the Nazis – the best rocks for fishing on a flowing tide, the best diving rocks, the most sheltered picnic spots, the best places for picking wild blackberries. Home ground. Comforting and reassuring. It had been wonderful to come back to in the vacations from university, and afterwards for briefer visits when she was working in Birmingham. She had been so proud and excited to show it all off to Michael, her then fiancé, when she had brought him over from England to introduce him to her parents. And he had been sufficiently impressed to look for an opening over here in accountancy so that they could settle in the island.

She looked round, whistling for the dogs. But the sound was carried away in the wind so fast not even she could hear it. Guessing they had followed their usual route, she headed off round the Martello Tower towards Fort le Marchant. I mustn't call it that any more, she reminded herself. It's Fort Le Plonque now. Nothing stands still. Things do change, like places . . . and people. Liz Cobb was small, barely five foot one, slim and dark with blue-grey eyes. But no one who knew her would describe her as *petite*. She was too vigorous, strong-willed and determined, which made her seem much larger than her size and why she had passed all her exams with honours to become a veterinary surgeon. Nor was she pretty, but her high-domed forehead and cheekbones, and the extra wide smile set over a pronounced chin made her very attractive . . . and popular, both professionally and socially.

From the top of the hill she could see the dogs way ahead, dashing from one clump of rock and bramble to the next, sniffing eagerly to assess which of their peers had been there last, before covering the scent with their own. Even from this distance she could see the parting combed through Cocoa's dark brown coat by the wind, and Horlicks' blond ears flattened back against his neck. They were both a Heinz mixture, second or third generation mongrel strays she had adopted from the Animal Shelter when she and Michael had split up. She had needed someone in the house to talk to, and

Cocoa and Horlicks had helped fill the gap. In fact there were times when she found them a far more sympathetic audience than Michael had ever been. They would sit listening, heads cocked on one side, waiting till she finished speaking. Never interrupting . . . Her sigh was lifted away, drifting with the spume blown up from the shoreline.

A few remaining seapinks bobbed, formation dancing in their clumps either side of her path, as Liz strode on towards the old Napoleonic fort. The breakdown of her marriage, and the divorce, still left a gaping void somewhere under her breastbone, sometimes so painful she felt winded, gasping for air. She could only be thankful they had parted before starting a family. Strangely, she and Michael remained friendly, and still liked each other . . . on a strictly social basis; it had been his boisterousness, his determination to laugh under any circumstances, in any situation, which had helped undermine her feelings for him. Big, blond, handsome, lively and hard–drinking, Michael Cobb was the life and soul of every party . . . and all life was a party. Whether he was burning sausages on the barbecue, discussing the mortgage or making love – he laughed. Everything was hilarious. Elizabeth le Tissier, in her last year at college, fun-loving and gregarious, had been enchanted, swept off her feet by Michael's slipstream. Though frequently exasperated by his idiotic pranks, she allowed herself to be convinced that marriage, home and responsibility would hone his excesses to an acceptable level. The thought made her grin into the wind. How naïve could one get? He had only become worse.

Standing in the lee of the granite walls of the fort, she gazed out over the boiling waters. It was a glorious day, the north-westerly still reasonably warm, but the air was ominously clear. To the north-east she could quite clearly see the white tower of the nuclear re-processing plant, twenty-four miles away on the French coast at Cap de la Hague, a sure sign that bad weather was on the way, though as yet the racing clouds looked benign.

Her watch said twelve, time to head back home; being Thursday she was not holding surgery this afternoon, but from two o'clock she would be on emergency call for the rest of the day. Not a situation she enjoyed, alone at home, trying to put her mind to autumn gardening, doing her small amount of washing and ironing . . . and wondering where her life was heading. This wasn't the way she had planned it. Oh yes, she had wanted a career as a vet, but she had envisaged taking a few years off for having babies and for turning their house into a family home, resuming work when the children were all at school. Instead, she was simply a career girl with no husband, no children and no prospect of ever having any. There was a never-ending stream of cats and cows, goats and gerbils, horses and hamsters requiring her time and attention, but all the eligible human males were either married, adulterous or gay. The prospect looked increasingly bleak, which tended to sap her confidence, and make her tense and irritable. Which was why she loved coming out on these walks. Even on a day like today, in the middle of a gale, L'Ancresse had a calming, tranquillizing effect.

The dogs were reluctant as ever to get back in the car. As a vet she found them embarrassingly disobedient; Horlicks even had to be caught, clipped onto his lead and physically dragged to the vehicle, fortunately taking it all in good part, grinning all the while as only a happy dog can. The car radio was tuned to Guernsey FM: suddenly the music stopped. "We interrupt the programme to bring you the latest update on the ship in trouble north-west of the Casquets. She is the *SS Trygon*, a cargo vessel, suffering engine failure, and currently reported drifting in heavy seas towards Alderney. That is the end of the bulletin. Stayed tuned and we will bring you further updates as they come in."

Just as well the shipping lanes had been re-routed miles further out into the Atlantic, Liz thought, remembering being driven as a child in her parents' car to see the wrecks of the *Prosperity*, the *Elwood Mead* and the huge oil rig *Orion* at Grandes Rocques. At least the crew of the *Trygon* stood a chance of getting their act together before before swept on to rocks.

"There's that fucking trawler again," remarked First Officer Lemayne. He leaned on the bridge screen, his elbows wedged, while he levelled his binoculars. It was a bright clear day, but the strong north-westerly had pushed up a big sea, and the *Trygon*, bereft of power, was rolling heavily. "Greenpeace," the mate added contemptuously. "You'd think they'd have better things to do."

Captain Glen Mahy was more interested in watching the light tower of the Casquets, and beyond, the high cliffs of Alderney, the northernmost of the Channel Islands. The protest vessel had been tracking his ship for the past four days, ever since he had rounded Cape St Vincent. He knew these waters very well. Born and bred in the island of Guernsey, clearly visible some twenty miles to the south, he had sailed in his father's boat before taking up the sea as a profession. He knew that in the Gulf of St Malo the tides were amongst the strongest in the world. Now this tide, a spring, was about to turn, and rush south at several knots – and south of him was a minefield of the most savage granite reefs to be found anywhere. "Where the hell is that tug?" he growled.

As if in answer to his prayer, his radio operator emerged on to the bridge. "Tug *Endeavour* bearing north-east twenty miles, skipper."

Glen gave a hasty glance at the horizon, then looked into his radar, and gave a great sigh of relief as he saw the blip, moving steadily closer. "Thank God for that." His entire body seemed to inflate with relief. He was a big man, heavy-shouldered, with prematurely-greying yellow hair and clear blue eyes. He exuded strength and the confidence of experience, but that experience had also taught him the power of the wind and the sea. "Speed?" he asked.

"Eighteen knots."

"Say just over an hour."

"What do you reckon, skipper?" Lemayne asked.

Glen looked in the radar again. The Casquets Reef was a flurry of broken water; the light tower showed clear, four miles off, bearing south west. Far too close. But the south-running tide had not yet gained force. "We'll make it," he said, and picked up the telephone. "Report."

"The fire is now extinguished, but there is no chance of repairing this bearing at sea, skipper," the engineer said.

"Right. Keep the generators going. We'll be under tow in an hour." Glen replaced the phone.

"Wind's freshening," Lemayne commented. "And take a look at that."

Glen looked to the north-west, where huge storm clouds were piling one on top of the other. The break in the weather had been forecast, as a fast moving secondary depression had come up-Channel, but according to all the information he had received, as well as his own instruments, it wasn't due to reach Alderney until two. This front looked much closer than that. There'd be storm force winds in that lot, to add to the tide. "Prepare both bow anchors," he said.

"Here?" Lemayne was astonished. "There's a hundred fathoms of water."

"It shoals pretty quickly close to the rocks. They'll check her speed of drift, anyway."

Lemayne swallowed. "Skipper, if we *did* strand . . ."

"There would be all hell to pay," Glen agreed. "There's going to be all hell to pay, anyway."

He knew his job was on the line – all because of a burned out bearing which should have been renewed before they left Nagasaki. But as always in this business it had been haste, haste, haste. No one wanted the ship blockaded in port by anti-atomic energy activists – the idea was to get to the waste disposal plant before anyone knew the nature of the cargo. But that would remain always a dream. He opened the door, and stepped on to the bridge wing. The Greenpeace trawler was very close now, and someone shouted up at him through a loud hailer. "You are endangering this entire area! Go away! We don't want you here!"

"Fucking cranks," Lemayne growled, and lifted his own loud hailer. "Keep clear when the tug arrives. Bastards," he added in a lower tone.

"Concerned citizens, Mr Lemayne," Glen said quietly. "Perhaps rightly so, in our circumstances." He returned to the warmth of the bridge, to peer again into the radar screen, comparing the distance between his ship and the Casquets and the ship and the tug.

Radio Officer Petersen was back. "It is humming out there," he remarked. "We have people calling from the Shetlands to Ushant."

"I can imagine." Glen looked up at the French Air-Sea-Rescue helicopter hovering overhead.

"Nice to see him there," Petersen remarked. "He wants to know if . . ."

"Nobody is being winched off this ship," Glen told him.

The tug came closer, now clearly visible to the naked eye. Everyone on board the *Trygon* knew she was travelling as fast as she could – they could see the immense white bone in her teeth – but she still seemed to be approaching with a deadly slowness: everyone on board the *Trygon* could also see the granite heads of the Casquets Reef as the tide turned.

Petersen returned. "Prepare to take towlines, skipper."

"Get your men up forward, Mr Lemayne," Glen said. "And Petersen, tell that goddamed trawler to stand off, and I'm serious."

Petersen nodded, and hurried back to his set. Glen went on to the bridge wing to watch the tug approach. Expertly handled, she manoeuvered upwind of the wallowing freighter, then the gun on her afterdeck fired, and again, and two expertly aimed light lines were thrown across Trygon's forward deck. These were gathered in by the oilskin-clad crew, equipped with thick gloves, and attached to the capstans. Lemayne, also on the foredeck, gave the signal, and the electric motors whirred. The heaving lines were taken in, and the huge steel-threaded hawsers dripped their way out of the sea, to be seized by the waiting hands and have their heavy eye-splices dropped over the steel bollards on the freighter's deck. Glen used the VHF set on the bridge to speak with the tug skipper. "All correct."

"Giving way."

The tug turned up into the wind, and the *Trygon* slowly followed, waves breaking against her hull and scattering spray high into the air. The crew gave a cheer, and Lemayne came on to the bridge, stripping off his gloves, oilskins dripping. "All under control, skipper."

"Let's hope it stays that way." Glen watched the huge cloud, now very close. A few minutes later it erupted in a flash of lightning followed immediately by a roar of thunder, and a gust of wind which had both ships seeming to stand on their sterns. The seas crashed against them, while the wind howled, the lightning flashed and the thunder roared, and above them all there came a crack as of a gigantic whip.

"Holy shitting cows!" Lemayne shouted, and dropped to his knees.

Glen followed his example as the snapped hawser curled through the air. This one did no damage, but the second parted moments later, and the snaking end flicked the bridge screens, shattering them and sending slivers of glass in every direction.

While heating some soup for her lunch, Liz switched on the kitchen radio. She was about to switch it off again immediately when she heard Lynn Battle's voice. Lynn was a local States Deputy, professional protester, and general pain in the neck! But with her hand on the knob Liz paused. ". . . carrying atomic waste to the Re-processing Plant at Cap de la Hague," the woman was saying. "Members of Greenpeace have been tracking the *SS Trygon* for some days through this storm."

"And you believe there is a serious threat to the islands?" the interviewer queried.

"Of course! But we have been saying this in Guernsey for years, ever since the French opened that plant!"

"What level of risk are you suggesting?"

"I'm suggesting nothing. I'm telling you," Lynn replied vehemently. "If that ship comes ashore and breaks up, our whole environment will be polluted with radiation within twenty-four hours. We are talking about lives! All our lives!"

"Well let's hope the ship regains power before that happens, Mrs Battle. A representative of the owners is reported as saying that they believe the fault is a minor one and the engine can be repaired at sea quite quickly . . ."

"Of course that's what they're saying! But I wouldn't like to stake my life on it," the deputy chipped in.

An ominous hiss warned that the soup was boiling over and blue smoke rose as it burned on the hotplate. "Damn . . ." Liz swore as she grabbed the saucepan and held it, dripping, over the sink. The phone rang. "Hell!" She dumped the pan on the drainboard, switched off the hotplate and picked up the phone. "Elizabeth Cobb," she murmured in her best professional tone.

"Oh God, Liz. Thank heavens you're home! Have you heard the news? About this ship?" It was her sister-in-law. Annabel was the sweetest, dearest person in the world, but not noted in the family as the most level-headed. She was plump, blonde and giggly, a delightful if scatty homemaker, a marvellous cook, cuddly wife to Pierre and a devoted mother. She spent hours each day driving the two girls to and from school and to their numerous extra-curricular activities in a clapped-out old Volkswagon Beetle which was held together by several layers of shocking pink paint, much to the embarrassment of Pierre's self-image as an up and coming banker.

"I was just listening," Liz said. I know it's the sort of

thing Lynn has been dying to get her teeth into for years, but I think she's over-reacting a bit."

"Do you really think so? Pierre is in a meeting. I can't get hold of him and I'm scared stiff."

Liz wasn't too happy about the news herself, but there was no way she'd let Annabel know that. "Look, there's nothing to worry about at the moment . . . Okay? If the situation worsens, then I'll come down to you till the problem's over."

"But what about the girls? Penny and Ros are at school. The ship could be washed on to the rocks within an hour, with all that radioactive waste. Do you think I should fetch them home?"

"I wouldn't muck up their afternoon yet. Wait a bit longer. Pierre will come home soon, if necessary. And I can fetch the girls and bring them out to you."

"Thanks, Liz, you are a dear. But what about the animals? Do we bring them all indoors too? Or are they radiation proof?"

The thought of sharing a house with Annabel's two dogs, three cats, rapidly breeding rabbits, the pony, the pigeons, the two budgerigars and an unlimited number of fantails gave Liz an uncomfortable few minutes as she fought to prevent her fit of giggles reaching Annabel. They would all need to be armed with shovels and pooper scoopers. And could an ordinary domestic loo cope with a pony's droppings?

However, it is all very well to laugh, she thought as she finally replaced the receiver: this drifting ship could become a serious threat.

"We are going to try again," the voice over the radio said. "Stand by."

"Get down there, Lemayne," Glen told the mate.

Lemayne hunched his shoulders and slid down the ladders to where the foredeck crew had already reassembled.

Glen stood beside the coxswain to peer through the shattered screens; the seaman had remained on duty although at the moment, with no steerage way, he was redundant. The rain was teeming and it was difficult to see anything in the gloom; the flashes of lightning only half-blinded him. He could just make out the tug, manoeuvering closer, but the Greenpeace trawler had disappeared. So, fortunately, had the Casquets; the brief period during which *Trygon* had been under tow had taken her clear of the reef. But there were a lot more reefs south of her, including Guernsey itself, now a solid mass on the radar screen.

"I have Guernsey," Petersen said. "They want to know our situation."

Glen continued to watch the screen. "The fire has been extinguished but our engine is out. Our position is eleven miles north by west of L'Ancresse Bay," he said. "Tidal current six knots, south by east. Wind northwest fifty-five knots. Estimated drift ten knots southeast over the ground. Am about to attempt to renew tow . . ." He did not finish the estimate; the Guernsey Port Authority could work out as well as anyone that if the tow could not be renewed *Trygon* – and her deadly cargo – would be in their midst in just over an hour.

"The lifeboat's coming out," Petersen reported.

"Big deal," Glen grunted, and watched a fresh line curving through the air. But this one fell short as *Trygon* rolled.

"Say, skipper," Petersen remarked. "Isn't that your home, Guernsey?"

"Don't remind me," Glen said into the thick neck of his jersey.

"Trying again," said the tug.

Glen went out on to the wing. The afternoon was wild, the sky, so clear a few hours ago, now obliterated beneath the huge, tumbling black clouds. The rain pounded down, clattering on the iron decks of the ship, streaming down the scuppers to pour over the sides, hurling water bullets from the surface of the sea. The force of the rain had a calming effect on the waves, and less were breaking, especially as wind and sea were now travelling together. But the speed with which the *Trygon* was drifting was frightening.

"*Trygon, Trygon*, Lifeboat here. Do you read?"

That was the VHF. Glen could see the lifeboat now, a high sided, modern ship, superstructure painted bright orange, punching into the storm and sending aside great cascades of spray. He went inside and picked up the handset. "Loud and clear."

"What is your cargo?"

As if he didn't know, Glen thought. "Atomic waste, bound for Cherbourg."

"Can you repair your engine?"

"Given time."

"Then you must pick up your tow. You must not, under any circumstances, approach Guernsey."

"Listen," Glen said. "Who is that?"

"This is Coxswain le Prevost, speaking."

"Toby?"

"Glen Mahy! By God!" They had been at school together. "You have got yourself in a mess."

"We'll get the tow," Glen told him, as another line snaked through the air. This landed safely and was secured. He gave another sigh of relief, and looked up, at the shadow looming through the rain mist. "Take it slow, and send another line," he told the tug.

The lifeboat was circling now, impotent to help, watching as a second line was again made fast, and *Trygon* was again pulled back up into the wind. Glen looked into the radar screen, and gulped.

Lemayne hurried in. "Let's hope this one works. That land is mighty close." He peered past his captain into the screen. "What's that big blip right there?"

"The Platte Fougère Light Tower," Glen snapped. "Not half a mile away." As he spoke, there was a scraping sound.

* * *

Liz was in the kitchen, cooking rice for the dogs, when the phone beeped on the counter. "Elizabeth Cobb."
"Liz! Have you heard the news? Do you know what's happening out here?" It was Michael, voice high-pitched with excitement. Just as though he'd won the pools jackpot.
But she was alarmed. "No. Er, yes, if you mean the ship. Where are you? What's that roaring noise?"
"Wind. I'm on my Celnet, out at Beaucette. There are hundreds of people here."
"Where's the ship?"
"We can just see her. She can't be more than a couple of miles away, heading full tilt for the Platte Fougère."
"You're mad. Why aren't you getting under cover?"
"And You're joking! I wouldn't miss this for anything."
"Even your life?" Lord! What an exasperating man he was. He still couldn't take anything, even this horrendous threat, seriously.
"Liz! Why do you have to go ape over this? I . . ."
"I must go," she interrupted. "I have things to do. 'Bye." She lifted the phone again to call Annabel. Better tell her she'd go and get the girls from school.

"Okay, you guys. Let's get these doors open." Willy Watts jumped down from his Land Rover to lead his troops up the grass track towards heavy, rusted iron doors set into a concrete bunker, another relic of the German occupation. Willy Watts was short and fat; most of his face and head were concealed by a bushy mass of hair and whiskers and he was a vigorous and enthusiastic senior member of the local Civil Defence. He had needed to be enthusiastic over the years; his troops, mainly angular spinsters in need of a cause, plus a small, retired bank clerk and a large, vague, amateur astronomer, had suffered a lack of impetus following the collapse of the Iron Curtain in 1989. They had lost their sense of purpose as they had realised that an atomic bomb was unlikely to be dropped at or near Guernsey – however remote that possibility had been even during the deepest dark days of the Cold War, it had still been there. Now they followed meekly behind Willy's strident voice, wanting out but not daring to resign. After all these years, at last they had an imminent disaster. Unfortunately none, except Willy, looked capable of doing much about it.

Willy wrestled with the padlock . . . which wouldn't budge. "Never mind. I've got some WD Forty in my Wagon." He bustled back down the hill.

"How many people did Mr Watts say we could get in here?" Miss Foster asked.

"Sixty," the bank clerk replied. "That's one per thousand head of population. But of course only the top brass will be allowed. You know the kind of thing . . . the Bailiff, the law officers, the Lieutenant-Governor, and their families, of course."

"Hmm," the astronomer commented, looking up at the sky. "Surely there's room for Civil Defence Personnel."

"Here we are!" Their leader returned to the padlock, and the spray can cleared the rust. "In we go!"

"Ugh! It feels so damp," one of the ladies complained.

"Bound to. Can't be helped. Now, let's check the First Aid equipment."

The team prowled into the dark recesses of the underground bunker, waving their torches. It had been built with all the thoroughness for which the Germans are renowned, and there could be no doubt that sixty people could live down here for years, if supplied with food, no matter what might be happening above them. But it was cold, and damp and neglected; it had stood empty for more than fifty years. And . . . "A rat!" screamed Miss Foster. "A rat ran over my foot!"

Willy's enthusiasm was stretched to the limit.

Hank Applegate balanced the heavy TV camera on his shoulder, finger on the trigger, while the Bailiff replied to Jane MacAvoy's questions. They had caught him as he was about to get out of his car in Court Row, looking hot and bothered. "Well, I really don't think I can comment on the situation at this moment in time . . . So much depends, you know, on . . . er . . ." he waved a hand vaguely in the direction of the sky.

"Do you consider the situation sufficiently serious to advise viewers to start sealing their doors and windows against radiation?" Jane was a tough interviewer: although her career had not progressed beyond the island, she had had twenty-five years experience of TV journalism and wasn't going to let the head of the island States – the local parliament – get away without admitting the authorities were unprepared for the emergency . . . if she could help it.

The Bailiff, on the other hand, was a lawyer – a necessary qualification for his job where he was also required to act as Chief Justice for the island – and equally experienced in the art of blinding the opposition with waffle. "There can be no harm in taking preliminary precautions, but until the situation becomes clearer it would not be wise to create unnecessary alarm. We must think of the effect this could have on the elderly . . ."

"Sir, would you tell us how you feel about cargoes of this nature passing, regularly, so close to our shores?" Jane switched tactics.

The Bailiff wished she'd go away. He said, "You may recall that the French assured us, in response to our protests back in '93, that they had every intention of closing the Cap de la Hague Re-processing Plant and re-siting in another part of the country."

"But the ships are still coming . . ."

"Not as close as they used to," he pointed out. "Before the *Amoco Cadiz* disaster they were much nearer inshore. Now, if you will excuse me . . ."

"With respect, sir, the *Amoco Cadiz* was carrying oil. The *Trygon* is carrying plutonium. What about . . ."

He had locked the car door. "I will speak to you later when more information is available."

They watched the Bailiff disappear into the court house.

Hank stopped the camera and looked at Jane.

She pursed her lips.

"Peter! Are you out there?"

"In my conservatory, dear." Mr Peter Barrington – he always insisted on the Mister to make sure everyone realised he was an FRCS – put down his plastic watering-can and pulled off his gloves, assuming Janet was calling him to the telephone. He knew she wouldn't interrupt him for any other reason.

"Peter!" His wife hurried in, face unusually flushed above her flat-chested jumper and pearls. "It's the television. They have just interviewed . . ."

"Television?" He looked appalled. "Have you been watching television at this hour?"

For once she ignored his censure. "It's a State of Emergency. The Bailiff was speaking . . ." she paused, unable to remember exactly what it was he had said.

"Good God! You say he has declared a State of Emergency?" He quickly took his hacking jacket off the peg and shrugged into it. One had to be properly dressed to cope with emergencies.

"We..ll no, not yet, actually. But he might any minute."

Her husband snorted impatiently, smoothed his hands over the hair on his temples and strode into the TV room to see what the silly woman was on about.

". . . have just learned that the *SS Trygon* is captained by a Guernseyman, Glen Mahy," Jane MacAvoy was saying. "The ship appears to be stationary at the moment, a short distance from the Platte Fougère lighthouse. As yet we do not know whether she is held there by hawser from the tugboat, under her own power or if she has already stranded on submerged rocks."

Peter frowned at his wife. "Why is the Bailiff involved?"

Before she could attempt to explain, the phone rang.

She lifted the receiver, listened, then held it out. "Andrew Driscoll for you. He wants you to attend an emergency meeting at the hospital . . ."

When he put the phone down the surgeon was white as a sheet. "What's the point of going to the hospital? Make more sense if we go straight to the old German Underground hospital. Safer there."

"Oh, my dear! Do you think so?" Janet immediately started a mental grocery list.

Liz Cobb steered the big white Volvo into a hopeless traffic jam at Ladies' College. Annabel had warned her about it but the rain was bucketing and there was no way she could leave the car down the road and walk up to collect Penny and Ros. She couldn't go forward and there were cars jammed up behind. Muttering under her breath she zipped up her anorak, grabbed her brolly and got out. It blew inside out the moment she put it up. Pulling her hood up over her head she threw the brolly back into the car and made a dash down the path, wriggling into the press of bodies inside the front door.

"Amy? Where are you?" An hysterical voice was calling.

". . . so I asked him where we should go . . ."

". . . and what did he say?" Others seemed less concerned.

"Mummy! Are we really in danger?"

"Will someone please clear the driveway! We need to get home, quickly!" A frustrated parent had rushed back in, shouting.

". . . absolutely outrageous that we weren't notified earlier!" One of the teachers was getting an earful.

Everyone was looking tense. Several of the girls were terrified.

"I've been saying this was waiting to happen, for years!"

"If I could get my hands on that Glen Mahy!"

"He should be ashamed, his own home and all!"

Liz's ears perked up as she hunted through the crowd for her nieces. Glen Mahy? What had he got to do with it?

"Liz! Have you come to fetch us? What's going on, then?"

"Thank goodness you found me. Where's Penny?"

"By the door. But tell me . . ." Ros, who towered above her aunt, was grabbed by the arm and propelled through the exit.

"Penny! Hang onto my jacket," Liz ordered in passing, and the three made a dash for the car.

"Good grief, I'm soaked to the skin," Penny complained from the back seat.

"Join the club," her sister growled.

"Where are we going, Liz?"

"To your house."

"Some girls are going straight up to the airport. Their parents have got tickets," Ros said.

"Tickets won't be much use without an aircraft and I haven't heard any go over since lunchtime. Where were they going?"

"They didn't know. Just anywhere, I guess. Away from here." The child sounded as though she'd like to be with them.

"We'll be better off all snug and cosy at your house, than sitting up at the airport waiting for non-existent planes."

"Are you going to stay with us?"

"Yes." She had eased out into the traffic. There seemed to be an awful lot of people leaving town.

"What about the animals? Will we be able to get them all into the house, too?"

"Should we put straw down for Tangle, or will newspapers do?"

Stationary at the traffic lights, Liz turned a grin on the girls. "Depends whether your pony is house-trained," she said, "And which room you think is most suitable for her." Both girls laughed, and Liz congratulated herself. She was beginning to feel very frightened, but she wanted to keep the girls calm. She was about to reach for the car radio, then thought better of it. She'd hear the latest soon enough, hopefully when the girls weren't around.

Pierre's car was parked outside their house when Liz drove in. She gave a sigh of relief: he would look after his womenfolk and keep them calm. "May I use your phone?" she asked as she walked into the kitchen.

"Take the one in the study," Pierre called from the top of the stairs.

She dialled and waited.

"GSPCA Animal Shelter. Can I help you?"

"Elizabeth Cobb, here. May I speak to Miss Ferbrache."

"Oh, yes. She's been trying to get you. Just one minute."

"Liz? I wondered where you were. Just want to keep in touch, for in case . . ."

"Margaret! How are things with you?"

"Ghastly. I'm nearly going round the twist."

"Why?"

"Fifty thousand cats and dogs. Every Tom, Dick and Harry has been driving in here dumping their livestock on us and telling us to look after them."

"Gosh! Where on earth are you putting them?"

"The pens were filled ages ago. Now folks are just leaving them in reception or in the yard and making a run for it. We've had two serious dog fights already. If I'd had time to open a book on them I'd have made a fortune."

"Well I'm glad to hear you haven't lost your sense of humour," Liz laughed.

"Got to hang on to that; it's the only sense I've got left."

"Shall I come up?"

"Whatever for? Nothing you can do here, unless you are planning to put an extermination programme into operation."

"Not unless I'm forced. We don't know for sure, yet, how serious the threat is. I'm going to be at this number for the time being," she gave Pierre's number. "I'll give you a shout later, if I hear anything. Meanwhile, don't hesitate to call if you need me." Though she couldn't imagine what she could do to help. She replaced the handset, picturing all the dogs in their outdoor runs, the cats in their pens . . . all open and vulnerable to radiation. Then she remembered that Margaret would be pretty exposed up there, too. A lot of people were at risk . . . but surely they were all grotesquely over-reacting, to a hidden fear all Channel Islanders had lived with for years It was never going to happen, surely!

"Oh, shit!" Lemayne said. "Oh, shit!"

Glen knew that his ship had touched a rock. On the other hand, she was not fast, and the towing hawsers were again taking up. He picked up the phone. "Damage report," he said.

"Nothing here, skipper. But it was a terrible noise."

"Get down into the skin, Lemayne," he said. "I want a report." He thumbed the phone. "Mr Briscoe, have your pumps ready."

"Are you hurt?" asked the lifeboat.

"I am finding that out."

"We have lift-off," announced the tug.

She was forging into the head seas, and this time *Trygon* was following steadily in her wake; the land began to recede astern.

Lemayne returned to the bridge. "We've buckled a plate, starboard amidships. We're making water, but nothing the pumps can't manage."

"Any risk to the cargo?"

"None."

Glen gave a sigh of relief.

"Have you suffered damage?" asked the lifeboat again.

"Nothing serious. No risk to the cargo," Glen said. "I'll see you around, Toby."

"Could be sooner than you think," the lifeboat coxswain replied. "I'm sorry, mate, but there's likely to be an inquiry into this."

* * *

Philippe looked up as the door opened, and turned down the radio. Small and dark, with handsome features and a quick smile, this was his first command.

"You should use the password before busting in like that," he said. His French was tinged with a Provençal drawl.

"So?" Monique asked. "Do you think it is not me? Let the Light shine tonight . . ."

"Until it is too bright," Philippe said, and stood up. Looking at Monique was always a pleasure. She was big in every way, her features too large for beauty but her breasts built for comfort. As were her thighs. Yet now he looked past her at the woman beyond. "This is Olga," Monique explained. She ushered the woman into the room, and closed and locked the door; the sounds of the bar downstairs became muted.

Philippe gazed at the thin features, the pale skin.

"I am the person you wish," Olga said. She spoke French with a foreign accent.

Philippe licked his lips. "You understand . . .?"

"Yes."

"Olga was exposed at Chernobyl," Monique said. "She came to France for treatment. But the treatment has not proved successful."

"It has kept me alive for some years," Olga said. "But now . . . I am told I have less than a year left." She smiled at Philippe's expression. "Have you Pernod?"

Philippe poured, and Olga sat in the chair. Monique sat on the bed.

"Have you heard the news?" Philippe asked.

"What news?"

He gave a wry grin. "We were nearly reprieved. A waste carrier got into trouble in the Channel this afternoon. Bound for La Hague. It nearly went aground on Guernsey. They are all very upset."

"Nearly?" Olga asked. "And where, or what, is Guernsey?"

"An island in the Bay of St Malo, about forty kilometres

from the French coast. They got the ship under tow in time. So, there will be much publicity . . ."

"That is good for us," Monique said.

"Not necessarily. It will mean a general increase of security. However, we will continue with the operation."

"There is a message from Georges." Monique opened her handbag, took out an envelope, and gave it to him.

Philippe opened it, frowning as he read the single sheet of paper inside.

"Well" Monique asked.

"There has been a change of plan."

"It has not been cancelled" Olga said. "I could not stand that. I should go mad, if it has been cancelled."

"It has not been cancelled," Philippe said. "We have been re-routed, that is all. Flamanville. Strange. He says it will be easier, because of internal difficulties. But he must have written this before today's near shipwreck."

"Will you query the command?" Monique asked.

Philippe struck a match and set the paper alight, then laid it in the ashtray to burn. "It is not our business to question commands," he said. "Georges has a much more complete picture of what is happening than us." He looked out of his window at the bulk of Saumur Castle rising above the Loire. Here there was no indication that the two enormous nuclear electricity plants were only a few kilometres away, at Chinon. "I was growing attached to this place," he said. "But . . . I am told Normandy is very pretty, in the summer."

THE FOLLOWING YEAR

Chapter 1

TUESDAY, 6TH JULY

"Ladies and gentlemen, in a few minutes time we shall begin our approach for landing at La Villiaze Airport, Guernsey. On our left at this moment is the island of Alderney, and beyond that you can see the coast of France. Will you please fasten your seatbelts, and return your seats and trays to the upright positions. Thank you."

Jackson Ridgeway looked down at the small, rocky island beneath him, the cluster of houses in the centre. That would be the town of St Anne's, he recalled from his pre-trip reading. He had the oddest feeling of *déja-vu*. Yet he had never been to the British Channel Islands before, although he had holidayed more than once in those other Channel Islands, off the Californian coast.

A hostess took his plastic glass, reaching across the man beside him to do so. As the aircraft descended, Jackson could see the outcrops of black rock against which the seas were breaking; the tide was low.

"First visit?" asked his travelling companion. He had obviously seen Jackson's name and home address on his briefcase, and made the right deductions, but this was the first time he had spoken since leaving Gatwick. He had to be British, Jackson reckoned with a private grin. Actually he was a pleasant looking man, big and heavy-shouldered, with graying yellow hair and brittle blue eyes; he looked tired. As Jackson was also a big man, tall and strongly-built rather than heavy, the two seats in the rather small aircraft felt very crowded: there was apparently no first-class seating on this Channel Island flight.

But the two men made a strong contrast, for Jackson was dark-haired and brown-eyed, and where the blond man's features were softly rounded, Jackson's were sharp and incisive. "Yes," he replied. "In a manner of speaking."

"Come again?"

"My ancestors came from Guernsey."

"Is that a fact? But you're American."

"True."

"Looking the old folks up, eh?"

"I don't think there are any of the old folks still around," Jackson said. "Are you a Channel Islander?"

"Yes. But I don't live there now."

"So you're going home to see *your* folks?"

The blond man grinned. "In a manner of speaking. Name's Glen Mahy." He seemed to be waiting for some reaction, but the name meant nothing to Jackson.

"Jackson Ridgeway."

They shook hands, then Mahy cleared his throat and returned to his newspaper, while Jackson studied the varying sea colours and contours beneath him. Even in July the sea looked cold. Someone had suggested he bring his scuba gear with him, but when he studied a map he had discovered that Guernsey was on the same Latitude as the mouth of the St Lawrence River, and he had never been tempted to dive there – he preferred the Caribbean. Besides, he was here to work, not play.

The aircraft taxied to a halt in front of the small terminal building, and the passengers disembarked. There were a great number of people standing just beyond the plate glass windows of the airport lounge. Although Jackson knew he was being met by someone from the local banking firm who were acting as agents for the Parks

Paramus Banking Corporation, he had no idea what this Pierre le Tissier looked like, so he did not spare them a glance.

They filed into the arrivals hall, where the conveyor belt was already rumbling, and an airport official hurried in. "There's quite a crowd out there, Captain Mahy," he said. "Would you like to be sneaked through?"

Jackson watched his companion considering. Then Mahy shook his head. "I have to face them, some time. Here's as good a place as any."

The other passengers were by now as interested as Jackson, but he wasn't going to pry. Mahy grinned at them. "Sorry about this, folks. Let me out first, and I'll draw off the pack."

He picked up his bag and headed for the exit.

"That's Glen Mahy," someone whispered. "Captain of the *Trygon*."

"The what?"

"You remember the *Trygon*?"

Jackson picked up his own bag, and passed through Customs unheeded. There certainly was a crowd out there, with flashbulbs glowing and at least two camcorders whirring, while other people with notebooks surrounded the blond man, who was apparently a shipmaster. "Now, listen," Mahy said in a loud voice. "You all know I can't say anything. Come to the inquiry. You'll get it all then." He strode towards the doors to the parking area, followed by the papparazzi.

"Mr Ridgeway?" The man was in his late thirties, well built and black-haired, with good features and dark eyes.

"That's me."

"Pierre le Tissier." They shook hands. "My car's in the park," Pierre said. "Only the one case?"

"Well, this is kind of a preliminary visit."

"Of course." Pierre ushered Jackson outside into the bright summer sunlight. "You're lucky you're seeing the island at its best. It was raining yesterday."

Having stowed the suitcase in the boot, he opened the door of the Rover. Jackson hesitated, then got in. "I'll have to get used to sitting on the wrong side of a car."

"When did you arrive in London?"

"This morning."

"Hell! You must be exhausted."

"Not yet. What have you got for me?"

"Well, I've some places for you to look at. We're a little over-catered with office space in Guernsey right now, so the choice is fairly wide. But for banking . . . how big an operation are you planning?"

"That depends on how big a clientele I can attract, right?" Jackson said. "But it will be strictly large investments for starters. What I want to do is look around, suss out the form. Like, fill me in on your political situation. You're independent but you're not independent. What does that mean?"

"The Channel Islands are all that is left, in British hands, of the old Duchy of Normandy," Pierre explained. "I know to you people yesterday is yesterday and not even last week, but in parts of Europe history has had a habit of standing still. This is one of those parts. In fact, there's an old joke that we don't belong to Britain, Britain belongs to us. That is because William the Conqueror ruled us long before he invaded England."

"That's great history," Jackson conceded. "What's the reality?"

"Not very different. We are a part of the British Isles. *Not* the United Kingdom of Great Britain and Northern Island. We are a self-governing part. I suppose you could liken us to a federal state. So, we have our own government, which we call the States of Guernsey, and which is elected by universal suffrage. The Crown is represented by a Lieutenant-Governor; the civil head of the community is our Bailiff, who is appointed for life by the Crown, acting on the advice of the Home Office, from amongst the members of our legal profession. We manage our own internal affairs, but in international matters the UK government looks after us."

"Sounds cosy. What I really want to know is, is there any prospect of your tax structure changing?"

Pierre grinned as he swung out of the airport on to the main road. "Not likely. The States is full of oddbods, but they do understand one thing: offshore banking is the lifesblood of the island economy, and low taxation is an essential of offshore banking."

"Is there nothing else?"

"Some tourism."

"I thought horticulture was a big thing in the Channel Islands?"

"It was once. But with our climate, we need to grow under glass and import oil for heating. That's expensive. Added to which is the cost of air or sea freight for all our produce. So we can no longer compete since Spain and Greece got into the Common Market."

"Then what about this Common Market? Can't they upset your low tax system?"

Another grin. "We're not in the Common Market, Mr Ridgeway. We're only associate members, and we intend to stay that way."

"Sounds like you have the best of both worlds."

"We don't complain. I've booked you in at the St Pierre Park Hotel. All right?"

"If you say so."

"It's just down here." The car swung round a corner. "Then I imagine you'd like to have a rest. We can get to business tomorrow. But if you feel up to it, why don't you come and have dinner with us tonight?"

"That's very kind of you. You don't have to, you know. I know you're acting as our agents here, but . . ."

"Annabel would like to meet you. So would Liz. She's my sister. I've told them you might come."

"Oh. Thanks." Jackson decided to change the subject. "What's with this guy Mahy? We sat together on the plane.

I didn't clue on he was famous. But that media crowd at the airport was waiting for him."

"He was skipper of a freighter which nearly stranded on the island a year ago. He's back for the inquiry."

"A freighter, nearly stranding, is that much news?"

Pierre gave another of his grins. "It is, when it's carrying atomic waste."

"Jees! Yes, I imagine it would be. But what was it doing off Guernsey?"

"He was bound for Cap de la Hague. That's the headland on France which sticks out towards Alderney. They've a re-processing plant there."

"You know, I saw what looked like an atomic power station there when we flew by. But I didn't reckon it was possible. That's not very far away, is it?"

"Twenty-four miles. You can see it from here on a clear day."

"Doesn't that bother you people? It scared the shit out of folks back home when Three Mile Island melted."

Pierre shrugged as he swung into the hotel drive. "I remember that. But the French aren't much interested whether we're bothered or not. Nothing we can do about it."

"Save get agitated when a waste ship comes too close."

Pierre braked. "Does that put you off opening an office here?"

It was Jackson's turn to grin. "It doesn't seem to have deterred any of the other hundred odd banks you have in the island."

Annabel took a mighty swing at Rosamund's service and drove it into the net. "Fifteen-forty," Penelope crowed, retrieving the ball and sending it back to her partner.

Liz waited on the base line; the next ball skimmed the net, clipped the corner of the service box and flew past. She hadn't even taken a swing at it. "Okay, little nieces, game, set and match to you. You're far too good for us poor old ladies."

"Poor? You're not poor," Rosamund argued.

"No. And a little less of the old, please," Annabel growled. She did not look her best in a tennis skirt: the knife pleats were expanded like a concertina, and her Aertex shirt hadn't a hope of staying tucked in the waistband. But no one could deny that she was a lovely woman. The open honesty and generosity of her nature shone in her face. Even now, flushed and perspiring from her exertions, the plump overlay of flesh could not mask her fine bone-structure, high cheekbones and arched brows, delicately shaped nose and small chin.

"Want your revenge?" Her two daughters knew they could run rings round her and their aunt, but were keen to continue play on the court in their back garden.

"What's the time?" Annabel asked, vaguely.

"Six forty-five," Liz told her.

"Oh glory be! I haven't turned on the oven yet for the baked potatoes, or laid the table!" She grabbed her towel and headed for the gate. "Sorry, darlings, no more now."

"I'll help," Liz hurried after her. "How many of us?"

"Er, us four and you. Milford and Katey and some banking chap Pierre's invited. Can't remember his name. Eight. We'll eat on the patio."

"I thought we were only going to be family. I haven't brought anything special to wear."

"I told the Martels to come casual. Not that it will make any difference to Katey. She can look like she's stepped out of *Vogue* when she's cleaning the oven. I'm just putting on a cotton skirt and tee shirt," Annabel assured her as she hurried into the kitchen and started crashing saucepans.

Liz had spent a lot of time with Pierre and Annabel since her divorce. Pierre showed brotherly concern to an almost irritating degree, but while maintaining her total independence, she remained grateful for their company. She loved family and was very fond of her tall, blonde sister-in-law. When she had set the mats, cutlery and glasses on the patio table, she skipped upstairs to the spare bathroom for a shower, replacing her tennis shorts with floral-printed slacks and an orange cotton shirt. She combed back her wet hair, clipped big plastic earrings onto her tiny ears and ran barefoot down the stairs. She hated shoes.

Pierre was in the kitchen mixing jugs of *sangria* when the big exterior doorbell clanged. "I'll take that," he said.

"Don't you dare!" Annabel exclaimed. "The girls will get it while you clear away your mess."

"Bossy woman!" her husband complained, hugging her round the waist and kissing her, whilst holding a large, plastic jug poised over a glass.

"Attend to what you're supposed to be doing, sex maniac," Annabel ordered, kissing him back.

"Got any more paper napkins?" Liz asked.

"Not white ones. You'll have to use red."

It was a happy, relaxed gathering. Jackson, arriving a few minutes later by taxi, was immediately at home and stood chatting with his hostess, a barbecue spatula in one hand and a drink in the other. "I just love your house. What age is it?" he asked, much impressed by the thick granite walls.

"The oldest part, at the far end, is seventeenth century, but it has been added to at intervals ever since."

"Wow! Seventeenth century! Back home we reckon nineteenth century is old. Have you retained the original features?"

Katey Martel sat watching, immaculate as ever: not a crease in her crisp shirtwaister, not one smooth blonde hair out of place.

Pierre looked from her to his skinny sister and then at his wife whose tee-shirt bulged out of the straining waistband of her skirt, her unruly hair blowing across her face in the soft evening breeze ... and resisted the temptation to give her another hug. He liked immaculate desks, secretaries and filing systems, but he wanted his wife exactly the way she was. "So when does the inquiry open?" he asked Milford.

"Monday. But it will all be preliminary details for the first day, then there'll be an adjournment . . . they'll drag it out."

"Are you going to get him off?" Annabel asked.

"He's not on trial, my dear. My business is to make sure he doesn't lose his ticket, and I hope to do that. Did you know John Marquand is on the case? You remember him at school, Pierre?"

"No! Is that a fact? Haven't seen John for years. Jackson," he turned to the American, "I omitted to tell you that Milford, here, is an advocate, attorney in your language, and is representing Glen Mahy at the inquiry."

"That is interesting, Milford. I don't really know your client, but we sat together on the plane earlier today and he seemed a very decent guy. Pierre was filling me in on a few details: can he be blamed that the ship's engines died in a storm?"

Milford peered through heavy spectacles, nodding gravely. "It is unfortunate that in the highly emotive circumstances which invariably attend incidents involving pollution, blame needs to be seen to be attached to somebody. It is equally unfortunate that Glen Mahy is a local man and therefore held by islanders as doubly culpable for putting the island at risk."

Liz smiled to herself, thinking that people don't change. Milford was six years her senior, but she could remember him when he was at school with Pierre; same glasses, same stiff manner and habit of swaying from the waist as he spoke. He had always looked very much the lawyer in a three piece suit, but was hopelessly adrift tonight in over-long shorts, suede shoes and a cravat that kept unwinding itself. When she looked away she accidently caught Jackson's eye . . . and imagined for a moment that he winked. She decided to sit herself next to him when the barbecue finally surrendered the steaks and sausages.

"I must apologise but I didn't get your last name," the

American murmured, holding the salad bowl while Liz helped herself. "Pierre introduced you as Missus."

"Was. Cobb is the name, but Michael and I are divorced."

"Oh. I'm sorry."

"I'm not. It's a great relief – for both of us. We like each other much more, now that we don't have to live together. Are you married?"

"No. Never got round to it. Cobb isn't a Guernsey name, is it? Is Michael English?"

"Yes. We met at university. What about you? Pierre said you had some Guernsey connection."

"My grandmother used to speak of it. Thought I might investigate sometime." He removed his sunglasses. "Ah! The evening isn't so advanced without those." He pushed them into a leather case.

Liz looked at the initials stamped in a corner. "J. O. R. What does the O stand for?"

"Orrville. My grandmother's maiden name."

"Really! Pierre, did you hear that? Jackson's grandmother was an Orrville!"

"Good Lord!" Her brother dropped his fork with a clatter. "That's amazing. Grandpa le Tissier's mother was an Orrville. The family had a place near Torteval Church. Way out in the sticks."

Jackson threw back his head, laughing. "How could it be out in the sticks? The island's only nine miles long, isn't it?"

"All things are relative," Annabel explained. "When you've been here a while you'll understand. It's bad enough nowadays, with fifty thousand cars on our narrow little roads. But in our great-grandparents' day, before cars replaced the donkey carts, even going to town was a major adventure. I bet they didn't attempt it more than half a dozen times in their lives."

"Dammit," Jackson shook his head. "This is just incredible! I must call Mom when I get back to the hotel and tell her about this. I mean . . . the fact that you not only knew the name, but that we are actually related!"

"Nothing very extraordinary about that," Milford pointed out. "Everyone over here is related to everyone else. We know each other's backgrounds and all the skeletons in everyone's cupboards."

"Wow! That must be like living in a goldfish bowl. Pretty uncomfortable."

"Yes indeed," Penny cut in. "Especially if you are in the habit of breaking the Ten Commandments."

"Penny! Shut up!" her sister hissed.

The younger girl gave her a sly glance, and grinned.

"I love our insular community," Liz said. "I like walking down High Street recognising so many people. I may not know their names but I certainly know their faces. It's a nice . . . comfortable feeling. Of belonging. When I do my round of house calls I know so many folk. There's a man down at the Capelles who used to drive our school bus. He has umpteen tortoises. And the man who used to deliver our milk has an old horse in an advanced stage of senile decay."

"I like it, too," Pierre agreed. "So many of the people I was at Elizabeth College with, have children at school with Penny and Ros."

"You mean they have lived here in the island all their lives and never gone away?" Jackson stared, wide-eyed with wonder.

"Oh, we've all been away, to university, then into our first jobs. Traditionally, over the centuries, islanders have gone abroad to the farthest corners of the earth, but a large proportion of them come back."

"You must be very happy with the way things are here," Jackson suggested.

It was Katey who laughed and endeavoured to correct him. "On the contrary. We criticise everything, all the time. The authorities and their decisions; the state of the roads; the level of water in the reservoir . . . the weather. Just about everything . . ."

"But I warn you," Liz wagged a finger at the American, "Just let a Guern hear a foreigner, some blooming Englishman . . . or an American, daring to criticise anything and he risks having the need of plastic surgery."

Pierre stood up, holding a jug. "I think I'd better make up another lot of *sangria*."

It was a lovely evening. The weather was perfect, the whole garden perfumed with Annabel's night-scented stock. The company was happy and relaxed and Liz enjoyed herself more than she had done for a long time.

Jackson enjoyed it, too.

Chapter 2

WEDNESDAY, 7TH JULY

Next morning Pierre picked up Jackson and drove him to the first building on his list. The offices were on the third floor of a block situated on one of the steeply sloping streets which led down to the town of St Peter Port.

"Don't you people indulge in elevators?" Jackson grunted, as they climbed the stairs.

"The new, custom-built buildings have them," Pierre said. "I have one of those to show you as well. But of course this place is much cheaper."

"I don't think Parks Paramus Banking Corporation is too concerned about a little extra rent," Jackson pointed out. "Anyway, if things go well we are going to want to buy, or build for ourselves." He waited while Pierre unlocked the door and then went into the bare rooms. "Um."

"You don't like it."

"Frankly, no. It has the smell of the last century about it. That's great if you're a hundred-year-old bank. We're not, especially as regards Guernsey. Our appeal has got to be that we are offering something new and exciting." He walked to the eastfacing window. "Pity. That's quite a view."

Pierre joined him. "Looks down on the town. Do you know that St Peter Port has more than once been voted the prettiest of all towns in Britain? Not that we are British. We are fiercely proud of our independence."

Jackson looked past the descending rows of roofs and the spire of the town church at the marinas and then the harbour a busy place on a summer's morning, with small boats and yachts entering and leaving and the large ferry to the mainland just preparing to depart. Beyond was a broad stretch of water, sheltered from the east by a cluster of islands. "That passage is called the Little Russel," Pierre said at his shoulder. "Those islands are Herm and Jethou. From this angle they look as if they're joined together, but there is a passage between. Beyond them is the Great Russel, and the island in the distance is Sark. To the south-east, Jersey is visible on a clear day. And that cloudbank beyond Sark is over France. Do you like boating?"

"I've done some."

"If you like, I'll take you out in my motor cruiser on Saturday, show you the waters. She's only a day-boat, I'm afraid, but ideal for island-hopping."

"Sounds great," Jackson said, and found himself wondering if that attractive little vet would be along.

He found the two floors of offices available on the Grange – the main thoroughfare running east-west out of the town – far more to his liking.

"This I could use, at least for starters."

"Right," Pierre said. "How long is starters?"

"Two years with an option to renew. By then I'll be more certain what I'm about. Will the electrics stand up?"

"To what?"

"We're talking about a dozen computers, a couple of typewriters, adequate heating . . . I only see one rad. per room."

"Well, you could probably have some more heat put in."

Jackson tapped the windows. "I'll need double glazing."

"In addition to extra heat?"

"It also keeps out noise." He looked down at the traffic on the Grange. "That looks, and sounds, like a busy street down there. But it's power that matters."

"That won't be a problem. We'll have the fuses checked out."

"It's the wattage I'll be wanting to know about. Forgive me for sounding like I'm pernickety, but a colleague of mine opened an office in Spain a couple of years ago and only after signing the lease did he discover that the building only had a total of five watts available. Every time the fifth computer was booted the other four blew."

Pierre grinned. "Compared with Guernsey, Spain is definitely a third-world country."

"I'm glad to hear it. Right. Can you set this up? I need to have it signed up by the end of next week."

"Hold on," Pierre said. "It'll take a bit longer than that."

It was Jackson's turn to grin as they went back down to the car. "You mean you're not *that* much ahead of Spain?"

Pierre decided to ignore the rebuke. "Don't you want to see the alternative possibilities?"

"This place suits me fine. It has reasonable parking at the back, and that seems more important in this island than a sea view."

"Point taken. I'm afraid I have a luncheon engagement. Shall I take you back to the hotel?"

"I'd prefer you drop me down in the town," Jackson said. "Let's talk about staff," he added, as they drove down the hill. "I'm going to need a secretary PR and a couple of computer operators for starters. Later I'll look for an accounts manager. Do I recruit locally or in the UK?"

"Locally," Pierre said. "As far as possible. You shouldn't have a problem. The money business has been operating here now for a generation; you'll find they're pretty clued-up. If you go to the UK, you run into housing problems, and a whole can of worms."

"Tell me about housing."

"Well, there's not enough of it. That goes for just about every urban community in the world, I suppose. But in Guernsey it's exacerbated by the fact that we're also a low tax area."

Jackson raised his eyebrows. "You don't describe yourselves as a tax haven."

"Certainly not. We have income tax as well as company tax. It's just that it's a lot less than in most other places, and we don't have absurdities like death duties, surtax, or valued added tax. Thus we obviously attract a lot of people trying to protect their assets, so the States had to take steps to protect the locals from runaway house inflation. So we have a two-tier system. Only houses over a certain rateable value can be occupied by people without residential qualifications; these properties – known as the Open Market – are obviously very expensive. Properties under that rateable value, the Local Market, are only available to Guernsey people or to people to whom a licence has been issued, men and women whose presence is regarded as essential for the island, but who are not in the financial bracket to buy open market houses. I'm talking about the specially qualified, like schoolteachers, engineers, etc."

"So if I wanted to bring in anyone from the mainland, I'd have to apply for a special licence" Jackson mused.

"And you wouldn't get one, so long as the job could be done by a Guernseyman, or woman." Pierre turned on to the Crown Pier, between the Careening Hard and the Victoria Marina, with the harbour and then the smaller islands in front of them and the town behind.

"So, do you have staffing agencies here?"

"Indeed. But sometimes word of mouth is better. If you like, I can have a word with my secretary. She may know of someone suitable who is looking for a move."

"Yes, please. I'll wait to hear from you. Well, thanks a million." Jackson got out. "It's all been most informative.

Will you call me the moment you have a date for signing up that lease?"

"Will do." Pierre drove off.

Jackson looked up at the town. He could well believe it was regarded by many as the most attractive seaport along the English Channel coasts. He looked forward to exploring it, after he had had lunch . . . not the brightest prospect as he hated eating alone. He walked to the traffic light to cross to the town side of the esplanade and saw, on the far side of the road, the person who might resolve that problem – the attractive little vet.

"Hi, there!"

Liz Cobb swung round and nearly collided with the American banker. "You made me jump. I was miles away."

"Where?"

"Trying to re-programme my day to fit in a possible emergency Caesarian Section on a beagle. A colleague is with her now, but we are hoping she can deliver under her own steam."

"Let me have that," he said, taking a huge plastic carrier from her. "Say, this is far too weighty for you to be toting around! What's in it, cannon balls?"

"Thanks. Yes, that's a fair guess; actually they're bottles of tablets for horses. I'm just taking them out to my car."

"Shame. I was hoping your new schedule might include lunch together."

"Ah . . ." she hesitated. Mr Ogier was coming to get these tablets from the surgery soon after two; and she'd promised to go and see Mrs Mahy's cat as the poor old lady couldn't bring it in herself. The bleeper in her pocket could summon her to the beagle bitch at any moment and she was due to start her shift in the surgery at five . . . but . . . "I'd love to, I'm starving. But I won't have time for more than a sandwich and a cup of coffee."

"Great. No problem. Where do you suggest?"

"Here?"

They were standing outside a small cafe built into one of the several tunnel-like cellars with rounded ceilings which had been used for storing cargo many years ago when sailing ships moored up alongside what was then the quay – now widened into a busy roadway. "Why not. Looks kinda cute."

The place was full of tourists, but a couple were just leaving a table in the window. The bag of horse tablets was stowed out of sight and the proprietor hurried over to take their order. "I'll have a couple of rounds of your lovely crab sandwiches, please," Liz told the beaming Italian. And to Jackson she suggested, "Why not sample some fried Guernsey fish?"

"Think I'd prefer to join you with crab sandwiches, thanks. How about a glass of wine?"

She hesitated, then nodded. "Just one."

"This place is really something," Jackson remarked looking around the small, flagstoned cellar, and then out across the road to the forest of masts in the Victoria Marina. "Does everyone in this island own a yacht?"

Liz laughed. "No chance. I, for one, have neither the time nor the inclination. Anyway, those boats you see there are all visitors."

"Where does Pierre keep his boat?"

"In the Elizabeth Marina, the other side of the White Rock."

"Uh? Come again?"

"The White Rock. Sorry, one forgets that other people don't know that is the name of our harbour. Just to the north, there."

"Sure. I get it. Pierre showed me from the window of an office we inspected today. This is a very beautiful little town."

Liz beamed. "I'm so glad you think so. I think we are very lucky."

"You'd better believe it! The whole island is lovely, or what I've gotten to see so far. Er, is there a chance you may get time to show me some more of it?" He watched her face, trying to assess her reaction.

"Only too happy to oblige," she said. But you do understand that I have a more than full-time job. It would have to be during an evening or at a week-end." She looked happy enough, though she was trying hard not to seem as keen as she felt. There was no doubt she was finding this American very attractive. Pity he should have caught her in old jeans and with her hair full of salt from her early-morning dip at L'Ancresse.

"I'll be tied up in business hours myself," he was saying, "I just have to get the act together here in Guernsey. We hope to transfer operations from Pierre's office to our own premises within the next few weeks." While he was speaking their wine and sandwiches arrived. He watched, fascinated, as her small, slim fingers carried one of the overflowing triangles of bread to her mouth. It was hard to imagine her wielding a scalpel.

"Mmm-mm," she giggled, as bits of crab clung to her upper lip and fell on the plate. "They put so much crabmeat in these it's impossible to eat them with any dignity." Her dark eyes twinkled, tiny crows' feet forming at the corners.

Jackson had a hard time taking his eyes off her and concentrating on his own meal. "The crab is great. Is it local?"

"You joke! It was caught out there last night and cooked this morning."

He raised an eyebrow. "That's a fact?"

"I often pop in here. I know the *patron*. There's no way he'd ever serve frozen crabmeat." She lifted her glass. "Cheers. I hope you'll enjoy Guernsey as much as I do."

"I don't reckon I ever met a person who appreciated their hometown like you do. That's nice. Really nice." She could see he meant it. "However, much as I am enjoying this meal, it doesn't exactly fill all the twenty-four hour requirements. What chance of sharing a real dinner tonight?"

This time she had to shake her head. "None." Then seeing his obvious disappointment added, "Maybe another day."

"Tomorrow?"

Her mind raced. She mustn't let this thing romp away out of hand too quickly. She hardly knew the man . . .

"Hell, I'm sorry. I guess I'm being very pushy . . ." he looked so contrite.

"I had said I might go to the theatre with a friend . . ." she began, and saw a certain flash in his eyes. "I don't want to let her down. Let's see . . ." She fished her diary out of her bag. They settled on the day after tomorrow, Friday.

"Where do we eat? My hotel?"

She gazed out of the window, through the harbour heads. "Why not Herm? We can take the Trident over, have supper at The Captain's Table at the White House Hotel, and come back on the late boat."

"That sounds terrific. Should be quite an experience!"

"Yes," she agreed, with a dubious note in her voice. "Especially if it's bucketing with rain and there's a howling gale blowing! However, the weather looks set fair at the moment."

"You're having me on!"

"No way! I can remember going over there for dinner and having to sleep the night on the floor."

"Why?"

"Fog came down during the meal and the boats couldn't risk the trip back. It was quite an hilarious night. The hotel was marvellous and gave us all breakfast next morning, a sort of second party!"

"You know something? This place is kinda special. Is everyone friendly like this?"

Liz laughed. "Until you start telling us how to run our lives or businesses. That's when the traditional Guernseyman turns to his chum and says 'They come. And they go!' And he's dead right. No end of foreigners settle here, puff out their self-important chests and try to tell us how much more they know of the world than we do. We just smile and wait for them to learn better. Those that don't are either obliged to shut up, or leave."

He noted a tinge of aggression in her voice as she spoke, and knew she was one islander who would brook no interference.

After leaving the tablets for Mr Ogier's horse at the surgery, Liz collected Cocoa and Horlicks from home before heading off to Cobo to see Mrs Mahy's cat. Normally she didn't do house visits for domestic pets; the islanders adored their animals, cats and dogs in particular; there were thousands of them and it would be impossible to see all the patients who needed attention if one had to drive round after them. But Mrs Mahy was different. Crippled with arthritis, it was impossible for her to bring the cat to the surgery and it had become the custom, each year when the annual booster jabs were due, for Liz to call at the cottage where a cup of tea was always waiting for her – with two custard creams in the saucer. Today, however, there was a difference: the door was opened by a very large, blond man who said, "Oh! I thought you would be the vet!"

"I am. Where's Mrs Mahy? Isn't she well?"

"Gran's in the back garden. She's okay. Not so stiff when the weather's fine. Won't you come through?" He led the way, ducking under each low lintel until they stepped out across the flagged pathway. The old lady was sitting in a deckckair on the lawn, surrounded by borders of geraniums, petunias and antirrhinums.

"Hello Mrs Cobb. Come and sit down for a few minutes." Mrs Mahy was one of the old school, insisting on addressing professionals formally, however many generations her junior. "Is the kettle on, Glen?"

"Nearly boiling, Gran. I'll go and make the tea."

"You remember Glen, don't you? He was at school with your brother," the old lady leaned forward, smiling.

"Glen! Oh, of course. I didn't recognise him, but then

I haven't seen him for years." Glen Mahy, captain of the nuclear waste ship that nearly stranded last year, over for the inquiry! They had been talking about him at Pierre's last night. Well, she had had no idea he was this Mrs Mahy's grandson.

"I don't see him very often myself. But he always comes to visit me when he's home." She sighed, shrugging her narrow shoulders. "You know why he's home this time, I suppose?"

"Yes." Liz didn't know what to say.

"I can't say I approve of him bringing that dangerous stuff into local waters, all the way from Japan, or wherever. But he has to take the ship where the owners tell him. That's what he's paid for." She gave a half smile. "About time he started obeying someone; he never took any notice of his mother. Ah well, I can't complain, myself. He's always been good with me."

"Here you are," Glen returned and put the tea tray on a small table by his grandmother. "How's your hand today? Do you want to pour or shall I do it for you?" He turned to Liz. "Half her trouble is she won't get someone in to help in the garden. Will insist on doing the weeding herself."

"There's nothing wrong with my hand today," the old lady snapped, and started filling the cups. "But if you want to make yourself useful you can fetch Smudge for Mrs Cobb. He'll be on the settee as usual."

"How is Smudge?" Liz asked.

"That's what I want you to tell me. He's been off his food for a while, now, but whether he has something wrong with him or he's just being pernickety I don't know."

Glen reappeared and placed the old tabby on Liz's lap, watching as she systematically ran her fingers carefully over him, reading the contours through the mottled fur.

"Here's the problem, I think. He has developed a lump."

"What is it?" Clen asked.

She didn't reply immediately, continuing probing for a few moments. "I'm not sure. It isn't giving him too much pain, yet, and it might resolve itself. However, if we leave it it could become serious. Risky. I think I should remove it."

"You mean operate on him?" Mrs Mahy looked devastated.

"Well . . . It's no use leaving it until he's really ill."

"He's getting too old for an operation."

"His heart is as strong as an ox," Liz assured her, listening again with her stethescope.

"Liz knows best, I'm sure," Glen said.

"Mrs Cobb, you mean."

"Liz, please," the vet insisted. She turned to him. "I remember going fishing with you and Pierre at Pembroke when we were kids."

He was glad she remembered. He had spent so much time at sea in the past twenty years he'd lost contact with most of his old friends and acquaintances in the island. "As I recall it, you were the only one who caught anything. Pierre and I were livid."

Liz released Smudge who promptly leapt on to his mistress's lap. "It was the first time I'd ever held a rod. Neither of you had wanted me along but Dad persuaded you. Pierre ignored me the whole time, but you were kind and showed me what to do."

"I was so small and skinny in those days, it was nice to be with someone I could look down on," the huge sailor grinned.

"Glen!" his grandmother admonished. "That's no way to talk! Now, what are we going to do about this poor old fellow" She stroked a loving hand over Smudge.

Before Liz could reply her bleeper sounded. "Oh dear. Do you mind if I use your phone?"

Glen took her into the house, and when she returned to the garden she said, "I'm afraid I must hurry. There are some beagle puppies needing help into the world. I have to operate on the mother. Glen, any chance of you bringing

Smudge into the surgery tomorrow morning? That is if you agree I should remove that lump, Mrs Mahy?"

Glen looked at his grandmother. "You must do what you think best, Mrs Cobb," the old lady nodded miserably.

"I'll bring him in. What time?" Glen asked.

"Eleven?" She entered the time in her diary. "Don't you worry, Mrs Mahy. Smudge will probably be back home with you in a little while. He'd best stay in for a few days, though, so we can keep an eye on him. Okay?"

The two oldies remained sitting there on the lawn as Glen walked Liz back to her car. She had left the windows open for the dogs, who jumped up at her approach, tails waving furiously. "Afraid you won't get your walk till late this evening," she told them. "You'll just have to run round the garden in circles till I get home again."

"Will Smudge need much looking after when he gets home?" Glen asked. "Only I won't be here to help the old girl. I'm going to be pretty busy over the next week or so."

"Yes, I know. Best of luck, Glen. We'll be rooting for you."

"You will? Thank God somebody's on my side."

"And don't worry about Smudge. We won't let him home till he's fit enough. I'll phone your Gran and let her know how he is."

"You always were a nice kid. Thanks."

Cheeky bugger, she thought as she drove off. But nice. She really did hope the inquiry cleared him.

Chapter 3

FRIDAY, 8TH JULY

Jackson insisted on collecting Liz from home, to take her down to the harbour for the evening Trident to Herm. He turned the car on the gravelled drive, switched off the engine and looked about him with interest. Apart from a couple of climbing roses, scattering petals on the breeze, there were no flowers: the clean lines of garden walls and drives were edged with small, neat shrubs and slim, decorative conifers. The one storey house was built back to front, obvious kitchen and bathroom windows and attendant pipes and drains facing the road. He wondered what the other side might be like.

"Hello! Sorry to keep you waiting," Liz hurried out, slamming her front door. "Ooh! You've bought a car." She walked round the blue, drophead Volkswagon. "That was quick!"

Jackson had jumped out to open the passenger door. "It didn't seem worthwhile hiring for an extended period so I picked this up secondhand. Don't want to buy anything new till I've been here long enough to size up what I'll need."

Liz fastened her seatbelt. "Where did you get it?"

"A garage not far from here. Parker Sales."

"Oh, Lord. Not Eddie Parker?"

"That's bad?"

Liz gave him a sidelong glance. "Oh, don't worry. No doubt the paint will hold it in one piece till you get your new one." She grinned. "No, I'm only pulling your leg. You see, Eddie Parker has earned himself a reputation, rightly or wrongly I can't say, for being a pretty sharp operator. They say he could sell ice to an Eskimo." She watched the turning they should have taken slip by on her left. "Er . . . which route were you planning?"

He grimaced. "I've gone wrong, huh? Tell me about it."

She navigated down to the North Beach car park, led him to the ticket kiosk and along to the Cambridge Pier where *Trident*, the large catamaran which served as a ferry between the islands, was embarking passengers.

The evening breeze scarcely ruffled the water. They stood out on the stern watching the sun dipping towards the silhouette of St Peter Port. "That's the Elizabeth College tower on the skyline," she pointed. "Where Pierre was at school." They waved to people in private boats lurching over their wake; watched seagulls wheeling overhead and distant cormorants diving. Then Liz tugged the sleeve of his jumper. "Come on, let's go forward."

Jackson followed her through the cabin onto the short bow deck. Herm and Jethou, bathed in the pink glow of evening, were enchantingly beautiful. He took a deep, contented sigh.

They were landed at Rosaire Steps, because the tide was low, after being told the return trip would be from the harbour. Climbing up the winding path round to the White House Hotel, walking mostly in silence, they both drank in the views, and the ambience. For Jackson it was unique, overwhelmingly impressive; to Liz every precious detail was familiar. It belonged to her, she was part of it . . . had been all her life. Yet it never failed to thrill her to the depths of her soul.

The bar was pressed full of bodies so they carried their drinks out onto the walled patio. "How often do you come here?" Jackson asked.

"Just as often as possible. Pierre often brings Annabel and the girls over in his boat. He and I used to come with our parents. We didn't have a boat of our own but would cross with friends or in one of the ferries. We camped here for our summer holidays several times."

"It is so fantastic. Haven't you ever wanted to live here?"

Liz tilted her head on one side, thinking. "No. I don't doubt there are problems, even in paradise; but when you experience them, then it is no longer paradise. I want Herm to remain this special to me, forever." Seeing the dreamy expression in her dark eyes, soft lips slightly parted in a subconscious smile, he had an urge to bend his head and kiss her. But of course he didn't.

They had seafood cocktail starters and queued at the carvery for roast ham with pineapple. Liz struggled to eat. The food was delicious but her mouth was dry and the wine didn't help. She was worried, stunned by the effect this man was having on her. Her heart thumped under her shirt – quite visibly she was sure; she had to hold her cutlery very firmly, pressing down on the plate to stop her fork rattling and betraying her shaking hand. This was not love-at-first-sight – she didn't believe in such nonsense; you couldn't possibly love a person you didn't know. No, this was purely and simply animal attraction. Lust. He was vibing the most basic sexual magnetism . . . A magnetism she must resist. It would be stupid to allow a wild, passionate affair to spoil what could develop into a really good friendship.

The American enjoyed his evening. The boat trip, the tiny island of Herm and the meal were all very special. The only disappointment was that Liz obviously did not reciprocate his interest in their relationship. He was disappointed too when he drove her home, that on some pretext about the next day's workload she excused herself from inviting him in for coffee.

Chapter 4

SATURDAY, 9TH JULY

"Sharon? Is that you?" Eddie Parker got up from his chair at the dining-table and opened the hall door. He was small, slim and neat, some might even say dainty, wearing his customary suit with a jazzy waistcoat, permed hair carefully combed over his ears. "Where the hell have you been? It's past teatime."

"Having my hair done!" His wife shouted back.

"What, again?" He went back to the heap of papers on the table.

Sharon came and stood in the doorway. "Yes, again. You're the one always bloody going on about my roots showing." She was short, too, but twice as wide, the rolls of fat round her middle making a travesty of the expensive matching silk blouse and pants.

"Can't think why you ever wanted to go blonde in the first place. It doesn't suit you," he grumbled, without turning round.

She stuck her tongue out at his back. "You was always complaining about how I looked before. That's why I did it. Trouble with you is you're never satisfied."

"And the trouble with you is you've never put a meal on the table on time since I married you."

"Where the hell do you expect me to put it, with that junk all over the place?"

"The only reason it's here is there's some important papers missing. It'll be that bloody slag sister of yours, messing things about again."

"You leave poor Wilma out of it . . ." she snarled.

"Poor Wilma nothing. We pay her a fortune to keep this place clean. And she never does. Her and her Social Security and child benefits and cheap housing . . . You realise I could be run in for paying her and her not declaring it, don't you?"

"She can't help being poor. She has an awful time trying to manage on what she gets . . ."

"If she cut down on her booze and fags she'd have more than enough. No wonder that bloody toe-rag husband of hers did a runner."

Sharon gave up and headed for the kitchen, shouting over her shoulder. "Anyway, what's your big hurry? We're not going out tonight, are we?"

"You're not, but I am." He stacked the papers into a tidy pile and slid them into his briefcase.

"Oh yeah? Where?"

He took the case into the hall and stood it near the front door. "Barrington's."

"Gawd! You still after that ruddy great barn of his? Here, what do you want for your tea? Sausage and chips?"

"No. Had that last night, and the night before. Haven't you got anything decent?" He watched her from the kitchen doorway. "And yes, I am still after his house. We need something bigger, if only to get away from the stink of frying chips."

Sharon muttered something indecipherable under her breath, opened the freezer door and pulled out a cardboard box. "Bird's Eye roast beef dinner do you? I'll stick it in the microwave."

"Did you have a good meeting, dear?"

Peter Barrington replaced the whisky decanter and held his glass under a syphon. "Hmm. Much the same as usual. Don't suppose the medical profession will ever be the same again, now we are stuck with all these young whippersnappers, imagining they know it all. They don't seem to understand that nothing replaces the old, well tried and tested methods."

Janet Barrington had replaced her twin set and pearls with a soft, silky dress: Peter always liked her to change for dinner. She wasn't really listening to his reply – it was always the same. And she didn't entirely agree with his attitude towards the advances in medical knowledge, though of course she wouldn't have dreamt of saying so.

"What are you drinking?" he asked.

"Just a dry sherry, please."

They took their drinks into the conservatory, to sit in the last rays of the sun with the evening paper. He would read it while she sat waiting for his comments. "They're talking of pouring more money into the Beau Sejour Leisure Centre again. What rubbish! Ridiculous that we tax payers should be expected . . ." He was interrupted by the front doorbell. "Damn! Who the devil . . ."

"Don't worry, dear. I'll go." Janet hurried away into the hall, her husband straining to recognise a voice.

He did. "Damn! Parker again."

"Peter, dear, it's Mr Parker to see you. Shall I ask him in here?"

"No! I'll go and speak to him in my study." He drained his glass and strode out to meet the foe.

"Ah! Parker. Reconsidered your offer, have you?" He opened the study door. "Do come in."

"Yes, doctor." Eddie knew Barrington hated being demoted from "mister". "I've thought quite a bit about it. You know," he settled himself in a studded leather chair, "I realise that now you are about to retire you will be relying on unearned income." He ignored Barrington's sharp intake of breath preparatory to a furious broadside. "So I am prepared to be generous. I am ready to raise my offer to three hundred and ninety-five thousand. Now what do you say to that?"

"Nonsense! Absolute rubbish. You're still fifty-five thousand short of my asking price." He wanted to say a great deal more, about rotten little Cockney double-dealers . . . but managed to restrain himself.

"Come on, doc! You know that figure you were asking was only a load of bull! Nobody in their right mind would . . ."

"Four hundred and fifty. That's my price. I have explained before, Parker, that we are in no hurry whatsoever to sell. We are very happy here." Peter Barrington stood over his visitor, glaring down his nose. He was appalled at the thought of this dreadful little man living here, anyway.

"Don't give me that. If you're not wanting to sell, why put the place on the market at all?" Eddie Parker stood up, realising he was not going to be offered a drink.

"Because we plan to spend much more time abroad and a smaller place . . ."

". . . would be easier to maintain in your absence. Yeah, I remember you telling me before . . . several times." He went to the door. "Okay, doc. You know where to find me when you drop your price. Give me a call." As he went out into the hall he added, "By the way, you wouldn't be interested in a nice little Porsche number I've just got in, would you? First class nick and only one careful owner . . ."

Peter Barrington's face was purple. "No! Absolutely not." He opened the front door. "Good evening, Parker."

Janet heard the door slam, and drooped even further. Her husband stamped into the drawing room and she heard the clink of a decanter before he rejoined her in the conservatory, breathing heavily. But for once he was speechless. She breathed a sigh of relief.

Jackson thoroughly enjoyed his trip out on Pierre's boat. They circled both Herm and Sark, and he was much impressed with Pierre's knowledge of the local waters, which apparently in the main consisted of razor sharp granite heads, either showing or lurking just beneath the surface. "Seems one has to be a considerable navigator to boat successfully around here," he commented, as they dropped the anchor in Belvoir Bay.

"It's pilotage more than navigation," Pierre explained. "One has to learn the rocks and the marks, but once you've done that, they don't change. The only shifting factor is the tides, but they also move to an unchanging rhythm, and once you've learned to understand your tables and your tidal charts, it's dead easy."

"I'll take your word for it." Jackson was disappointed that Liz wasn't along. She'd accepted his dinner invitation readily enough, but he had gotten the impression that her mind had been elsewhere much of the time. Of course a woman as attractive as that, and a divorcee into the bargain, probably had a string of admirers jockeying for position; his only asset was that he was a new face.

She was, without question, the most interesting woman to happen along since Joanne. The two were vaguely alike. Nothing odd in that: men were always supposed to go for the same physical types. The difference had been in their lifestyles. Liz Cobb worked hard for her living, and, he suspected, her satisfaction; she took her responsibilities, and her patients, seriously. Joanne had been a total hedonist, independently wealthy enough to live life exactly as she chose. Which had been what had killed her. Yet he had loved her dearly, had actually asked and been accepted only a few weeks before that dreadful day in Colorado she had lost control of her skis. They had buried her wearing his engagement ring.

Ten years, and he had not thought seriously about another woman, until now.

Chapter 5

SUNDAY, 10TH JULY

Jackson did want to see Liz again, but not to appear too pushy, so he decided to leave it until next week. He then discovered what a dead place Guernsey was on a Sunday, if you were not a member of the community. After breakfast he did some exploring, driving across to the west coast, and stopping at an attractive looking pub – to discover it was locked up tight.

"It's Sunday, mate," said a man digging in his garden next door.

"I know that," Jackson said.

"Pubs don't open on Sundays," the man said. "Unless they're serving meals."

"You mean no one can get a drink on a Sunday?"

The man grinned. "It's no problem if you belong to a club. Clubs can open. But not pubs."

"That's a bit rough on your visitors, isn't it?"

The man shrugged. "They complain, especially if they're here on bed and breakfast terms. But what the hell? That's what they come for, right? The olde worlde charm."

"I'm not sure that's what I'd call it. Okay, can you tell me where the nearest garage is? I'm a little low on gas."

"Gas?"

"Ah . . . petrol, right?"

"Right," the man said. "There's a garage just round the corner. But you can't buy petrol on a Sunday, either."

"You must be joking."

"Listen," the man said, "if you don't like our laws, you can always leave."

"That's a fact," Jackson agreed, and drove back to the St Pierre Park. "You're not going to tell me I can't have a drink," he said to the waiter, somewhat aggressively.

"Of course you may have a drink, sir. You are a resident of the hotel."

There seemed nothing for it but to spend the rest of the day reading and watching television. It was not particularly interesting until after the six o'clock news, when the local station put on a special programme. Jackson, reading a crime novel with one eye on the box, was not really interested until he saw the face of his acquaintance Glen Mahy. Mahy was not appearing on the programme – it was a library shot – but there could be no doubt about the subject. He put down his novel and turned up the sound.

There were three people facing an interviewer. She was a rather well-worn blonde whose name he gathered was Jane MacAvoy; Jackson indeed remembered seeing her at the airport when Mahy had come in. "I'd like, first of all, to ask you, Deputy Battle, what Greenpeace hopes to achieve from this inquiry, for which you have campaigned so hard."

The camera picked up a short, stockily built woman with short hair, who wore trousers and an aggressive expression. "What we want," the woman replied – Jackson gathered she was a member of the local parliament – "is a complete banning of all nuclear waste ships from Channel Islands waters."

"But that's not on, Lynn," said the man seated on her right, large and bluff and red-faced. "The inquiry is into the shipping accident, not the cargo."

"Now, Paul, seriously, do you suppose there would be an inquiry at all, but for that cargo, and the risks that were involved, for every living creature on this island? Risks," she went on, slightly raising her voice as the man she called Paul would have spoken, "about which we have been complaining for years, without any notice being taken of us."

"I'd like to ask you, Conseiller Pritchard," Jane MacAvoy said, anxious to defuse the tension, "as President of Tourism, if the island has suffered at all, financially, from the *Trygon* incident. It has received a great deal of publicity, hasn't it?"

"Why, yes, it has," Paul Pritchard was apparently one of the island's senior statesman, and as president of a States Committee, the nearest equivalent to a minister there was in Guernsey. "But it has had almost no effect on the number of visitors coming to the island. I mean, everyone knows that there is going to be a major earthquake in California some time in the near future, but that doesn't stop people going there."

"Then you feel that there is going to be an atomic accident close to Guernsey in the near future?" Jane MacAvoy asked.

"Now, I didn't say that," Pritchard objected, his colour deepening.

"Of course there is going to be a nuclear accident close enough to Guernsey to be highly dangerous, at some time in the future," Lynn Battle declared. "The States is merely living with its head buried in the sand."

"Well, perhaps we should bring in Mr Watts," Jane MacAvoy decided, and turned to the third studio guest. He is a short, heavy man, entirely lacking a neck, it seemed, with wild hair and his face half hidden by bushy whiskers. "You are a member of the Civil Defence Committee, Mr Watts. Was the island in any real danger last year, from the *Trygon's* cargo?"

"Ah, not *per se*, to be sure."

"Just what do you mean by that, Willy?" Lynn Battle demanded.

"Well, all the waste is secured in sealed containers. If the *Trygon* had struck and broken up, those containers would have sunk to the bottom, where they could do no immediate harm. They would have to be recovered before they started to corrode and leak their material into the sea, but that would not be for some considerable time. The damage would be mainly psychological."

"Do you seriously suppose that if the *Trygon* had gone down off the Platte Fougère, anyone, ever again, would have been prepared to eat any fish caught in Guernsey waters? The industry would be killed at a stroke."

"As I say, the danger would be mainly psychological," Willy Watts said stubbornly. "The fish would be quite unaffected by any radiation until and unless those containers were allowed to corrode. Why, more radiation goes into our seas every day from the atomic power station at Flamanville than could possibly come from one ship."

"Aha," Lynn Battle said. "Now, let us talk about this deathtrap on our doorstep."

"I say," Paul Pritchard muttered. "That's pitching it a bit strong."

"Deathtrap," Lynn repeated, with great deliberation. "You know about these things, Willy. Is it not true that there were four 'incidents' at the two French stations on Cap de la Hague, last year?"

"That is correct. But all were classified as level one, that is, with little or no risk of any significant escape in radiation. Certainly no increase was registered here."

"Possibly. But is it not also true that the French electricity industry remains government controlled, and that governments habitually minimise mishaps in their industries?"

"Now really, Lynn, that's going over the top."

"Is it not also true that of all the nuclear incidents in France last year, and there were about twenty of them, a third were caused by human error?" The angry woman bounced in her chair. "There are people over there, not thirty miles away from us, handling the most lethal material on earth, and making mistakes. But there is no danger, the French say. And so do the States here in Guernsey. That's like saying we are employing a bus driver who habitually crashes his vehicle, but no one is in any danger, because he hasn't killed anyone yet!"

She appeared to run out of breath, and Jackson grinned as he switched off the set. All small communities drummed up these vital local issues to gnaw at. He rang down for room service. He had no problems; if there was a serious accident at Flamanville, he would simply step on the next plane out. Then his smile faded into a frown. But what about those who couldn't do that?

Philippe stood at the window of the apartment building in Cherbourg and looked down at the street. A car had just pulled into the kerb, and Monique was getting out, looking as alluring as only Monique could. Then she bent over to thrust her head through the open window, obviously kissing the driver of the vehicle. He turned back into the room, and winked at Olga. "She's away."

Olga lay on the settee. She spent a lot of time doing that, or lying in bed. She was a desperately unhappy woman. Well, that figured; it was difficult to walk around with a bright smile when one knew one was dying. But Philippe no longer feared that she would not go through with it. Sometimes he wasn't quite sure whether she was dying of radiation exposure or of hatred for the people who had inflicted such a terrible fate on her, for the millions who were going to live after she was dead.

Like Monique, she frightened him. He watched the door open. "Tell me."

"He is one of the pumproom operators," Monique said. "Name of François. Very serious stuff. He is a very serious man."

"I can see that," Philippe said. "As it has taken you five weeks to net him."

"Fucking hard five weeks too. But it's done." Monique kicked off her shoes and poured herself a Pernod. "Anything in?"

"Yes, from Georges."

She turned, so abruptly that she spilt some of her

drink. Although she was as dedicated as any of them, and although *her* role did not necessarily involve suicide, she could not help but hope their mission might somehow be aborted.

"We are to wait on the decision of the Inquiry in Guernsey before making a move."

"What has the Guernsey Inquiry to do with us?"

"The lawyers acting for the sea captain have subpoenaed a security man from Flamanville. There will be a lot of questions asked. Georges is hoping something may develop. If this man could be forced into making any damaging admission, and if as a result public pressure was such that Flamanville, or any nuclear station, was forced to close, then we would know we were winning, without having to resort to violence."

Monique finished her drink and poured another. "Well . . . he's a nice engineer," she said. "Good in the sack. I'll have some fun, anyway,"

Chapter 6

MONDAY, 11TH JULY

Pierre had fixed an appointment for Jackson with an advocate, to go into the ramifications of Guernsey Company Law, particularly with reference to banking. "I'd put you on to Milford Martel," he said. "The chap you met at our house last Tuesday. But he's all tied up with this inquiry. The man you'll be seeing, Jerry Quentin, is also very good, though. He's in the same practice as Milford."

Jackson, happy to accept the recommendation, was given a thorough grounding in local practice at their first meeting, gathering that his main objective must be to keep himself, and any employees he might accumulate, squeaky clean when it came to financial matters. When the island had first begun to attract offshore banking because of its favourable tax structure, the lawyer explained, one or two cowboys had moved in, cleaned up a few million in shady dealing and left behind some unpleasant scandals. "The new laws are to prevent these incidents recurring," said Jeremy Quentin, from behind the mountain of books and papers on his old-fashioned mahogany desk. Like the whole building, the office was tiny, cramped, and the shelves lining the walls were bowed with the weight of antique leather tomes and files.

"Absolutely. Does the banking industry no good at all. Just scares off the customers," Jackson agreed.

Their business complete, he shook hands and went down the narrow, twisting stairs into the street called

Court Row, on the other side of which were the broad granite steps leading up to the Royal Court. Here quite a crowd was waiting, for the inquiry was about to convene. He saw Captain Mahy, deep in conversation with Milford, and also both Jane MacAvoy and Lynn Battle, the Deputy once again in trousers.

Tempted, he went inside, and took a seat in the public gallery. The procedures were interesting enough. The jurats – life appointed senior citizens who acted as a jury in all cases, civil or criminal – clad in their flowing robes and their Norman clerical headgear, took their places. The initial evidence was, as Milford had warned the previous Tuesday at the Le Tissier's barbecue, entirely concerned with how and when and where, charts being produced and studied and various expert opinions offered.

"Bloody boring nonsense," said the man sitting beside Jackson. "Let's go and have a drink."

Jackson turned his head. He had not paid any attention to the other spectators when he had taken his place, but now he realised there was something familiar about this man. His was not an easy face to forget, foursquare and craggy – a description which equally applied to his body – he had great bags under his eyes and his jaw. "Don't I know you?" he asked.

"Ssssh," someone hissed, and heads turned, censoriously.

The big man jerked his head, and they tiptoed out into the corridor. "Everybody knows me," he said.

"Good lord! You're David Beaufort."

"Right first time." David Beaufort headed for the stairs. "The nearest pub is just round the corner."

"I must have seen nearly all your films," Jackson said.

"I'm sorry about that. Most of them were bloody awful." Beaufort ignored the steps up to the main bar, continuing round the curved building to open the door into a cellar bar. Brown with nicotine and woodstain, thick with smoke and the smell of beer it was intimate, welcoming and gloriously old-fashioned.

"Oh, I wouldn't say that," Jackson followed him through into the small room at the end. "The fact is, my cousin directed several of them."

"Your cousin? What'll it be? Beer? Local brew. Not bad."

"I'll try it," Jackson agreed. "Harrison Briggs."

"Harry? You're a cousin of Harry Briggs?"

"Well . . . in a manner of speaking. He is the son of my mother's brother-in-law by her first marriage."

Beaufort drank deeply while considering this, but Jackson's attention was caught by another, older, barman who had just appeared. "Something wrong?" he asked.

The barman jerked his head. "Get 'im out," he whispered, hoarsely. "Mr Beaufort. 'E breaks things, when 'e's 'ad a few."

"What's that runt saying?" Beaufort demanded.

"That you get violent when drunk."

"Doesn't everyone? Same again, friend."

"You 'aven't finished that one."

"I'll bet this pint is gone quicker than you can pull the next."

The barman sighed. "One more, Mr Beaufort, and that's it."

"Fucking little Hitlers, these people," Beaufort remarked, without malice. "So. Fancy you being a cousin of old Harry Briggs. He was a bit of a shit, mind you. But he made good films. You know he's dead?" Jackson nodded. "Cirrhosis of the liver. Could happen to anyone." Beaufort contemplated his empty glass. "Let's switch to shorts. What's your favourite scotch?"

"Well . . ."

"No more, Mr Beaufort," said the barman. "And if you start trouble, I'll call the police."

"Shit," Beaufort commented. "I'm going home." He went outside, and waved for a taxi.

"I'll drive you," Jackson volunteered; he'd only drunk one beer. "My car's in Hirzel Street. It's parking time is just about up, anyway."

"That's very decent of you, old boy."

They got into the car. "So where is it?" Jackson asked.

"The airport, old boy."

"You live at the airport?"

"I live in Alderney," Beaufort said. "Why don't you come and have a drink? Stay for lunch, if you like."

Jackson thought that might be rather amusing. The man did drink like a fish, but there was nothing much for him to do until the lease for the office was signed.

The local bus-stop airline, known as Aurigny, which was indeed the French name for Alderney, maintained a frequent service. Although they did not have long to wait, in that time Beaufort downed two double scotches; Jackson contented himself with one single.

"It sure is small," he commented, as the twin-engined aircraft began its descent to the airstrip on the highest part of the island.

"Three miles long," Beaufort agreed. "You can walk round it in a couple of hours . . . if you're good at that sort of thing."

"And that's France."

"Cap de la Hague. The strait is only eight miles across. It's known as the Race of Alderney. You cotton race?"

"Ah . . . a very fast flowing body of water, over an uneven bottom, which makes for a good number of overfalls."

"And then some, especially if there's wind across tide."

"And that's the famous atomic station about which everyone is so het up." Jackson gazed at the tall white tower.

"One of them," Beaufort said. "Silly shits. They're het up, twenty odd miles away. We don't bother about it, and it's only eight miles from us."

"What's the main occupation of the island?" Jackson asked as the plane touched down.

"Drinking," Beaufort said.

* * *

There were a surprising number of cars at the airport, including a very old and battered Bentley, into which Beaufort climbed. "Are you sure you can drive?" Jackson asked.

"Of course I can drive. I haven't had a drink for half an hour." Jackson got in beside him, and they weaved their way out of the airport, Beaufort blowing his horn regularly. "That's to let them know I'm back," he explained.

"Who?"

"Everyone."

"Ah. How long have you been away?"

Beaufort looked at his watch, causing the car to lurch from side to side of the narrow road and forcing two cyclists into the ditch. "Three hours."

"I see." Jackson looked over his shoulder at the cyclists, who were shaking their fists and shouting. "Don't you have any police on the island?"

"They send a couple of chaps up from Guernsey for a month's tour," Beaufort said. "But if they're sensible they keep out of the way. Home." They had driven just about the length of the island from the airport, and were turning down a short drive to a surprisingly modern-looking house, a place of tinted glass and steeply sloping rooves. "Shangri-la," Beaufort said, and braked in front of the door.

Jackson got out with some relief. Then the door opened and a vast Pyrenean Mountain Dog shot out to greet them, jumping up on its hindlegs to place a paw on each of Jackson's shoulders and gaze down into his eyes from a massive six feet, a slobbery tongue dripping down the guest's collar. "He likes you," Beaufort commented.

"Is that a fact?" Jackson kept very still. "What happens if he doesn't like me?"

"You'd be dead. Down, Trouble. You're at it again."

The dog reluctantly stopped breathing into Jackson's face and dropped to all fours. "Is that his name, Trouble?"

"Absolutely. Ah, Forsythe."

A tall, somewhat cadaverous man had emerged from the door. "Just two for lunch, Mr Beaufort?"

"You have it. His name isn't really Forsythe, of course," he explained to Jackson. "But one can't have a butler with a name like Jones, now, can one? Through here." He led Jackson through a spacious lounge to a conservatory set on the edge of the cliff. "That fort over there is Essex. Quite a history."

Jackson peered down at the sea breaking on the rocks a hundred feet below them, then up at Cap de la Hague; seen from this angle the French promontory looked very close. So did the tower on the atomic station. "It's very lovely," he said. "The view. But I'm not sure I could live here."

"Drives a man to drink," Beaufort agreed. "Down here."

He led Jackson down a short flight of steps at the side of the conservatory, opened a door, and led him across a lawn to a large garden shed. "What's in here?" Jackson asked, as the actor unlocked the door. "Your etchings?"

"My booze." The door opened, he gestured Jackson into a perfect replica of a cowboy-western bar. "When I drink up at the house I break the windows, and Forsythe starts nagging like a woman," he explained, and went behind the bar.

"What about the mirror?" Jackson pointed above Beaufort's head.

Beaufort grinned. "Plastic. I can throw bottles at it all day. I often do. Now then, Jackson my boy. Let's get down to the serious stuff."

Chapter 7

TUESDAY, 12TH JULY

Liz Cobb peeled off the thin rubber gloves, pressed the pedal-bar of the surgery bin and dropped them in. The lid clanged down as she stepped away. "I won't be in here again till this evening, Polly. If you're busy you needn't bother to move this fellow yet; he won't be round for hours."

"Okay, Mrs Cobb. I promised to help Angela put away the new stocks of equipment today." Polly leaned over the inert young poodle on the operating table. "Poor little thing. I do hope he'll be all right."

"Don't see why not. His heart is strong and steady. Better put his Eton collar on so he can't gnaw the stitches when he comes round. I must go and phone Mrs Mahy, now, and let her know that Smudge is ready to go home." She removed her plastic apron and overall, before returning to her office.

First she rolled the poodle's file up on to her computer screen and typed in the details of his operation and medication. She then accessed Smudge Mahy's file for the telephone number. "Good afternoon, Mrs Mahy. Elizabeth Cobb here."

"How is Smudge today, Mrs Cobb?" The old lady was beginning to sound more confident.

"Fit as a flea. We took the stitches out this morning and the wound looks fine. He can come home as soon as you like."

"Glen promised me he'd get him for me. I'll telephone him. I'll be glad to have him back."

"I bet you've missed him," Liz smiled, thanking God the tumour had been benign. "Glen can collect him any time before seven this evening."

Glen. He was such a good sort, so kind to his old Gran. She wondered why he had never married. Her diary lay on the desk; she checked it, ticked off the day's achievements, closed down the computer and picked up her medical bag . . . there was still Ben Ozanne's heifer to visit before she called it a day.

Once in the car and heading out into the country her thoughts returned to Glen . . . and Jackson. Amazing. Suddenly two eligible men had moved into her orbit – a rare situation indeed. Not that she had any intention of marrying either of them, but a woman in her mid-thirties has to think about these things – decide if she really wants to risk another run on the matrimonial stakes or choose to remain single for the rest of her life. Neither prospect seemed very attractive at the moment, but at least if she did want a man around there were two waiting in the wings . . . at the moment. Yes, why hadn't Glen married? Maybe because he spent too much time at sea. Jackson, on the other hand, had explained to her about his fiancée's death. Awful. She was attracted to Jackson. He made her feel quite giddy every time she saw him, her tummy tying up in knots at the very thought of him. But there was no way she wanted to get seriously involved with him. He would only be here in the island for two or three years and then he'd be off back to the States again.

She turned on to the Forest road, glimpsed an aircraft coming in to land, shiny against a cloudless sky, and gave a contented sigh. She never wanted to live anywhere else but here, in the island. It was great to get away on trips, holidays, but even better coming back home. So that was Jackson ruled out. And Glen? Good, solid Guernsey stock. He might spend two-thirds of his life at sea, but there was no doubt Guernsey would remain his home.

He was big, strong and good looking; kind, gentle and caring. A shy, quiet man who was obviously attracted to her . . . but there were no responding sparks in herself. She liked him a lot, felt sad, angry, that he had to face this awful inquiry, but he excited no animal instinct in her at all. So, did that matter?

She swung the Volvo on to the track that Ben Ozanne laughingly called a drive, and bounced all the way down to the farmhouse. Ben came out to meet her. "Was wond'rin' when you was comin'," he called.

Liz brought her bag out of the car. "Hello, there. Afraid I couldn't get away any earlier. So where's your heifer?"

"Here in the field." He led the way round the barn to a gate. "Now will you just look at her. She's off 'er 'ead. Talk about mad cow disease." He wasn't exaggerating. The young animal was charging round the field in circles, kicking her heels high in the air. "I should 'ave known better than to buy her off 'Arry de la Mare. All 'e's ever been able to raise on his farm is a glass of beer."

"Let's have a closer look at her," Liz said, lifting the heavy iron ring off the gatepost. "Can you catch her for me?" Silly man, wasting time like this. He should have had the heifer in the barn, waiting for her.

The animal had disappeared to the far end of the pasture, but when she saw the two figures by the gate her head went down and she charged back up the field . . . straight at them. "Watch yourself!" Ben shouted.

The heifer swerved at the last moment but still managed to catch Liz a hefty bump on her side, sending her rolling over on to the grass, and causing great amusement to the man and his animal. Liz muttered a number of very unprofessional and unladylike words she had picked up in the course of her career. "Ben, that has to be the healthiest animal in the island!"

"Bot she'm mad!"

She got to her feet, staring down the side of the field. "Let's just go down there, a minute," she suggested.

"What for? There's nothing down . . ."

"I think we may find the source of your mad cow disease." She strode off, stopping fifty yards along the hedge. "Look!" she pointed at the apples which had fallen off an overhanging tree. "She's not mad. She's drunk!"

The farmer stared at the fermenting fruit. "You reckon? Well I'm damned! Trust 'Arry to raise a dronk. And I never thought alcoholism was an infectious disease. At least, not in cows."

Liz related the story later that evening at Pierre and Annabel's Pimms and Quiche party, given for a team of bankers who had flown over for a golfing week-end, plus a few local friends. "Such a waste of time, though," she complained to her laughing audience. "And he'll be mad as hell if I bill him for the visit."

"How do you structure your scale of charges?" one of the visitors asked very seriously.

"By the seat of my pants," she replied, unwilling to get into a heavy financial discussion; she was tired, had a bruise on her hip, and had accepted Annabel's invitation only to help provide a little feminine balance to a predominently male evening. Seeing Glen wearing a glum expression in the doorway of the conservatory she moved in his direction.

The sea captain's face immediately lit up. "Hi, there. You did a good job on old Smudge."

"Not difficult. He's a fine, healthy old fellow. You fetched him home, did you?" They talked about his grandmother and her cat for a few minutes, then to get off the subject of shop Liz said, "Do you play golf?"

Before he could answer, Pierre joined them. "In a fashion. When he connects he knocks the cover off the ball."

"*When*, being the operative word." Glen made a moue, and drained his glass. "Which is why I've never got my handicap into single figures."

"I wouldn't have thought you had a chance of much practice," Liz said.

"Didn't you know? He takes bags full of old balls to sea with him, each trip, and practices driving them at the horizon," Pierre told her, with a deadpan expression.

Glen nodded. "That's right. But the trouble is the horizon is so wide it's hard to judge if one's on target."

"Excuses, excuses. Refills?" Pierre asked, taking Glen's glass and calling as he walked away, "Ah, there you are, Jackson! Thought maybe you were going to give us a miss, tonight. Pimms?" The American came out onto the patio.

"Sorry I'm late. Er, no thanks. Do you have a plain soda?"

Liz noted the unusually bowed shoulders and black rings round his eyes. "What's up? You look totally pole-axed."

"Yeah. Yeah," Jackson nodded, immediately regretting the sudden movement. "I guess that's as good an assessment as any. It happened yesterday."

"What did?" Glen joined them.

"I went to Alderney . . ." he winced at the memory.

"Whatever for?"

"A drink before lunch. All because of you, you understand." He levelled one bloodshot eye at Glen. The other was closed.

"Me! How come?"

"Went to sit in on your inquiry . . ."

"What's that got to do with going to Alderney?"

". . . and was sitting next to a bloke who lives there, and somehow found I'd gotten into a drinking session with him."

"Say no more." Pierre grinned. "Which one was it?"

"David Beaufort . . ."

His audience shouted with laughter. "And you're still standing?"

"Soda nothing! What you need is a *Fernet Branca.*"

"Did you meet Trouble?"

"Trouble? You'd better believe it!" Jackson lowered himself on to a padded lounger. "Oooh!"

"Trouble . . . the dog."

"You mean the hairy white pony that stands on its hind legs and slobbers all over your face? He was the least of my problems. David asked me to stay for lunch but, as I recall, we never got round to consuming solids. He decided to take me on a guided tour of the island . . . in his Bentley." Accepting the proffered Scottish hangover remedy he drank, grimaced, coughed violently and drank again. "Look," he raised the sleeve of his shirt. "There are the bruises to prove it."

"How did that happen? What hit you?" Liz asked.

Jackson shook his head . . . and winced again. "Can't say I'm dead sure about this but I believe it was while David was arranging a few extra bends in a wall exiting the town. Of course it could have been when we took on a team of local footballers. Because there were only two on our side David recruited some cows . . ."

Most of the guests surrounded the lounger, listening with great glee to the tale of Jackson's suffering. Liz was amused herself, but seeing Glen sitting on a low granite wall some distance away she wandered over to join him, jug of Pimms in hand. She topped up his glass without asking, placed the jug on the grass and perched on the wall beside him. "They say alcohol doesn't make you any happier: only intensifies the mood you're in when you start drinking." Glen sighed and took another swig. "So I supposed I shouldn't be having this."

"Worried?"

"Wouldn't you be?"

Liz thought. "I certainly wouldn't like to be in your shoes. I'd hate it. But one has to face facts. Your main critics are the cranks and weirdos. You can't take them seriously."

"Someone does, or there wouldn't be an inquiry."

"Surely the only question is whether or not they can prove negligence on your part."

"Always supposing that the result depends solely on physical and material facts. The trouble is that fear of pollution has become a very emotive factor at these hearings. Not helped by my being a Guernseyman." He turned to stare at her, his intensely blue eyes filled with misery. "Don't you realise I'm regarded as a traitor?"

"Come on! That's going over the top. No one with any nous would suggest . . ."

He bowed his head to run the fingers of both hands through his hair. Then he picked up his empty glass and stood up. "Sorry I'm being such a party pooper. I really shouldn't have come tonight, but when Pierre asked me I thought it might take my mind off things . . . Let's go back and join the others."

Shortly afterwards, when Liz looked round to see if Glen had got over his fit of blues, she couldn't find him.

He'd gone home.

Jackson wasn't particularly exhilarating company that evening, either, but Liz found herself gravitating in his direction . . . too often. Pierre's potent Pimms gradually washed away the gloss banking image of the visiting team who decided on an extremely rowdy game of torchlight tennis after supper. Liz, herself, was tired and Jackson's head was in no condition to withstand the noise. "I'll just finish helping Annabel with these glasses, then I'm going home," she told him.

"Good. That means I won't have to be the first to leave. Where's the telephone. I need to call a cab." Jackson made three attempts to leave the lounger before he finally succeeded. "I didn't feel up to driving this evening," he explained.

"Very wise, seeing that you've put some of Pierre's Pimms on top of what's already in there," she teased. "Don't worry with a cab. I'll give you a ride."

"I'm mad as hell this has happened," he said later as he lay back in the passenger seat. "I just never met anyone before coming here who drank like that."

"I've never met David Beaufort, myself. I understand that drinking with him in Guernsey is hazardous enough, but joining him for a session on his home ground in Alderney is generally reckoned to be fatal."

"You're not kidding." He pulled himself up in his seat and turned his head to watch her profile as she concentrated on the road. "I hope you understand . . . this kind of drinking is not my scene. I've never been in this state since leaving Harvard."

"I'll believe you. Thousands wouldn't." She pulled up at the yellow line at the bottom of the Rohais.

"I should ask you in for a drink . . ."

"Don't even think about it," she stopped him.

"Hell, I'm mad. I mean mad! I was really keen for you to think me a nice guy. Dammit, you're such a honey. You're beautiful and intelligent . . ."

". . . and you're still tight as a tick!" She swung the Volvo through the hotel gateway, circled the fountain and drew up at the front doors. "There. And I hope you feel better in the morning."

"That depends."

"On what?"

"Whether I have the prospect of lunching with you to give me an incentive to live."

She giggled, and without thinking leaned across to give his cheek a goodnight peck. "Okay, you're on. Now, out!"

He lurched towards her, wanting more, but she hastily backed off. "Where?" he asked, before shutting the door.

"Collect me at the surgery at twelve thirty. We'll decide then. Goodnight."

Jackson stood in the pool of light from the lobby, swaying slightly, as she drove out. He was smiling. So was Liz.

Chapter 8

WEDNESDAY, 13TH JULY

The waiting room was full all morning. Every time Liz emerged from her room there seemed to be more people rather than less. Cat baskets and wire cages sat in rows on the floor . . . the more fortunate felines hidden in downmarket cardboard boxes which concealed them from the interested attentions of canine patients. By twelve-fifteen she was hot and thirsty, but there were still several owners waiting, clutching leads and baskets. A large boxer was sitting peacefully, pretending he hadn't noticed the rude remarks being made by a miniature Yorkshire Terrier; a mongrel with a bandaged leg was out-staring an embarrassed Dalmatian. One of the other vets in the practice collected the boxer and his owner; Liz re-dressed the mongrel's leg and returning for the Dalmatian, saw Jackson sitting with the little Yorkie on his knee, chatting to the big fat man on the other end of its lead. It was nearly one when she finished. "Is it like that every day?" the American asked as they got into his Golf.

"That was pretty average. Unfortunately, when there is a breather one feels one has to operate on the backlog of bookwork. What about you? Successful morning?"

"Yes, amazingly, all things considered." He flashed a repentent grin at her. "Sorry about last night."

"Forget it. Could happen to anyone. Tell me where you're taking me."

"Jerbourg, but you may have to direct me. I picked up a couple of packed lunches at the hotel. Does that suit you?"

"Er . . . yes. But you do realise there's a grim bank of cloud coming up from the southwest?"

Jackson gave a quick glance around. "Which way is southwest?" Then swerved on to the pavement to avoid a bus.

"Hidden behind the trees my side. How come you chose Jerbourg?"

He smiled. "Asked the breakfast waiter where he takes his girlfriend. Wanted to have you all to myself. There always seem to be so many people around. I think we need the opportunity to get better acquainted."

Luckily his attention was wholly involved in a tricky manouevre past a lorry, so he couldn't see her reaction. Alarm bells were pealing in her ears . . . while her tummy was leaping with excitement. "Leave the car up here on the right," she told him. "Then we can walk on in that . . ." she pointed, ". . . direction."

Lunch was chicken legs, bread rolls and tomatoes, apples, bananas and a bottle of Frascati. They didn't have anything to sit on, but the grass was dry.

"Top marks. They even remembered the corkscrew." Jackson stood the bottle on the ground between his knees and worked on the cork.

"And glasses. Good," Liz took them out of the bag, "I hate drinking wine out of polystyrene cups."

He poured, touched her glass with his and said, "Here's looking at you, Liz."

"Cheers." She gave a weak smile and tried desperately to think up something to say. A thousand topics came to mind, but none seemed suitable.

"Signed the lease on my new offices this morning," Jackson told her.

"The place in the Grange?"

"Yes. You must come and see it. I've sketched some

plans for the lay out. Now I have to find a contractor to take the work on board."

"Does the lease permit you to make alterations?" she queried.

"There won't be any. Just the computer cables, phones, screens and desks in the main office. And some re-decorating. I'll have a room to myself and the mainframe will live in a storeroom at the back."

"How many access screens will you have to start with?" she tried to sound computer-wise.

"The system I'm bringing in will take thirty. We'll access as many as we want when the need arises. "Here," he opened a foil dish. "Are you going to tackle one of these chicken pieces?"

Liz took a leg and holding it to her teeth, tore a strip of flesh from the bone. Between mouthfuls she asked, "How long do you intend staying in Guernsey?"

"Depends . . ." he watched a seagull swing past below them.

"On what?"

He turned to look at her. "Several factors, too numerous to mention. Tell me, what did your ex do?"

A sudden switch of subject! "You mean for a living, or to make me divorce him?" She helped herself to a tomato.

"I meant his job . . . profession. Whatever."

"Accountancy. He still does."

"Here in the island?"

"Yes. You must meet him some time. You'll like him."

"I doubt that."

She swung round to look at him. "Why?"

His eyes held hers. "Jealousy, maybe?" Without looking away he refilled the glasses.

A red stain crept up her neck. "Come off it. We only met a week ago."

"Long enough." At last he dropped his gaze.

When the food and wine were gone they lay back on

the grass, a few feet apart, looking up at the clouds. "We are going to have to make a run for it in a minute," Liz said.

"I'd come to think you only had blue skies here. Won't this pass soon?"

"It might. But we need the rain. The reservoir is getting low." She pulled a stem of grass, put it in her mouth and closed her eyes. Moments later the stem was drawn from her teeth . . . and Jackson's mouth was over hers, his lips softly nibbling her own. Soothing. Magic. She scarcely wanted to breathe for fear of breaking the spell. His lips moved over her face, caressing her eyes, brows, hairline.

This was not meant to happen! She'd intended to remain friendly, but aloof. Keep cool and calm . . . and instead there was a burning, aching response right through her body, the almost imperceptible touch of his fingers gently stroking the front of her shirt, making a nonsense of her plans. Her arms slid up round his neck and her mouth sought his.

What seemed like only a few moments later, Jackson said, "It's okay for you, down there, but my back is freezing." He rolled away from her.

"Why . . .?" she began, then as water rolled down her cheeks realised for the first time that it was pouring with rain. "Oh hell! Grab the bag, and let's get out of this."

"Won't do us much good. I never put the car roof up."

They ran together, hand in hand, laughing as the rain washed their hair down over their faces.

Chapter 9

THURSDAY, 14TH JULY

The arrival was a dapper little man with a pencil moustache. He carried only an overnight bag and a briefcase, and looked around him with an air of dissociation from his surroundings, eyeing the ground officials and the other passengers who had just disembarked from the Aurigny Cherbourg-Guernsey flight as if they were creatures from another planet. "Monsieur Dubois?" Milford Martel hurried forward with outstretched hand.

The Frenchman took it somewhat reluctantly. "Dubois, *c'est moi.*"

"You do speak English?" Milford asked anxiously.

"That is why I am 'ere," Dubois pointed out. "I speak Engleesh."

"That's great. My car is right here. We'll have to hurry. The Inquiry reconvenes in half an hour."

"Eet will finish today?"

"Well, I can't promise that. However, I am sure your evidence will be a great help."

"I 'ave zee overnight things," Dubois said. "But no 'otel. I should not be 'ere, you know."

"Well . . ."

"Today, een France, ees holiday. Bastille Day! I should be on zee beach, weez my wife. Yes?"

"Oh, well, I'm terribly sorry. We didn't fix the hearing for today. It just fell out that way. If you do have to stay over, we'll fix you up with a place to sleep, don't you worry about that."

"That ees very kind of you. Now tell me what ees eet you weesh me to say."

"Eh? I can't tell you that, *monsieur*. I just want you to answer any question I or the Comptroller or any of the Jurats may ask you, with absolute truthfulness. Remembering always," he added with a grin, "that it is in your interests as well as my client's to make it plain that there is no radioactive danger whatsover emanating from the plants on Flamanville."

"But of course," Dubois said. "Zere ees no radioactive danger, whatsoever, from zee plant at Flamanville. Or zee one at Cap de La Hague."

"You mean that's true?" Milford was surprised.

"But of course."

"Sit down, *monsieur*." Jacques Blaisdel indicated the chair before his desk. He also had intended to spend Bastille Day on the beach, and had not been at all pleased at being informed by the Director that he was needed to be in his office to receive an important visitor. Now he looked at the card in his hand. "Monsieur Etal? From the . . ." he drew a sharp breath. "Deuxième Bureau?"

"Why, yes. You have been visited by us before?"

"Indeed. But . . ."

Etal walked to the window and looked out at the sea, the Race of Alderney, Alderney itself. To the south-west the island of Sark loomed large, and beyond it, the dark patch on the horizon that was Guernsey. "What a delightful spot you have here."

"Thank you." But Blaisdel was not in the mood for pleasantries. "Is something the matter?"

"One never knows, in our business," Etal said, and sat down. "We understand that you have been requested to supply representation at this absurd inquiry now being held in Guernsey."

Blaisdel nodded.

"And you have have complied?"

"I have sent one of my assistants. Etienne Dubois."

"Is he a sound man?"

"Oh, very. He will tell them nothing they should not know. But . . . I do not see what this has to do with the Secret Service."

"Everything to do with nuclear energy is the business of the Secret Service," Etal said severely. "However, I am not here because of any agitation in Guernsey. Have you ever heard of an organisation known as The Shining Light?"

"I think so," Blaisdel said uneasily.

"This organisation is dedicated to the elimination of the use of nuclear power, for whatever reason, civil or military. A laudable aim, you might say. Unfortunately, these people are not open anti-nuclear campaigners, such as Greenpeace. They are fanatics, who believe in the use of violence, and who are not averse to causing the deaths of large numbers of people to achieve their objectives. As we in France are more heavily reliant on nuclear power than any other country in Western Europe, it follows that the main thrust of their effort is here in France."

"I understand this, *monsieur*," Blaisdel said. "And I can assure you that security at Flamanville is second to none."

"That may be. But these are dangerous, cunning people, who are quite prepared to commit suicide if they think that may help to bring down your industry. I am here because some months ago we believe we located a cell of this organisation in Saumur. As you are no doubt aware, Saumur is close to the nuclear generating plants at Chinon."

Blaisdel nodded. "Have you apprehended these people?"

"Unfortunately, no. As I say, we were in receipt of information concerning them, but we had nothing concrete to go on. Then, several weeks ago, they disappeared. Without making any attempt to gain access to either of the establishments at Chinon. We entirely lost track of them until four days ago, when we received a report that their leader, a man called Philippe Morin, had been seen in Cherbourg."

"Cherbourg?!" Blaisdel sat up straight.

"This is a very dangerous man, and if we are correct, he will be accompanied by a woman named Monique Lesbirel, who is even more dangerous. Unfortunately, while we do have a description of the man Morin we do not have one of the woman. All we know is that she has been responsible for two deaths already." He placed a sheet of paper on Blaisdel's desk. "There is a photokit of the man."

Blaisdel gulped as he looked at Philippe's picture. "You think they mean to attack Flamanville? That is simply not possible. No one can attack us here with the slightest hope of success."

"I do not know *what* they intend to do. We will do all we can to locate this man and arrest him. However, you are a nuclear generating station, and Morin is in the business of destroying them, regardless of the consequences. Therefore I must warn you that your security must be at its maximum level until we have made the arrest. I will wish you good day."

Chapter 10

THURSDAY, 14TH JULY – (continued)

Cocoa and Horlicks barked joyously when they heard Liz pick up their leads, dashing through the utility to the door and back, impatient for her to tie the belt of her mack. She cursed the sand all over the floor, brought in after previous damp expeditions, and vowed to do some housework that evening. Not that there was too much, living alone, but the dogs made twice as much mess each, as any human being. Of course now that dogs were banned from the popular beaches it was necessary to visit the more obscure areas where they had to scramble over rocks to reach the shoreline. These two idiots loved the sea so much and 'fishing' in rockpools, that she couldn't deny them a beach for ever more.

Her hand was on the doorknob when the phone rang; she toyed with the idea of ignoring it . . . then it crossed her mind it could be urgent – it was only a quarter to eight – or it might be Jackson. She went back to the kitchen phone. "Elizabeth Cobb," she murmured, and held her breath.

"Liz, dear! Trish here. I'm in Guernsey!"

"Trish! How marvellous. Where are you? When did you arrive?" The flash of disappointment at not hearing Jackson's voice was quickly overcome; Trish was her favourite aunt, her mother's younger sister.

"Just driven off the ferry. I'm at the Richmond, but they can only give me a bed for two nights . . ."

"You should have called me: there's tons of room here." She turned to shout at the dogs to shut up.

"What's that? Are you busy?"

"No. Just about to walk Cocoa and Horlicks. Want to come?"

"In this weather? No thanks. I'd rather have some breakfast and join you later for coffee."

"I have to be at the surgery by nine. Make it about twelve forty-five, and we'll have lunch. Afraid it will only be something out of the freezer."

"Couldn't be better. Twelve forty-five. See you then."

Liz drove off to the coast with the dogs through heavy drizzle, in happy anticipation of a *tête-a-tête* with Trish. She wanted to talk about her career; she longed to tell her about Jackson, about her otherwise non-existent love life . . . men in general, and the direction her life was or was not taking. Trish was twelve years younger than her mother, known in the family as The After-Thought, and so much nearer her own age: old enough to be experienced, young enough to sympathise with her feelings, which Mum did not. Mum was of the old school, a leftover from the Victorian era, and there were too many subjects it was just impossible to broach with her. Anyway, the Wrinklies were abroad at the moment on a three-months world cruise.

She was a few minutes late for surgery; the dogs were stinking so much in the car she had had to take them into the back garden and hose them down. The odour was still pretty strong but at least the worst of the sand and seaweed was washed off. After seeing three dog patients, all suffering from overfeeding, a beautiful Persian cat with furball, a gerbil, two guinea pigs and a canary, she neutered two cats, scrubbed up and dashed home to make a salad to go with the steaks and French bread she'd removed from the freezer before leaving.

The Bailiff coughed. "You may sit down, Captain Mahy."

Glen sank into a straight chair, while the court rustled with anticipation.

The Bailiff gave a brief tap of his gavel, and the rustling subsided. "Now, Captain, you are aware, I am sure, that we are not sitting as a court of law. You are not charged with any crime, you are not under oath, and of course you are not obliged to answer any of the questions that may be put to you."

"But if they find him guilty," David Beaufort whispered to Jackson, "he's going to lose at least his master's ticket. I hope he knows that."

Jackson Ridgeway and David Beaufort had not arranged to meet in court; they had just happened to arrive at the same moment. Amazingly, the actor did not seem to have suffered the slightest after-effects from his monumental binge. Jackson was still feeling a little tender – but that might have been because of Liz Cobb. He had really gone overboard yesterday, something that had not happened for a very long time, since Joanne's death, in fact. Though she had not been unresponsive he had pushed his luck, and if she hadn't managed to keep her cool their relationship, still very new and fragile, could have turned into a cheap, one-night stand affair . . . albeit in the middle of the day. Not something of which either of them would be proud.

The most reprehensible thing of all was that, in hindsight, he didn't regret a moment of it. He had fallen very heavily for the little vet, and not only because she was so darned sexually attractive. She was bright and colourful, fun to be with; and yet she could be so sensible and serious when the need arose. The question now was, what did he propose to do about her? His masculine ego was sufficiently developed for him to feel quite certain that he *could* take the relationship to include bed on a fairly continuous basis, without making any firm commitment. The question was what came after that? Just a friendly wave good-bye? Circumstances had made him a bachelor for more than half of his allotted span. Could he cope with marriage? Or even a live-in arrangement? Anyway, from what little he had seen of Guernsey, such an unorthodox step would not encourage people to place their money with the Parks Paramus Banking Corporation.

And such reflections took no account of *her* feelings. She had tried marriage once and given up on the idea. Then there were all those animals with whom she appeared to be personally involved, unlike most of the vets with whom he had come into contact, who seemed to regard animals as mere lumps of flesh to be dealt with as quickly as possible and then forgotten. He wanted more from their relationship than mere physical gratification. But there . . . Admit it! He did want a relationship with this woman . . . on almost any terms.

He tried to concentrate as the Bailiff continued. "Our purpose here is to attempt to establish whether or not the island of Guernsey and its inhabitants were put at risk by your ship the *SS Trygon*, in September of last year, and whether there was any negligence on the part of yourself, or your crew, which caused the near catastrophe. However, the Royal Court has determined to widen the terms of reference to include the whole situation of Guernsey, and by consequent extension, the other members of the Channel Islands, with regard to the possible effects of a radiation accident in our seas and our skies. Yes, Mr Martel?"

Milford, seated next to Glen, was on his feet. "With respect, sir, my client cannot be expected to offer an opinion on these matters, nor can he be held responsible for any finding of this Court of Inquiry into such matters. He is here to answer questions pertinent to the endangerment of his ship."

"Quite, Mr Martel; your remark will be noted. I just wish Captain Mahy, and indeed the Court, to be aware of these larger issues, which perhaps we in the Channel Islands have been neglectful in not having raised publicly before."

"You can bet your bottom dollar they've raised them privately often enough," David whispered to Jackson.

"With what result?"

"Sweet Fannie Adams. The nuclear industry is France's sole source of electricity. But it's such a profitable source they are just about the only country in Western Europe which can actually export the stuff. Shit, a sizeable proportion of Britain's electricity requirements are imported from France, and there's even talk of Guernsey buying from them. So you can see nobody's going to bother too much about a fuss kicked up by a bunch of cranks."

The Bailiff had handed over the inquiry to HM Comptroller, the Guernsey equivalent of an attorney general. "Now, Captain Mahy," the Comptroller said. "I would like to take you through your voyage. You sailed from Japan on . . ." he checked his notes. "25 August last. Is that correct?"

"Yes, sir," Glen said.

"Your cargo was atomic waste, bound for the re-processing plant at Flamanville?"

"Yes, sir."

"You had made this voyage before?"

"Six times."

"Always with the same cargo?"

"Yes, sir."

"Has the point ever been made to you, Captain, that this is a highly dangerous and anti-social trade?"

Milford looked as if he would have objected to the question, but Glen merely grinned, sadly. "There are several re-processing plants in Western Europe, sir. There is one in England. My firm happens to deal with one in France. As to the undesirable nature of the cargo, nuclear waste is there. It is going to be there as long as nuclear energy is used, for whatever purpose. As it is there, it has to be got rid of, in the safest and least environmentally hazardous manner possible. Nobody has yet come up with a better idea than the re-processing plant."

"Good for you," Jackson muttered.

"So therefore, you have no compunction whatsoever about transporting such a potentially deadly cargo close to a heavily populated area?" the Comptroller pressed. "An area in which you yourself were born and grew to manhood."

Milford stood up. "Mr Bailiff, I must protest. As you have just made clear, my client is not on trial."

"Quite, Mr Martel," the Bailiff agreed. "I don't think you need answer that question, Captain Mahy." The Comptroller revealed no discomfort; he and the Bailiff were socially the best of friends.

"But I wish to answer the question, sir," Glen said.

Milford sat down with a sigh. "Yes, Captain?" asked the Comptroller.

"As I have attempted to explain, sir, atomic waste is a fact of life. It is also a dangerous substance. As it is going to be shipped from A to B no matter what any of us may think about it, I personally feel happier that I should be in charge of it when it is passing close to my homeland, yes. My family lives in Guernsey, as you know, and it is not my intention ever to endanger either them or my home."

If Glen had hoped to score a point, it failed to register on his examiner. "And, of course," the Comptroller said, "you are a professional seaman, who goes where the pay is best. Is that not correct?"

Again Milford opened his mouth, but Glen beat him to it. "Why, yes, sir, or I would not have been able to command the ship."

The two men glared at each other for some seconds, then the Comptroller smiled, "On what could have been her last voyage, eh, Captain?" He picked up some of the papers from his desk. "I have here a marine engineer's report, following an examination of your ship's engine, which indicates that a main bearing was so worn it was in a dangerous state. In fact, am I right in saying that it was the overheating of this bearing, and the consequent fire it caused, that was responsible for your engine failure off the Casquets?"

"That is correct, sir."

"I also have here a copy of a letter from you to the marine superintendent of your shipping company, dated last summer, in which you draw his attention to the condition of the bearing and request that the ship be dry-docked for extensive repairs, and . . ." he waved a third sheet of paper, "a copy of his reply, in which he agrees that the engine needs an overhaul but insists that this cannot be carried out until your return from the delivery to Cherbourg. Again, what might be termed, the last voyage of the *Trygon*, Captain."

"As you say, sir," Glen agreed equably.

"I assume you feel that, having pointed out the condition of the ship's engines, and been told to proceed with your delivery, you are entirely exonerated from any blame in the matter?" He hurried on before Glen could reply. "But do you not, on reflection, consider that, in view of the length of the voyage required, and the nature of the cargo you would be carrying – the highly dangerous cargo – that you should have taken the matter of the engine further? That, if necessary, you should have refused to captain the ship in such unsatisfactory circumstances?"

"I would simply have been sacked," Glen said. "And somebody else given the command. Shipping is a hard business nowadays. Profit margins are tight. Any personal action I might have taken would not have prevented the ship from sailing. I at least knew what to expect, and I am better acquainted with local waters than any other captain on our staff."

"Quite. And equally, you had no desire to be made redundant in this, as you say, hard business. Now Captain, let us deal with the events of 21 September last. I have here your log book . . . may I ask if these entries were made as the events happened?"

"No, sir. Those entries were copied from the deck log, which is a rough book. You should have the deck log there also."

"I do. But as you say, it is a rough book. May the Court

take it that the entries in the Ship's Log are an accurate transcription?"

"They are accurate as to the timing of events, and the events themselves. It is normal procedure, when completing the Ship's Log, to add whatever observations may be thought pertinent in the light of any later information which may have come to hand."

"Very good. Now . . ." he glanced at the Log Book, "the engine-room staff reported overheating in the bearing at eight o'clock that morning. There is no additional entry at this point, except course and speed."

"I was within six hours of Cherbourg, and overheating did not necessarily mean that the engine was going to fail. Having due regard both to my cargo and my circumstances, I decided to attempt to make my port of destination."

"So you maintained your course. But the engine did fail, following the fire, at nine-fifteen. Yet it was ten o'clock before you called for assistance. Can you give a reason for that delay?"

"I instructed the engine-room staff to see if they could repair the damage. As soon as they reported that they could not, I called for assistance."

"You allowed your ship to drift, for forty-five minutes, carrying a dangerous cargo, and so close to land?"

"When the engine failed," Glen said, "the ship was in no danger of stranding. We were six miles north-west of the Casquets Reef, and the tide was running north out of the Bay of St Malo. That north-running tide turns north-east when it reaches the Casquets and the Race of Alderney. At that time the tide was carrying us away from land and out into the Channel."

"But the tide would turn?"

"Yes, the tide was due to turn just after twelve. When I called for assistance, at ten hours, I was assured that the tug would be with me in just over an hour. It was delayed, but even so it arrived just as the tide turned. Unfortunately, weather conditions had by then deteriorated to a considerable extent. The tug managed to get two lines aboard us but they both parted soon after we were taken in tow. We were then in the grip of the south-running tide, but it had not yet gathered pace."

"But it was doing so. Your ship was in grave danger. Yet you do not seem to have realised this. Is it not true that you refused an offer of assistance from a French Air-Sea Rescue helicopter?"

"I was still confident of saving my ship," Glen asserted. "So were my crew. I needed all my hands. It would have lessened our chances of saving the ship had anyone been winched off by helicopter."

"But was that not a miscalculation? You say you were confident of saving your ship. And you did. But purely by fortune. Did you not touch a rock off the Platte Fougère Light Tower?"

"I did. The weather was so severe that it took longer than I had anticipated for the tow to be made secure. However, it *was* made secure, and although my ship was holed, it was not critically damaged, nor was there any risk of the cargo being lost."

"You say the weather was very severe by then. How would you describe that in layman's terms, Captain Mahy?"

"The wind was out of the north-west blowing a steady forty knots, with gusts to fifty. There was heavy rain limiting visibility."

"And the sea state? Was it very rough?"

"No, the sea was rough, but not extremely so. This is because wind and tide were travelling in the same direction. Also, rain as heavy as that has a calming effect upon the waves."

"However, conditions were pretty unpleasant?"

"Yes, they were unpleasant."

"Then can you tell us this, Captain: did you not, with all the meteorological information at your disposal, anticipate such a deterioration in the weather when you delayed that call for assistance?"

"No, I did not. I had no reason to, on the information I had received. When the engine failed, the wind was north-westerly force four to five, that is, about twenty knots. The sea was moderate to rough, because of the wind across the tide. Visibility was excellent."

"You had no knowledge of an approaching storm? I find that difficult to believe, Captain."

"I did have knowledge of the approaching storm, sir, but the information I had at my disposal indicated that it would not affect my ship until after two that afternoon. By then I anticipated being under tow and well away from land."

"What was this information based on?"

"I had three sources of information, sir. One was my barometer. The second was my weatherfax machine. The third was the weather bulletin from the Channel Islands. The Channel Islands weather forecast was received at zero-seven-forty-five, and on request I received a verbal update from Guernsey, at ten fifteen. Both are recorded in the Ship's Log."

The Comptroller picked up the Log. "The earlier forecast says: 'Small but vigorous secondary depression moving quickly up Channel. Contains heavy rain and wind strengths of Force Eight to Nine, direction north-westerly. Will reach Alderney early afternoon, and be followed by brighter, showery weather.' Will you tell the court what speed is represented by a Force Eight to Nine wind?"

"One would expect wind speeds of thirty-five to forty knots," Glen said.

"Which is in fact what happened, with gusts of considerably more than that."

"That is normal," Glen said.

"But you still felt your ship was safe?"

"Anticipating the promised time of arrival of the tug, and comparing that with the estimated time of arrival of the storm, yes, sir."

"Your weatherfax machine and your barometer did not indicate to you that the storm was in fact travelling faster than forecast?"

"With respect, sir, I was somewhat busy between nine o'clock and the time the storm struck. Up 'til nine o'clock the barometer was falling steadily, but slowly. This indicated that severe weather was approaching but was not imminent. The barometer did not fall sharply until after ten. I last took a reading from the weatherfax at nine-thirty, and although I could see the storm centre approaching again it did not appear to me, in the brief time I had available to study it, that it was travelling any faster than originally forecast. However, I did call for that update from Guernsey. Owing to traffic, that was not received until ten-fifteen, as shown in the Log. By then there was nothing I could do about it."

Once again the Comptroller and the Captain gazed at each other for several seconds.

"I think," the Bailiff remarked, "that it is time for lunch. Court is adjourned."

The Press and TV people were out in force. When Glen emerged on to the steps of the Court House they crowded around him, shouting questions, but he said nothing, leaving it to Milford Martel to fend them off.

Hank Applegate cursed aloud as Milford's head obscured a perfect shot of Glen's pensive expression; he had stood there for an hour, drizzle running down his neck, camera protected by its black plastic cover, waiting to record Jane's interview with the star of the show . . . for damn all.

Jane said several very rude words. "I'd give my eye teeth to record what was behind that solemn face of his," she said to Hank. "Not full of confidence and good cheer, I'd say."

They watched Glen disappear into Milford's office. "Let's go," Hank muttered. "I could murder a couple of hamburgers."

Jane was correct in her analysis of Glen's mood, but she would have been surprised at the cause. Left alone in Milford's office while the lawyer went off to deal with other matters, Glen was not thinking about the hearing: he had said his piece with total honesty and now it was up to the court to decide his fate. Naturally a lump of lead remained in his stomach, but there was nothing more he could do. No, it was another matter entirely which was exercising his thoughts: whether there was anyway he could extend his acquaintance with Liz le Tissier – well, Cobb really but he always thought of her by her maiden name – into a closer friendship . . . or more. He had found it difficult to get her off his mind since seeing her again at his grandmother's place: what a dinky little doll she was – he longed to tuck her tiny frame under his arm. He had half hoped she might have been in court . . . but of course that was impossible, her being a vet. Funny to think how that skinny baby sister of Pierre's had grown into such a tough, determined little body. And she could be so kind and gentle with it. Look at the way she handled Smudge, and Gran. All loving concern and caring. Was it possible she could ever be interested in Glen Mahy? Of course the le Tissiers had always been better off than his family, but he'd done well for himself . . . And she had seemed very, very friendly at Gran's. Trouble was, he would be flying off to London in a few days time – if the court cleared him and he still had his ticket, of course. If not he wouldn't expect any girl to be interested – so he wouldn't have much time to make his number with her . . . He'd have to work out an excuse for seeing her again.

Liz was chopping up tomatoes when her aunt arrived. "Welcome to sunny Guernsey!" She leaned forward in the doorway to kiss Trish before relieving her of her mack and brolly. "Fancy bringing this weather with you."

"Don't give me that! I left glorious sunshine behind in England." Patricia Moorhead, wife of a Tory MP, shook out her mane of red, shoulder-length hair and followed Liz into the conservatory. Her emerald green jeans matched her eyes, her sweat-shirt was white with a spray of flowers splashed across the front, and her feet were tucked into white leather toe-thongs. The varnish on her finger and toenails, and her lipstick, toned perfectly with the flowers on her top.

"Sit down, and tell me how it is you always make me feel so old and drab when you walk into a room?" Liz grimaced at her own faded denims and washed out tee-shirt.

"I see I shall have to take you in hand again. With a figure like yours you can look a million dollars. You don't know how lucky you are, not having to fight the flab constantly."

"You don't appear to be having a problem . . ."

"You joke! Paul and I spend half our lives attending elaborate dinners, and the other half giving them. I go to a fitness factory three times a week in an attempt to keep my backside under control." Trish smacked the rear of her jeans before lowering herself into a cane armchair. "Now, are you going to offer me a drink?"

It wasn't till after they had eaten, and were relaxing with coffees, that Trish introduced the subject of men. "So are you going to tell me about the current local talent?"

"What makes you think there is any?"

"You've developed a dreamy look since I last saw you. Who is he?"

Liz told her. "The trouble is," she ended, "he'll only be here for a couple of years, then he'll be off back to the States."

"Wouldn't you want to go with him?"

"Probably, at first. But I have no wish to spend the rest of my life there."

"What's the alternative?" Trish sipped her coffee, the green eyes studying her niece's face.

"Not a lot. Men of my age are thin on the ground; at least ones who are footloose and fancy free." She stretched her legs across the rush matting.

"I imagine you get propositioned by some who are not free?" Trish grinned.

"True. But I have no intention of getting involved with someone else's husband, and playing the role of scarlet woman. You'd be amazed the effect it would have on people's opinion of my veterinary competence."

"Darling, you don't have to tell me. I was born here, remember? And there's no one else?"

"Well . . . yes. Do you remember the Mahy's from Hougue de Haut? Their son, Glen . . ."

"You don't mean this boy who is appearing at an inquiry . . .?"

"Yes, that's him, although I'm not sure boy is an entirely appropriate description, any more. He is one of life's really nice people. A type one automatically likes, immediately."

"Well? What's holding you back?"

Liz rubbed her fingers into her scalp. "I've nothing against him whatsoever, but . . ."

". . . he just doesn't turn you on."

Liz's head jerked up. "You're right on the button – as usual."

"Love versus lust. The oldest problem in the book." Trish drained her cup and held it out. "Got any more?"

"Yes." Liz looked at her watch. "But I mustn't be long. I'm operating at three." She refilled the cup and passed it back.

"Just kick me out when you have to go."

"Will do. Now tell me if you think it's possible to love and lust after the same person?"

"Definitely."

"Which comes first?"

"You mean could you develop a lust for Glen . . . and get to love Jackson?"

"One or other, preferably. Not both – that would be far too confusing."

Trish laughed and put down her cup and saucer. "I must apologise, I forgot to pack my crystal ball. How long have you known these two boys?"

"One for twenty-five years, on and off, and the other, let me see, what's today . . . Thursday . . ." she counted on her fingers ". . . just over a week."

"Great Scott! From the sublime to the ridiculous! Dear, dear, dear. You always were in a hurry. Slow down. Give yourself and your possibles a bit of time."

"There isn't any time. Glen will go back to sea as soon as this inquiry is over . . ."

"And Jackson?"

"Seems he can't wait to get me in the hay."

"And you're standing on your mother's principles, I suppose?" She saw Liz look at her watch. "I'd better be going, but before I do I want to know when I can meet this American."

"What about Glen? Don't you want to meet him, too?"

Trish gave a coy smile. "I don't think I need to. I knew his father."

"Not in the biblical sense, I hope?"

"Why on earth not? Now," she stood up. "When did you say I could move in?"

"Captain Darwin," the Comptroller said. "You are the Guernsey Harbourmaster, am I correct?"

"You are correct," Bert Darwin said.

"Now, you have heard the evidence given by Captain Mahy, and also by the tugmaster and the signalman on duty at the White Rock on that fateful day. I also understand you have had the opportunity to examine the Ship's Log of the SS *Trygon*."

"That is correct."

"Would you give this Court of Inquiry your professional opinion as to the way the incident involving the breakdown of the ship's engines was handled?"

"Willingly," Darwin agreed. "It is my opinion that Captain Mahy behaved in a thoroughly professional manner throughout, and that he took every possible action to save his ship."

The Comptroller raised his eyebrows at so forthright an endorsement, and David Beaufort squeezed Jackson's arm – he had had, for him, an amazingly teetotal lunch, consisting of one pint of beer and a bottle of wine, which he had shared with Jackson.

"Both seamen and both Guernseymen," he whispered. "They're thicker than thieves."

"I happen to agree with the harbourmaster," Jackson said. "Don't you?"

"Don't know anything about it, old boy. I'm just here for the beer."

"Now, Mr Marquis," the Comptroller said. "You are a States Meteorologist, am I correct?"

"That you are, sir." Walter Marquis was short and bald, with strands of hair carefully combed back and forth to cover his shining crown.

"Were you on duty on 21 September last?"

"Well, we all were, like," Walter said.

"Yes, but you were in charge on that day?"

"Well, I was senior, I suppose. Mind you, there's only a week in it between me and Dave Picquerel."

The Comptroller uttered a very audible sigh. "Mr Marquis," he said. "I have here your various charts and the observations you received on that day, and for the previous twenty-four hours."

"That's right," Walter agreed. "You would have 'em. They was sent to your office."

"Now, according to your charts, the whole of the British Isles was in a low pressure area on that day."

"You could say that, sir. Low. But not very low."

"What do you mean by that?"

"Well, sir, if you look at the charts, you'll see that the barometric reading over the Channel at dawn on 21 September last year was one thousand and eight millibars. Now that's low, sir. Oh, yes, low. But kind of slack, see? A real low, now, that'd be well under a thousand."

"I see," the Comptroller said, not very convincingly. "However, on this big, shall we say, not-so-low low you have a notation, here, just off the Isles of Scilly, of a barometric reading of nine hunded and eighty-four millibars. Now that is low, is it not?"

"That is what we call a secondary depression, sir," Walter explained. "You often gets them where there is a big area of slack, low pressure. They're small, fast-moving, and unpredictable. They're also short-lived."

"But in the immediate area of the centre of this secondary depression, one would expect very bad weather, would one not?"

"Well, sir, there'd be strong winds, for sure. And some rain. It's there in my report."

"I see that. Now it was dawn when this secondary low was reported, and it was your job to plot its course."

"Not my job alone, sir, oh no," Walter protested. "All the stations were plotting it. They can be dangerous, those secondaries. Oh, yes."

"Quite. But you, or someone, arrived at the conclusion that it would travel up Channel, and reach Alderney just after lunch?"

"Well, sir, depressions like to stick to water where they can. Land kind of breaks them up, you see? As for speed, well, like I say, secondaries are unpredictable. But fast. Oh, yes, fast. We estimated about eight hours to Alderney, yes, sir, given the speed it was travelling at dawn. It was travelling fast, sir. Secondaries always do. It was making twenty knots. That's fast."

The Comptroller frowned. "You mean that it was only carrying wind speeds of twenty knots?" He was not of the yachting fraternity.

"Oh, good lord, no, sir. Twenty knots is the speed at which the centre was travelling. That's got nothing to do with the speed of the winds circulating round that centre. No, sir. They was strong, they were. Yes, sir."

"So, you estimated that this secondary depression, travelling at twenty knots, would reach Alderney at two in the afternoon?"

"That's right, sir. It's one hundred and sixty miles from the Scillies to Alderney. That were an easy one, that were." He looked around the court with a broad smile.

The Comptroller gave another sigh. "But it got there quicker than you estimated?"

"It's true, it did. It began to travel faster and faster. It was a maverick, you see."

"And you no doubt advised Captain Mahy of this increase in speed, Mr Marquis?"

"Well, sir, it weren't that easy. The increase was gradual, like, you see? It wasn't until ten o'clock that we realised how fast it was travelling. As it happened, just about then the *Trygon* called asking for an update. They'd have known about the secondary, see, both from their instruments and the regular forecast. I said I'd call them back with the details, but when I did I couldn't get through the traffic. Well, I knew they was having some trouble, but they was busy talking with the tug people, we could hear them. So we had quite a job making the signals, like. I reckon they got the update about ten-fifteen. But by then there was nothing they could do about it, with a dud engine and all."

"Thank you, Mr Marquis." The Comptroller was looking tired.

"Your name is Etienne Dubois?" asked the Comptroller.

"Zat ees correct."

"And you are Chief Security Officer at the Atomic Re-processing Plant, Cogema, at Cap de la Hague?"

"No, no, zat is not correct."

The Comptroller looked up, somewhat sharply. "That is what it says here."

"Zen what you 'ave zere is not correct. I am a security officer at zee *Centre Nucleaire de Production d'Électricité de Flamanville*."

"You are Head Security Officer at the Flamanville Power Station?"

"No, no, zat is not correct. I am a security officer. But zee 'ead, *non*."

The Comptroller looked about to tear up his notes. But he resisted the temptation. "Then may I ask, what exactly are you doing here, *monsieur*?"

"I am 'ere because I was asked to be 'ere."

"I understood that we had requested the Head of Security at Cogema to be present."

"Monsieur Blaisdel is a very busy man," Dubois explained. "And 'e do not speak zee good English. I am 'ere because I speak very good English."

"I see. Well . . ."

"I am also an expert, on matters *nucleaire*."

"Hm. Well, then, *monsieur*, let me ask you, firstly, how dangerous, in your opinion, is the transfer of nuclear waste by sea?"

Dubois shrugged. "Eet ees not dangerous at all."

"Oh, come now, *monsieur*. Radioactive waste is surely the most dangerous substance in existence."

"Eet ees dangerous when eet ees left lying around, eh?" Dubois conceded. "But in zee sheep, zey are een zee canisters, eh? Zees canisters cannot leak."

"But if a ship, such as the *Trygon*, had struck a rock and sunk, those canisters would have been scattered around the seabed. Is that not so?"

"Maybe. Maybe zey stay eenside zee sheep."

"Either way, in the course of time, they would start to rust and break up. Would you not agree?"

"Eet would be a very long time before zat 'happened."

"So, in your *expert* opinion, there is no danger whatsoever in transporting atomic waste from, say, Japan to France?"

"Zat ees correct."

"Very well, *monsieur*. Now, one of my colleagues would like to ask you a few questions. I hope you have no objection to this?"

Dubois shrugged.

"I wish you to understand, very clearly, Monsieur Dubois," said the Bailiff. "That you are not required to answer any questions which you feel are inappropriate, either for reasons of national security, or for . . . any other reason."

"What he means is, any that might incriminate himself or his business," David whispered.

But Dubois was shrugging again.

"My name is Mrs Battle," Lynn said importantly, standing up, and waiting for a moment, just in case he had heard of her connection with Greenpeace.

Dubois barely restrained a third shrug of indifference.

"Now, Monsieur Dubois, you have asserted that the transportation of atomic waste is a perfectly safe business. I assume that you would further assert that once the waste reaches Cap de la Hague it is also perfectly safe."

"Eet ees safer," Dubois said.

"Very well. However, I hope you will not assert that the use of atomic power, for whatever purpose, is also absolutely safe."

"'Ow am I to say zat?" Dubois asked. "Eef you make zee *nucléaire* bomb, and you drop it, zat ees not safe, for zee people underneath, eh?" He looked around the courtroom with an ingenuous expression, and there were several smiles.

"I am speaking about the use of atomic power for so-called peaceful purposes," Lynn snapped. "As at Flamanville."

"Zat ees for zee manufacture of *électricité*. Zat ees safe."

"Yet you cannot deny that there are emissions into the atmosphere and into the sea." She looked at her notes. "Monsieur Dubois, will you tell us, what is a Becquerel?"

Dubois looked pained at the idea that there could be anyone present who did not know what a Becquerel was. "A Becquerel, *madame*, ees a unit of measurement."

"What does it measure? What is its meaning?"

"It measures zee radioactivity, *madame*. One Becquerel equals one radiation emission per second."

"I see. And is it not true that your power station at Flamanville emitted one billion Becquerels last year?"

Dubois shrugged. "Zat ees about right."

"And you still claim it is safe?"

"Zat figure ees zero-point-nine-one per cent of zee permitted amount."

"Permitted by whom?"

"Zee Atomic Energy Commission, *madame*. Zat amount ees less zan what you get from zee sun. Much less."

Lynn gave him another glare. "Very well, Monsieur Dubois. However, there is a considerable discharge of radioactive material into the sea, is there not?"

"Last year zere was about zirty-five million Becquerel."

"Is that not an enormous amount? A dangerous amount?"

Dubois shrugged. "Eet ees forty-zree per cent of zee permitted discharge."

Lynn looked ready to explode. But she checked her notes again. "Then let me ask you this, *monsieur*. What is the effect of radiation, any radiation, upon living tissue?"

"Eet ees not possible to . . . 'ow do you say? Generalise. Eet ees deefferent in deefferent species, eh? Zo, we measure by what ees called zee Sievert. Zee Sievert ees zero-point-zero-one per cent of a rem. You understand?"

Possibly Lynn Battle did understand. Very few other people in the courtroom did. Thus she decided to clarify the issue. "Then what is a rem?"

Dubois sighed at encountering such ignorance. "A rem, *madame*, ees a measure of radiation equivalent to one rad of X-rays."

It was Lynn's turn to sigh. She went for the jugular. "All right, *monsieur*. Will you tell us what is regarded as a lethal dose of rems, or Sieverts or anything you like to call them?"

"Zee maximum permitted dose for any 'uman being ees zree rems in zirteen weeks, but eet ees considered zat any 'uman being could take, once een 'ees lifetime, a dose of twenty-five rems."

"And your emissions, whether into the air or into the sea are below that figure?"

"Oh, yes, of course. A fraction of zose figures."

Lynn realised she was not winning this battle, so she changed tactics. "However, if there were to be an accident, at Flamanville, the amounts of radiation released would be far greater."

"Accident? 'Ow is zere to be an accident?"

"I am thinking of what happened at Chernobyl."

"Zat could not 'appen at Flamanville."

"How can you be so sure?"

"Because our rods are cooled weez water. At Chernobyl zey did not use water."

"So as long as you have water, there is no risk. What happens if your water supply fails?"

"'Ow can zee water supply fail, *madame*? We 'ave water from zee land, we 'ave water from our own reservoir, and we 'ave water from zee sea. All are used. Zere is always water."

"Three Mile Island was a water-cooled reactor, was it not?"

"Zat ees correct."

"And it had a very serious accident."

"Zat was a long time ago, *madame*. Zeir water supply was not foolproof, and when eet failed, zey did not applay ze right procedures. Zat could not 'appen at Flamanville."

"But there could *be* an accident," Lynn persisted. "Suppose a big aircraft, a jumbo jet, was to crash on to your station?"

"You expect a zhumbo to crash on zees courthouse?"

"Well, of course not. But it could happen."

"Eet ees, 'ow do you say? A beellion to one chance? Maybe many beellions to one chance. But even eef eet 'appen, eet could not damage zee Flamanville units. Zey are too well protected. Maybe . . ." he looked around the courtroom with a broad grin. "Zree zhumbos, all crashing togezzer at zee same moment . . ."

Lynn offered her last card. "You still cannot rule out sabotage."

Dubois considered. "Sabotage ees a possibility. But eet must be a beeg operation. Zee sea, zee land supply, zee reservoir . . . 'ow ees anyone going to do all zat at zee same time?"

"Monsieur Dubois, is there not an organisation in France so dedicated to the ending of the use of atomic energy that it has already carried out several acts of sabotage?" She looked at her paper. "It is called The Shining Light."

Dubois shrugged and appeared to blow a raspberry at the same time.

"You have not heard of this organisation? You are a security officer. You must have heard of it."

"Maybe I 'ave *'eard* of eet."

Lynn scented that she had at last made a breakthrough. "Well, then, Monsieur Dubois, can you assure us that there is no risk of this organisation ever infiltrating your station? Or ever perhaps attacking a ship carrying atomic waste?"

"Zose people are mad," Dubois declared. "To save life, as zay say, zey will take life. Many lifes. Zey are mad. But zey will not get into Flamanville. Zere is no chance of zat. I am Dubois. I 'ave said zis."

He glared around the court, defying anyone to challenge him.

Chapter 11

FRIDAY, 15TH JULY

Next morning the Jurats sat listening intently to the Bailiff's summing up before filing out into the ante-chamber. Jackson had been called to the offices by the electricians and arrived in court only moments before they filed back in again and took their seats on the high bench to either side of the Bailiff's chair. "They've only been out for half an hour," David whispered. "That has to be good for Mahy."

The Bailiff re-entered, took his place and cleared his throat, looking over the expectant faces in front of him. "Having regard to all the evidence presented to them, the Jurats have come to the following conclusions. Firstly, that there was a grave dereliction of duty on the part of the marine superintendent of the shipping firm which owns the *SS Trygon*, in allowing, indeed insisting, that the vessel put to sea for a lengthy voyage with its engine known to be in need of an overhaul, and especially when carrying a dangerous cargo."

He paused, and a rustle spread through the court.

"This conclusion will of course be passed on to the Board of Trade in the United Kingdom for further action," the Bailiff went on. "The second conclusion is that no blame for the near disaster can be apportioned to Captain Glen Mahy, master of the *Trygon*. He was aware of the situation, he did his best to prevent it, but when commanded to take the vessel to sea he felt it his duty to do so. When the accident which he had anticipated took place, he did all in his power to avert a catastrophe, and his efforts, thankfully, were eventually successful. For this we owe him our thanks."

Another pause, and David began to clap. The Bailiff and other court officials gave him a censorious stare, and he subsided into silence. "It is the third conclusion of this court, that the whole business of the transportation of atomic waste to the re-processing plant at Cap de la Hague should be reassessed and discussed with the French government, in view of the extreme hazard presented to the Channel Islands with the passage of every ship carrying such a cargo. The States of Guernsey will immediately instigate urgent talks with the Foreign Office in London in this regard."

"As if they haven't been talking about it for years," David muttered. "Without anyone taking a blind bit of notice. But you know what, Jackson old boy? I think we could both do with a drink."

David and Jackson were perched on stools at the end of the bar, when Milford and Glen came in with Walter Marquis and Bert Darwin, all having posed for Hank Applegate's camera and fielded Jane MacAvoy's loaded questions. David winked significantly at the barman who responded with an almost imperceptible nod before fulfilling the newcomers' orders.

Glen took out his wallet, but the barman tilted his head in David's direction. "Thank you very much . . ." Glen began.

"Congratulations," David smiled. "A popular finding, I'd say."

"With a lot of people, but not all."

"Like the belligerent Battle, you mean," Walter laughed.

"That bloody woman is a pain in the ass," Bert growled. "Always binding on about something. Usually what she finds floating in the marinas. But like I say to her, how the hell does she expect me to stop a hundred yachts from flushing their heads in the middle of the night, eh?"

"P'raps you should issue them with corks as they arrive," Glen suggested. "But that little Frenchman gave as good as he got, eh? He was a treat."

"Hello, Glen, how did it go?"

He swung round to face the newcomer. "Pierre! What are you doing here?"

"Come to share a liquid lunch. So?"

"They've delayed the hanging."

"Thank God for that. Public executions tend to put me off my beer." Pierre looked past the court party and saw Jackson and David. "Hi! Were you in court for the kill?"

David shook his head, sadly. "Very disappointing finish. No dramatics. Lynn Battle wasn't allowed to get up and shout at the verdict . . . No one was garrotted . . . What about the Press and the media? I didn't even see them."

"They were there, all right." Jane had come in behind Pierre.

"Hi Jane! How's my favorite TV journalist," David quipped. He and Jane were old antagonists.

"Waiting for a sensational episode in the life of David Beaufort with which to entertain the viewers," she responded, drawing a long draught of nicotine into her lungs.

A tray of crab sandwiches appeared on the bar counter. More people flooded in from the hearing and the barman rang through for assistance. At ten to two Pierre looked at his watch. "Sorry you guys, but must get back to the million dollar deals." He leaned towards Glen and Milford. "You two like to come down to our place for a bite of burnt barbecue this evening? Wives and girlfriends welcome."

Glen hesitated. "I'd like to, Pierre, but I think Mum and Dad would want me to be with them . . ."

"No problem! Bring them, too. And you, Jackson?"

David stared at Pierre, waiting. Pierre gulped. "And you too, David." Hell, Annabel would kill him for this.

"That is extraordinarily kind of you. I am delighted to accept." David made a mock bow.

When Pierre dashed out of the door and down the hill to his office, he seemed to have invited almost everyone in sight!

This was going to be quite a party.

A dress, Liz decided, standing in front of her wardrobe in bra and briefs; the tartan-printed shirtwaister was crease-resistant and shouldn't, in theory, need ironing. It wasn't too bad so she slipped it on, pushed her toes into flip-flops and hurried into the bathroom to examine her hair and face. The trouble with suntan was matching it up with a make-up base. She tried two: one looked as though she was wearing army camouflage, the other gave the impression of having fallen head first into a sack of flour. She should have bought an in-between tone: if only life wasn't such a rush. She scrubbed it all off, abandoned hope of concealing her freckles and settled for eye make-up and lipstick only, hoping Jackson would approve.

Just as she had finished operating this afternoon he had phoned to ask if he could show her his new offices. He had sounded a bit odd, very happy to inform her that Glen had been cleared by the court of inquiry, and adding that she was invited to Pierre and Annabel's barbecue that night. Another one! The white Volvo swung off the Grange into the deserted car park at six o'clock.

"You look gorgeous!" was Jackson's greeting.

"You don't have to sound so surprised!"

He put an arm round her shoulders and guided her in through a back door. "I wanted you to see what I'm planning, here. Tell me if you agree."

Liz pondered that remark, wondering why her agreement mattered, but said nothing, and followed him upstairs into a nice, airy suite of rooms. There were screen partitions dividing the main room; some desks appeared to have been arranged in order, others stood stacked in the middle. There were wires springing out of the floor at odd intervals, and several cardboard boxes stencilled with the international symbols for This-way-up and Fragile – arrows and cocktail glasses. "Those are the computer terminals," Jackson explained. "They'll have to wait until the mainframe is installed and programmed."

"You have a lot of desks. How many people are you taking on?" Liz wandered round the partitions.

"That's a variable. Not too many to start with, but I must have room for early expansion. Being hopeful, you note."

"You already have quite an operation here through Pierre's bank, don't you?"

"Absolutely. It is because they have done so well for us that I have been commissioned to open up independently and hopefully expand."

"Your other bank is in New York, isn't it?"

"One of them. We are also in LA, Singapore, Hong Kong and Sydney."

Liz swallowed. "I thought you said it was your family banking concern?"

"It is."

"Oh." What does one say to a man whose family own banks all round the world? Change to safer ground. "Do the terminals stand on the desks?"

"Only for the full-time operators. Fund managers have them mounted on sidetables leaving the desks clear for phones, intercoms, message screens and paperwork." He watched her move from one area to the next, her slim fingers touching desktops and screens, testing textures, her green, red and yellow dress bright against the plain cream and beige paintwork and teak furniture. She looked so delicious he could almost eat her. Glancing over her shoulder to ask a question she saw his expression, and smiled . . . which was his undoing. "Is this angle of light . . ." she began.

He reached her in two strides and wrapped his arms round her. "Dammit, Liz, you are having a devastating effect on me." He bent his head low to seek her mouth, softly, gently at first but, encouraged by her immediate response, his kisses became hard and passionate. It was a long time before they separated. He picked her up, sat her on a desk and stood in front of her, shaking his head. "I didn't ask you here for this . . ."

". . . but we both knew it could happen. Right?" she said, eyes riveted to his.

"You too?" She nodded. "I haven't felt like this . . ." he pushed back the hair that had fallen over his face. "I'm not sure where we go from here," he said, then regretted it. She had visibly bridled. "I mean . . . I don't want this just to be some casual thing . . ."

"Okay." She slid off the desk and went to the window. "So we turn each other on, but we can't possibly be in . . ."

"You may not be, yet, but I think I am."

"You can't. You don't know me . . . any more than I know you."

"Sweetheart, we're not teenagers. We've been around long enough to read the signs. I know damn well you are one in a million for me, and . . ."

"Slow down, Jackson. We are also old enough to face the practical aspects of this. Do we want to get deeply involved? Our origins are a world apart. We may find the differences destroy our . . . feelings for each other, and splitting up can be a very painful business, even after a brief affair . . ."

He could see he was making her nervous. After the celebrations with David and Glen he was feeling bold and brave, wanting to make sweeping decisions, statements. Idiot. Liz was right: their embryonic relationship wasn't ready yet for major decisions . . . commitment, but their feelings were too strong to bear a brief romp and good-bye. He smiled. "So can we agree on a getting-to-know-you period?"

"That makes sense."

"How long? A week?"

"That does not!"

"Open-ended then. You can't argue with that."

"Right. Now, since you assure me you didn't lure me here with an ulterior motive in mind, would you like to tell me what it is you wish me to comment on?" She surveyed the office, frowning with concentration.

Jackson tried to re-focus his thoughts. "You were about to query something about angles a few minutes ago."

"Yes. A matter of window light reflecting on screens. Bad for the eyes."

"Good point. Those desks should be re-aligned." He grasped the end of one, tugging it round. Liz helped with the next. Then Jackson asked her about curtains or blinds, and the subject of their friendship was not raised again before they left for the barbecue.

Annabel was definitely fraying at the edges when Liz and Jackson walked into the house. "Thank the Lord you've come early," she said. "Can you carry on with microwaving the potatoes, Liz? Get them to about two-thirds done."

"Give me a job, to" Jackson offered.

"Here's the roll of aluminium foil. You can wrap the spuds in it individually, ready to go on the barbecue."

"Where's my little brother?" Liz asked. "Will he really be able to barbecue in this weather?"

"Your bloody brother has been sent out to buy vast stocks of bread and booze. Do you have any idea how many people he has invited here tonight? In this weather!" It sounded like a rhetorical question.

Liz shook her head. "No."

"Nor have I! But he has confessed to at least twenty."

"More than that, I reckon," Jackson warned.

"How would you know?" Liz asked.

"I was there. There were at least two dozen of us in the bar, helping Glen celebrate."

Annabel's eyes widened. "And he invited everyone?"

Jackson scratched his head. "I don't want to talk out of turn . . ."

"Come on," Annabel's expression was grim. "Out with it."

"Well, we were all men. So Pierre told us to bring wives and girlfriends." He held his breath, waiting for the explosion.

When it came it was not what he'd expected. Annabel threw back her head and shrieked with laughter. "Oh boy! This is going to be hilarious. Come on, Jackson. You can help me fetch paper cups and plates from the utility. I'm sure as hell not washing up for that lot."

He rolled his eyes at Liz and followed as ordered.

Later, as people were drifting in and Jackson, now detailed to pour drinks, was standing at the kitchen table tilting a two-litre bottle of red wine over trays of polystyrene cups, Pierre finally returned. Triumphant. "Annie!" He shouted. "Come and give us a hand, will you?"

She had been upstairs trying to do something with her hair, unsuccessfully. "You've got a nerve," she shouted back. "Where in heaven's name have you been?"

She was soon mollified. First by her adoring husband's affectionate greeting, second by the sight of supermarket bags full of sausages, pre-cooked chicken legs and spare ribs, and thirdly by the vision emerging from the back of his car. "Trish!" she yelled, dragging the older woman in, out of the rain, and sweeping her into her arms. "Wow! What a wonderful surprise!"

Trish handed her dripping brolly to some man she'd never seen before who happened to be passing. "Pierre came up to the hotel to ask me. Never could resist a party, darling. Seems you have quite a crowd."

"You ain't seen nothin' yet," her niece-in-law warned. "Hey, Milford. You remember Pierre's aunt Trish. Get her a drink and introduce her round, will you?"

Discretion being the better part of valour, Pierre and Annabel abandoned all thoughts of barbecueing in favour of double ovens and microwave. Jackson watched with interest how everyone, all of whom seemed to have known each other since birth, mucked in together cutting up bread, prodding sausages, making salads and conversation.

The front and back doors were left open to let out some of the smoke, steam and noise, so the late arrival was suddenly in their midst, unannounced. Annabel, carrying a pile of paper plates and napkins through to dump on the dining table, looked up, and there was David Beaufort. She'd seen most of his films, and although he had never met him, she knew him well by reputation. The corners of her mouth lifted in polite greeting . . . while, fearful for the safety of her crockery, her spirits drooped. Forty dripping bodies and eighty wet shoes were bad enough, but she could handle that. This hellraising drunk was something else. "David! How lovely to see you," she cooed. "So good of you to come on a dreadful night like this. Just a mo." She off-loaded her burden onto the hall table, "Now let me take your . . . oh, you haven't got a brolly. You are absolutely soaked!"

"You, dear lady, must be my charming hostess." David took her hand and raised it to his lips. "Ah! Chanel Number Five!"

"Wrong," she corrected. "Never use it. In fact I fear all you will detect is garlic, right now."

"Shoot! I must be pissed out of my mind." He swayed gently.

"Well there's only one cure available for that. Jackson? Another goblet of wine needed."

Jackson was kept very busy. Trish took command in the kitchen, Annabel was doing her hostess bit and Pierre was trying to prevent his daughter Ros from taking off into the nether regions with her boyfriend, Niall. Having finished the potatoes, Liz drifted out into the conservatory and found Glen Mahy with his parents. "Congratulations, Glen. Wonderful. You must be feeling relieved, now it's all over." She was genuinely delighted to see him. And it showed.

"Thanks. You could say that." He swallowed hard; she was looking lovelier than ever. "You remember Mum and Dad, don't you?"

"Of course. Lovely to see you again. It's been ages."

Adele Mahy smiled. "Yes. A very long time. But I . . ."

"Mum's worried," Glen explained. "She thinks she and Dad are too old for the party."

"What!" Liz frowned. "What a load of rubbish! Don't let Trish hear you. She'd be livid!"

"I didn't know she was over here." Adele's face brightened.

"She arrived yesterday. And already she's taken over Annabel's kitchen."

"Is there anything I can do to help?"

Liz was quite sure there wasn't, but the shy little woman would feel much more at home if a job could be found. "Trish would be so grateful for a hand," she nodded eagerly. "Would you mind? The kitchen's just through that door, there."

Glen winked. "Thanks, she'll love to see your aunt."

"And thanks for seeing to my mother's cat," his father said. "The old lady was scared stiff she was going to lose him." He recounted a number of Smudge's adventures until he received a resounding smack on the back.

"John Mahy, by golly! It's you!"

"Well I'm damned. Walter Marquis! Fancy seeing you here. I say, you spoke well for the boy at the inquiry." John tilted his head towards the large 'boy' towering over him.

"Inquiry! Bah! There never should have been one. Your boy knows his stuff. He did everything right that day. It's only the loonies getting up in arms about the bloomin' environment. Bah!" After several hours celebrating, Walter Marquis' long tail of hair now trailed forlornly over one ear down to his shoulder, exposing a shiny brown pate.

"Never mind, Walter. You told them." Milford joined the group.

Glen and Liz sidled away. "At least it's given me an extra bit of time back home," he told her.

"You must miss the island, being away so much."

"That's right. I wish I could be here more."

"I don't think I could ever live anywhere else."

Glen saw the pensive look in her eyes, her beautiful eyes, and wondered if he might ever give up the sea, just to come home and be with her, always. "Must have been awful for those who evacuated from the island in the war, not seeing their home for five years."

"Your mother and Trish were evacuated together, weren't they?" Liz asked.

"That's right. What about your mother?" He wished he could think of a more interesting subject; it was extraordinary how his mind went a blank whenever she was around. What he wanted to say was how much he liked her dress; that her hair was nice, now that she'd let it grow a bit longer; that he wanted to buy a house for when they were married and he'd never go back to sea and leave her . . . He noticed her shoulders twitch, eyes sparkle – and turned to watch the American coming out of the kitchen with more wine, heading straight towards her. He saw their eyes meet, an extremely intimate message passing between them. So that was the way it was.

Glen sighed. So, you win some, you lose some, he thought. But not usually both in the same day.

Everyone drifted into the sitting-room after supper, following the strains of Annabel's grand piano. But not played by her. It was David, extemporising, leading the party in an endless selection of well-known tunes accompanying words known mostly amongst the rugby fraternity. He was being remarkably good, considering his reputation, singing la la la in place of the rudest words, mindful of the presence of Glen's parents. Having met Trish he knew nothing would faze her, but shy Mrs Mahy might be upset. Niall produced a trumpet and rendered *A Lighter Shade of Pale* almost unrecognisable. Rosamund plucked a guitar and Milford was found to be a splendid bass baritone when well oiled. Then Penelope, who had been told to go to bed hours ago, produced some pop CDs and people started dancing.

Glen agreed it was time to go, as soon as his mother suggested it. It wasn't easy standing there, watching Liz dancing a dreamy number with Jackson, her head leaning on his chest, eyes closed. But he had to be honest. She needed a full-time husband, not one who was away three-quarters of the year. Would he really have given up the sea, stayed home in a humble desk job so as to be with her?

"They have acquitted the sea captain," Philippe said. "Well, he did his best. But the Guernsey court has condemned the shipment of waste, and indeed, the use of atomic energy at all."

Monique was drinking Pernod. "You think that will make a difference? Sixty thousand people on an offshore island?"

"Of course it will not make a difference. But Flamanville is news, right now. So now is our time."

Monique put down her glass, and Olga, stretched on the bed, sat up. "When?" she asked.

"Next Friday. A week today. I have arranged the tour, and Georges has rented the boat."

"François is not on duty on Fridays," Monique said.

"That is all to the good. He can still get in and out of the complex. You wish to see how the pump room works, right? It is your day off, as well."

Monique finished her drink and sat on the edge of the bed, shoulders hunched.

"So," Philippe said. "Now you are all afraid."

"I am not afraid," Olga said. "It is just that . . . all those innocent people."

"Think of the millions who are at risk if we do nothing." Philippe told her. "Anyway, I have checked the forecast. It is for relative calm at the end of next week. The fall-out will simply fall up."

"It must come down eventually," Olga said. "Anyway, it will not stay calm for more than a few hours. It never does."

"One does not make an omelette without breaking eggs," Philippe said. "And you, Monique?"

Monique grinned. "What a way to go."

Chapter 12

THURSDAY, 21ST JULY

"Pierre?" asked the voice on the phone. "Glen here. I was wondering if you had those papers ready yet for me to sign? Only I'm off Monday."

Pierre flicked the corners of a pile of documents on his desk. "Hold on, Glen. I'll just check with my secretary." He pressed a switch on the intercom. "Karen. Are those documents ready yet for Captain Mahy?"

"I should finish them in about half an hour." Her voice sounded hollow through the unit on his desk.

"Thanks. Let me have them when you're done." He switched back to Glen. "Can you get down here before five?"

"You want to leave sharpish, do you? All right for some with nice cushy jobs."

Pierre was well accustomed to Glen's ribbing. "I'll have you know I'll probably be here till six-thirty, but we'll need a couple of secretaries to witness your mark, and they won't love you if you keep them out of the arms of their boyfriends." Pierre didn't add that his in-tray was stacked with work accumulated over the past few days' hangovers, much of which associated with helping Glen celebrate the outcome of the inquiry. And there was the regatta yet . . .

"You coming down to the Town Regatta tomorrow night? Join our party. A fitting farewell specially designed for seafarers."

"Sounds great. Where are you all meeting?" His answer

was automatic, but then suddenly he had doubts. Would Liz and her American be there?

"On the Crown Pier, down at the far end. We'll want you to give a big shout for the bank's entry for the harbour dinghy race."

Glen hesitated.

"You still there, Glen?"

"Er, yes. That's fine." If they were there it wouldn't matter. He could soon lose them in the crowd. "Anyway, I'll see you in a couple of hours, pen in hand."

"Sure. *Ciao*." Pierre smiled to himself as he replaced the receiver. Glen had a modestly healthy income, out of which he set aside a goodly amount each year to ensure that whatever happened to him, his family would be well looked after, including his married sister and her children in England. A really decent bloke, Glen. Pity really; much as he liked Michael Cobb, it would have been much better if Liz had married someone like Glen.

"Ah, Etienne." The Chief had been in Paris, and had only just returned. "How did it go?"

"As we expected," Dubois said, sitting down before the desk. "There can be no doubt that the entire idea of an inquiry was inspired by Greenpeace. They have a sympathiser in the Guernsey parliament. A formidable woman. She even interrogated me herself."

"You told her nothing of importance?"

Dubois grinned. "Nothing that is not known already."

"Still, the publicity, this is not good for us. That kind of publicity."

Dubois could understand the Chief's concern. The whole business of atomic power stations was coming under increasing criticism, world wide, as more and more pressure groups got into the act. Not that they were likely to get very far with the French Government: there was simply no other source of electricity available, without increasing the cost astronomically. But it was still worrying. And . . . "I must tell you," he said. "She asked questions about The Shining Light."

The Chief's head jerked. "What questions?"

"Just if I had heard of them. With regard to possible sabotage attempts."

"What did you tell her?"

"That it would be impossible." He spread his hands. "Unless two or more people were prepared to commit suicide. But I did not say that."

"And she did not suggest the possibility?"

Dubois shook his head. "Which shows she knows nothing about the Light. Because they are sworn to do just that."

The Chief got up and walked to the window, which looked out over the presently calm waters of the Alderney Race. "While you were away, I had a visit from the *Deuxième Bureau*."

Dubois frowned. "Why are they interested in us?"

"Because of this Shining Light. Apparently they feel we may be a target."

"That is impossible."

Blaisdel turned to look at him. "Nothing is impossible, Etienne." He gave a little shudder. "To think that there are people out there who are willing to risk contaminating vast areas of France, and perhaps southern England . . ."

"And the Channel Islands," Dubois put in, "if they attempted anything here."

"All those people," the Chief mused. "Going about their businesses, going about their pleasures . . ."

Dubois began to wonder if the Chief was not ready for retirement. Now the older man turned again, fiercely. "Those *sods* must never get in *here*, Etienne."

"Never!" Dubois promised him.

Chapter 13

FRIDAY, 22ND JULY

There was a large number of visitors due on Friday afternoon; three guided tours. Dubois prowled the exhibition hall as they came in, just after lunch. They were all young people, so enthusiastic. Or sad. There was one girl in particular . . . from her face he would have said she was ill, but her body looked plump enough, although it was difficult to be sure, because although it was quite a warm afternoon she was wearing an anorak zipped up to her chin. Probably she had a cold, he thought. She would have been pretty, but for the thinness of her face.

He turned to look at the next group, and saw François Leclerc, accompanied by a rather splendid looking young woman. "Hello, Etienne," François said. "This is Monique."

"Yes?" Dubois said. François had a great eye for the ladies, and came up with a different girlfriend almost very month. But this Monique looked a cut above the average. "Mademoiselle! But . . . aren't you off duty, François?"

"Yes. But I thought I'd give Monique a private guided tour. You do not mind?"

"Why should I mind?" Dubois eyed Monique's somewhat large shoulder bag. "I hope you have searched that, thoroughly?"

François winked. "I have searched all of her, very thoroughly."

Monique gave an attractive simper.

"Well, then, enjoy your tour."

Dubois followed the guided parties into the main building, and stood well back behind them as the guides explained the workings of everything. The visitors were not allowed to see anything vital, of course, or go within any distance of the core, but it was all very exciting for them, obviously. They whispered to each other and pointed. All except the sad-looking, ill-proportioned girl, who always stood a little apart from her group. She was interested in everything, certainly – that was quite apparent. But it did not excite her.

It occurred to Dubois that she might be intending to make a demonstration. These happened from time to time. Although he would not have associated this young woman with demonstrations; she did not look the type. But he continued to watch her as the group filed through the control room and arrived at the reservoir. At that moment he was distracted by a buzz from his bleeper. He moved away from the group, and picked up a house phone. "Dubois."

"There is a report of something in the harbour."

Dubois blinked. "What do you mean, some thing? A boat?" The harbour was not really a harbour, although supply ships did use it. But it was more important as a catchment area of sea water for use as a reserve for the cooling system for the reactors.

"Not a boat, Monsieur Dubois. They think it is a man. A frogman."

"I'll be right there." Dubois slammed down the phone, and glanced at the tour group before running for the door. The guide was giving his spiel about the various sources of water, and Dubois, as he reached the doorway, saw the ill-looking girl move, with remarkable speed. Before anyone else could react she had jumped the barrier and hurled herself into the pool; as she struck the surface there was a vast explosion, and an enormous plume of water shot up to the roof.

The party dissolved into a kaleidoscopic scream. Several, including the guide and Dubois, had been thrown down by the blast, and there was shattered glass flying in every direction. Alarm bells jangled. People scrambled to their feet. So did Dubois, blood streaming down his face from several jagged cuts. He ran forward to look at the reservoir. The young woman had disappeared, although where she had jumped the water was discoloured with blood, but the concrete walls had been cracked by the explosion, and even as he watched, the water level began to drop as it seeped away.

The nearest phone had been shattered by the blast, but the one in the corridor was undamaged.

"Evacuate the building," he snapped. "Now! Switch . . ." there was another booming explosion, some distance off. "What the hell . . ."

"The pump room," gasped the voice on the other end of the phone.

"Holy shit! Get everybody out. Shut down the operation. Get me Blaisdel."

People flooded past him, still screaming their pain and terror. The bells still jangled. Sirens now began to wail.

"Dubois! What in the name of God has happened?" Blaisdel shouted.

"At least one person has committed suicide, blowing herself and the reservoir up with it." Christ, he thought; almost all of that apparent extra weight must have been semtex, wrapped round her body, together with a detonater. But the fanatacism needed to do it . . . "Another seems to have got to the pump room."

"Who the devil can have got into the pump room? Nobody is allowed in the pump room."

Save an operator, Dubois thought. And his new girl friend! Holy Mother of God!

"I have a report," Blaisdel said. "But . . . this cannot be true."

"What is it, sir?" Dubois asked. The corridor was empty now; he was alone with imminent catastrophe.

"The sea water intake has been blocked by an explosion. My God . . . that frogman!"

"Chief, we have got to get water."

"Have you not shut down?"

"Yes, I have shut down. But those rods are still several thousand degrees hot. If we cannot get water, very quickly, there is going to be a meltdown. We must have water!"

"You islanders take your pleasures very seriously, I reckon." Having elbowed and edged his way through the tight-packed crowd, Jackson Ridgeway was now leaning over the harbour railing, pressed hard against Liz by the hefty young father on his other side who held a youngster perched on his shoulders: the wife was inadvertently jabbing Jackson's calves with a pushchair containing a toddler – complete with candyfloss.

The wet of the past few days had steamed away and the evening sun, soon to sink out of sight behind the town, still reached the outer ends of the piers and jetties. Castle Cornet basked in a warm, pink glow. The flags and bunting festooning the entire town and looped right round all the harbours, marinas and piers from high street-lights and overhead cables, scarcely stirred; only the bunting on the hundreds of boats, dressed overall, which were currently parading on the water below the crowd, were moving. Every conceivable type of craft was taking part. In the Victoria Marina, where most of the harbour games and fun took place, were the smaller boats: dinghies and canoes, dories and inflatables jostled with small fishing boats, day boats with little cabins. Out in the harbour pool tall-masted yachts flying proud ensigns, burgees and pennants and much aware of their own importance, looked down their noses on the sleek sharp bows of powerboats and beamy cruisers. And Jackson could see that every single craft was filled with happy families and their friends.

"Absolutely," Liz agreed. "We love every form of sport and hobby. You name any leisure activity in the world and it's represented by a really active, enthusiastic island club."

The crowd let out a series of shouts and wolf whistles. Looking down, directly below them a bunch of girls appeared on the pontoons dressed up as waitresses and displaying a considerable area of bare thigh and suspenders between black skirts and stocking tops. "Now the fun starts," Liz declared.

"What are they doing?"

"Lining up for the Ladies' Harbour Race. Look. Here comes Pierre's team."

These were in skimpy red Santa Claus suits with red pompom hats, long white beards and sporting several pairs of bare legs ranging from the long and glamorous to the short, mauve and dimpled. 'The Barclays Secretaries' were very smart in white collars and bow ties, black swimsuits and horn-rimmed spectacles. 'Greenpeace' was represented by girls in brown costumes sewn all over with green leaves. A team of cooks wore tall hats and white aprons which did little to conceal the backsides of their bikinis, and a rowdy gang of pirates in bandannas and eye-patches stormed into place on the pontoon.

"Where do they race?" Jackson asked.

"Across the inner harbour mouth to the pontoon the other side, see?" she pointed, "where another member of each team is waiting to be collected and brought back. The difficult bit is that they don't have any means of propelling their inflatables, other than paddling with their hands."

Jackson was watching the parading boats withdraw when he felt a hand on his shoulder, turned and grinned at Pierre who had somehow wriggled through the crowd with Glen and Annabel, to join them. "Hello!"

"Hi! Thought I'd better come up with supplies while I had the chance." He swung the haversack off his shoulders and passed round cans of beer. "You can put the empties back in here," he added, hooking the bag over a rail post. "Look! They're off!"

Some teams had obviously practiced more than others. While the 'Waitresses' and 'Secretaries' paddled off in orderly fashion, the 'Pirates' spun round in circles and the 'Santa Clauses' became entangled with 'Greenpeace'. In the resulting pushing and shoving, and accompanied by high-pitched squeals and hysteria, one pirate's headscarf became a blindfold and a white beard was seen floating away with a tall white hat. The two leading teams then jousted in true tournament style and, eventually arriving at the far pontoon, tried to prevent the waiting crew members of their opponents from boarding their respective craft. A Waitress gave the Secretaries' dinghy a tug just as the waiting Secretary was boarding, leaving her poised daintily in mid air before disappearing into the water. Later craft boxed in the leaders, the Santas crept in behind, their waiting team mate made a successful leap and they were on their way back to the cheering crowd.

"Santas!" Pierre yelled.

"Barclays!" shouted the man beside Jackson.

"Greenpeace!"

Liz swivelled round, wondering who that was, and saw Lynn Battle. Glen glared the woman in the eye and said "Boo!" in a loud voice.

A big shout went up as the waiting Pirate leapt from the far pontoon into her dinghy, landed on the gunwale and turned it upside down, depositing the crew in the harbour. A few more bandannas and eye-patches were lost in the ensuing skirmish before the inflatable was righted and the squealing girls scrambled aboard. The fattest one never made it, but swam energetically behind the boat, butting it forward with great determination, to renewed cheers of encouragement.

Despite his fervent shouts, Pierre's Santas were pipped into second place by the Barclays' team. But it didn't seem to matter who won. Everyone had an hilarious time, contestants and audience alike. Rosamund and her beloved Niall, with Penelope in tow, joined them as the party of friends drifted away towards the games booths; Glen bought a clutch of tickets and won a giant blue teddy bear which he promptly gave to Liz. Jackson got a box of chocolates . . . the chocolate had gone white with age but must have tasted all right – they didn't last long.

Liz and Penelope bought candyfloss which stuck all over their faces. On the Albert Pier they watched tinies on the swingboats and roundabout and bouncy castle, listened to the band, then agreeing on the need for sustenance, they headed for the nearest cafe. Several bottles of wine and platefuls of hamburgers later, they emerged in time for the launching of the latest in aircraft inventions . . . from a platform built high over the harbour. The amazingly contrived machines were brightly coloured, some modelled in serious vein, others pricelessly Heath-Robinson . . . but all doomed to ultimate malfunction, depositing their hapless pilots into the water in pretty short order. All to cheers and gales of laughter from the crowd.

The sun had disappeared completely, the town, harbour and marinas now illuminated by necklaces of fairy lights, all reflected in the water. Boats, similarly illuminated, circled the harbours again, while their crews ate and drank their suppers and the public address system relayed popular music. The music was interrupted from time to time to announce other attractions or to ask missing parents to claim their worried children.

"The castle looks very romantic when it's lit up at night," Jackson commented.

"Would you like to stroll along there?" Liz suggested. "There's nothing much happening for another half hour."

"Sure. Let's go."

Watching them, Pierre and Annabel winked at each other.

Glen sighed, and opened another can of beer.

"I wanta go on the bouncy castle!" one child howled for the umpteenth time.

"Well ye can't!"

"I wanna go wee wee," wailed the other.

"Bloody hell. You only jus' went five minutes ago!"

"Wanna go again."

"Y'll 'ave ter wait a bit," Wilma snapped, draining her third glass.

"I told you you should never 'ave asked 'er!" Eddie snarled at his wife.

"Shuddup, she'll 'ear you. Anyway, I wasn't to know she'd bring the kids!" Sharon smoothed the smart collar on her sailor suit.

"It was obvious she would. Well, now you can 'elp 'er keep 'em quiet."

Sharon gritted her teeth and reached for the younger one. "Come an' sit on yer auntie's knee, Francesca. And stop yer whingeing." The child tried to pull away but was dragged without ceremony on to her aunt's lap. "You'd better pour me another drink. Just ter keep up me strength."

Eddie made a grimace at his two mates who'd come along for the jolly . . . and Eddie's gin, and held the bottle over Sharon's glass.

Francesca continued to howl.

"Look, love, at all the lovely lights on the boats. Aren't they pretty?" The howling stopped and Sharon thought she'd scored a success, until she felt the hot liquid trickling through her designer pants and down her thighs. "Shit!" she shouted. "The little devil's peed all over me!"

"Francesca!" her mother complained. "That's the second time yer done that terdiy!"

"Come on, Eddie! We're goin' home!" Sharon ordered.

The men were all creased up, laughing. "No we're bloody not. We're just beginning to enjoy ourselves. Aren't we, fellas?"

Sharon threw her gin over him.

"Fearful racket coming from that flashy motor cruiser," Peter Barrington remarked to no one in particular.

"Simply ghastly!" agreed a rather busty female in a Guernsey sweater and Breton fisherman's cap.

"Who on earth are they? Surely not members of the

Club." Her husband adjusted the casually knotted kerchief at his throat.

"Lord, no! We may be short in the kitty but we're not reduced to letting the riffraff in, yet." His host smiled, glancing appreciatively at his burgee.

"Who on earth are they?" asked the busty guest.

"I believe it is a car salesman by name of Parker," Janet told her.

"Not Eddie Parker? Well! Now we know why he's such a sharp dealer. Maintenance on that craft must be at least ten thousand a year."

At that moment the cruiser's engines rumbled into life and she swept past the doctor's yacht. "Hiya, Peter!" shouted Eddie.

Peter turned away, pretending not to hear. But he swore viciously as his sleek vessel lurched wildly in the cruiser's wake, spilling whisky down his blazer.

Jackson and Liz strolled along the town side of the Albert Marina, watching the neat rows of locally owned craft swaying gently on their pontoon berths. They turned down towards the castle, round the model yacht pond and on along the castle emplacement to the end of the breakwater. The light tower flashed continuously into the darkening sky. "This is an enchanted island," Jackson murmured, gazing back across the harbour at the lights of St Peter Port. "There cannot be a more magic place on earth to live."

"Until you want to get off it."

"There are boats and planes . . ."

". . . and fogs and storms and faults in the engines of the ferries. Not to mention the expense."

"Are you trying to discourage me from setting up home here?"

"Setting . . . Are you serious?" Jackson live here? Permanently? The implications sent her mind spinning. Not that the possibility hadn't crossed her mind . . . as a sort of pleasant daydream, unrelated to reality. Now . . .

"Does the thought of having me here as a fixture faze you?"

"Er . . . no. Of course not."

He noticed her hesitation. She waited for him to say something but because he remained silent she felt obliged to explain. "I just wondered how you could be sure . . . but then you would only stay for a couple of years I suppose, until Parks Paramus was established . . ."

"And then fade away into the sunset? Is that what you're thinking?"

"Well, something like that."

"We would have to discuss it," he said, watching her profile being intermittently lit by the light above them.

Liz's head jerked round to face him. "We . . .?"

His arms reached out for her. "Yes, my darling. We. Us. Is it still too soon for you to talk, to think of us as an item? I know the week has only just passed . . ."

Her tummy was turning somersaults, wine, hamburgers and all. Apart from a small voice nagging at the back of her brain her entire being screamed at her to tell him No, it's not too soon. I've fallen for you like I never fell before in my life. But should she wait, and listen to the nagging argument, the cautionary note telling her that she must find out more about this dreadfully attractive and persuasive man before committing herself? She gasped for breath: without realising it she had stopped breathing. Slowly her arms crept up to circle round the back of Jackson's neck. His head bent over her till his mouth found hers. Several minutes passed. "May I take that as your answer?" he asked.

She leaned against him. "You may take it that I'm giving the matter serious thought. But I think as two sane, adult human beings we should talk things through; there are so many factors involved, quite apart from us being attracted to each other."

"Tell me what you have in mind," he muttered into her hair.

"Jobs, for instance. Your job. My job. Where you want to live for the rest of your life . . ."

"With you . . ."

". . . here or in the States. And where I want to live."

"And whether we have ten children, or stop at eight."

"Jackson! I'm trying to be serious!" She tried to sound stern, but couldn't stop a gurgle bubbling up in her throat.

"Did anyone ever tell you how gorgeous you are when you try to be serious? Hell, sweetheart, I love you so much I'm melting. Why are you so cruel?"

"Me! Cruel? How come?"

"I'm asking you to marry me and you won't give me an answer."

"Darling, Jackson. Ask me again tomorrow when you're one hundred per cent sober. Then we'll talk about it and I promise I'll give you an answer."

"Do you think we ought to sleep together, first. Kinda try each other out for size?"

Liz laughed and wriggled out of his clasp. "No! I want to make an unbiased, calculated decison."

"Dammit! And I'd once thought you were a romantic!"

"I was. That's how I finished up a divorcee." She grabbed his hand. "Come on. Let's get back to join the others before the fireworks display. They set them off on the castle so it's better to watch from the town."

She was right, of course. He knew he wouldn't have said anything yet if he hadn't had those glasses of wine to loosen his tongue. However, the fact remained that he had made up his mind. He wanted this little woman in his orbit for the rest of his life. "I'm sorry, Liz. I really didn't mean to faze you."

"Faze me? That's the understatement of the year! You and I have known each other only two weeks and tonight you blew my mind."

Smiling to himself, he allowed her to lead him by the hand between the Albert Marina and the bus terminus, to the crowded pier.

They were hunting through the throng of dancers when the music stopped, and the loudspeakers crackled back to life with a long roll of drums. A fusillade of rockets screamed into the sky from the castle and burst high over the main harbour, myriads of red, blue and white gems competing with the stars, streaking across the night and cascading to the surface of the water.

"They're good, eh?"

Liz peered about her. "Oh, it's you, Walter! Yes, spectacular. Say, have you seen my brother?"

"He was with Glen, up by the cafe just now. Hey, that was a good party the other night, eh?"

"Yes. Fun. What time did you finish?"

Walter scratched his head. "I don't rightly know. The missus drove home and she wasn't speaking to me at breakfast next day. So I s'pose I'd had a drop or two. But it was that film star chap, eh? Not a bit toffee-nosed. He was good on the piano, too . . ." He pointed. "There he is, your brother. Hey, Pierre!"

They all stood together watching the firework display, Pierre and Annabel, Jackson and Liz, Walter, Ros, Penelope and Niall. Walter's wife and daughter found him; Glen could see his parents had brought his Gran to sit up on the seats above the cafe for a grandstand view. Trish was with Paul and Wendy Pritchard's party, chatting with Willy Watts. "The entire island population seems to be here," Jackson remarked to Liz.

"Lord, no. Only a fraction. Some people just don't like these noisy gatherings. There are even a bunch of old biddies who reckon fireworks should be banned."

"For why?"

"They object to the noise. Mind you, I do feel sorry for some of the animals; terrifies them out of their wits. Ooh! Look!" A huge golden fountain showered the castle.

After a prolonged dislay a particularly elaborate set piece lit the entire town, followed by a continuous fusillade of rockets . . . and then a deafening silence. The crowd burst into cheers and clapping and the loudspeakers crackled into action with more dance music.

David threw the script onto the coffee table with a thump and sat staring at it, morosely. He hated it. Lousy plot. Lousy characters . . . and once again they wanted him to play a lousy drunk. Huh! Classic case of type-casting. He stared, dull-eyed, at the booze cabinet, and for once he had not the slightest desire to pour another drink. That was the problem. Either he had had too much of it or he hadn't had enough. And tonight he was too bloody sober for his own good.

His mind drifted back to the party in Guernsey, after the end of the *Trygon* inquiry. At Pierre Somebody's house. Nice party, nice people with their families and friends. Real people, not poseurs calling each other "Dahling!" and pretending they could fathom deep meanings in crazy, meaningless prose and infantile paintings. God Almighty, he'd had that lot up to the back teeth. Had the Arts always been full of such idiots? But who was he to talk? Hadn't he once been one of them?

Sitting alone in the solitary circle of light from his reading lamp, he threw back his head and laughed aloud, remembering what a cake he'd made of himself . . . and so many times! Like so many others fondly imagining he could change the world.

Suddenly Trouble growled and lumbered to his feet, staring at the big picture window with his ears back.

"What's up, old chap? You don't usually bother when I laugh at myself." David leaned over to scratch the enormous white head.

"Did you call, sir?" Forsythe stood in the doorway.

"No. Just laughed," David explained, then added, "Don't know what's up with Trouble. He's got the jitters tonight."

"Funny you should say that, sir. When I was in the kitchen this afternoon all the plates rattled on the dresser.

Like when we were in San Francisco. And Trouble was most upset."

Trouble whined, crossed the room to the settee and proceeded to wedge his vast bulk behind it.

"What the hell's got into him?" David said, getting out of his chair. "Come on, boy. What's the problem?"

Forsythe had gone to the window. "Wouldn't be anything to do with that, would it?"

"With what?" David joined him, gazing out into the darkness. "What the devil . . .?"

A dull, red glow was spreading upwards into the sky from the south-eastern horizon.

Ben Ozanne was driving home from the cinema with his wife, when he saw a figure leaning over the gate of the top field by the turn off. He slowed to a stop and lowered his window. "You're working late tonight, Harry."

"My herd was spooked this afternoon," Harry de la Mare told him. "I don't know what got into them, haring up the field here and all huddled in a bunch. They still haven't settled down."

Ben switched off the engine, got out and joined his rival farmer friend at the gate. "Whassat, over there?"

Harry peered in the direction of Ben's finger. "You mean that red in the sky? I dunno. Never seen it before."

"Nor me. Hey, Joan. Come an' look at this." His wife came to stand with them. "What you reckon it is?"

She stared for a minute. "The *aurora borealis*?"

"Don' be daft, woman! You don' see the *aurora* at this time of year, nor over there. That's not north."

"Eh? What you two on about? What's this rora thing?" Harry wanted to know.

Joan ignored him. "It's getting bigger."

"Some French farmer's rick gone up in smoke over on the mainland?" Harry suggested.

"'Ave to be a bloody big rick." Ben shrugged. "Well, I don' know. Anyway, I'm for bed. Come on, Joan." They got back into the car. "'Night, Harry. Hope your cows'll be okay."

"That's funny," Joan said as the car bumped down the farm track. "Our lot are all up here in the west corner of the field."

Caught in the headlights, the whites of the cows' eyeballs were wild with fright.

"What are they doing in Herm, do you suppose?" Mrs Mahy pulled at her son's sleeve.

Glen had been watching the dancing and turned round to see what his mother was talking about.

"That red glow. They must be burning a bonfire."

The music stopped at that moment and the dancers were rejoining their friends.

"You think they're having a party in Herm, Glen?" his father asked.

"You talking about that red on the horizon? That's not Herm, that's France," Glen replied. His hand came up to cover his mouth: he knew exactly what part of the French coast it was, and a great band of fear tightened round his chest.

"What are all those people looking at?" Jackson wanted to know.

Pierre saw a crowd gathering on top of the cafe. "Someone clowning round in the harbour, I suppose. Anyone coming back to our place for a coffee?"

"Just a minute," Liz held his arm. "Is it my imagination or is the sky turning red over to the north of Herm?"

"Red? Where?"

"She's right, you know," Jackson said. "Looks like something's on fire."

They saw the Mahys leaving the pier. "Say, Glen," Pierre called out. "You seen that light in the sky over there?"

"Yes." The sea captain's face was serious as he approached.

"What do you reckon it is?"

With a jerk of his head Glen beckoned Pierre away from the others. "Don't want to scare the girls, but I don't like the thought of where it's coming from." He spoke very softly.

Pierre frowned. "You mean . . ."

Glen nodded. "Yes. Flamanville."

Pierre's mouth dropped open. "Oh God!"

"Ssh! Don't say anything. I could be wrong. It might not have anything to do with the place." He wanted to believe that.

Pierre returned to the others, his brain frantically concocting a lie. "What did Glen say?" they asked.

"It's probably another Nato exercise. They often have them out there." His voice was bright and cheerful, so cheerful that the painful lump of lead in his stomach began to shrink. Dammit, it was millions to one against it being anything serious.

Chapter 14

FRIDAY, 22ND JULY – midnight

Philippe stood at the window and looked down at the street beneath him. It was filled with people. He estimated every street in Cherbourg was filled with people. They stared at the glow to the west, and they shouted at each other. The more knowledgeable looked up at the sky, and tried to estimate the wind direction and force; there was almost no wind, but what there was came from the west. Thus whatever might escape from the damaged plant would be coming their way . . . unless the wind shifted.

Philippe had had a hot bath, and felt better; even in July and clad in a wet-suit, the water off Flamanville had been cold. Or perhaps he had simply been afraid. But it was done. By now Georges would be down at Granville, he supposed, stepping ashore from his boat after an afternoon's fishing. He would board a train, and disappear. The authorities would become curious soon enough about the abandoned speedboat, but they would never trace the chartered vessel back to Georges. Georges had wanted Philippe to go with him, rather than be put ashore on Dielette Beach. "It is very unlikely that Monique got out," he had argued. "You have done a great job. Why expose yourself?"

Philippe had refused. He loved Monique. If there was a chance she might have got out, he wanted to be there; they would escape together. Besides, there was something exciting about returning here. Over the last month he had come to know quite a few of the bourgeois little people in the town, all smug in the regular pattern of their lives. Now he had forever disrupted those lives. They did not know it yet, but Cherbourg would have to be evacuated, closed down, bulldozed. And it would remain uninhabitable for years, perhaps forever, depending on how much radioactive material escaped the burning station. That would make them think again before opening another re-processing plant.

The door behind him opened, and Monique was in his arms. "Oh, my darling," he said. "My dearest girl. I could only hope."

"There was no problem." But her cheeks were pale.

"François?"

"I hit him with the hypodermic, as Olga said, and left him with the bomb." She stared at him, defiantly. Philippe swallowed. He had never actually, knowingly, killed anyone. Monique terrified him. But that made her the more compelling. His hands moved over her back. "Later," she said, slipping out of his grasp. "Let's get dressed and get the hell out of here. I don't want to be about when that cloud arrives."

Liz and Trish pushed Annabel on to the settee. "You stay there and relax. We can cope," Liz said, and headed off into her sister-in-law's kitchen, their aunt at her heels.

"Coffee?" Trish opened and shut a couple of cupboards.

"In the bread bin," Liz told her, pouring water into the coffee machine. "Don't ask me why – just another of Annabel's little idiosyncrasies. I think she finds the life of a housewife becomes boring if one always does the obvious."

"Adorably original, our Annabel!"

"You girls need a hand?" Pierre poked his head round the door.

"Can't find many cups . . ."

"Dishwasher," he said. "But did little wifey put it

on before we went out, I ask myself?" She had. Her idiosyncrasy always amused the family, but she was, nevertheless, efficient.

By the time Trish and Liz carried the steaming mugs into the sitting room, Pierre had produced a bottle of Armagnac and the men were swirling the dark liquid in balloon glasses. Before leaving Town the family had been joined by Toby le Prevost and his girl friend, and by Bert Darwin the harbourmaster, who had finally stopped chasing offending boat owners round the harbour in his Dory. They had all accepted the general invitation to coffee, and Niall had come back with them, too, and was nonchalantly copying Pierre's brandy-warming wrist action – though not quite sure of the purpose. Ros watched him adoringly, while her younger sister played with the dogs on the carpet.

Pierre looked at the carriage clock on the mantlepiece and wondered if he should switch on satellite news at midnight. He was convinced Glen was worrying unnecessarily: he had attended a banking dinner last year, shortly after the *Trygon* near disaster, when the guest speaker had explained in boring detail the extensive, foolproof safety precautions in force at all French Nuclear Power stations. It was quite impossible for any real crisis to occur . . . Having said which, he supposed it would do no harm just to see if anything was reported. "Mind if we get Sky headlines?" he asked, addressing no one in particular. They were all chatting and no one bothered to reply.

Jackson twisted in his chair to look at the screen. The Prime Minister was getting into a car outside Number 10, but Pierre had pressed Mute so he didn't gather why; the Shadow Chancellor mouthed silently, face flushed with self-righteous anger, then the newscaster returned to the screen briefly before the usual round of adverts.

Pierre finished topping up Toby's glass and reached for the control to turn off, when the newscaster's face reappeared with a 'Just in' caption, so he turned up the sound instead. ". . . unconfirmed reports from Cherbourg, of an explosion at or near the Nuclear Power Station at Flamanville, on the west coast of the Cotentin Peninsular, Normandy. There is no further information available at present but we will bring you updates on that and other news stories as they come in. Now here is Bill Chambers with the latest sports results from around the world."

Pierre pressed Mute again. Everyone had gone quiet. "So that's what the red glow was in the sky, this evening," Trish said. She stood up and began stacking empty coffee mugs on the tray.

Toby's girlfriend gaped at him with her mouth open. "A nuclear explosion? Just a few miles away? He . . . ell!"

"Twenty-four, to be exact." Bert liked to get facts straight.

"But they didn't say it was a *nuclear* explosion. They don't even know yet if it happened at the station," Annabel pointed out.

"The newscaster will be back in a minute with an update," Liz said.

"I hope not. That yucky tie of his makes me feel ill." Ros hadn't appeared to take her eyes off Niall, so Liz wasn't sure how she could have seen it.

"I didn't realise you girls were still up. Come on, time you were in bed," Annabel ordered.

"Oh, Mu . . . um!" Penny rolled over on the rug. "There's no school tomorrow!"

"Your mother said bed!" Pierre attempted his stern father act. "Off you go. And yes, you too, Niall. It's long past time you went home." The three youngsters bade protracted farewells to each person in turn, and while Penny headed upstairs, her sister led Niall through the front door for an amorous farewell session in the front garden.

The offending tie flashed back on the screen and Pierre brought back the sound. ". . . we have Monsieur Jacques Labalestier on the telephone from Cherbourg . . ."

"Whoever he might be," Toby growled.

". . . er . . . we think we have him; are you there sir? . . . Monsieur Labalestier, can you hear me?"

"Yes, yes, I hear you." A map of Normandy was framed in a small window on the right of the screen.

"Can you tell us what has happened at Flamanville?"

"There was a minor explosion."

"Is it serious?"

"No, no. Not at all." His voice crackled over a bad line.

"Are you saying there is no cause for alarm?"

"There is nothing to cause alarm."

"Then can you tell us where exactly the explosion occurred and what caused it?"

The line crackled again. "I am sorry. I cannot hear you. Would you repeat the question, please?"

While the question was being repeated there were more hisses and crackles and the map in the window disappeared. "I'm sorry. We seem to have lost Monsieur Labalastier for the moment. We will hope to come back to him later. Meanwhile, let's have an update on the weather."

Pierre switched off, but somehow the news had dampened the earlier festive spirit, though no one, except Toby's girlfriend Jackie, seemed gloomy or worried. Jackson looked round from face to face wondering if the others were really unconcerned or simply displaying the renowned British 'stiff-upper-lip'. He drove Liz and Trish home in his car, and the latter immediately headed for bed, leaving the lovebirds alone to say their goodnights. "You're very quiet," Jackson said. "Worried?"

"I don't know about worried. But it certainly makes you think." Liz led him into her sitting-room.

"Think about what?"

"The mind-boggling enormity of the ensuing crisis . . . if it *was* a serious nuclear explosion."

"The chap in Cherbourg stated categorically that there was nothing to worry about."

"Mmm." She dropped into an armchair. "He would,

wouldn't he? But supposing he was wrong . . . do you realise that a moderate north-easterly could have radiation raining down on us, here, in a matter of hours?"

"If there was any radiation leak. Which we don't know."

"If there is, I'd like to know now."

"Why? To allow time for evasive action? Or maybe make a run for it?" He got up to come and perch on the arm of her chair. "Talking of which, unless you were thinking of inviting me to stay, I suppose I will have to make a run for it myself."

Liz leaned her head against him. "I'd like you to stay, but to be honest I don't think I'm in the right frame of mind."

Jackson stroked her hair. "I'll try to restrain myself for another day. Anyway, we don't want to shock Trish."

"You have to be joking!"

"Tell you what. Pierre was telling me one can dial a Guernsey number for a weather report. Shall we try?"

"Why not? Be my guest." She waved a hand at the phone. "The number is eighty eighty."

He punched the digits and listened. "There. Light south westerly. So if, by any remote chance, there is a great pall of nasty hanging about up there it's heading away in the opposite direction. Does that make you feel better?"

"Yes sir, Mr Jackson Ridgeway, sir!" She jumped out of her chair, stood to attention and saluted. "Now we'll away to our respective couches. Dear Jackson," she stroked his cheek, "I really would love to sleep with you but I'm so tired I think I'd flake out before anything was achieved."

"I can't say I'm flattered to learn just how stimulating you rate me."

"Come off it! We are neither of us in our teens, remember. Come to breakfast and we'll discuss it then." She stood on tiptoe to kiss him, then pushed him unceremoniously out of the door.

Chapter 15

SATURDAY, 23RD JULY –
pre-dawn

"No, sir. The Chief Inspector is not on duty at the moment. Can I help you?" WPC Susan Johns picked up the polestyrene cup of revolting, lukewarm coffee and took a quick swig. "No. We have not received any information about an explosion . . . Possibly, sir. But until we are notified I'm afraid . . ." She raised her eyes to the ceiling. "Yes of course, sir. I'll see he gets your message when he comes in." She flicked a knob on the switchboard and drained the coffee.

"Not another one?" Sergeant Collins looked up from the charge sheet he was perusing.

"That's the . . . fifteen . . . sixteen . . . seventeenth call about this so-called nuclear explosion. Do you suppose there's anything in it?" Hoax calls were a normal feature of police work, but this was different . . . She was beginning to feel quite edgy.

"Amazing how many of the general public take TV dramas for real, you know. I wonder what was on the box tonight." He slipped the sheet of paper into a file on the desk and glanced up at the clock. "That's not too bad for regatta night. Twelve thirty and only three arrests for drunkenness and two for brawling outside the chip shop. Needless to say, that Shaun Scott's lot."

"So far," Sue added with a grin. The switchboard buzzed. "Here we go again. Guernsey Police," she said in her official voice. "How may I help you? . . . No. I'm sorry the Chief Inspector is not on duty . . ." The sergeant saw her mouth fall open. "Would you like to speak to the Duty Sergeant . . . Er . . . Yessir. Yes. Just one moment please." She stared up at Collins, her face drained of colour. "It's someone from the Home Office in London. He insists on speaking to the Chief. What do I do?"

"Put him through to me." He picked up his receiver. "Duty Sergeant here, sir . . . Yes, so I understand. If you would like to hold on for a moment I'll try to get him at home." He laid the receiver on his desk and crossed to the switchboard. Sue plugged in another set of headphones as she dialled, and handed them to him. "Collins here, sir. Yes, I'm sorry to disturb you at this time of night but there's a gentleman from the Home Office who insists on speaking to you immediately on a Red Alert Emergency matter. Will you take the call?" He nodded to Sue.

She connected the two exterior lines through her board, then sat back staring up at Collins's face. He was a tall man with a long, thin body and long thin head. His turned down eyes and mouth and beaky nose gave him a gloomy expression at the best of times . . . of which this was not one. "Maybe all those callers were right . . . There *has* been some explosion at Flamanville. Do you think it could be really serious?"

He lifted his bony shoulders and sighed. "S'pose we'll know soon enough. Want another coffee?"

"Yes, please. At least it's warm and wet. Sarge, is it all right if I ring Barry?"

Collins paused with his hand on the door. "Not to tell him anything, mind. If there is anything wrong the authorities must be notified first."

"He wouldn't pass it on . . ."

"Sue! No. Sorry, love, it's against Police rules. You know that."

"Yes. Of course. Okay."

The switchboard buzzed again as the sergeant left the room.

Fifteen minutes later Chief Inspector Joseph Thompson burst in. "Johns, get the Bailiff for me and put him through to my office."

"Yessir."

"Collins. Call in Pike and Williams, will you?"

"Yessir."

"Remember. Not one word to anyone about this until you're given the go ahead. Understood?"

"Yessir," they replied together.

Sue's throat went dry – her heart was pounding.

Twenty minutes later the Bailiff arrived with the Governor. The Bailiff had been an Advocate of the Royal Court before graduating to the senior island post. He had been around a long time, seen many emergencies and had himself been evacuated as a small child with Elizabeth College on a Dutch cargo boat only a few days before the island was invaded by German troops in 1940. But he had never been faced with the responsibility for any situation remotely as serious as this. After speaking with the Home Office he had immediately phoned the Governor who, as Queen's representative in the island, insisted on being involved from the start. They agreed that any action would stem initially from the Police Station, and it would be better for them to meet there with the Chief Inspector and possibly set up an Emergency Control Room.

The Governor was a retired Vice Admiral, as much admired and respected in Guernsey for his enthusiastic interest in all aspects of island life and relaxed, friendly manner, as he had been throughout his service career.

They were met at the door by the Chief Inspector of Police. "Would you gentlemen care to take over the Police Committee room for the time being?" he asked.

"Have you plenty of phones in there?" asked the Bailiff.

"Four, sir."

"That will do."

Joe Thompson led the way. The room was dominated

by a long mahogany table surrounded by padded chairs. A leather chesterfield, armchair and coffee table stood at the far end and a small, secretary's desk near the door. There were phones at each end of the table, one on the desk and the fourth on the coffee table. The three men seated themselves at one end of the committee table where Bill Collins had placed quarto notepads, pens and a water carafe with glasses. "Could either of you gentlemen face a revolting cup of vending machine coffee?" the Chief asked.

"Can't be worse than Naval brew. Yes please. Must try to get the sleep out of my eyes." The Governor, wearing a jumper and open-necked shirt, tilted his chair back and looked at the Bailiff.

"Well if you can face it, sir, I suppose I'll have to." He nodded at Collins who was waiting to take the order. "Now," he pulled a pad towards him, "where do we start?"

"Civil Defence, sir," the Chief said briskly.

"Ye . . . es. But we haven't been informed yet whether or not this incident is definitely dangerous to us. We don't want to spread unnecessary alarm."

"Quite," the Governor agreed. "But the fact that the Home Office rang so promptly indicates they regard the situation as *potentially* dangerous. So all vital emergency services should be alerted well in advance, don't you think?"

"Good theory, Mark. Trouble is you might just as well broadcast the whole thing from the rooftops. You have no idea how fast rumour, let alone genuine news, can travel round this island. Leaves Concorde standing."

"Shall we make separate lists of people to be alerted at each stage of development of the situation, sir?" Joe suggested. "If, of course, it does develop . . ." He ran fingers through his thick grey hair "Though I can't honestly believe it will."

"I can't, either," the Bailiff agreed. "However, we can use the opportunity to test the efficiency of all our emergency services. Yes, Chief Inspector, that's the best plan. Separate lists. Starting with Civil Defence, Fire, Ambulance . . . I say, if there is a great cloud of radioactive dust out there, how long do we have before . . . what's the term . . . fall-out, reaches the island?"

"That would depend entirely on meteorological factors, Hugh," the Governor pointed out. "Wind. Atmospheric pressure and moisture content."

Collins returned and set a plastic tray on the table, bearing three polestyrene cups of coffee and three little packets of custard creams. "Anything else, gentlemen?" They eyed the offering and declined. "Doctors. They ought to be told early," the Chief said.

"Yes. Who's head of BMA at the moment?"

"Andy Driscoll."

"And all the hospital units. Got to give them time to get the hatches off their emergency resources."

"Haven't the Civil Defence people got all these lists worked out already?" the Bailiff asked.

"Quite possibly, sir. Trouble is, I think their head man is on holiday. Hasn't he gone to Barbados with his wife?"

"I believe you're right. Yes, he told me he was going when we were fellow guests at a dinner party a couple of weeks ago. So who's in charge?"

"It'll be Mr Watts, Sir."

"Oh Gawd! Not Willy!"

"What's wrong with him?" the Governor wanted to know.

The Bailiff and the Chief Inspector looked at each other, each waiting for the other to explain. The senior man accepted the task. "There is nothing wrong, exactly, with Willy Watts. He is hard working, enthusiastic, industrious. One of the few Guernseymen to make money out of the horticultural industry in recent years. Trouble is he is such a bouncy little bugger . . . if you'll excuse me saying so, Mark. Always full of bright ideas which he brings into my office quite regularly on Monday mornings. An absolutely exhausting fellow." He was tearing open a packet of custard creams. "Once he gets wind of this he'll take over the whole operation. Drive all over the rest of us like a bulldozer."

"Do we have any option but to get him in?"

Sir Hugh shook his head. "No. I had hoped the Home Office would call back, by now, to tell us it was all a false alarm. But as they haven't I suppose we should get hold of Willy right away."

"Yes, Sir. And Dr Driscoll?" Joe asked.

"Yes." He bit a biscuit in half and masticated with much deliberation. "I say, these are rather nice. Try one, Mark."

The Queen's representative took a custard cream with customary diplomacy.

Peter Barrington grunted, snorted and finally reached a hand out for the light switch before grabbing the phone. "Yes," he yawned. "What is it? Who? What? What the hell . . . oh!" He sat up in bed in his crumpled red silk pyjamas. "Yes, Sir Hugh. So sorry. Yes, sound asleep. No, no. Don't mention it. Yes, Driscoll has taken his yacht to France, somewhere. No, carry on; it's obviously important."

Janet, on her separate twin bed, lifted her head from the pillows and stared at the awed expression on her husband's face.

"Oh my God! Oh hell! Seriously? You're sure? Well, what do you want me to do?"

Janet swung her legs out of bed, looked at the soft pink negligee which matched her nightdress, shivered, and fetched a warm towelling robe from the dressing room. "Was that the Bailiff?" she asked.

"Yes." Peter stared at her, unblinking, his eyes as big as saucers.

"What on earth did he want at this time of night? Good gracious, it's one thirty!"

"He says that the Nuclear Power Station at Flamanville has blown up, or melted down, or whatever these things do, and we are all going to be engulfed in radioactive fall-out. Wants me to organise the profession. This *would* happen with Driscoll away!"

Janet gaped at him. "I think I'll go down and make a mug of camomile tea. Do you want some?"

Peter was scratching his thin, grey hair into a frenzy. "Yes. No. I think I'd prefer a brandy."

"Are you sure?"

"Yes. No! Oh, for heaven's sake, Janet. I don't care! Don't you realise what's about to happen to us?"

"Did Sir Hugh say it was definitely confirmed?"

He was dragging on his clothes. "Yes. No! Well, not exactly. He is still hoping the Home Office will phone back to say it was all an unfortunate mistake. But what if it isn't?"

Janet giggled. "If it isn't, then I would say it was a pity you didn't sell the house to that Parker man, when you had the chance."

"What good would that do?"

"Well, we could sail off in the yacht to safety and buy a house somewhere else. Now, are you sure you want a brandy?"

Peter sat slumped on the edge of the bed, shoes in his hand, studying her. She was no beauty even when she was dolled up to the nines, but in the middle of the night, without any make up, she'd petrify Dracula. Then he registered what she'd just said. Sail off to safety . . . South of France, maybe? And buy a house somewhere safe . . . Sometimes, just sometimes, she did show a modicum of intelligence. Well, after being married to him all these years something was bound to have rubbed off. Yes. If only he had sold the house . . .

"Hank? Hank, is that you?"

"Ugh? Yes, of course it's bloody well me." Applegate gave a huge, loud yawn. "What the hell time is it . . . Christ, it's twenty-to-two, woman! What the . . ."

"Listen, Hank. I've just got home . . ." Jane began.

"Early for you. Did lover boy get fed up with your snoring and kick you out?"

"Shut up, you clown, and just tell me why the Bailiff should be driving the Governor down the Grange ten minutes ago at the rate of knots, both in scruff order . . ."

"How the hell should I know? For chrissake, Janey, gimme a break. I only got to bed an hour ago."

"I can smell something, Hank. I'm going down into Town to see what the hell's going on. Are you coming?"

"You're not serious," he said hopefully. But he knew she was. Jane McAvoy was very experienced – a tough cookie in every sense of the word. She swore and drank like a man, interviewed with the cunning of a fox after a rabbit, took her work and sexual activities equally seriously. And when Jane's nose started to twitch, there was invariably a story waiting to be dug out.

"You'd better believe it. Get your skates on. I'll wait for you at the War Memorial."

"Shit!" he complained, swinging his legs off the bed. "This had better be good."

Twenty minutes later he joined her.

"There's nobody in Court Row," she said. "I've checked. Let's go down Hirzel Street and see if there's any activity at the cop shop."

For the fourth time Zelda Marquis shook her husband and shouted in his ear. "Walter! Will you wake up. It's the police on the phone!"

Walter snorted, coughed and tried to lift his head off the pillow, but the effort proved too much. "Whassat?" he mumbled without opening his eyes.

"Cor, you had another skinful tonight. You're still plastered." She tore all the bedclothes off and clicked her tongue with annoyance. "Really! That's the second time in a week you've got to bed with your shoes on."

"Ah, that explains it."

"Explains what?"

"Why I couldn't get my pants off. Hey, put the covers back on, Zelda!"

"I keep telling you, the police are waiting to speak to you. For heaven's sake get yourself downstairs to the phone." She shivered in her cotton nightie, clutching a cardigan round her shoulders.

Walter sat on the edge of the bed and with a supreme effort heaved himself to his feet and headed for the bedroom door. He didn't get very far. "Dammit!" he shouted as, hobbled by the crumpled trousers round his ankles, he fell on to Zelda's dressing stool.

"Mr Marquis?" Sue Johns said, when at last he reached the phone.

"That's me." His voice wasn't much more than a low rumble.

"I have the Bailiff on the line for you. Just one moment, please."

Walter glared at Zelda who'd followed him down. "You silly cow. It's not the police! I'll bet it's that bloody brother of yours trying to be funny."

"It *is* the police! That was Sue le Poidevin as was, married the Johns boy last year. She's been in the police for three or four years. I recognised her voice."

Walter stared at his wife's serious expression. "Are you having me on?"

"Is that you, Mr Marquis? I believe you are the next meteorologist on duty today?"

Walter's jaw dropped. Not even his brother-in-law could mimic the Bailiff that well. "Yes, sir. That's right. You want me, sir?"

"I need an up-to-date detailed weather forecast, Mr Marquis."

"Well, I don't usually go up there till five . . ."

"Now. It is essential I have it immediately."

"Yessir. Straight away. I'll go up straight away."

"I'd like you to report to me at the police station as soon as you have the information. I'm particularly anxious to know the wind speed and direction."

"Yessir." He replaced the receiver, his jaw still hanging open.

"Well? What is it? What have you done?"

"I haven't done anything." He almost sounded surprised. "It was the Bailiff! He wants me to go and get him an up-to-date forecast, now! In the middle of the night! I suppose he wants to go out on his boat at dawn, or something."

"He'd hardly be ringing from the police station then, would he? No," she shook her head. I reckon there's some sort of emergency. I wonder what it is, eh?"

David Beaufort sat by the window with the lights off, staring out across the eight miles of water to the French coast, Trouble at his feet. The huge red glow had dwindled somewhat, but the fire continued to burn. News reporters were scurrying about London and Paris trying to find anyone willing to divulge what was going on, and whether there had been a radiation leak. Officials were still saying "Yes, there had been a minor accident," and "No, nothing serious had been reported." But he didn't believe them. He was horribly convinced that whatever it was might prove disastrous and that he ought to be doing something. People should be warned, prepared to evacuate; they couldn't remain trapped here on Alderney, so close to danger. Not a nice, clean, violent danger, as when an earthquake or an explosion suddenly tears apart the lives of an entire community. This was different. He had starred in a film a few years previously, about a radiation disaster, and had read a mass of literature on the subject while researching the role. It was a slow, seeping, sly, invisible danger, its effect perhaps not apparent for some time after its onset. Then would come the vomiting and weakness, the mutations in plants and children, the slow death from leukemia. The people here needed to be shipped or flown out as quickly as possible, while there was still time . . . But nothing official had been announced. The French authorities hadn't admitted, yet, that their foolproof safety regulations had failed.

If they had . . . So if he went round knocking on people's doors, telling them to pack a suitcase and prepare to flee, the entire population would assume he was drunk again, or suffering another attack of DTs.

Evacuate. So what would he pack for himself? He looked towards the shelves of albums, framed photos, memorabilia of his career. It was too dark to distinguish one photograph from the next, but there was a dull reflection from the statuette . . . his only Oscar. Clothes meant nothing at all, they were replaceable; it was these things, amassed all over the world during the past forty-five years, that really mattered.

Trouble raised his head, and gazed questioningly at his master . . . who shuddered. Oh God! His dearest friend for the past ten years. The friend who had shared good times and bad, drinking sessions and hangovers, listened to endless private rehearsals. His most constant companion. Women and children would go first, then as many men as possible. But what chance was there of transportation for pets?

Liz turned her pillow over again, thumped a hollow in the middle with her fist and tried to settle. She felt hot and sticky, unsure if it was due to a rise in atmospheric temperature or simply the fact of eating and drinking too much during the evening. She had been a fool to have coffee at Pierre and Annabel's. She rolled over to look at the clock . . . it was nearly three. Thank heavens it was Saturday tomorrow – today, actually. Fifteen minutes later she gave up and sat up, turned on the light and reached for a book: anything to get her mind off nuclear power stations and radioactive fall-out.

A few minutes later there was a scratching at the door. Liz jumped out of bed to let Cocoa and Horlicks in, lest they woke Trish. They dived on to the bed and lay absolutely still, chins on paws, watching her, waiting until she smiled before letting their tails drum happily on the bedsprings.

"Demons!" she hissed at them.

They grinned back.

Walter Marquis stood in the doorway, twisting his hat in his hands. He wasn't used to mixing with the top brass.

"Come in, Mr Marquis," Joe Thompson invited. "You know Walter Marquis, Sir Hugh Your excellency, this is Walter Marquis, one of our meteorological experts."

"Marquis," the Governor acknowledged.

"Now, what have you got for us, Walter?" The Bailiff spoke gently, using his Christian name in the hope of easing the man's embarrassment.

"Well, sir, you wanted the weather for the next few days, right?"

"That's right."

"Well, sir, it's set fair. Yes, sir, not a drop of rain in sight." He paused, hopefully.

"We're more interested in wind direction, Walter. Right now it's south-west, force two to three, right?"

"That's right, sir. But it ain't going to stay there. No, sir. There's pressure building over the Continent. Yes, sir. That wind is going to shift, to the east."

"Did you say, the east?" the Governor asked.

"That's right, your excellency. Fine weather wind, that is. No rain."

"Jesus!" Thompson muttered.

The meteorologist looked pained. No pleasing some folk.

"When will this happen, Walter?" the Bailiff asked.

"Well, sir, that pressure is building now. I'd say today and tonight is likely to be dead calm. Tomorrow too, most likely. But sometime on Monday the wind should shift to the east."

"Monday," the Governor said. "Would you estimate the wind strength?"

"Oh, nothing to worry about, your excellency. Not

much above force two. Could be a three. Real gentle breeze." He beamed at them. "You gentlemen planning a yachting trip?"

"No," the Bailiff said, adding, "I wish we were. Thank you, Walter. You have been most helpful."

Walter hesitated, then backed through the doorway. The constable waiting in the corridor closed the door.

"What exactly is force two?" Thompson asked; he was not a sailor.

"Four to six nautical miles per hour," the Governor said. "Force three is seven to ten miles per hour. And therefore if Flamanville . . . ?"

"Is twenty-four miles from Guernsey," the Bailiff said.

"So anything emanating from Flamanville would be over Guernsey in something between two and a half and six hours."

"But not until late Monday," Thompson said. "Whatever is up there will have drifted some miles to the north-east in the present breeze."

"Whatever *is* up there," the Bailiff said. He lifted the phone. "Is my call to the Home Office through yet? . . . Very well, then the minister . . . He's away too? God Almighty . . . All right, I'll speak with the person who telephoned us here earlier, or if he is off duty, whoever has replaced him. Do make them understand that this is urgent. They seemed to think it was urgent enough at midnight." He tapped his fingers on the table, gazing at the two other men while he waited. "Yes? Oh, good morning. Are you the person who called me before? Oh, good. Would you put us in the picture, please?" He listened. "Waiting on the French? . . . Yes, I know the Channel is sixty miles wide at that point, but that isn't very far, is it? . . . I see. Just Cherbourg? . . . The whole north end of the Cotentin Peninsular? Yes, that makes sense. But the French are claiming the radiation levels are low? How low . . . forty Rem? My God, man, that would kill any living creature . . . I see. Yes. I think you should know that we have a forecast here that says the wind is going to shift to the east within seventy-two hours . . . I'm afraid I cannot adopt that point of view. When do you expect the Secretary of State back? . . . Well, I would very much like to speak with him just as soon as he is available. Thank you." He gazed at his two companions. "Silly, pompous twit."

"Did I hear you say, *forty* Rems?" the Governor asked.

"Yes. However, London says that is the strength that came out of the plant, last night. According to them it is naturally dissipating in the air. The cloud is of course still lethal, but at the moment it is hovering over the Channel just off Cherbourg. The entire Cotentin Peninsular north of Carteret is being evacuated, and experts are rushing down from Paris and various other places. London claims we are in no danger; they are obviously more worried about the Sussex and Kent coasts. When I pointed out that the wind is going to shift some time in the next seventy-two hours, he said, well, hopefully the cloud will have risen into the atmosphere by then."

"Do you believe him?"

"Of course I don't believe him. I don't think he believes himself. He's just stalling to avoid a panic. The French experts haven't got there yet to cap whatever is escaping. So that forty Rems level is being maintained at the moment. If the wind does shift . . ." he sighed. "As you heard, I have asked to speak with the Secretary of State as soon as he gets in. Seems he is at his country home but has been summoned. Meanwhile . . . we had better call a preliminary meeting. Where's the list?"

Chapter 16

SATURDAY 23rd JULY – morning

"Would you like another cup of coffee, dear?" Janet asked, poking her head round the study door.

Peter Barrington looked up, frowning. "Bloody annoying, Driscoll being away at this time, leaving me stuck with all these calls to make. Eh? What's that? Coffee you say. What's the time?"

"Nearly six o'clock."

"Great Scott! I don't know about coffee. I'm feeling damned hungry. How about some porridge, and toast and marmalade?"

Janet thought bed more appealing than the kitchen stove, but dutifully said "Yes, dear," and staggered off to start cooking.

Peter's face was grey, with black circles round his eyes, when he came and sat down behind the dish of steaming porridge. "I just rang the Bailiff again to check if he'd heard anything more. The Home Office have confirmed a serious radioactive leakage."

Janet gaped at him, porridge dropping off the wooden spoon in her hand on to the floor. "Serious? What do they mean? How serious? As bad as Three Mile Island?"

"Worse. Much worse, they believe." He stirred the milk and Demerara sugar into his porridge and conveyed a spoonful of the mixture to his mouth.

"What's going to happen?"

"Who knows? But I can't imagine it can be anything short of disaster."

"What will we do?"

"Get out, as fast as we can."

"I didn't mean us, personally – I meant the island as a whole. You can't leave, can you? I mean, with Andy Driscoll away . . ."

"What the hell can I do? Stand on top of Jerbourg Monument blowing the damn stuff away?" He pushed the plate across the table. "Too bloody lumpy. Can't eat that. Where's the toast?"

Both of them knew there was nothing wrong with the porridge. Janet knew his appetite had vanished because he was scared out of his wits. Peter knew she knew, and it made him furious. He managed half a slice of toast and a few mouthfuls of coffee before mumbling something about a shower, and stomping out of the room.

It was almost eight o'clock when, both dressed and looking a little better, they met crossing the hallway in opposite directions. "Anything I can do to help?" Janet asked bravely.

"You can go and pack a bag, I suppose. Ready for a quick getaway." He didn't add that he had spent the past half hour with a pile of *Adlard Coles* navigational books plotting a course of escape. The phone beeped. "I'll take it." Peter hurried into the study.

"Barrington? Just thought I'd let you know the latest." It was the Bailiff. "Seems what little air movement there is at the moment is carrying the threat away in the opposite direction for the next few hours. However, we will make a public announcement later this morning. Can you be down here about nine-thirty?"

Damn! That was the last thing he wanted to do! "Yes, of course. As soon as you like, Sir Hugh." His fingers fiddled irritably with a piece of card. When the Bailiff had rung off he turned it over and saw it was Eddie Parker's, with his latest offer for the house written on the back. Eddie Parker! He wondered if the little bounder had heard about the explosion yet. If not, of course, that idea he had had about selling the house and getting out with the cash . . . He lifted the receiver and pressed the numbers on the card.

It was long time before anyone answered. "Yeah?" Eddie sounded very sleepy.

"Parker? Barrington here. Look, I've been thinking over your offer . . . Are you there?"

There was a long drawn out yawn. "Bloody hell, Barrington. It's only ten past eight on a Saturday morning. You got insomnia or summat?"

"Beautiful day, you know. Been up for hours . . ."

"Well maybe when I get to your age, I'll get up early too. But in the meantime I've still got to service the little lady," Eddie cackled at his little joke. He didn't add that he and the little lady hadn't spoken since the flaming row they'd had on the boat last night, and that after all the booze he'd had at the regatta the only thing he was capable of servicing this morning was an Alka Seltzer. But the house . . .? Was the bloody man changing his mind about the offer? Surely he wasn't serious! "I'm listening," he said.

"Wondered if you were still interested?"

Blimey! If he was prepared to talk at all at that figure, he must be desperate. P'raps he'd come down even further. "Well, to be absolutely honest with you, old man, we have been looking at a couple of other rather attractive places. The wife has gone potty on the kitchen in one of them. I'll have to see what she says."

Barrington knew the man was lying, trying to lower his offer. However, a bird in the hand . . . "Perhaps we could convince her, between us, that the one here is better?"

"You mean, like, for three hundred and forty . . ."

"No, no. Your offer was three hundred and ninety-five . . ."

"Was. But considering what the other places are going for I don't think . . ."

"Well what do you think?" Little bastard, Peter muttered to himself.

"Like I say. Three hundred and thirty-five thousand."

Dammit! Another five thousand gone in thirty seconds! "Well I do think that's a ridiculously low figure, but maybe we could talk?"

"You in for lunch? I might pop up then."

"Excellent. We can have a drink." His voice was all charm and hospitality. He ground his teeth.

"You lot still in yer bleedin' beds?" Wilma's voice reached them from the kitchen doorway.

"Shit! The voice that breathed o'er Eden! Go an' shut your bloody sister up, Sharon." Eddie pressed the volume-plus button on the children's Saturday morning cartoon on the bedroom telly.

"You bloody well go." Sharon sniped back, glaring through yesterday's smudged mascara.

"She's your sister!"

"True. But it's you she's botherin', not me."

"I'm telling you. If I go down, she goes out, plus her bloody kids. And what's more, she doesn't come back."

Sharon seethed. Not at the thought of Wilma no longer coming in to do the housework – her kids made more mess than she ever cleaned up – but because she had always felt sorry for her sister and knew she needed the money. She swore at her husband long and loud. But Eddie was so used to it he hardly noticed: he was concentrating on a huge green dinosaur. Three minutes later Sharon was back. "Here. You'd better get up. Wilma says there's been an explosion at that nuclear place in France."

"Yeah? So where did dear Wilma get this stunning bit of info? And what nuclear place in France? They've got dozens of them."

"It's the one we can see on the French coast, when the weather's clear. Her neighbour's boyfriend works for the cleaning service that does the police station. They went in at six this morning and the Bailiff and the Governor were there. Been there all night, it seems."

"And they called this bloke in to the room to tell him all about it and ask his advice, I suppose. You women start more rumours . . ." Of course, if by any chance it was true, that would explain why Barrington had suddenly changed his mind about selling . . . He must've heard something, some rumour that scared him rigid. It certainly wouldn't take much: the pompous, stuck up bastard was all mouth and yellow liver. Nuclear explosion! Balls. They were always dreaming up some terrible emergency or other. But still, as long as Barrington was scared witless, then Eddie Parker could make himself a bloody killing! He jumped out of bed. "Where's my pants, girl? I'm going out."

There was a tap on the door. "Mr Watts is here, sir," the constable said, "and Dr Barrington."

"Oh, right. Ask them to come in, will you?" A few moments later Peter Barrington strode into the room looking suitably serious and important, Willy bustling in his wake, face redder than ever. "Peter, my dear fellow," the Bailiff stood up and shook his hand. "So glad you could come down so quickly. And you, Willy. Wretched business this. And just when you were considering retirement, eh?"

Willy scratched his head. "Morning, Hugh. Your excellency," he nodded at the Governor. "Some thing this, eh?"

"Have you monitored our air?"

"Yes, sir. The instruments show no increase in radiation. Could be the whole thing is a big mistake."

"I think we must thank the wind direction for that, Mr Watts," the Governor said. "What we would like you to do, Willy," the Bailiff said, "is very quietly and confidentially, arouse your people and put them on stand-by. The one thing we must avoid is any suggestion of panic, so there will be no letting off the sirens at this stage. We do not want to be held responsible for a whole series of heart attacks and people taking to the boats, as it were. The operative word is *quietly*. As you say, the whole thing might be a colossal mistake."

"Yes. Yes, quite. Definitely quietly." Watts was looking very worried, then his face brightened. "At least I can assure you gentlemen that the Command Bunker is in splendid nick. I checked out every detail last year, when that ship nearly came aground, and I've renewed the food stocks. We keep it well maintained and you'll be as safe as houses. Well . . ."

"Thank you, Willy," the Bailiff said.

The Governor tapped the table. "How many people is the Command Bunker supposed to hold?"

"Sixty. That is, you and me, and Joe here, with other persons considered essential to the island. As per these lists we've prepared."

"Hugh, do you seriously intend that you and I and our support groups should take what shelter there is while everyone else is exposed to a lethal dose of radiation?"

"Well, of course I don't. That bunker system was set up when there was a chance of the Cold War getting hot."

Peter Barrington's head swung from *he* to the Bailiff and back, Wimbledon style, wondering just how essential these two men regarded senior members of the medical profession.

"So, supposing, just supposing, that radioactive cloud does start to drift in this direction . . . what is the population of this island?" the Governor asked.

"With summer visitors, something close to eighty thousand, at the moment."

"Yes. Just what are we going to do about that?"

Peter coughed, significantly. The Bailiff stared at him, and waited. "I was wondering what preliminary evacuation plans you, or the Civil Defence people, might have?"

"Those plans were formed back in the fifties," Willy told him. "They've been updated from time to time."

"I'm glad of that! Hate to think of us been flown out

in relays in de Havilland Rapides." Peter couldn't resist the note of sarcasm.

Willy bridled immediately. "I can assure you that Guernsey's Civil Defence Force is completely *au fait* with all the latest . . ."

"Yes, yes, Willy," the Bailiff snapped. "We know all that. Now . . . ah, Gordon, just the man."

Gordon Nugent, Managing Director and chief shareholder of Sea Transit Ltd, one of the island's main lines of surface contact with England and the Continent, was ushered into the room by Bill Collins. "Good morning, your excellency, Sir Hugh, gentlemen. How may I be of use?"

"Sit down, won't you." The Bailiff waited while the newcomer pulled up a chair. "You've heard the news?"

"You mean that the Australians were three hundred and fifteen for four overnight?" He could think of no other news which could be of vital interest to Sir Hugh.

"No, no. The explosion at Flamanville."

Gordon, a large, genial man with a shock of thick brown hair and deceptively lazy green eyes, looked slowly round the table at the faces staring at him. "Jeepers! You mean it? This isn't just some Civil Defence mock exercise?"

Willy shook his head. "'Fraid not, old man. Though we are all still hoping it might be a false alarm, or at least the seriousness may be exaggerated."

"While we are waiting for the various States Committee presidents and the conseillers to arrive for a meeting, I wonder if you would mind giving us a run down on what shipping might be available should it be deemed necessary to commence evacuation of the island."

Gordon's eyes closed, his face screwing up in horror. He took a deep breath. "I cannot say for sure what ships are in the harbour at the moment, but I can state quite categorically that we own only two passenger ships, carrying twelve hundred people each, and three cargo vessels with a very limited capacity. Say twenty each."

"But far more than that if people are put in the holds?"

"Mmm. True." He grimaced, and looked unsure. "They are not licenced . . ."

"I don't imagine anyone will be worrying about licences at a time . . ." the Governor began.

". . . except the insurers. If you'll pardon me," the shipping man added, balancing due deference with business.

"Surely people would rather get away than worry about compensation if they lose a suitcase," Joe Thompson said impatiently.

"How many might be transported by other sea carriers? And by air? What about Condor?"

"Depends how much time we have."

"It could be as little as twenty-four hours."

Gordon shook his head. "I'd have to work it out, but off – hand, I'd say less than a third of the population could be got out in twenty-four hours."

"And how many can be accommodated in your various bunkers, Willy?" the Bailiff persisted.

"If you're talking about any length of time, around six hundred, at most."

"Can the population make safe areas within their own homes?"

"Some. For a limited period." Willy shrugged.

"What about the hospital patients, Mr Barrington?"

"Uh? Oh, er I'm not sure of the current situation. With all the new buildings . . ." he looked vague, quite understandably as he hadn't been listening to the discussion, concentrating his mind on personal arrangements.

"What about medical care?" the Governor wanted to know.

"Wouldn't be much use. Once one absorbs a certain level of radiation . . ."

Everyone glared at him, and he shut up.

Eddie Parker's Mercedes convertible was parked in the driveway when Peter swung up to the garage and flicked the remote control at the automatic roll-up-and-over doors. He half wished he hadn't bothered about re-starting the sale . . . there was still a chance that the wind might carry the threat away, but on the other hand, once they knew for sure, then Parker wouldn't buy anyway. The successful Cockney car dealer was waiting in the sitting-room. "Hello, old chap. Been down at the new nick with the Bailiff? Quite a scare going on, eh?"

Barrington stared at him. "How the hell . . . Janet tell you where I was?"

"No, I guessed where you'd be. This scare about Flamanville, it's all over Town."

"So much for keeping it quiet," the doctor muttered.

"Did you mention something about a drink when you rang? Hot day, today."

Peter hadn't forgotten, but now that Parker knew about the explosion there didn't seem much point in being that hospitable. However . . . "Yes. What'll you have, a beer?"

"I'd prefer a nice long gin an' tonic with a lotta ice." Janet appeared at the door, so Peter passed on the order, plus a beer for himself. "So, you'd like to sell, huh?"

"Yes."

"You realise that this radiation threat makes a difference?"

Peter frowned. "What to?"

"Well, let's face it, there'll be a lotta people hastily putting their places on the market as soon as they hear the news, for one thing. And for another, whoever buys is taking a big risk. I mean to say, I could lose the lot if the island's a write off, couldn't I?"

"Everything, I imagine," Peter replied, coldly.

Janet came in with the drinks. "Thanks, love." Eddie took his glass from her tray. "Cheers. But don't worry about me, mate. Most of my investments are abroad."

Janet glanced at her husband, who was not about to reveal the whereabouts of any investments he might have made. "You didn't bring Mrs Parker with you, to see the kitchen," Peter observed.

"Not necessary. She could remember it. She still prefers

the one at Torteval. But I reckon between us you and I could change her mind. Now what was the last figure you mentioned? Three fifteen, wasn't it?"

"Dammit man, you know bloody well it wasn't. You were the one who said three four five . . ."

"Ah yes, you're absolutely right. But that was before the explosion. Things are different now."

"How different?"

"A straight three?"

"What!" A red stain crept up Peter's neck. "Have you forgotten my asking price was four fifty?"

"Well, that was a joke, for starters. When you rang this morning I thought you wanted to talk serious," He drained his glass and stood up. "Well, Torteval it is, then."

Peter and Janet stared at each other. She had her mouth open, waiting . . . He was breathing hard, trying to control his fury. "Well, come on man. What sensible figure are you prepared to offer?"

"Three ten?"

"Three forty."

"Three fifteen?"

"Three thirty."

"Three twenty?"

Peter's chest heaved. "Very well. Three twenty." If there was an all clear before they signed the agreement, at which time Parker was supposed to pay the ten per cent deposit, he could always back out . . .

Parker opened his leather, continental style handbag and pulled out a paper. Unfolding it he said, "I always carry one of these on me when I discuss a property deal. No time like the present?"

The colour drained from Peter's face as he stared at the official, printed property conveyance contract. "Er . . . well, I like to get the cheque cleared before . . ."

"Never bother with cheques for deposits. Always carry a bit of spare cash, see?" From the bag he withdrew a vast fistful of banknotes. "There's two bundles of hundreds, makes twenty thou. Two bundles of fifties makes it thirty thou, and a bundle of twenties." He piled the notes on the coffee table.

Peter knew he was trapped. As he took the pen Parker offered him for the signing, his mind swam in circles and he looked at Janet, perhaps hoping to read in her expression a way out. She smiled bleakly, stooped to collect the empty glasses and carried them out to the kitchen. No doubt she would be blamed if the beastly fall-out didn't fall on Guernsey! Of course if it did, then Peter would doubtless claim credit for a brilliant stroke of genius.

Monique yawned, and stretched. "God, is it morning? Shit, where are we?"

"Coming up to St Mére Église," Philippe said.

"And it's . . . She looked at the clock on the dashboard. "Eight o'clock? We have been on the road for twelve hours and travelled thirty kilometres?"

Philippe waved his hand at the bumper to bumper traffic in front of them, and behind them too. "At least we haven't had to stop and get gas, eh?"

Quick as they had been, Philippe and Monique hadn't been quick enough, last night. By the time they had loaded their gear into the hired car, all Cherbourg was on the move, alerted by radio and television, and by the police, who were everywhere, telling people to leave town. It was a slow business. Getting a Frenchman, or even more, a Frenchwoman, to abandon her home when there was no immediate visible threat, was difficult. But the streets had already been crowded, with vehicles, belongings, animals, and people, all shouting and gesticulating, the whole being marshalled by the police, not very successfully.

"Shit," Monique had remarked. "We might as well back upstairs and gone to bed. We're going to be here all night."

"If we had left the car, somone would nicked it," Pierre said.

Monique shuddered. "All these fucking policemen make me nervous."

"Forget it. They don't know who we are, and they don't care. But I agree it could be a long night. Listen, nip across the road and buy some bread and sausage and a couple of bottles of wine." He had grinned. "May as well enjoy ourselves."

Monique opened the door, and gave another little shudder. "Do you think it's in the air, yet?"

"By now, sure; it's had twelve hours, for God's sake."

"Then . . ."

"You're going to be contaminated? Sweetheart, all these people are contaminated by now. They're all going to get sick and die, sometime. Soon. So what the hell?"

Chapter 17

SATURDAY 23RD JULY – MORNING (continued)

Eight-thirty! Liz jumped out of bed and her legs nearly crumpled as the weariness of the previous night hit her behind the knees. The bathroom mirror revealed a horrifying image, not much improved by a rapid cold shower. She teetered on one leg as the other groped in her jeans for an exit, slammed the drawer after grabbing a tee-shirt, pulled a comb through her wet hair and ran into the kitchen. Cocoa and Horlicks showed no inclination to follow, so she scribbled a hurried note asking Trish to walk them. Trish wouldn't mind, she was an enthusiastic walker.

The waiting room was full, as usual on Saturday mornings. Polly, frowning into the phone in reception, put her hand over the mouthpiece. "This is the second call about what to do with animals if there is a fall-out!" She looked totally confused, behind her thick spectacles. "What are they talking about?"

Liz took the receiver from her. "Elizabeth Cobb, here. Hello, Mr Le Maître. . . . yes, terrible. But frankly until we know quite definitely what is happening, I think we had better not make any decisions. As far as we know this may well be a false alarm." Polly was staring at her like a zombie.

"There was an explosion in France last night and some people are thinking there is a risk of nuclear fall-out or something." Liz handed back the phone. "No point in worrying about it. We'll know soon enough if there is any serious problem." *At least I hope it will be soon enough,* she thought!

"How will we know?"

"The sirens will blow off I suppose and there'll be some announcement on radio. Now, how many patients have I this morning?" She was trying to think logically, overcome the nagging in the pit of her stomach . . . which could well be the fact of missing breakfast.

Later, she emerged from her room having just prescribed another lot of worm tablets, this time for an emaciated moggy, when Polly called to her. "Mrs Cobb. An American gentleman has left a number for you to ring when you're free. Do you want me to get him for you before your next patient?"

Jackson! She smiled to herself, realised that Polly was watching her expression and quickly straightened her face. "Yes, please. I'll take it in my room."

His voice sounded thick. "You're an early bird."

"Early! I've seen seven patients, so far."

"Bully for you! Heard any more about the explosion?"

"No. Have you?"

"It was reported as a third item on the news this morning."

Liz gave a sigh of relief. "Thank goodness. Can't be that serious."

"What time will you be finished ministering to the dumb?"

"About twelve-fifteen. And if you could hear the racket out in the waiting room at the moment, you wouldn't call the little beggars dumb! Are you coming round for lunch?" She made a mental note to slip down to Rocquaine for fish on her way home.

When Liz arrived Trish was reading the local paper, armed with a gin and tonic. She was frowning. "I don't get this. The BBC have interrupted their sports coverage to update viewers on *'the situation at Flamanville, site of last night's nuclear explosion*,' as they put it. Yet it is only mentioned in a single column strip on page two of your local paper. Look!" She held up the broadsheet. "If, as it claims, it's an evening paper, then it won't have been put to bed before this morning. So why no current information?"

Liz dumped her bag on the kitchen table. "They would be very chary about scare-mongering. But it is quite possible they've been gagged for fear of terrifying all our OAPs unnecessarily. Not to mention our tourists."

"Gagged! Wish we could do that in London, sometimes."

"We don't have party politics here. Or gutter press."

"Lucky you." Trish folded the paper. "Lots of super shots of the regatta in there. I'd like to take a copy home with me. By the way, Jackson phoned at the crack of dawn . . . just before ten. I don't think he believed me when I said you weren't here."

"He got me at the surgery. He's coming to lunch."

"Well, I won't be here. Promised to go out in the boat with Pierre and the family. Do you think they'll still go?"

"Oh, yes. The weather is lovely. Not a breath of wind. It may be a bit misty, though."

Trish stared at her. "That's not what I meant."

Liz stared back, sighing. "I know. Look. I'm trying not to think about it. I may be over-optimistic but I can't believe . . . I don't want to believe, it could happen. Okay. I know it's stupid to play ostrich," she headed for the door. "Let's put the local radio on."

"I think I'll call Pierre. See what they're doing. If they are going out I'll have to leave now."

Jackson drove in as Trish's hire car pulled out of the driveway. She waved but didn't stop. He found Liz in the sitting-room on the settee with a bowl and knife, stringing beans. The TV was on, muted, and Abba was singing an oldie on the radio. "Not outside on a beautiful day like this?" he asked.

"Long may it last." She often got depressed when hungry.

"You're worried." He leaned over to kiss her.

"You bet your sweet life I am." She responded with a perfunctory peck.

"Tell me." He sat beside her.

"First, the fact that despite all the speculation on UKTV, nothing has been said on local media: which can only mean they are too seriously worried to refute alarmist reports. And second, if there is a serious risk of radiation fall-out here, I have one helluva responsibility looming, for the animal population." She dropped the knife in the bowl and swung round to face him. "Do you know, by the end of the morning we had had seven calls from people wanting to know what to do with their pets? And now they're starting to ring me here."

Jackson's comforting arms slid round her and she gratefully abandoned the beans. Abba finished . . . to be replaced with only a faint crackle. Jackson and Liz sat up, looking at the radio, waiting. The programme presenter came on air. "We are interrupting this programme to bring you an important announcement given by Guernsey's Bailiff."

"Ladies and Gentlemen. Following a meeting this morning of senior States representatives and their advisors, I have been asked to assure the islanders and our visitors that, after last night's explosion in France, our Civil Defence Committee and all relevent public service personnel have been alerted of the possibility – and I assure you, it is only a possibility – of a radiation leak from the Nuclear Power Station at Flamanville. However, we are informed that, at this moment in time, there is absolutely no reason whatsoever to be alarmed as there is no threat of any possible fall-out on the island. Experts are constantly monitoring the situation and the public will be kept informed on this radio channel of any changes. In the meantime we suggest you enjoy your week-end as normal. Thank you."

Acker Bilk's clarinet filled the air. Liz fried the fresh Guernsey whiting which they ate in the sitting-room from trays perched on their knees, flicking from one TV channel to the next, the radio presenter delivering a continuous string of taped music interspersed with local chatter.

Liz was just finishing a last mouthful of the delicate white fish when the phone beeped again at her elbow. "Elizabeth Cobb," she said, smiling politely at the receiver. The smile quickly vanished. "I don't think we have any reason as yet to take such drastic action. The authorities . . ." Her mouth tightened. "Yes. Well, possibly they don't but . . . No. Quite. . . . Yes do. Goodbye." She replaced the receiver. "Some self-confessed expert wanting to tell me how much more he knows about the situation than the authorities do, and the appalling effect of radiation on animals. He wants to know what am I intending to do about it?" She gave a weak grin. "He seems to be advocating mass slaughter."

"Amazing how some people appear to go through life looking for dramatic opportunities to panic!" Jackson got up and carried his tray out to the kitchen.

Liz followed suit. "I wonder what your friend David Beaufort is thinking about the situation. If he's at home he is a lot nearer to the problem than we are."

"Hmm. I'd wondered about him. Shall I give him a call?"

"Do. I'll make some coffee."

David was staring across the Race of Alderney at the atomic tower. The light winds of the last couple of days were having their inevitable result, and a sea mist was gathering so that the tower emerged from a white cloud in an almost disembodied state. Of course, nothing had happened at the Re-processing Plant, and the mist even with his binoculars was too thick for him to make out the domes of the electricity generating station eleven miles down the coast. That was where the glow had come from, last night. And that was where it was happening, whatever it was. However, despite the hysterical reaction on the part of the media, there had been no massive explosion, just a fire. But if there had been a leakage . . . Of course atomic radiation clouds were invisible, and of course the wind – such as it was – was still south-westerly, but that station was still damned close, visible or not.

"Excuse me, sir," Forsythe appeared on the terrace carrying a cordless phone. "Mr Jackson Ridgeway for you. Do you wish to take the call?"

"Indeed." He held out his hand. "Jackson? How are things shaping up over there?"

"Did you get the Bailiff's announcement?"

"Yes, for what it's worth. I imagine he is reluctant to start a mass exodus from Guernsey. However, I think the threat is infinitely greater here."

"You coming over to Guernsey?"

"Reckon everyone should get out of here, certainly. I mean, if and when a State of Emergency is declared it will be too late for anyone here to get away, except those lucky enough to have a private plane or fast boat on standby."

"Would everyone agree to leave Alderney at this stage?" Jackson queried.

"I doubt it. Specially if it's suggested by a drunken old actor."

"You don't sound drunk to me."

"Thanks for those few kind words. As a matter of fact I'm horribly sober and shit scared at the moment. I think I may go into the town and suss out the general feeling. Where are you right now? I may call you back."

"At Liz Cobb's." Jackson read out the number. "I don't think we're going far from the TV or radio for a while, so we'll be here."

David switched off the phone, and went into the house. "You there, Forsythe? I'm going into town. Want to come with me?"

"Perhaps it might be better if I stay by the radio, sir?"

"Yes. Good thinking."

Trouble sat in the passenger seat as the Bentley bounced off down the drive to Longis Road, swaying as they lurched at speed round corners. Braye Street was remarkably empty so David drove straight down to the harbour. Three large sailing yachts were motoring out round the breakwater, heading south, and he could see people on board two others in the harbour, stowing cardboard boxes and suitcases.

"Rats deserting the proverbial ship which hasn't even started to sink, yet," he muttered to himself. But he couldn't blame them: there were children on board both. Trouble was sitting with his chin on the sill of the open window. "We can't very well ask them to take you, too. So we'll have to charter an aircraft. Let's go up to the airport."

It was a five minute drive. There was a queue at the ticket desk, but an old drinking acquaintance was on the tarmac preparing his Cessna for departure so, leaving the dog in the car, David walked out to speak to him. "You heading for the mainland, Tim?"

"David! No, actually. I'm going to Guernsey. Looking for a ride?"

"Not for myself. Just my dog, Trouble. I'd make it well worth your while," he added, seeing the man's grimace. "Two hundred be okay?"

"Quite a responsibility," Tim hedged. "Dogs can be pretty unpredictable . . ."

"Five sound better?" Drinking pal he might be, but obviously one who reckoned there was no room for sentiment when discussing business. And what did cost matter, or where Tim was going? He could always catch up with Trouble later, wherever he was. All he wanted was to be sure the dog was safely off the island.

"What do I do with it when I get there?"

David hated hearing Trouble referred to as *it*, but he kept his cool. "I've got a friend over there who'll look after him. I'll go straight home and phone him. Just put

Trouble in a taxi to Elizabeth Cobb. Her address will be in the phone book."

"How are you paying?"

"I'll write you a cheque, now."

Chapter 18

SATURDAY, 23RD JULY – NOON

"Ow! Oh bloody hell my neck!" Hank Applegate groaned and sat up, bumping himself on the steering wheel. He pulled the car duster off his face and blinked at the strong sunlight. He yawned long and loud . . . and suddenly realised that Jane was in the seat beside him, sound asleep. "Hey, wake up!"

She was awake and alert immediately. "Yes, what? What's happening?"

"Nothing. At least not since that announcement, earlier."

"Then why the hell did you wake me?"

"One, for the sheer pleasure of turning the tables on you, and two, to share my agony. I can't move my head."

"It won't matter, as long as you focus the camera right."

"It does matter. And do you realise we've been staked out here for more than twelve hours?"

"Nonsense. You went off for an hour and had a revolting great breakfast."

"And now I could happily wrap myself round a revolting great lunch. I don't know how much longer you plan to stay here, but I've had enough. I'm . . ."

"Wow!" Jane exclaimed. "Look at this lot."

They were parked in Hirzel Street, and trouping down the hill past them was a large group of States members, the Guernsey equivalent of MPs.

Weariness forgotten, they leapt out of the car, and within moments Hank's camera was recording.

"Are you attending an Emergency Council meeting?" Jane shoved her microphone into the group.

"Not to my knowledge," Paul Pritchard said.

"Would you tell us if you are meeting to discuss . . ."

"Nothing to say . . ."

"Are you personally worried about the situation?" Jane persisted.

"What situation?"

"Yes. Very worried," said Lynn Battle. "I'm going to see the Bailiff now to find out what he's doing about it."

"About what?"

"Lynn! That's enough. You know what the Bailiff said!" Paul warned.

"What did he say?" Jane asked.

"Nothing. There will be a statement soon, no doubt. When the Bailiff sees fit."

The journalist followed them as far as the police station, followed by her reluctant cameraman, but they were prevented from entering by Bill Collins.

"That's it, Jane." Hank eased the camera off his shoulder. "I'm going home to shave, shower and shampoo. Eat. And then I'm going to sleep. In bed!"

"You can't! Anything could happen at any minute."

"Quite. But on the off chance that nothing is going to happen for hours, I'm off."

Jane capitulated. "Okay. Go. I'll call you if things hot up." She watched him put the precious camera in the car and drive off.

She was weary, too. But nothing would persuade her to leave. Not now.

"That you, Adele?"

"Hello, Ma. John was going to ring you. You okay?" Adele reached with her free hand to lower the sound of the radio. Seeing how seriously Glen had reacted to the news from France, she and his father had taken turns listening in all morning.

"I'm okay," her mother-in-law said, but there was a doubtful tone in her voice.

"But you're worried, eh?"

"To be truthful, yes. My heart's going fifteen to the dozen. I don't like what's going on one little bit. What do you people think about it all?"

"We don't know what to think. We keep the wireless on so we'll hear if they make any announcement."

"They won't. Not till it's too late to do anything about it. Just the same as in nineteen-forty. They argued in the States for days – this one saying people should leave, that one accusing him of panic."

"I don't remember all that," Adele said.

"You wouldn't. You were too young. But there was so much confusion. Some saying the Germans would kill us all and others saying they'd never dare come here at all."

"But you stayed here, in the end." Adele wasn't quite sure of the whole story, though she'd heard it often enough. The trouble was, when it didn't affect you, you tended not to listen.

"Well, we couldn't very well leave the old people, see. We sent John off with the school, as you know, but we thought it would only be for a few weeks at most. Had we known it was to be for five years we'd never have let him go alone. We'd have found a way to take the old people too. Even if we were accused of running away."

"People didn't really say those things, did they?"

"And more. But then, there were families split in two over it, let alone the States. You know the le Hurays from up here by me?"

"Yes."

"Well it wasn't till years after the Liberation that Sheila and her brother ever spoke to each other."

"Why?"

"He and his wife left in a hurry, and when they came

back five years later there was all hell let loose. They reckoned Sheila should have stored all their stuff for them . . . all their furniture and their clothes and everything. Instead, the Germans took over the house and all the contents disappeared."

"I can't see how they could blame Sheila for that?"

"They believed she'd gone in and taken some of their things for herself."

"And had she?"

"Well, I saw her wearing her sister-in-law's fur coat, myself. She said she had saved it from being stolen and kept it in her wardrobe for years. But dash it, Adele, by 'forty-four we'd worn out all our clothes and it was jolly cold, that winter. I can't honestly say I blame her borrowing it."

"Didn't she give it back after the war?"

"Of course. But her sister-in-law was so furious she'd worn it she threw it on the bonfire in the backyard."

"It's no wonder they weren't speaking for so long," Adele commented. "Now look, Ma, we don't like to think of you there alone, worrying. Why don't I pop round with the car and fetch you for tea? And then, if you like, you can stay the night."

The old lady looked round her room. She didn't want to leave it, or all her things. And she would certainly be more comfy in her own bed. Yet she wasn't keen to stay alone all evening. "Would you mind if I bring Smudge? He's been all on edge since last night. Makes you wonder if he knows something we don't, eh?"

"He probably does. Anyway, you can bring him. You know he's welcome." Which wasn't entirely true, but it would make her mother-in-law happier.

The phone beeped yet again. Liz glared at it. "I've half a mind not to answer," she told Jackson.

"I'll take it. It might be David Beaufort." He crossed the room. "Hello? . . . Who is wanting her? Mr Thomas. I'll see if she is at home." He put his hand over the mouthpiece, looking up at Liz. She shook her head. "No, she is out at present . . . No, I have no idea when she'll be back but I'll leave a message to say you called. Goodbye."

"Well done," she grinned. "Let's take the radio outside onto the patio. We can at least lie out on the sun loungers for half an hour." She loved her garden. It had been a wilderness when she and Michael had bought the place but she had worked hard to remove the old bits of decayed greenhouse wood and broken glass, and designed the layout to include the huge natural boulder at the foot of the hill at the back, the clump of tropical-looking dracaenas and the small lily pond in front of the new summerhouse. She treasured the few chances she had to relax and enjoy the results of her work.

"Why only half an hour?"

"I don't know. Maybe because I have a feeling I ought to do some provisional packing."

He found it heart-wrenching to see her face so drawn. But he didn't refer to it. Instead he said, "Why don't you go and put on a swimsuit?"

They placed the loungers close together so they could touch, clasp hands and occasionally reach over to kiss, eyes locked and scarcely blinking. They both knew the moment was close when they would have to accede to the demand which was swamping their minds, gradually eliminating all other thoughts . . . and fears.

Liz was about to suggest they retire to her bedroom when the phone beeped from the sitting-room. She sighed, and Jackson got up to take it again. "Darling," he called. "It's Annabel for you."

"Bad moment?" her sister-in-law asked as Liz took the receiver.

"Could have been worse," was the wistful reply. "What are you doing at home? I thought you were all going out in the boat."

"Pierre changed his mind. It's very thick on the water. Now listen . . . June next door just popped in. She says the supermarket is packed with people stocking up on supplies. Huge trolleyloads of food waiting at all the checkouts. I'm going there now to get what I can before they run out. What about you?"

Liz was gazing through the French windows at Jackson's lean, hard body. "Er, I hadn't thought of it." Which wasn't entirely true; she had thought of it several times, but at that precise moment it didn't have priority rating. "Yes. I suppose it wouldn't be a bad idea. Thanks for letting me know."

"What did she want?" Jackson asked.

"To warn me that food supplies are selling out fast. Maybe we should go and stock up in case we find ourselves trapped here."

"If that's what you want to do."

"It isn't," she grinned. "But I suppose it makes more sense."

"Than what?" he asked, pretending he didn't know.

"Hm. If that wind were to shift, the whole south west of England would be at risk, as well as us," David remarked to Forsythe. "Trouble's on his way to Guernsey and when I've organised someone to look after him, I'll go down to the Yacht Club and find out what our Alderney States members are doing." He took the cordless phone out onto the terrace, gazing pensively at the now invisible French coast while the digits clicked through and cursed as Liz Cobb's phone gave the engaged tone. Moment's later he pressed re-dial, and still it was engaged. So he tried the number of the Alderney States President, and that was engaged, too. When at last he got Liz's number it beeped and beeped, but there was no reply; she had switched off her ansaphone. David referred to his vast repertoire of blasphemous curses, and minutes later the battered Bentley was hurtling down Longis Road into the town.

"I have had a report from Mr Watts, sir," Joe Thompson

said. "He has checked all the monitors, and there is as yet no increase in the radioactivity reading."

The Bailiff nodded. He had bathed and shaved and changed, and still looked distinctly the worse for wear, having as yet had no sleep. The Governor had gone home, but had been replaced by several States members, all looking anxious.

"We've received a up-date from France, via the Home Office," the Bailiff said. "It seems certain that there was an act of sabotage, carefully planned and in fact suicidal. The various explosions and the initial fire are really of very little importance. But the saboteurs did achieve what they set out to do, which was to cut off the water-supply to the plant. This was an enormous undertaking, as it involved three separate sources, and of course they all had to be cut off at the same time. Thus one of the saboteurs, a woman, actually blew herself up in the reservoir; another, again a woman, managed to get herself into the pump room and plant a bomb – that caused the explosion. The man who was with her, an engineer who she had apparently seduced, died in the explosion. No one knows what happened to the woman. And the third source, the intake from the sea, was destroyed at the same time. They have no details about this, but they suspect it was done by a frogman placing an explosive charge within the inlet itself. The result of all this was that, before any replacement source of water could be brought to bear, there was a meltdown. That was the big glow we saw last night. I don't have to tell you what is involved, or what the after effects can be."

"Good God! But who can have done all this? The Russians? Gaddafi?"

"I don't think so, Paul. Neither do they. They are going for a French terrorist group which apparently is out to destroy their atomic program, no matter how many lives it costs – including, apparently, their own."

"Ah," Thompson said, having just taken a phone call.

"Yes. Talking of which I should tell you that Lynn Battle has arrived, demanding to speak with you."

"She's all we need," Gordon Nugent muttered.

"I suppose I'll have to see her," the Bailiff said.

Lynn Battle led the group of deputies into the room, obviously determined to emulate her name. "Now, look here, Sir Hugh! How long are you going to keep misleading the public?"

"Really, Mrs Battle," Thompson protested.

"That's all right, Joe," the Bailiff said. "Why don't you sit down, Lynn? You know Mr Gordon Nugent?"

"Aha!" Lynn said, seating herself at the table. "So, we are discussing evacuation."

"Should it become necessary," the Bailiff said. "You'd better explain it to her, Gordon."

"These are of course precautionary measures only," Nugent said. "I'm afraid the number of ships available at short notice are extremely limited. In addition to our own fleet, I believe I could arrange to have another two ferries or small freighters here within twenty-four hours, if it became absolutely necessary."

"What about aircraft, man?"

"Well, we could obtain a large number of medium-size jets. Our runway won't take jumbos, as you know. And the whole operation would be limited by the fact that there is only one runway. And each aircraft would have to be loaded, as it came in. I think we could handle something like one every ten minutes. So working round the clock, that would be one hundred and forty-four sixty-seaters in twenty-four hours. That would be eight thousand, six hundred and forty people. Now I believe we could take off another ten thousand by ship, in that time . . ."

"The Navy would send what they have," the Bailiff put in. "I have already confirmed this with the Home Secretary."

"In other words," Lynn said, "the entire island could be evacuated in three days."

"Weather permitting," Joe put in.

"Weather? The weather's perfect."

"That's it. You looked out of the window recently?"

"Sea mist. The sun will burn it off."

"Maybe. But it'll be back tonight. And if there's no wind, it'll be a lot thicker tomorrow, which will hamper the aircraft."

"Well," Nugent said. "We will just have to cope with the fog, if necessary."

"We also have the visitors to consider," the Bailiff said. "We estimate about fifteen thousand of them at the moment."

Paul Pritchard gave a wry grin. "A lot of them are trying to get off the island now. Next thing there is going to be a whole batch of cancellations for the rest of the summer. What this is going to do to the tourist industry . . ."

Nugent nodded. "My ship was turning people away this morning, simply because every place was taken."

"Is money the only thing you can think of? We're still talking about not more than four days," Lynn said. "When does the evacuation start?"

"There's Alderney as well, of course," Nugent said. "We'd have to send transport there."

"And Sark," Joe Thompson said.

"What's Jersey doing?" Pritchard inquired.

"Sorting out their own problems, I should imagine," Nugent said.

"Just so long as they don't try to pinch any of the transport we have available."

"When does it *start*?" Lynn shouted. Heads turned, expressions somewhat pained. "Or has it already started?" The men exchanged glances. "You mean nothing has been done as yet?" Lynn demanded. "At least tell me the ships are on their way."

"The ships are not on their way, as yet," the Bailiff said.

"Why not?"

"Simply because, Mrs Battle," Joe said, rallying to the aid of the Bailiff, "there is no guarantee that we will ever need them."

"But, good God, man . . ." she looked from face to face.

"Do you have any idea how much an operation such as I have outlined would cost?" Nugent asked.

"We are talking about people's *lives* . . ."

"No we are not," the Bailiff said, somewhat snappishly – he was very tired. "At this moment, no one's life is in danger. The wind is in our favour, the melted reactor is being isolated, so that the build-up of radiation will be halted, and anything that may have escaped . . ."

"May?" Lynn shouted.

"May," the Bailiff repeated firmly, "is dissipating into the atmosphere over the English Channel. The south-east coast of England is at much greater risk than us."

"And *they* are evacuating," Lynn said triumphantly. "I heard it on the car radio."

The Bailiff nodded. "I understand all children in the area which could be affected are being moved further inland, with their mothers. But no mass evacuation has taken place as yet, simply because there has been no significant rise in radiation levels. The place that has been seriously affected is the Cotentin Peninsular."

Lynn glared at him, then said, in a softer tone. "At least show me the lists that have been drawn up, the orders of priority."

"They are being compiled now," the Bailiff said.

"The children . . ."

"Would go first, of course."

"Very well." She stood up. "All I can say is, you had better pray all your prognostications are proved right."

"I can only act upon the information given to me, and upon the recommendations of the Home Office."

"Ha," Lynn said, and stalked for the door.

The Bailiff pointed. "There is not to be a word about this to anyone. Especially your friends in Greenpeace."

"They have a right to know what is going on, especially as they have been telling you for years that this was bound to happen one day."

"They, no one, has any right to start a panic," the Bailiff said. "That is not to happen."

"What are you going to do? Lock us up?" Lynn demanded belligerently.

"If I have to, yes."

"You make me sick, the lot of you." She banged the door behind her.

The men gazed at each other. "If that cloud were to come this way, we aren't going to have four days," Nugent said.

"Don't I know it," the Bailiff said. "But to start a mass evacuation, before anything happens . . ."

"It'd kill the island," Pritchard said. "Just as much as if the cloud actually comes here. You remember they evacuated Alderney at the beginning of the Hitler War. How many of those people ever went back?"

"But others did," Joe pointed out. "And Alderney is there, as a community."

"Obviously, we have to have Alderney uppermost in our mind." the Bailiff said. "And Sark. You'd better get the President and the Seigneur on the phone for me. But there's something else. I'm going to get back to the Home Secretary, and ask him to give the Governor emergency powers. If there *is* a panic, he's going to need them."

Chapter 19

SATURDAY, 23RD JULY – AFTERNOON

Several shelves were bare, others sparcely littered with upturned tins and bottles. Only the stacks of smart plastic utensils, storage boxes and bins, mops and buckets had survived the onslaught. Liz reached for a solitary tin of Spam but lost it to a shoulder-charge from a dear little old lady with white hair and an impish grin. Others were less charming. There were a few packets of dried Chinese-style food left. "I tried one of these once, ages ago and concluded that the box might have tasted better. But there doesn't seem to be much choice." Liz heaped them in her trolley. "I do have some room in the freezer. Let's see what we can find." There was an awful, niggling feeling that this whole drama would blow over in the next twenty-four hours and she would be faced with months, if not years, of eating up all this revolting stuff.

When the trolley was full of items she would never dream of buying in normal circumstances they joined a long queue at the checkout where Jackson's bulk guarded their purchases from marauding housewives. There were endless arguments at the tills when shoppers found they had insufficient cash. Tempers frayed. One checkout girl dissolved into tears, while smart-suited managers and store-buyers waved their arms and tried to achieve some sort of order.

"Hell! I feel completely pole-axed!" Liz gasped, subsiding into the passenger seat of Jackson's car. But she felt doubly so when they turned into her driveway to find a taxi waiting with its engine ticking over, and its driver standing on the front doorstep beside an enormous white dog.

"Afternoon, ma'am. Would you by any chance be Elizabeth Cobb?" the man asked hopefully.

"Yes?" she climbed out of the car.

"Hi, Trouble!" Liz and the cab-driver turned to stare at Jackson. "Here, boy," he called to the Pyrenean mountain dog, who bounded across the drive and hurled himself happily at the friend.

"Thank gawd for that," the driver said. "When there was no reply I thought I was going to be stuck with him. Er . . ." he coughed. "That will be five pounds sixty, with the waiting time."

"Come again?"

"The fare for the dog."

"But where's Mr Beaufort?"

"Who?"

"The owner."

"Search me. Some bloke put him in my car at the airport and told me to bring him here. Said you'd be expecting him." He smiled cheerfully. "Now if you'll excuse me, I've got to get home to the missus. She's panicking at home about this so-called threat of radiation. Load of nonsense if you ask me."

Liz's mouth hung open as the taxi disappeared down the road. "What are you going to do with him?" Trouble grinned at her.

"I don't have a clue. We'd better call David and ask what's going on."

"But where is he going while you phone?"

"Can't he wait inside?"

"With Cocoa and Horlicks? I don't know that they'd approve."

"Oh shit." Jackson scratched his head. "Shall we try them? Maybe one at a time." Mongrel strays they might be, but they weren't stupid. One sight of Trouble's bulk was enough to convince Cocoa and Horlicks that the visitor would make a more amenable friend than an enemy. They led him away to show off their estate, fertilising as they went, while Jackson helped Liz unload the car and deposit frozen foods in the freezer.

It was Forsythe who answered the phone. "Yes, sir. Mr Beaufort called the number you gave several times. I understand you were engaged for a while, then when he tried later there was no reply."

"What does he want me to do with Trouble?"

"He didn't tell me exactly what he had in mind, sir. But I imagine he is hoping that you will be kind enough to look after the dog until he gets over to Guernsey himself."

"Will he be over by tonight?"

"Oh no, sir. That I do know."

Jackson sighed. "Well when is he coming? Have you any idea of his plans?"

"When he left here half an hour ago, I believe he had the intention of evacuating the Alderney population."

"He what! Don't tell me he's been on another party?"

"Strangely enough, no, sir. He was complaining of being horribly sober today. And he is taking the threat of radiation very seriously. You understand, Alderney is far more vulnerable than Guernsey: it's only a dozen miles from Flamanville."

"Yes, of course. Well, perhaps you'll ask him to call me when he gets back, please."

Jackson found Liz kneeling on the floor of the kitchen, trying to work out where to put the stocks of unwanted food. "Well?" she asked.

"He isn't there . . ."

"Not to worry. He will probably turn up here any minute."

"No. Not today, according to Forsythe."

She stood up, brushing the hair off her face. "You mean we've got that monster overnight? Oh, well, maybe he's into dried Chinese food."

When Jackson had finished repeating all Forsythe had told him, Liz was looking strained. "Oh, darling, I'm beginning to feel very frightened."

He put his arms round her, but he could think of nothing cheerful to say. He was feeling pretty sick himself.

"Let's turn on the TV and the radio and hope there's some good news."

"First of all," the Bailiff said, "I wish to repeat what I said when I spoke to you this morning: at this moment in time Guernsey, together with its dependencies of Alderney, Sark, Herm and Jethou, is in no immediate danger. I am not going to attempt to disguise what has happened. There has been an act of sabotage at the French Nuclear Electricity Generating Plant at Flamanville. This act has resulted in the closing down of the plant, and there has been some leakage of radioactive material. Just how serious this leakage is has not yet been ascertained. But I can tell you that, as I have said, it represents no threat to these islands at this time. The amount which has escaped is small, and the weather is favourable. I know you will have seen on television or heard on your radios that the French are evacuating the entire Cotentin Peninsular. This is a necessary precaution. You will also have heard that children and pregnant women are being evacuated from the south-eastern coastal areas of England. This again is a sensible precaution, given the wind direction. Now you may be certain of this: should we here in Guernsey receive any indication whatsoever that any radioactive fall-out is likely to reach the islands, then we also will put an evacuation programme into effect, for those most at risk, and a protective programme into effect for the less vulnerable. But I know every one of you will agree with me that it would be senseless, indeed it would be criminal, for us virtually to shut down the island, with the attendant disruption not only of the present, but of the future, all of our futures, for fear of an event which may never occur. I ask you to trust your government, and the measures it is already implementing for your safety, should the need arise. Finally, however, I must make clear that it is the intention of the Island Government to maintain peace and law and order. There is, sadly, an element in our society, as in every society, which seeks to use critical situations for their own advantage. Already there are reports of panic buying. This must cease. There must be no panic. There *will* be no panic. In this regard I must tell you that His Excellency the Lieutenant-Governor has been granted emergency powers by the Home Secretary, with the right, should he consider it necessary, to impose a curfew and martial law upon this island. Make no mistake about this: he will implement this right, with the full support of the States of Guernsey, if it becomes necessary. But I know that with my my fellow Sarnians, trusting in God and in each other, we will see this crisis through as we have coped with other crises in the past. The very moment it becomes necessary to take any further action in this situation, you will be informed. May God bless you all."

"I hope your face is as red as mine," Liz said, as she muted the set.

"It would be, if I could convince myself that that was anything more than a load of bull."

"You don't believe what he said?"

"I believe that when the head of a community has to make a statement like that there is a disaster in the offing," Jackson replied. "Still he's right about one thing, panic is the last thing any of us need. We may not believe the guy, but as he's the boss, we have to trust him. So . . . what are your plans? I would ask you to come back to the St Pierre with me, except we can't very well take the dogs."

"I think I'd rather be here, anyway. But darling, I would like you to stay with me, will you?"

"Nothing would persuade me to leave, honey. But I think I should fetch some things from the hotel. I haven't a clean shirt or my shaver."

"Makes sense. And while you're gone I need to talk

to some of my colleagues and get their feelings on what must be done with the animals in case of evacuation."

Liz phoned three other vets and got three totally different opinions; one said cattle and horses could be left in the fields but domestic pets should be put down in preference to slow starvation, another said no, it might never be bad enough to warrant such extreme measures and everyone might return in a matter of days. The third was quite snappy at her queries and said he hadn't a clue. Then her friend Margaret Ferbrache at the Animal Shelter left her more confused than ever. Lastly she tried Pierre. "I was about to call you," he said. "We don't like to think of you alone, up there. Why don't you come here? We've plenty of room. Trish is going to stay the night and may try to leave in the morning. If she can get a flight."

"Good. But don't worry about me, Jackson is keeping me company. Thanks all the same."

"Oh yes? We thought there was a certain electricity between you two! So tell me, are you going to try to get away?"

"No. Not yet, anyway. I think it would be awful to abandon all the island's animals. Even if no radiation got here, with everyone gone they would be left alone to starve. I've already had umpteen calls from owners about putting them down. Are you thinking of going? What are you doing about your menagerie?"

"We haven't decided. If the authorities advise evacuation and lay on boats, we'll certainly go. Or even take off on our own, weather permitting. There is no way we'd keep the girls here sealed up in the house indefinitely. But they'll break their hearts if the animals have to be put down. Oh God, Sis, what a bloody awful catastrophe this could be." There was a break in his voice and he could no longer speak.

Liz was nearly in tears herself, for him and his family. It was so much easier for her, in a sense, having no one but herself to think about . . . except Jackson, of course. "Look, don't worry about the animals at this stage. If you do decide to go I'll move into your house and bring my lot with me. Which, by the way, currently includes David Beaufort's giant dog!"

"Liz, you are a dear. I can't tell you how relieved Annabel and the girls will be. But how come you've got Beaufort's dog?"

"What you might call an on-going shaggy dog story. I'll tell you all about it over a celebratory glass of champagne when this emergency is over." She was attempting to sound brighter than she felt.

"We'll pop up later to get Trish's gear. And keep in touch, eh?" Pierre appreciated her efforts.

"What's the matter dear?" Janet asked.

Peter Barrington had been pacing the lawn, pausing only to scan the sky for the faintest indication of weather change. "Matter? What the devil do you think is the matter? This damn awful emergency, of course."

"I have packed all the clothes and food I think we can stow aboard. When do you plan to leave?"

"I'd go now if we'd completed the conveyance for the house with Parker. But it seems stupid to go without his money."

"He wouldn't be able to pay us the balance in cash," Janet pointed out. "And we couldn't be sure his cheque will be honoured."

"If it's certified by a London bank, it should be all right."

"But conveyances are only done on Tuesdays and Fridays, aren't they? Can we wait till then?"

"How can I know? No one seems to know anything, least of all the States. If necessary I might persuade someone to put it through on Monday." He headed back into the house, Janet on his heels. "At least we can load everything possible onto the boat, in waiting. I'll need a couple of big holdalls for papers and files from my study."

Obediently, Janet climbed the stairs to the attic to fetch them.

*   *   *

Pierre and Trish didn't stay long. While Trish packed her belongings Pierre sat with his sister and Jackson discussing the impending disaster. Liz offered him a drink and he chose tea, in which she joined him. The two men talked about the banking facet. There was little they could do over the week-end but enormous problems loomed ahead of them on Monday morning. "If we are all still around by then," Pierre added, then cocked his ear. "Who's that?"

"Hi!" a voice called from the hall. "Are you there, Liz?"

"Michael!" She leapt up, spilling her tea.

A boisterous blond giant, Michael Cobb bounded into the room. "The front door wasn't locked so . . . wow!" He found himself pinned to the door post by the shoulders, a vast, shaggy white face examining his, large slavering mouth huffing over him while a pair of dark-brown eyes analysed his intentions.

"Down, Trouble!" Jackson ordered. The newcomer apparently passed scrutiny and the dog lumbered off onto the patio with his faithful mongrel admirers.

"Your pony, I presume?" Michael said to Jackson, somewhat miffed.

"Wrong," Liz corrected. "He belongs to David Beaufort. So tell me, to what do we owe this honour?"

"Thought I'd better pop in and check you hadn't blown your mind. Didn't like to think of you here alone and scared witless, but I see you are surrounded by family." He grinned at Pierre and Trish.

"Indeed." She felt quite touched that he had thought about her, though suggesting she might be scared witless was irritating. "And Jackson Ridgeway. Have you two met? Jackson is opening a branch of Parks Paramus here." She turned to the American. "Jackson, meet Michael Cobb, accountant, my ex husband." Jackson stood up and they shook hands.

"Opening up before blowing up, huh?" Michael roared with laughter at his quip.

Jackson forced a smile but no one else laughed. "Like a cup of tea?" Liz offered.

"Tea! You have to be joking! I'll settle for a beer if you're not offering anything better." While Liz went to fetch it he settled himself on the arm of her chair. "Here for long?" he asked Jackson.

"For the forseeable future."

"Which might, radioactive fall-out permitting, be two or three days, huh?" Another roar of laughter.

There was an embarrassing silence, which Michael failed to notice.

"God alone knows," Pierre sighed, shaking his head. "If we do have to evacuate, when will we ever get back? How many years will we have to live as refugees in another country?"

"What the hell? As long as the beer's drinkable. Ta, love." He took the can from Liz. "Cheers."

"They can't evacuate everyone, surely?" Liz had lived with his hearty humour long enough to ignore it. "It isn't humanly possible. Sixty-odd thousand locals and . . . how many visitors?"

Pierre shrugged. "The turnover is around fifteen thou per fortnight I believe, but some of the current batch will have beaten a hasty retreat if they've any sense."

"Not many," Trish said. "Folks don't abandon their annual hols unless they're forced. Maybe some of the yachting fraternity will be moving on."

"Wonder what the Normandy yachtsmen will do? You heard the Bailiff say the Cotentin Peninsular is being evacuated." Pierre was the most pessimistic of them all. "Anyway, Trish, we'd better be getting back home."

Michael made no attempt to move and watched in surprise when Jackson, too, remained. When Liz returned from seeing them off he got up and put an arm round her. "Thought you might like me to move back in. I don't like to think of you here by yourself."

His ex-wife gave a wry grin. "I won't be. Jackson has promised to stay."

"Ah, ah! Can't have that. Think what the neighbours will say! No, you needn't bother, mate," to the American. "I'll look after the little woman."

"On the contrary, Michael," Liz said quietly. "It is all arranged. Jackson is staying, regardless of the neighbours."

Michael remembered Liz's quiet voice, of old; it always meant she was digging her heels in and about to get angry. He frowned. "You two an item or something?"

"Definitely," Jackson and Liz chorussed.

"Oh!" Now it was his turn to feel angry. "Well, I suppose I would be the last to know." He drained his beer. "I'll be off then. Don't bother to move. I know the way out."

Liz and Jackson stared at each other, waited till the front door slammed shut, and burst out laughing. "What a burke! Oh I'm sorry, darling. I shouldn't say it but . . ." he shook his head, "how the hell did you get to marry him?"

"Met him at university. He was good fun at a party. Wasn't till after we were married I discovered he wasn't such fun to live with." She kissed his nose. "Don't worry, I shan't make that mistake again."

"You'd better believe it!"

They took their supper out on the patio, the radio beside them; at any minute the taped music on Radio Guernsey might be interrupted for the broadcast of an evacuation order . . . a warning that their lives were in danger. Neither was hungry but they forced themselves to eat because they knew they should.

"I wonder if they've sent for any ships yet?"

"I swung round the Town and along the front after leaving the hotel, and there didn't appear to be any waiting outside the harbour. There were a lot of people down there and several small craft going out. Seemed an odd time of day to be setting off. Where might they be going?"

"South, I should think, if they have any sense. Lots of

the locals know the French coast quite well, even after dark. Lezardrieux is reasonably close but they may go on round the Brittany peninsula to Benodet or further. Depends on the type of craft and fuel consumption."

"You obviously know all about it."

"Mum and Dad had friends with a boat. We went cruising with them every summer, and on fine week-ends we'd occasionally pop across for a couple of nights and a good *plateau de fruits de mer*. We'd come back each time with the obligatory bags of French bread and bottles of wine."

"Carrying on the island's smuggling tradition," he teased.

Liz was too overcome with memories to respond.

Crickets filled the air with their high-pitched rasp. A few late garden birds sang evensong and gulls were mewling in the distance. Liz left her flip-flops under her chair to walk bare-footed through the dew-wet grass. It needed cutting. If she went away it would be a hayfield by the time she returned . . . if she ever did return. If there was a serious fall-out what would happen? Would it kill off everything including all vegetation? A sob caught in her throat as she bent to fondle the dahlias she had so lovingly raised from seed and planted out about ten weeks ago, in May . . . long before they had dreamed this situation could happen. She shivered. A goose had walked over her grave. Jackson joined her. "Better come inside, sweetheart, you're getting cold."

"Must be the dew," she said.

Later, when they had cleared the meal, settled Trouble in his new quarters and locked up for the night she continued with bouts of shivering. "I know it's only ten-thirty, but I think I would like to go to bed. It's been an extraordinarily long day and we did have a late night last night." Was it really only twenty-four hours ago they were dancing and singing on the Albert Pier?

"Of course. Which room do I sleep in?"

She grinned weakly. "Mine, please?"

"I hoped you'd say that."

"I can't think of anything I want more at the moment than to snuggle up safely in your arms."

"I'm not guaranteeing you'll be safe," he warned.

"I'll qualify that. Safe from the world . . . not from you."

"Might I interpret that as an invitation?"

She smiled, picked up the radio somewhat reluctantly, and led him out of the sitting-room, turning off the lights as she went. The windows in the bedroom were big plate-glass sliding doors opening on to a small patio enclosed with hedges. Liz waited till the lights were out before drawing one back, so as to avoid being inundated with moths and daddy-long-legs, and with the curtains open the room filled with moonlight. It was an enormous relief to get into bed, stretch all the muscles which ached with tension . . . and reach out to touch Jackson's face, trace the line of his brows, his cheek and the smiling lips.

He knew he had never been so emotionally confused. He was at last in bed with a woman he loved – yet a woman he had known for only a matter of days. She had roused an animal desire in him the first time he'd set eyes on her.' From the moment of their second meeting, he realised that he actually loved her and that this was much more than a mere lusting for a one-night-stand. He had resisted the desire to haul her into bed. He preferred to wait, praying she might fall in love with him, too. It hadn't been an easy discipline: the desire to possess her had built rapidly, almost gotten out of hand when they picnicked on the cliffs . . . And then the miracle had happened. She *had* fallen in love with him. Although the waiting had been only a matter of days it had seemed like a lifetime . . . but now just when the waiting was over and the big moment had arrived, now she was actually lying here beside him in bed . . . an invisible cloud of radioactive dust was hovering only a few miles away, threatening to destroy everything she had ever held dear in her whole life, and possibly themselves as well. Poor sweet darling Liz. He slid one arm under her shoulders, and with the other drew her against him. Her sigh became a deep, shuddering gasp, a release of emotional tension and fear. His body heat permeated through her icy skin, through her flesh and deep into her bones. Moonlight shone on the white pillowslips and duvet, revealing the dark silhouette of her tousled hair and suntanned features, until she nestled further down tucking her head under his chin.

He thought about his parents back home in the States and allowed himself to wonder, just momentarily, if he would ever see them again. He wondered what David Beaufort was doing – drinking? Or was he really trying to organise some evacuation as Forsythe had suggested? It seemed unlikely; amusing as he was as a drinking partner, David's will to do anything definitely appeared soluble in alcohol. His mind focused again on the woman in his arms; she was so small . . . yet tough. Determined. When he first met her it was hard to imagine such a tiny, feminine creature as a vet. She admitted having neither the size nor strength to cope with difficult calf and foal deliveries: her arms were too short to reach into the depths of a bovine uterus to correct breach presentations, she had explained. And he had wanted to laugh at the very idea. But she did attend sick cattle, nevertheless. And she operated in surgery at least three times a week. Suddenly he became aware of her quiet, regular breathing, and realised she was asleep.

Jackson remained wide awake. The radio continued to produce muted music-by-the-yard, as his mother used to call it, and he watched as the moon shadows crept across the carpet. Trapped under Liz, his arm ached but he wouldn't move it for fear of waking her. Strange creatures whistled from the bushes in her garden and the air was heavy with night-scented jasmine. He was dozing, stroking her hair in a half-dream, when she moved her body against his, sensuously. Her hand caressed softly down his back, nails scratching slightly over his buttocks. He wasn't too sure if she was awake until her reaction to his body's involuntary response left him in no doubt. She pulled his head down to kiss him with frantic urgency, then her arms and legs twined round him, drawing his body over and into hers. He was terrified of crushing or smothering her, but this frail looking creature demonstrated her tremendous strength and energy.

It was over as quickly as it had begun. Not the long, slow, erotic lovemaking he had been dreaming about for days . . . but in the present circumstances he supposed it was a miracle it had happened at all. "Don't move," she whispered into his neck. "Don't leave me. Stay, just where you are." She wanted him to remain there for ever. But of course that was impossible, and when he eventually withdrew it was like a bereavement. She inhaled . . . a half gasp, half sob.

"I'm hungry," she announced later. "What's the time?"

"Two thirty."

"I'm going to make some cocoa. Want some?" she slid out of bed and padded across the carpet to unhook a bathrobe from behind the door.

"I don't think I ever had any." All he wanted to do was sleep.

"You coming or shall I bring it to you here?"

The thought of leaving a warm bed to go out and face the three dogs and a cup of cocoa, was not appealing, but the desire to be with Liz, wherever she went, persuaded him. And in the event the dogs merely registered their disapproval of the disturbance at this unearthly hour by opening one baleful eye apiece, briefly. The hot cocoa was good. Liz stuck her nose in the steaming mug and allowed her eyes to focus over the rim on to Jackson's strong, sinewy feet, up his athletically muscled legs to his boxer shorts, and over the pale blue sweatshirt until they reached his smile. "Here's looking at you, lover boy."

"I see you, baby."

"I suddenly feel quite human again."

"What brought that on. The cocoa? Or was it something else?"

"A bit of both."

"Well when you've finished your drink we'll see if we can enhance the improvement to a superhuman state, shall we?"

This time it was just the way he'd planned it, and later, a long time later, they slept soundly, fears for the future forgotten, until the room was filled with sunlight . . . and the sound of barking dogs.

Chapter 20

SUNDAY, 24TH JULY – PRE-DAWN

Walter Marquis sat at his desk and became aware that the sky was lightening. Golly, he thought: I've sat here all night. The missus is going to brain me, especially as she liked them to attend early communion together. But he wasn't the least sleepy, only stiff and exhausted. He had been receiving fax messages and phone calls from up and down the Channel, and places as far apart as Cork and the Faroes. Now he studied the weather chart he had composed. And there could be no doubt about it. Equally, sitting here and brooding on it wasn't going to help. He picked up the phone, and dialled the emergency number he had been given. "I'd like to speak with the Bailiff, please."

"Oh, is that you, Walter? Bill Collins here. Look, I'm afraid the Bailiff's gone home for a kip. He's been up for more than twenty-four hours."

"I'll call him at home, then."

"I wouldn't do that, Walter, unless it's really urgent. You're liable to get your ear blown off."

"It's really urgent," Walter said. He hung up, looked up the number, and dialled again.

"Yes?" This was the Bailiff's wife, who sounded every bit as tired as her husband would be.

"Sorry to bother you, ma'am, but the Bailiff said to let him know the moment there's a change in the weather."

"And there's a change?"

"Yes, ma'am."

"Can you give me the message? The Bailiff is asleep."

"I think I should speak with him, ma'am. This is very important."

"Oh, very well. Wait a moment."

Walter listened to voices in the background, and was sure he heard the phrase 'silly man', from the Bailiff's wife, but a moment later Sir Hugh was on the line. "Yes, Walter."

"Good morning, sir."

"Yes, Walter. What's on your mind?"

"Well, sir, I've been getting figures in all night, and checking our own observations here. That High I was talking about, well, it's building kind of quicker than I estimated."

"Building where?"

"Well, over Normandy like. And the barometer here is high and steady. So . . . it looks like there could be a wind shift to the East."

"You said that would happen, maybe Monday or Tuesday."

"Yes, sir. But that's changed. I think it may be sooner than that."

There was a moment's silence. Then the Bailiff asked, "How much sooner?"

"Well, sir . . . I reckon it could go east by tonight."

Chapter 21

SUNDAY, 24TH JULY – MORNING

The Bailiff replaced the phone, slowly, and sat on the edge of his bed for several seconds.

"Bad?" asked his wife.

"Wind change. I suppose it had to happen." He got up and went into the bathroom.

She followed. "What are you going to do?"

Rubbing his face with a towel he hurried back to the phone and tapped the numbers. "What can I do? . . . Joe? You still there? Haven't you had any sleep yet, man? . . . Look, I don't want you collapsing on me. Listen, just do this for me, first, then get yourself a couple of hours rest. Now, I want everyone at the command room within half an hour . . . No, hold the media for a bit until we decide exactly how we are going to handle this. But Nugent must be there. I'll call HE myself. Thank you.."

He replaced the phone and began to dress.

His wife watched him. "We're not talking about evacuation?"

"What else can we do?" he asked again.

Hank Applegate stood in the kitchen with his hands clasped round a mug of instant coffee, staring blankly across a sink full of dirty dishes and through the open window at the yard wall, only a few feet away. His one-time wife Brenda had done a runner years ago and he'd never replaced her. Not for the want of trying, but his peculiar working hours hampered the establishing of a reasonable relationship . . . which was why it would have made sense to team up with Jane on more than a professional basis. But she was determined to remain freelance – in every respect. She had told him quite adamantly that she had no intention of washing dishes and socks for any man. He could do his own or get a daily. So he'd taken her advice – but dailies seldom stayed long and anyway, he wanted someone to come home to, to share his life with. So if this nuclear threat was for real, maybe it was fate taking a hand in his life, forcing him to leave the island for pastures new. He'd have no regrets. This flatlet was a dump, and his friends were really only drinking pals. The only person he'd miss would be Jane. The phone beeped while he was shaving.

"Hi. You awake?"

"Of course! Up and dressed." He was smiling – he always did at the sound of her voice.

"Thought I'd mosey on down to the cop shop and see what gives."

"I'll be there. Ten minutes."

There was a line of cars going down Hirzel Street and into the Police Station courtyard, so he drove in with them and parked beside Jane. "Looks like we're just in time," he said through his driving window. "Must be serious for this lot to be called out again at the crack of dawn."

"And HE, driving himself. Let's get over to the front steps." Jane slung her bag over her shoulder and strode across the paving.

Hank caught up with her. "Surely at this stage they should let us inside. Time for a filmed statement from the Bailiff."

"I had it in mind," Jane said, climbing the steps amongst the conseillers and deputies. "Conseiller Heaume! Have you been summoned here by the Bailiff?"

A stocky, sunburnt man of medium height and weary expression nodded. "Yes. Half an hour ago." He put a hand up to smother a yawn.

Yawns were catching, several of the group were at it. But not Sergeant Crowe. He had arrived on duty less than an hour ago fresh from a long night's sleep. "Excuse me, Miss MacAvoy, have you been requested by the Bailiff to attend this meeting?" He stood in front of her, politely barring her way.

"No. But we would ask you to inform him we are here, waiting for an interview and full statement on the situation."

"Certainly, Miss. If you and Mr Applegate would like to wait in here," he ushered them into an interview room, "I will see he is given your message. No doubt he will want to see you as soon as the meeting is over." He stood aside to allow Hank to follow her. "Please take a seat." He closed the door behind him.

They sat on the hard chairs, equipment piled on the table between them. "I saw a vending machine on the way in. Think I'll go and get a coffee," Hank said. "Want one? This could be a long wait."

A bell was chiming away nonstop in the back of the building in response to the constant pressure of David's finger on the button. He waited. A distant dog barked. Eventually a sash window was flung up and a head emerged. "For crissake what the hell do you want at this hour of a Sunday morning . . . oh God, it's you! Go away, man. You're drunk!"

"Steve, I am not drunk. I'm here to warn you that there is a state of emergency on. A lethal radioactive cloud is heading this way and we have to evacuate the island."

Behind the stubble of beard Steve's face bore all the telltale signs of the whisky habit that was corroding his liver. His red, watery eyes focussed briefly and with some difficulty on the caller below, then he said, "That's not funny. For God's sake go home to bed, Beaufort. I'm not receptive to practical jokes at this hour." He slammed the window down.

David sighed. He had known that with his reputation

it was going to be hard getting the message across but he would have to persevere. Fortunately the Alderney President had finally come round to accepting the urgency of the situation, once he had received a call from the Guernsey Bailiff to say that warships were on their way. Between the two of them they had rounded up the Alderney States members and together they had divided up the island map into a grid, with different people responsible for warning the sleeping islanders to prepare for the exodus. Response had been various. Some couldn't scramble into their clothes fast enough, others like Steve dismissed the idea as ludicrous, and there were those who, while accepting that there was a serious threat, flatly refused to leave their homes, possessions and livestock. "I retired here to die fifteen years ago, David. And here I stay," one householder had declared.

David's hand remained on Steve's bell until the window was opened again. "Look, Beaufort. I'm getting bloody annoyed. Are you going to let up or . . ."

"The President and all the Alderney States members are telephoning and going from door to door with this same message. I'm trying to save your bloody neck, you stupid drunken idiot."

"How?"

"By getting you down to the harbour with your piddling little suitcase and on to one of the warships that are coming to our rescue. You blithering great ape!" he added for good measure.

"Shit! How do I know you're on the level?"

"Turn on your radio. And listen for the bell of St Anne's. When it rings head for the harbour. Okay?"

"I can't believe this is happening. Must be an attack of DTs." Steve slammed the window again and David hoped the message had got through.

His next call was at Mrs Lawson's cottage. "I'm afraid we are all having to leave the island because of nuclear fall-out," he explained when she opened the door, clutching her dressing-gown round herself.

"Eh?" It was hard to hear above the din of her three dogs.

He got through to her eventually, and she broke down in tears, abandoning her hold on the dressing-gown to put her arms round her pets. "Can they come too?" she asked. "And what about my budgie?"

How do you tell an old lady of nearly ninety that she'd have to wring her pet's tiny neck or release it to be pecked to death by wild birds? David had never felt such a desperate need of a drink in his life. Why the devil had he got himself involved in this business anyway?

The men and women crowding into the command room all wore the same look. They were exhausted, and they knew that the Bailiff would only have called them out at dawn, several hours before their next scheduled meeting, if there had been a serious deterioration in the situation. The Lieutenant-Governor was also present, although he indicated that the Bailiff should take the chair.

"According to the local Meteorological Office," Sir Hugh told them, "we can expect an east-north-east wind of about six knots by dawn tomorrow morning. The wind will probably freshen up by tomorrow afternoon, to about fifteen to twenty knots."

"With respect, Sir Hugh," Paul Pritchard said, "their forecasts have not always proved accurate in the past. Especially with regard to timing. They nearly always err on the side of immediacy. They could well be twelve hours premature."

"It's flat calm over the Russel now," the Comptroller added, optimistically. "There's thick mist out there."

"I'm afraid we cannot take the chance that Walter Marquis may be mistaken," the Bailiff said. "In any event, what is certain is that there is going to be an east-north-easterly wind some time in the next twenty-four hours. That is, a full day sooner than we had anticipated. I have been on to the Home Secretary. He is going to secure an update from French Government sources – we cannot afford to act on all the rumours and speculation that are being pumped out by the French media – and he hopes to come back to me with some accurate data in a couple of hours. However, going on what we do know, the highest radiation levels are presently being recorded on the eastern side of the Cotentin Peninsular and in the Bay of the Seine. These levels are still lethal, but they are dissipating into the atmosphere. Of course the long-term effects of this are going to be pretty horrendous, but that is not our concern at this moment."

He paused to clear his throat. "What does concern us is the next few days. We are fairly sure that there is still radioactive material escaping from Flamanville itself. The French are being very cagey about this, as one would expect, but the fact is that they do not claim to have succeeded in sealing the plant, although they are frantically working on it. I am hoping the Home Secretary will be able to give us an update on this also later today. However, what we have to consider are two waves of radioactive matter. The first one being the continuing emissions from Flamanville itself, which we must regard as absolutely lethal. This you can see is roughly located here . . ." he jabbed his finger onto the map he had spread on the table, "and the second, in this area, is hopefully less serious, but its long term effects may still be considerable. Now . . ." He waited until everyone came forward to peer at the map. "Let's assume that Barfleur is the centre of the already escaped cloud. The French obviously think so, and the port has been entirely evacuated. As the crow flies, or the wind blows, Barfleur is fifty miles from Sark, something over forty miles from Alderney. That means, if the wind shift comes at . . . say midnight, the radioactive cloud could be over both those islands by dawn."

"And over Guernsey an hour later," Nugent commented.

"Any further emanations from Flamanville could be here in four hours," Pritchard said. "And over Alderney in less than one."

"So we have something like twenty hours to play with," the Bailiff said, and looked from face to face, his gaze coming to rest when he reached Nugent.

"My people are all standing by," Nugent told them. "But . . . twenty hours . . . I just don't have the capacity."

"This is a life and death emergency," Paul Pritchard pointed out.

"Jersey will be saying the same thing."

"Right," the Bailiff said. "We must do the best we can with what we have. I have already arranged with the Home Secretary that two naval ships will be in Alderney Harbour later this morning. They will evacuate the entire population. I have spoken to the Alderney President and he has a team out rounding up the people."

"They won't like it," Prichard said.

"They will have to like it. Now, there aren't any other warships immediately available . . ."

"God, to be back in the old days of the Royal Navy," Darwin said. "We'd have had an armada in here by now. Aircraft carriers . . ."

"I've asked for a carrier," the Bailiff said. "But she can't get here until Tuesday at the earliest."

"By which time . . ." Thompson shrugged, his face white with exhaustion.

"Nugent?"

"One of my passenger ferries is here now, the other is coming in this morning," Nugent said. "Plus two of the cargo ships. If we do cram people into the holds and fill the vehicle bays with foot passengers only, that should take us up to nearly five thousand. There is a complication, however: the tides. We're in the middle of a big spring, which means that St Sampson's will be dry about three this afternoon until nine tonight. St Peter Port will also be affected; my ships will be able to get in, but only one at a time. However, as I say, one is here now, and I have told her not to leave until instructed, and the other can be here by noon. Unfortunately, neither of my cargo vessels can get here in time to use the midday tide out of St Sampson's, but we can load them in St Peter Port."

"You say your ship in the harbour is loaded and ready to sail? What or who is she loaded with?" the Bailiff inquired.

"Tourists mainly, headed for home."

"Then I suggest you instruct her to sail immediately, so that she can be back here on this afternoon's tide."

"Will do."

"How long will the turnaround take?" Pritchard demanded.

"Something like eight hours. So it's not good. The passenger ships will be able to make at least one other roundtrip before midnight. It's the best I can do," his voice rose an octave.

"Wouldn't it make sense to evacuate our people to France?" someone asked. "Then the turnaround would be a quarter of that."

"No sense at all," Nugent replied. Apart from Cherbourg itself, "the only close French port capable of handling big ferries is St Malo, and if that cloud moves this way they will be as affected as ourselves. Roscoff is only marginally closer than Weymouth, and it too lies in the direct path of an east-north-easterly blowing off the Cotentin Peninsular. Now, I've been talking with the airlines, and we can start the aircraft rotation by mid morning, as long as this fog doesn't thicken right up."

"Even if it does," the Governor said, "it's a risk worth taking, to get people off."

"Well, maybe you'd better speak with the airline people yourself, Sir Mark, and convince them of that. If you can . . . it's a matter of organising people to go."

"The hydrofoils are standing by; as they can do Weymouth and back in four hours, plus say loading and unloading two hours, they should be able to run four trips in twenty-four hours; they aren't affected by the tides. Say a thousand people."

"But we're still talking about a maximum of twenty

thousand people by the time the wind shifts, if it happens tonight," Thompson said.

"Yes." The Bailiff leafed through his notes. "Well, everyone under the age of sixteen goes first. Now where the devil is Barrington?"

"I called his house, but there was no reply."

"At this hour? You'll have to find him, Joe, right away. He will have to prepare . . ."

"In fact he was only standing in for me while I was out of the island," Dr Driscoll, currently head of the local BMA, interrupted. He and his wife had been summoned home from their yachting cruise by ship to shore radio; fortunately they had been in St Malo and had been able to catch an Aurigny flight out of Dinard. "I was about to ask about the sick and the elderly. If any people are left here to fend for themselves in sealed homes or underground shelters, it should surely be the most able-bodied."

The Bailiff looked around the table for reactions. Rod Frazer from the Housing Authority coughed significantly.

"Well Mr Frazer?" Sir Hugh asked.

"I hate to sound cold-blooded, but I'm afraid some of our decisions will need to be just that. I am asking myself whether it is right to risk sacrificing comparatively young and healthy people with fifty years or so of their potential lifespan yet to run, in favour of geriatrics with up to . . . say five years at best, and sick patients with limited prognoses."

"What are you suggesting?" Andy Driscoll glared angrily. "Leaving the helpless to die either of radiation or starvation, or would you prefer a rapid round-up for mass euthanasia?"

"There's no need to get up in arms, Doctor!" Rod came back. "I'm not making any suggestions, only saying we should consider these factors . . ."

"Gentlemen!" The Bailiff held up his hand. "Let's try to keep calm, please. You have both made valid points which will need consideration. However, in the meantime I must prepare an announcement."

"That's not going to be easy," Pritchard said. "There'll be a panic."

"I see no reason why there should be a panic," the Bailiff objected. "According to my father, there was no panic in 1940, when the Germans were about to land."

"With respect, Mr Bailiff," Frazer said. "The Germans didn't mean certain death for the mass of the population."

"They were regarded as sadistic murderers, thanks to the press propaganda."

"Again, with respect, Hugh, but that was a long time ago." The Lieutenant-Governor spoke quietly, but every head turned towards him. "In 1940, discipline was a key part of life. Children obeyed their parents, their parents obeyed the law. And all obeyed authority. I'm afraid that is all changed. I am quite sure your solid old-fashioned Guernseyman and his wife will do whatever you require of them, but I cannot have the same faith in all the younger element, either islander or visitors, which you estimate at approximately fifteen thousand people. Besides, even if there is no panic, once the news is released the streets will be crowded, with people trying to get to their parents, parents trying to get to their children, even people just wishing to gawk. This would hamper the emergency services, and we simply can't permit it."

"Just what are you proposing, sir?" Pritchard asked, while the Bailiff considered the Governor's remarks.

"I'm afraid I feel it necessary to invoke the powers given to me by the Home Secretary to declare martial law. In that, I would include a twenty-four curfew, which will commence at twelve noon."

"Twelve noon?" Pritchard cried. "You can't have a curfew beginning at noon. With respect, sir!"

"We can have a curfew beginning at any time we decide, Mr Pritchard. By twelve noon the evacuation will have begun, right? Or at least, the first evacuees will have been assembled for embarkation. By then everyone will have gone home for lunch. Those who have not, will be instructed to return to their houses and remain there until told to leave by the proper authority. We *must* keep the streets clear. Those who leave their houses after that hour will do so under escort, either to the airport or the dock. You will have all your men turned out, Mr Thompson, and they should be armed. By this I do not mean they should wander around brandishing Kalashnikov rifles, but they should wear whatever sidearms you have available."

Thompson gulped; he had never received such an order before – he had not ever expected to receive such an order in Guernsey, probably the most peaceful place on earth. He looked at the Bailiff. "Do you really think such drastic steps are necessary, Sir Mark?" the Bailiff asked.

"I do not think we can take the chance that they may become necessary, and, having done nothing to anticipate it, find ourselves with a situation we cannot control. I would regard that as the gravest dereliction of that duty we accepted when we took office."

The Bailiff swallowed. "What do we do with people who are already out?" Thompson asked. "It's a fine day. If they haven't heard the news they'll be picnicking."

"Maybe you'll be expected to shoot the buggers," Darwin growled. He could not see any of this was necessary.

He pursed his lips. "You'll round them up and send them home."

Thompson pulled his nose. The idea seemed ridiculous. "How do we evacuate the children, sir?" Nugent asked, anxious to prevent any unpleasant confrontation. "I mean, supposing we can only get half the population off by dawn tomorrow. I would say there are probably more than twenty thousand under-sixteens in Guernsey. And of course the very small will have to have their mothers with them. So, where do we start?"

The Bailiff glanced round the table. He was as aware as anyone that this was a red-hot political potato. He drew a deep breath. "We will start with those nearest the approaching cloud," he said. "All qualifying residents of the various esplanades, overlooking the Russel, then moving inland in waves. In each wave, children first, with their mothers. Then schoolchildren. Then adults."

"And the sick," Andy Driscoll insisted.

"But . . . with respect, sir, the island is only five miles wide. What difference does it make which area the children come from?"

"We have to start somewhere, and there can be no question of privilege," the Bailiff insisted. "Thus, I want everyone off Herm and Sark, by mid-morning. The children, and, where appropriate, their mothers, will count as residents of Glategny Esplanade, as will the adults, when their turn comes. Yes, Dr Driscoll, and the sick. The Sark boat will leave immediately. Darwin, you'll send whatever local boats you can round up to help in that evacuation. And when they get here they too will be treated as residents of Glategny Esplanade. Understood?" The Harbourmaster nodded. "Right. Now let us consider those we cannot get off in time. Willy, you and your people will have to work on a house to house basis."

"The German Underground Hospital will hold several hundred, for a start," Willy said brightly.

"Willy," the Bailiff said with considerable patience. "We are not talking about an atomic blast. We are talking about an invisible cloud of lethal dust which may be around for a while. Your business it to make sure that everyone understands that if they cannot be evacuated before that cloud gets here, they must stay indoors, with every exterior opening sealed. That includes all pets and livestock."

Willy gulped. "Until when?"

"Until they're told to come out."

"But . . . that could be a thousand years from now."

"Of course it won't be a thousand years from now. As soon as the planes and ships are free, we will continue with the evacuation, using protective clothing. I agree that use should be made of the Underground Hospital, but only for those people whose houses are incapable of being adequately sealed."

"What about Beau Séjour Leisure Centre?" Pritchard asked. "We could put a few thousand in there."

"I'm not sure that Beau Séjour can be adequately sealed. We'll keep it as a reserve. As regards evacuation after the cloud gets here, if it does get here, I shall be organising protective gear with the Home Office. James, I'm relying on you, as head of the Electricity Board, to see that electricity is rationed but maintained. We'll hope the oil stocks last out as long as needs be. Likewise those who head the water, gas and Telecoms. The pumps for the main drains must be kept working, too. Mr Heaume, once I have spoken with the Home Office, we must have protective clothing brought over on every incoming flight and distributed to essential personnel. Will you take responsibility for that?"

"There's one other matter, Sir Hugh. Where do the tourists rank in this priority list?" Paul Pritchard asked.

"Same as anyone else," Darwin snapped. "Wherever their hotel happens to be situated."

"I don't agree," Pritchard argued. "These people were, in a sense, invited to come here by our promotion campaigns, advertisements and brochures. Surely we have a responsibility to them?"

"Responsibility hell," Darwin said. "We would be the only country in the world that has ever accepted responsibility for the well-being of tourists in the event of a national catastrophe. You're still thinking about afterwards, when the tourists will be coming back. Well, think about this, Mr Pritchard: if that cloud gets here, there isn't going to be an afterwards, so you can stop bothering about it."

"Surely it's academic," Nugent said. "It's July. Nearly all the tourists here right now are people with school-age children. They will have priority anyway."

"Yeah? What about those visiting with friends and relatives here?" another Deputy asked. "Where do they stand?"

"Jesus, I don't know," Pritchard said.

"Gentlemen," the Bailiff said. "We do not have time for a States debate. I agree with Paul, that tourists have high priority. Children and mothers first, of course."

"That's not going to be very popular with our own people," Darwin muttered.

"Bert, right now, nothing that we do is going to be very popular. And you can bet there will be sixty-five thousand different opinions on what should be done." He gave a bleak smile. "Well, let's get to it."

"There's one further point, Hugh," the Governor said. "A very large percentage of the population of this island own or have access to, boats. Would it not ease the evacuation problem if they were allowed, or indeed, encouraged, to use their boats to leave with as many people on board as practical?"

"And go where, your excellency?" asked the Comptroller.

"Well, the small craft could at least make western Brittany, which would remove them further from the cloud, and from there should be able to obtain transportation out of danger. Larger boats could of course go further afield."

"That would be quite an operation, your excellency," Darwin said. "You're right about the number of boats. But getting them all to sea within twenty-four hours in these tides . . . and I don't know we'd have enough fuel to fill them all."

"Well, you will have to see what can be done," the Bailiff said. "I agree with his excellency that it should be tried, and I will say as much in my address."

"What about all the large yachts in places like Beaucette, belonging to English owners, just lying there vacant?" Driscoll asked. "Each of them could take fifty people at a pinch, certainly as far as Brittany."

"Have we the legal power to requisition them?" Nugent asked.

"Once martial law is proclaimed, we have the legal

power to do virtually anything," the Bailiff pointed out. "And besides, provided we can put a competent crew on board each boat, we'll actually be doing the absentee owners a favour, by saving their yachts from contamination."

"What about money?" Pritchard asked.

"Eh?"

"Your average yachtsman, when he is about to take a trip to France, collects some cash. Not everyone accepts credit cards, and in these circumstances maybe nobody will. There is also the point that a lot of people will wish to take as much cash as possible with them, anyway. And today is Sunday. Cash dispensers won't be too much good, because they only disburse Guernsey notes."

"Damn, I'd forgotten about that. We'd better call a meeting of all the clearing bank managers immediately. They will have to make cash available; I assume all accounts are on computer somewhere in England so actually transferring money should not be a problem. Obviously we don't want queues up and down the High Street, but there will have to be some plan for those heading for France. Well, gentlemen, we have a lot to do."

Rod Frazer cleared his throat, and every head turned towards him. "There is one other matter, Sir Hugh. I . . . ah . . ." he looked from face to face. "My house is in Havelet, overlooking the bay. That would count the same as Glategny Esplanade, wouldn't it?"

"Yes, Mr Frazer," the Bailiff said. "But I am confident we are all agreed that no one in this room leaves the island until everyone else has gone."

Frazer opened his mouth, but not to speak.

"The Bailiff is absolutely correct," the Governor said. "Order and government must be maintained."

"Until there's no one left to govern," Darwin grinned.

"Quite. Mr Watts, you tell us that the command bunker is ready for use?"

"All ready to go, your excellency. Phones, computers and all."

"Very well. Should this cloud arrive, we shall move in and govern from there. Meanwhile I think that as much as possible of the Admin. should be transferred there immediately, together with a senior authority. Sir Mark, would you be prepared to fill that role? I will remain here for the time being."

"Yes, of course," HE agreed. "I'll get down there right away."

"Can we take our families?" Frazer asked.

"No, I'm afraid there will not be sufficient room. Unless they have been evacuated in the order I have outlined, they will have to be sealed into your house like everyone else. Thank you, gentlemen."

"We must go," Pierre said forcefully. "We'll load the boat and get down to Perros. We can be there by lunchtime."

"What about money?" Annabelle asked.

"I have some left over from the last time we were in France. And we have our cards and Eurocheques. There'll be no problem."

"Daddy we can't! Who'll feed Tangle?" Penelope was near to tears. "And what about Tuppence and Sixpence?" The two cats who shared her bed were almost as precious as her pony.

Trish had listened in silence as her nephew and his family agonised over their decisions, but now she clenched her fists tightly in her skirt pockets, and said, "I've decided I'm staying here with them, just leave a list of instructions. I'm not too well versed on the inner needs of ponies and budgies."

"Oh, Aunt Trish! Would you?"

But Penelope's hopes were soon dashed. "No, she wouldn't. I won't hear of it," Pierre insisted. "You must get back to the UK as you planned. We cannot expect you to risk your life . . ."

"And who the hell do you think you're talking to, kid?" Trish pointed a bright red finger nail at him. "I was making my own decisions before you were even a twinkle in your father's eye, and I don't intend handing over that prerogative to you or anyone else." She grinned at him. "If I say I'm staying, then that's it. Understand?"

Penny's mouth hung open in awe.

Annabel knelt on the floor beside Trish's chair and put her arms round her waist. "What have we ever done for you, to deserve this?" she asked.

"Nothing . . . yet. But you just wait! You may well find yourselves nursing your sick old aunt indefinitely, in years to come, as payment." The older woman pushed Annabel away. "I'll cash in on the investment, never fear." She laughed. "Guernsey is my home. Where else would I choose to be in an emergency? Now you've got things to do. Get to it."

"You always were a bossy old woman," Pierre growled. But the loving humour in his eyes belied the words. "Anyway, Liz said that she'd move in here, remember? If she doesn't change her mind then there is no need for you to stay."

"She has the island animal population to take care of. She'll need someone at home to run the show. Now stop arguing." He got up, squeezing her shoulder affectionately. "I'm not arguing. Just very, very grateful. Well, I'll go down and fuel the boat now, if I can."

Despite the flamboyant clothes and make-up, Trish was a very practical person. Soon she was at work with a tube of Gripfill, sealing gaps round the windows. They might never open again, but at least no radiation could get in.

Penelope ran outside to Tangle in the paddock, wondering whether to put him in the stable or leave him where he was. She felt sick.

Annabel hurried upstairs to the bedroom for a secret howl. She had been bottling it up for hours. The dogs went with her, sensing her distress, and leapt on the bed to lick the tears off her face. "Oh, my darlings. What is going to happen to us all?" She hugged them in turn, burying her face in their golden fur. Suitcases? No, bin sacks would be easier to stow on board. She got up, sluiced water over her face in the bathroom and dried herself fiercely on a towel. One big sack each for clothes, and the rest for food . . . no, they could buy food in France. Better leave stocks for Trish and Liz . . . Where on earth is Rosamund, she wondered.

"Are you still sure about this?" Niall asked. He was flushed and nervous, not happy with the idea of doing this in her house.

"Absolutely sure. I lay awake all last night thinking about it and I've quite made up my mind." Rosamund's arms wove themselves round the back of his neck and pulled him over her. "Darling Niall, for all we know this could be our very last day on earth. Wouldn't it be awful to die, never having consummated our love?"

Niall frankly thought it would be awful to die, period. But he had adored Ros for nearly a year and his feelings had never been purely platonic. Now, with the added stress of impending doom, and with her naked body under his, it was impossible to resist. It took about fifteen seconds. Niall felt totally gob-smacked . . . and so excited he wanted to do it again almost immediately.

Ros felt sore, and wondered what the other girls at school who had already done it had been raving about. But the sensation beforehand had been terrific, and the kissing was wonderful . . . Mmmm . . . Neither heard the door open, nor were they aware that Ros's mother was standing, staring at them, completely stunned. "Er . . . excuse me," Annabel stuttered. What the hell was she supposed to say in this situation? "Really, Rosamund . . ."

The lovers scrambled off the bed, clutching at corners of sheet. "Mum!" Ros gulped. Niall was speechless.

Annabel started to giggle. She felt an absolute fool, but she simply couldn't help herself. As if their lives were not in sufficient crisis already . . . And the reaction to her giggles on the kids faces, Niall's expression changing from horror to relief, and Rosamund looking mortally offended, made it impossible to stop.

"Mum!" Ros exploded. "I can't think what you find so funny!"

"Oh my darling. I'm so sorry. I know losing one's virginity is a very serious business . . . I presume this was the first time?" Ros nodded. "But with all that is happening around us right now, it just seems like the last straw . . ." Then she burst into tears again.

Margaret Ferbrache had also shed some tears but not for long, there was too much work to be done for the residents of the Animal Shelter. Technically she wasn't supposed to be on duty this Sunday, but Mavis was worried about her family and Jimmy, who had popped in to help with cleaning out, earlier, said he'd come back if his wife calmed down a bit: she wasn't a Guernsey girl, had no relatives here and according to Jimmy was scared out of her wits.

The animals greeted Margaret in turn as she delivered their food. They all loved her – and it wasn't just cupboard love. She had a natural empathy with even the most truculent dogs and nervous cats. She would cuddle them against her soft bulk muttering sweet nonsense, calming their fears at their strange surroundings . . . but for how long could she keep it up? She studied the buildings as she did the round: it wasn't going to be possible to seal this place, so what could she do? Take them all home with her? Well, she might be able to accommodate the cats in her cottage, but there'd never be room for the dogs. There were fourteen in at the moment. To house and feed them would be difficult enough, but the biggest problem would be the messing. Two piles each per day meant twenty-eight, multiplied by seven is . . . one hundred and ninety-six per week, for how many weeks? "Shit!" she exclaimed out loud. It was not a word she normally used, but there was no one around to hear, these were hardly normal circumstances, and it was an appropriate expletive, she thought. Of course it wouldn't be too hard scooping up the poops but how could she cope with all their tiddles? She gazed lovingly at a little Cairn Terrier who she had rescued from a very bad home and nurtured back to health. A lump was forming in her throat and she felt the corners of her mouth beginning to droop. "Darn it, love. We'll make it work, somehow!" she vowed. "As soon as I've finished this we'll get to work on a plan."

"Ready?"

Janet looked up from the stack of photo albums in alarm.

"What for, dear?"

"To leave, of course," Peter spoke savagely. He wanted to savage someone, blame someone for what was happening.

"Already? But we don't know that it will be necessary . . ."

"Yes, we do. If you insist on bringing that little tyke of yours you'd better put it in the car now."

"But . . . how can you leave before all the patients are evacuated . . ."

"They are Andy Driscoll's responsibility, not mine." Which wasn't true; caring for the island's sick and elderly was the duty of everyone in the medical profession. Mr Peter Barrington knew this perfectly well, but he refused to think about it and was livid with Janet for mentioning it. He had made up his mind yesterday, that he would take an unscheduled holiday with his wife on their yacht should the threat become imminent, and he was damned if he'd wait any longer.

"There hasn't been any official warning . . ." Janet ran a finger over a precious Dresden figurine, stared gloomily at others of her beloved collection in the glass cabinet, "and we haven't passed contracts on the house, yet."

"For God's sake stop prevaricating. We've got to go now. I want to be well past St Martin's Point before the tide turns." He picked up his briefcase. "Is the back door locked?"

Janet stumbled across the room. For some unaccountable reason her thighs felt weak . . . perhaps it was because they were walking out on their entire lives.

"My friends, visitors, fellow Guernseymen, what I have to say to you this morning is of the gravest concern to us all. Yesterday I promised to keep you all informed of what was happening, and of the measures your government is taking to secure the lives of you all. Now I have to tell you that it is probable that a shift in the wind, occurring some time in the next twenty-four hours, will bring some of the nuclear fall-out released from the Flamanville meltdown over the Channel Islands. It is not possible to gauge the degree of radiation we may receive, as yet. It *might* be low enough to create no serious ill effects. But equally it could be high enough to prove lethal within thirty days. And, I must tell you, it might just be bad enough to kill any living organism within twenty-four hours."

The Bailiff paused to let that sink in. "We are therefore, with the most serious possible scenario in mind, implementing our plans. Guernsey, and all of its dependencies, will have to be evacuated. This evacuation has already commenced as regards Alderney, Herm, Sark and Jethou: the inhabitants of Alderney are being shipped to England by the Royal Navy, those from the smaller islands will in the first instance be brought to Guernsey. From Guernsey, they, together with everyone on Guernsey itself, will be evacuated, either to France or mainland Britain. Now, the first thing I wish to make clear to you is that *everyone* will leave. Let no one doubt that. However, equally it will be clear to you that this cannot be done all at once. We shall begin with the visitors to the island, the sick, and those unable to care for themselves. Their evacuation has already commenced.

"They will be followed by all children under the age of seven, together with their mothers, and then all other children up to the age of sixteen with their schools. Now, I must repeat what I said yesterday. There must be no panic. This would be a catastrophe for us all. To make sure of this, His Excellency the Lieutenant-Governor will invoke the powers granted him by the Home Secretary, and declare a State of Emergency, placing the island under martial law, commencing at twelve noon this morning. That is two hours from now. Between now and noon, I wish every one of you not already at home to return there and remain there. You will be visited by members of the Police, WRVS or Civil Defence Service. They will advise you when and where you are to assemble for transport by special buses to the airport and harbours. In the meantime, repeated instructions will be broadcast on radio and TV on the best methods of sealing up your houses to await your return. I must repeat, these measures are essential for the protection of us all. Anyone breaking the curfew will be committing a criminal offence and may be imprisoned without trial until the emergency is over.

"Now I wish to speak with those of you possessing boats capable of reaching either England or Brittany. These boats may be used for those purposes, but here again, it must be done in an orderly and civilised manner. Harbourmaster Darwin and his staff have a list of all boat owners in the island. They will be contacting you in turn and inviting you to leave, by yacht, if you so wish. Do not attempt to leave the harbour or any of the marinas, unless invited to do so by Captain Darwin. This again will be treated as a breach of the curfew. However, any experienced seamen or yachtsmen who do not have boats of their own are requested to contact the Harbour Office with a view to manning vessels belonging to absentee owners and taking them to safety.

"I wish to assure you that all members of the Emergency Committee, together with all people appointed to officiate or care for others during this emergency, and persons necessary for the maintainance of essential services, will remain at their posts until the last person has been evacuated. For those of you with particular queries, Guernsey Telecoms have a block of lines available through their advice number, one hundred. Anyone who has essential duties to perform, for example doctors and nurses, should apply immediately for special permits allowing them to disregard the curfew and for special anti-radiation suits which are now being obtained from England.

"This concludes my announcement. Until we are united again in happier circumstances I will say Good bye, and God Bless you."

They sat in silence, holding hands, gazing into space. "Stay tuned to Guernsey Radio for instructions from Mr Willy Watts. He will tell you how to seal your homes against radiation," the announcer said. "In the meantime we will play some records of music we hope will help while you are preparing your departure."

"You classify as a visitor, so why don't you get back to the St Pierre while you can? You will be evacuated from there." Liz squeezed Jackson's hand and got up from the settee.

"I'll ignore that insulting suggestion." He stood up beside her. "Now what do you want . . ."

"It wasn't meant as an insult. I'm serious. There is nothing for you to do here . . ."

"Nothing? I'm of no use to the woman in my life?"

"I have a duty here, in Guernsey. You have a duty to your family and Parks Paramus . . ." She walked round the settee, put her hands on the back and faced him. "I love you, Jackson. But I have to stay . . . you don't. Why risk throwing away your life . . ."

"We won't have a spat over it. I'm staying. Got it? So, what's first on the agenda?"

Their eyes were locked across the room. Liz allowed her shoulders to sag in submission to his decision, though she'd known all along he wouldn't leave without her. She blew him a kiss and said, "My special permit. Then we must get the three dogs and our food down to Pierre's place, which will need to be sealed and their animals sorted out. Do you want to try contacting David again, about Trouble?"

"I did, while you were making the coffee. Forsythe says David is down at the harbour helping with the evacuation. The old chap seems to think David is some kind of hero!"

"Emergencies do bring out the secret strengths and weaknesses in us all. Right now I'm trying not to wet my pants with fright. I never knew I could be so scared, before." She collected a notebook and ballpoint from her bureau. "Better start writing lists."

"Sure. Just anything and everything that comes into our heads. We can put them all into order of priority later. And, when and if you have to go off attending your patients, I'd like to come with you, as your assistant. If you can get a permit for me too, that is."

"Yes. That would be great. Permits must have high priority but I think before we go out to get them I should call some colleagues in the veterinary fraternity. We will have to meet and decide who, how and what. Divide up the jobs."

Charles Daley, the island's senior vet, answered his phone immediately. "Yes, Liz. Thanks for calling, I was about to buzz you. We are meeting at my surgery in half-an-hour."

"I thought I should go into town for my special permit, first."

"I've called in to the Police and they are issuing permits for us all, plus a few extra for our assistants. My receptionist is fetching them now and we'll distribute them here."

"May I claim one for the man in my life, who has volunteered his services?"

"Certainly. Great stuff. Do I know him?"

"I doubt it. He's a banking Yank with a yen for heroics," Liz said, grinning at Jackson. "May I bring him with me, now?"

"Indeed. The more helpers we have the better."

Liz had barely replaced the receiver when the phone beeped.

It was Polly from her surgery. "Mrs Cobb, there's a man here at our house from the Civil Defence who says Mum and my little sister Karen must leave straight away. That means I'll be left by myself. I wondered, could I be of any use if I could get up to your place?"

Liz thought, quickly. There wasn't much chance of the girl getting a permit, but she would be useful down at Pierre's, looking after the animals until . . . God, the thought of putting them all down . . . "Yes, Polly. You could be a great help. Do you know where my brother lives?"

Polly didn't, but was able to follow Liz's directions and promised to go straight there.

Again the phone went, and Liz grabbed the receiver. This time it was Pierre. "We are going to leave on our boat, Liz. As soon as we're called, of course. Trish is staying, but there's room on board for you if you want to come."

"I'm part of essential services, Bruv. Jackson has enlisted as my assistant and we are just off to a veterinary meeting. Sweet of you to offer, though." She knew the boat would be pretty uncomfortable with extra passengers anyway, and there certainly would not be room for Jackson or the dogs. "But listen. We'll be bringing our dogs down, soon. And Polly, one of our receptionists, is on her way to your place. She can help with the animals until her turn for evacuation. And she can help with sealing the house . . ."

"Don't worry about that. Trish is already working on it. None of the windows will ever open again, I'm afraid."

"She's very efficient. Okay, *mon veille*. See you soon." She stifled the sob in her throat.

"Stick in there, Little Sis," he choked. "There's some champagne in the cellar. Put a couple of bottles in the fridge for when we all get back."

"Will do." Tears were streaming down her face as she replaced the receiver on its rest, and strode out, lists in hand, to put the dogs in the car.

Jackson saw, but remained silent. There wasn't a damn thing he could say that wouldn't make her feel worse.

"We're all gonna die, just like in Hiro . . . Hiromi . . . that place in Japan where the atom bomb went off," Wilma wailed. Her mascara had created a zebra effect down her face during repeated bouts of weeping.

"For gawd's sake dry up, Wilma!" Even Sharon was getting fed up with her.

"Why the hell won't the telly work? What's happened?" Eddie stood in front of the set punching buttons on the remote control – with no response.

"I think one of the kids was playing with the gadget," Sharon said over her shoulder. "Look, love," turning back to her sister, "you and your kids'll be fine. You'll all go off on the big boats. The Bailiff said."

"Why can't we come in your boat with you? I can't manage the three little ones on me own."

Sharon glared at her husband.

"I said no, and that's final!" The prospect of going off to France saddled with that lot was almost worse than staying here. Almost. But he bloody wasn't doing that, no matter what the Bailiff said.

"We can't leave her to cope on her own, Eddie. It's not fair," Sharon whined. "If they can't come on our boat with us then we'll have to stay."

"That's up to you. Go, stay, it's your choice. All I can tell you is, I'm off. Now. Are you coming or not?" He was shaking all over with fright, at the thought of the death cloud rolling nearer and nearer with every minute.

"You have to wait to be called . . ."

"Bugger that. You think I'm going to wait for some fucking little Hitler to tell me whether I can live or die? In another hour the tide'll be so low I won't be able to get out. I'm going, now!"

"We can't leave Wilma here alone . . ."

"We'll drop her and her brood back home on the way to the marina. The buses are collecting everyone with toddlers from the States houses. Get them into the car. And for chrissake hurry."

"Well, I'm bringing Rover."

"You're not."

"I bloody am."

"No!"

"We can't leave the poor little bugger alone to starve to death!" she screamed.

"Right. So you get your sister and her lot sorted out. I'll see to the dog."

Sharon didn't know what he meant by that, but she hoped if she got Wilma into the car she still might persuade Eddie to let her come with them. Wilma had to be half dragged out of the front door, still howling, and the kids bundled into the back seat of the car with her. Just as she slammed the door closed she heard the bang from the back garden . . . and ran. "Eddie! No, Eddie you bloody murdering rat, no!"

They met in the hallway. "I had to do it, love. You were right, we couldn't leave him to starve to death." He dropped the revolver into his holdall. "Let's go."

"You bloody bastard! You bloody murdering bastard. I'll never forgive you for that. Never!"

When they arrived at Wilma's housing estate, both the women and two of the children were still howling, one of them, Francesca, because she'd wet herself again on the car seat. The third was silently demolishing one of the ashtrays. Sharon got out, pulled the kids after her and finally Wilma heaved her bulk on to the footpath, balancing precariously on the remains of her stilettos. "Good-bye. And good bloody riddance!" Sharon slammed the car doors as hard as she could, took Francesca's hand and led the group through the litter up Wilma's front path to her door.

Eddie shouted across the back of the open car. "What you playing at? Are you coming, or what?"

Sharon turned round long enough to direct an extended middle finger in his direction and shout, "You eff off, you bloody murderer. I'm going with Wilma." And followed her sister into the house.

"Thank God for that, you stupid cow," he shouted after her. "And good bloody riddance." As no one had told him that radioactive dust is invisible, Eddie kept peering up at the sky as his car careered down to the marina. He stopped at the top of the pontoon where he was berthed, dragged his bags out of the boot and hurried down the bouncing walkway. He didn't even bother to put the roof up or lock the car. Five minutes later his motor cruiser roared out over the sill leaving an enormous wash rocking every craft in the marina. Bert Darwin, taken completely by surprise, didn't get a chance to stop him.

"What do you reckon, Ben?" Harry de la Mare called over the hedge.

"You mean about leaving home and that?"

"Yeah. Did you hear the Bailiff?"

"No, but the wife did. Says we've got to evacuate, like Mum and Dad did in nineteen-forty. You going?"

Ben finished examining a cow's troublesome hoof and stood leaning against the animal's flank. "How the hell can I? Who'd see to the cows, you?"

"You joke! But Joan's packing, right this minute. She's going to Jenny's to help with the grandchildren. Jenny's husband flew off to Hong Kong on Wednesday on banking business. He's not due back for another week, so she's all alone, see?"

"And you, you're staying put?"

"It's like you say. Who'll see to the cows?"

Jackson sat in the car, waiting for the vets meeting to end. He had made the diplomatic decision to stay put when he realised that only members of the profession were gathered in the waiting-room, being the largest room in the building. They had opened the windows and from time to time he heard a voice raised, in anger or in anguish. There were so many decisions to make, and no one could possibly be sure which would prove to be correct. The most hellish scenario would be of the radioactive cloud heading straight at them and the vets hurriedly putting down every animal in the island before rushing off to their sealed homes or bunkers – only to discover later that the cloud had by-passed them . . . Dear Lord – he was not a church-goer or even much of a believer, but this seemed like a good time to be talking to the Man Upstairs, always supposing He was actually there – Dear Lord, tell us what we should do. Help us to decide what's best. He wished Liz didn't have this responsibility to stay, but even without that she would hate to leave: Guernsey, its atmosphere, aura, was her life's blood. She would vigorously oppose abandoning it . . . and he had to try to understand that. The island was certainly beautiful and somehow encapsulated within its twenty-five square miles all the enthusiasm and participation in every business, trade, hobby sport and cultural activity imaginable. Yet it remained hard to assimilate her absolute obsession, her total sense of belonging. Maybe if he had ever had a settled home life . . . but he hadn't. His parents had moved from California to Philadelphia, then to New York and for the past ten years made their home near Boston – so nowhere was truly home. He seemed to remember adoring the west coast as a child, making a host of friends in Philly and still hated the idea of living in New York . . . Maybe there was something in the saying, "home is where the heart is". And his heart was definitely where Liz might happen to be . . .

He wondered how she getting on in there . . .

Even with the windows open the atmosphere in the waiting-room was close and oppressive. Most of the veterinary surgeons wore open necked sports shirts, two were in shorts and the only other female vet, Winifred Potts, a large, angular woman in her late fifties, wore a floral cotton skirt, yellow tee-shirt, and her grey hair in a ponytail. Charles Daley was the only one wearing a tie;

being short, round and bald with a shiny red face, he fondly believed the more formal look lent him dignity. "We are instructed to be extra careful with these lethal drugs," he was saying. "Ensuring they are constantly kept under lock and key."

"Which blithering bureaucrat dreamed that up at a time like this?" someone interjected.

"No doubt the one that's running the fastest to get away from the lethal dust," another suggested.

Charles ignored them to continue. "Willy Watts will notify us when the anti-radiation suits arrive so we can collect our allocation. He doesn't know yet how many are expected, so I cannot say if there will be enough to go round."

"They'll be jolly hot to work in at this time of year," Winifred complained.

"I'd rather be hot and safe than dead cold," retorted the new young vet. Fortunately he was impervious to one of Winifred's withering stares.

"I assume everyone here has a pager?" Charles asked.

Everyone except Winifred agreed they had. "No!" she said. "I find all these high-tech gadgets far too time consuming."

"In which case, Miss Potts, we may have difficulty contacting you. For the others, this will be the collection spot for drugs and equipment. Please fetch your requirements as soon as you are notified they've arrived."

"When do we use what?" Liz asked. "Do we agree a joint policy on the timing of slaughter?"

"Certainly not!" A young man with longish hair and very thick glasses spoke for the first time. "We are not planning euthanasia for the human population. What right have we to slaughter the animals?"

"Don't start all that again, Jeremy!" a colleague begged.

A voice growled something about bursting udders and milk fever, while another snapped at him to shut up.

"Yes, Liz. I think you have a point there. We should

aim at a united policy. One was agreed years ago, but most of the people who signed it are no longer with us. Apart from the dissenting Jeremy, are the rest of us in accord on the subject?"

"Worded how?"

Charles looked at his notes and read, "That we, the undersigned veterinary surgeons practicing in Guernsey, Channel Islands, agree to exterminate as many as possible of the animal population in the island, in the event of the imminent threat of radioactive fall-out becoming reality and their being abandoned by their owners – this being the less harrowing alternative to the misery the animals would suffer in dying from starvation, neglect or the effects of radiation sickness." He looked solemnly round the room at the unhappy faces. "That sound all right?"

"What do we need to sign it for?" Winifred asked.

"To absolve individuals from any blame that might be laid on them for the slaughter, when this is all over."

"Damn silly, if you ask me," she retorted. "Surely it's only common sense."

Knowing her of old, Liz was perfectly aware that Winifred was quite capable of going out with a twelve bore if she thought it would alleviate suffering. She also remembered seeing the large woman collapsed in tears in her car after putting down a beautiful young horse who had broken his leg. Personally, Liz always had horrors of administering death. It was ghastly enough when it involved creatures who were strangers to her. But thinking about Cocoa and Horlicks, Trouble, Tangle and all the other pets at Pierre's place was horrendous.

"I'm not signing any death charter," Jeremy announced. I'll leave you to it." He walked out.

Everyone else signed.

Chapter 22

SUNDAY, 24TH JULY – NOON

The yacht rocked violently, bouncing off her fenders against the pontoon. Janet squealed in alarm as she watched her husband teetering on the sloping foredeck, arms full of luggage.

Peter dropped one of the bags to grab a halliard. "Dammit!" he shouted. "Who the hell was that?" as the powerboat shot out into the open sea.

Janet had recognised Eddie Parker, but she didn't say so. Peter was in a bad enough mood as it was. "Are you all right, dear?" she asked.

Peter grunted, picked up the bags and edged carefully aft to dump his load in the cockpit before collecting the next lot from Janet's outstretched hands. He looked at his watch. "Quick, get aboard, we're only just going to make it. We can stow the gear once we're under way."

"What about the car?"

"Well, what about the car? Did you want to take it with us?"

She loathed his sarcasm. "It's parked in the middle of the road!"

"If it's in anyone's way they can move it. The key is in the ignition." He stretched awkwardly. "That jolt nearly put my back out again. God, if I could get my hands on that swine . . ."

"Poor dear," Janet said sympathetically. But she was wondering what Parker was doing, shooting off like that.

He had been so loud in his confidence when he paid over all that cash.

Neither of them realised they were being watched. Bert Darwin was on a far pontoon, checking up on various departing yachtsmen and wondering what one of the island's senior medics was up to. Presumably he was preparing his yacht for departure . . . if the time came when he could feel justified in leaving. That, of course, wouldn't be until all his patients were evacuated . . .

He was below decks explaining local tidal movements on a visiting yachtsman's charts when the Barringtons motored out of the marina. He excused himself and hurriedly stuck his head up through the hatch, watching in amazement as the large craft disappeared from sight. Surely . . .? He shrugged and returned to the chart in question.

At first sight the normally well-ordered hospital appeared to be in a state of total chaos. Trolleys with patients, drip feeds and appropriate attendants weaved down the corridors around waiting wheelchairs, work-trolleys laden with clean laundry, and miscellaneous patients wearing pyjamas and degrees of terror, while others, too ill to care, lay in their beds being pushed gently by nurses towards the lifts and exits. However, it was not as chaotic as it looked. Andy Driscoll and his team of doctors had done an excellent job of organising the evacuation of the building and, with the co-operation of Admin, almost everything was going according to plan. As many patients as possible had been returned to their families, all clutching their medical files to be handed on to whomever it may concern. Children on stretchers were taken to the airport for immediate transportation to England with their mothers, other patients were being transferred to comparatively safe havens which were believed to be radiation proof.

Andy had expected hitches, problems, but the only one bothering him at the moment was the fact that they were unable to contact Peter Barrington; he was answering neither his beeper or his phone. Some of his patients were proving difficult, not wanting to accept other doctors' decisions on where they should go and what treatment they required in transit. When told that his surgeon was not available, one patient had accused Andy of lying. Most of Barrington's patients tended to be wealthy inmates of the Victoria private wing, insisting on preferential treatment in all matters. "He is obviously not at home," Andy said to a harrassed nursing sister. "I wonder if he has been called into Town by the Bailiff for another meeting?"

"Shall I get someone to phone the Police Station?"

"Might be an idea, if we are to avoid a Vic. Wing riot."

A WRVS lady was asked to make the call. She returned a few minutes later with the request that Dr Driscoll go to the phone.

"Driscoll here. Who is that?"

"Sergeant Collins, sir. I spoke on the phone to Bert Darwin a few minutes ago. He said he'd seen Doctor Barrington and his wife load their yacht and leave the marina."

"I can't believe it!"

"He was quite positive, sir. I thought maybe I should tell you direct, rather than pass on the news through someone else."

"Quite right. Thank you." Christ! The rat! And how was he supposed to tell all these people here, professionals, auxiliaries and patients alike, that one of the island's senior medics had done a runner? Walking back to the ward, he decided to say nothing. Would be bad for morale.

The meeting in the waiting-room had broken up but only Jeremy had left when the door opened and an Alsatian bounced in, dragging a harrassed young man in its wake. "I'm afraid the surgery isn't open," Charles began.

"I can't 'elp that," the young man said. "I'm deliverin' it for me muvva. She's gorn off wiv me dad on ve plane. 'E's sick, see. She said for me to 'ave 'im put down." For all his tattoos and macho image he looked desperately unhappy about it.

"We have not commenced putting down . . ." Charles stared at the happy canine face ". . . why don't you take care of him until we are sure it's absolutely necessary . . . ?"

"I can't, see. Me girlfriend's just 'ad a baby an I gotta go wiv 'er an' the uvva little one ter England. Ve perlice said."

"Can't a neighbour . . ."

"We lives down the Front, see, an' ev'rybody's packin' up. So I'll 'ave ter leave 'im 'ere. I gotta go. They're waitin' fer me, see?" He took out his wallet which was stuffed with a huge wad of money. "'Ow much?"

Charles shook his head. "Nothing. It's free," and accepted the proffered lead with a dazed expression.

The door opened again before the young man reached it, and two young, boisterous terriers came in with their weeping mistress, followed by a man with two cat boxes. "I think I had better get down to my own surgery," Liz said. "I presume this syndrome is island wide."

"What are we going to do with them all?" a colleague asked.

"Take them to the animal shelter?" Charles suggested.

"Maggie's in the process of taking them all to her own home," Liz told him. "Isn't there a German bunker, or somewhere else we could use?"

"That's a totally impractical idea," Mick, the young vet said scornfully. "It would be impossible to house them all in one room without them tearing each other to pieces, and the mess would be unbearable."

"What's the alternative?" Winifred Potts demanded. "We have agreed not to start the slaughter till it's absolutely necessary."

"Who's going to feed the brutes?"

"There must be warehouse stocks of feed we could commandeer," Winifred insisted. "Charles?"

Charles said he would call a wholesaler friend and ask if they could do a deal. "Are we assuming the States will pay for it?" Mick sneered.

"That can be sorted out when the emergency is over," Liz snapped. "We have made our decisions. Now let's get to work. We will each have to make our own arrangements for animals dumped at our respective surgeries but I, for one, refuse to put down any healthy animals until absolutely necessary."

"Here, here!" Winifred applauded. "Let's get to it, chaps."

There were dogs, cats, hamsters and a pet pig waiting for Liz when she and Jackson drove into the surgery yard. "At least we shouldn't run out of bacon," the latter commented.

"Let's try to get them all down to Pierre's place," Liz said. "What we need is a truck."

"I'll check through the yellow pages." The American jumped out of the car to a vociferous greeting. "Where's the phone?"

Within half an hour a truck drove in. "Can I stay to help?" the driver asked. "Name's Owen Clark." He was tall, thin, bald and welcomed with open arms.

"Marvellous!" Liz beamed. "I'm Liz, a vet. This is Jackson and here's what we have to do."

"These are the instructions given to us by Mr Watts of the Civil Defence." Isobel Marquand handed out the photocopied leaflets to her band of Women's Royal Voluntary Service ladies. "Unfortunately we haven't time to run off sufficient copies to hand out to each household, so you will have to explain and demonstrate, especially to the elderly. Marion has obtained vast quantities of heavy duty tape and various other sealants, but basically each householder should decide on one or two rooms only to be sealed. Otherwise the supplies will run out. It is also very important to make sure that when we say sealed, it will also be necessary to leave some air access, or we'll have some suffocations on our hands."

"If air is allowed in, won't radioactive material go in with it?" someone asked.

"I don't know. We'll have to ask Mr Watts. But they must have access to air. Now, you will see on your copies further instructions and helpful hints on alternative methods of sealing which, hopefully, the people will be able to implement for themselves. These include the hygenic disposal of all types of waste matter. We are asked to keep records of who we have visited and note any special cases where extra provisions are necessary." She paused to smile briefly at the serious faces of her listeners. "Now we come to the problem of food. We have no idea how long people may be required to remain in their sealed rooms. The Bailiff intends to get everyone evacuated as soon as possible, but in the meantime we must ensure that each home has sufficient foodstocks to last for at least two weeks. A suggested list is on the back of your leaflets. Again, you are asked to make note of anyone who has insufficient provisions. Now, does anyone have any questions?"

"Yes," said a voice from the back. "What do we do when we find some old dear who has nothing in the cupboard, is not capable of sealing the house and refuses to leave?"

"Telephone the police immediately. They will send someone out to move the person to safety," Isobel told her.

"What about pets?"

"They can keep their house pets sealed up with them, if they can cope. If not they will have to be taken to a vet to be put down."

"And cows and horses?"

"Notify a vet."

When the meeting closed and the ladies dispersed in their cars, all displaying their special permits, Marion and

Isobel locked the door of Jubilee House and set off on the planned route of their grid.

Annabel felt numb. Throat tight and tears threatening, she had worn a brave face for the sake of Pierre and the girls for the past couple of hours, and now she was feeling exhausted. Wandering from room to room she had tried to make up her mind which most precious items to take – or leave behind. But everything was precious – she couldn't bear to leave anything. Wedding presents they'd been given eighteen years ago: she remembered who had given them each one. Photos taken on holiday, the beautiful Mother's Day card with lovely words written by Ros when she was ten. She whipped it out of its frame and into her bag: it wouldn't take any extra room. The huge, framed photo of the four of them with the dogs and cats – that had been such an hilarious session in the photographer's studio. She stroked the back of the little antique nursing chair Pierre had given her when Penny was born, the tapestry seat covers she had worked for the dining chairs . . .

"Annabel!" Pierre's voice reached her from the garden. "Are you ready? Where is Penny?"

"Penny!" she shouted up the stairs. There was no reply. She ran up to her daughter's room and opened the door. It was as chaotic as ever, clothes flung over the bed and the chair, collections cluttering every available surface accumulating dust – but no Penelope. The fact that the big enlargement of the girl taken riding Tangle was not on the dressing table gave her a clue, and from the window she glimpsed the pair together in the paddock. She called, but Penny didn't appear to hear. When Annabel reached the paddock she saw why: arms wound round the pony's neck, Penny was crying uncontrollably, her thin shoulders shaking, eyes red and swollen, face soaked with tears. Annabel put an arm round the girl's waist. "Come, my darling. We have to leave. Now."

"No, Mummy, no. I can't leave Tangle. I can't!"

"Trish and Liz will look after him. They've promised."

"If they stay, and if they survive!"

"Nobody can ever be sure what's round the corner, darling. My father knew a man who survived years of shelling in the trenches, and was run over by a bus the day after he was demobbed." Dear Lord, did that story help? "Please come, darling. Daddy and Ros are waiting in the car."

When they reached the car Ros was sitting in the back, white-faced, with a wooden expression, and a small case perched on her knees neatly packed with her most precious pieces.

The corners of Pierre's mouth quivered downwards as they drove away from their home.

"Why carn I take me doll's pram?" the child whined.

Sharon gritted her teeth. "I told you! There's not room on the boat for it, Francesca."

"Why?"

"There's too many people."

"Why?"

"'Cos everyone's leavin'."

"Why?"

Her mother had a shorter fuse. "Shurrup, will yer!" she yelled, advancing with hand raised.

Francesca ducked. But she was saved by the thumping on the front door. "It's the WVS people," Sharon said. "They'll want us to go. Got everyfing?"

"Yeah," Wilma said.

"Turned off the fridge?"

"Reckon I should?"

"Yeah." Sharon picked up the younger boy. "Come on, sweetheart."

The lady in the smart green pinny held the gate open while the group of women and children came out to join the bus queue. "Are you Mrs Doherty?" She smiled politely at Wilma.

"Yeah." Wilma nodded.

"Then who is this other lady?"

"Me sister, Sharon. Wiv 'er little boy," she lied.

"And these two are yours?"

"Yeah. Got a problem?" she challenged.

The nice lady smiled again. "It's just that there is no other lady on my list from this address."

"She's 'ere on 'oliday," Wilma explained.

"Oh. I see. And where is your other child?"

"Eh?"

"I have you down for three children, Mrs Doherty."

"Oh, that one. 'E's away visitin' 'is dad."

"I see." She was quite sure there was some hanky panky going on, but she wasn't prepared to start an argument. "Well, would you all get on the bus, please."

They sat in one row at the back. "There," Wilma said. "I tol' you it'd be dead easy." She winked at her sister.

Sharon didn't reply: she was trying to remove chocolate from her smart linen skirt, deposited there by her newly acquired "son".

It was sweltering on the road down to the harbour, and along the Alderney breakwater. Queues of people stood on the tarmac and concrete, edging slowly forward a few feet at a time as those on the dock moved up the gangways on to the deck of the destroyer. It was a subdued crowd. No one pushed or shoved, no one raised a voice except to call a straying child. Occasionally a potential wag attempted to lift the spirits of those near at hand with a quip, or caustic comment on the ill-timed activities of the Ruddy Frogs. Someone broke into *Ten Green Bottles* but only one other voice was with him by the time they were down to five. The sea inside the long arm of the breakwater was like glass, only tiny ripples snaking over the wet sand. The remarkably empty sand, for today was Sunday . . . a hot sunny, summer Sunday when despite the mist which hid the rocks on the far side of the Swinge the beach below the town should be full of squealing children with buckets and spades, and hotel waiters playing football. Rows of bikinis and bright coloured towels should be laid out on the drier sand, while tourist cameras clicked and gulls wheeled over incoming boats in hopes of a hand out. There was not one solitary soul on the beach today. Not a bikini in sight. Everyone was fully dressed, standing with one suitcase apiece, waiting to leave.

Sweat was pouring down David's face, half his shirt hung out of his shorts exposing an ample beer-gut and there were dark circles round his eyes. "Okay folks, that's it," he shouted, spreading his arms wide. "No more passengers on this trip or the poor old tub will roll over." He looked into the face of a distraught young woman who was supporting an elderly man. "Don't worry, love," he told her. "There'll be plenty room on the other one. She'll be alongside in five minutes."

"Stand clear, there," a sailor yelled as the ropes were unhitched from the gangways. "Mind yer toes!"

"Thank God this happened in mid-summer," the elderly man remarked. "Grim down here in the teeth of a winter's gale."

Grimmer than you realise, old man, David thought, if it was carrying radioactive dust. He was into his fourth "wind" at least, having passed through the exhaustion barrier several times. Forsythe had come down on a mysteriously acquired bicycle with a flask and sandwiches and the news that Trouble was with Jackson and his girlfriend, the vet. David sent him back to pack a suitcase each, seal up the house as best he could and return in time to leave on the second destroyer . . . if there was room. There probably would be. Several plane loads of people had taken off and nearly every available pleasure and fishing craft had left, too, easing the pressure somewhat. But David had ideas of his own on where he wanted to go. Trouble was in Guernsey, and there were still one or two fishing boats left in the harbour.

"Hi, Dave, how ye doing?" Steve, of the bad humoured cirrhosis, hailed him from the crowd.

"Great. But I'm working up one helluva thirst!"

"Makes me dry just watching you."

The loaded destroyer had pulled away from the end of the breakwater and her replacement was edging up to the men waiting to take her warps. David returned to the shepherding of his flock.

In the farmhouse sitting room Trish's hands and face were pitch black as she greeted them. Liz burst out laughing. "What on earth . . .?"

"I'm trying to seal up the chimney, but everything I shove up there just keeps on going. I don't seem to be making any progress."

"Wouldn't it be a might easier to cap the top of the stack?" Jackson grinned over Liz's shoulder.

"Great idea!" she grinned back. "Do it!"

"Why do I open my big mouth?" Jackson groaned. "So where might Pierre keep a step ladder?"

"You can go out through the attic window," Liz said, "Later. Let's get these animals unloaded first. Has Polly arrived?"

Trish was rubbing her nose on the back of her hand . . . which didn't help. "She's out in the barn, I think. She was feeling a trifle fazed when she got here."

But Trish had done a good morale job on the girl who was busy wielding a shovel, mucking out Tangle's loose box. Shovel perched on top of her loaded wheelbarrow she staggered out into the yard. "Oh! Mrs Cobb, I didn't know you were here already. Anything you'd like me to do?" Her voice was brighter than when they'd last spoken on the phone and she was smiling cheerfully, though her cheeks were still smudged from weeping.

"Yes, please. Can you help us unload the truck? It's full of animals."

Caged birds and hamsters were not a problem, they were placed upstairs in their cages in the spare room. Cocoa, Horlicks and Trouble had taken charge of the canine contingent, assisted by Pierre's Goldens – intrigued rather than upset by this invasion – forcibly subduing any discordant dog in the ranks. Extra rabbit hutches were stacked in the stables along with a pair of guinea pigs, while a pet goat, together with the pig, was released into the enclosed paddock with Tangle – who wasn't overly impressed. They could all be housed indoors later, if necessary. But it was the cats who presented the big problem. For a start they were terrified out of their socks, howling continuously from their boxes and baskets, which stank. "We can't possibly let them out, other than into a closed room," Liz said, frowning.

"What about that old dairy where they keep all the outdoor furniture?" Trish suggested, drying her hands and face after a rather unsuccessful attempt to remove the soot.

"Brilliant. And I suppose we should begin with cat loos."

"Penny has one in her room for Tuppence and Sixpence," her aunt told her. "We'll need more than one."

"Roasting tins?"

Jackson was sent to get buckets of soil to fill them while Owen Clark and the women carried in the cats in their containers ... which the occupants seemed reluctant to leave once they were opened. Polly was left in charge. "Will you need me for anything else, Mrs Cobb?" Owen asked.

"Not right now. But the odds are we'll have loads more animals to shift by this evening. Will you still be available?"

"Sure thing. My daughter and her kiddies are off on the boats and I've no one else to think about 'cept myself."

"Would you be prepared to help move animals for the other vets if necessary?"

"Yes. Who?" It took only a few minutes to establish his help was necessary and he drove off to Charles Daley's, promising to keep in touch.

"I think I'd better transfer my calls to this number," Liz said when they returned to the kitchen.

"You realise you're going to be swamped?" Jackson said.

"Yes. But I don't have a choice."

"Is your gas tank full?"

"Yep. Yours?"

"Yes. I filled up on Friday. If you run out while doing your rounds you can use my wheels. Meanwhile I'm going to try to get through to Boston if that's okay. I should fill my folks in on the latest."

The four of them set about their allotted tasks, converging in the kitchen an hour later. "Heavens, what happened to you?" Trish exclaimed at the sight of Polly's bleeding arm.

"The beautiful, pedigree Persian puss was terrorising the others. I tried to stop him."

"You'd better let me clean and dress that." Trish reached for Annabel's First Aid box. "Did you succeed?"

"I'm afraid so."

"Afraid?"

"I got so angry when he turned on me I kicked him rather hard," Polly admitted. "He's been cowering under a chair ever since."

"Good for you. Ah, here's Liz. Come on, you're the medical expert. You have a patient. Fix Polly's arm will you, while I dish up?"

"Dish up?" Liz looked at her watch. "Gosh! So that's why I'm sagging in the middle. Starvation!" She studied Polly's wounds. "Nasty. The claws have gone quite deep. You should have a shot of penicillin, I think."

"Do you have some?" the girl asked.

"Oh, no. You'll have to go to your doctor . . ." Liz began, then stopped. "Hm. Difficult."

"Surely you carry it in your bag?" Trish suggested.

"Of course. But I'm not qualified to treat humans."

"Good girl," Trish approved. "You stick to the rules

of the game . . . as long as no one moves the goalpost. Unfortunately they just did. So the sooner Polly gets her shot the sooner she'll be safe from septicaemia. Come on, Liz," she added, seeing the professional's continued reluctance to contravene her training. "Where? In her bottom?"

Polly was bent over the kitchen table with her skirt up and briefs down when Jackson walked in. Liz was rubbing the spot with a pad of alcohol where the needle had jabbed, then pulled the skirt into place. "There. And don't tell anyone I did it or I'll be struck off!"

"Do we assume that was not the commencement of your euthanasia programme?" Jackson murmured.

"Ooh!" Polly exclaimed. "I didn't know you were watching!"

"I wasn't. My stomach was following my nose. What's cooking?"

"Only a fry up. Bacon and eggs and sausages," Trish told him.

"That I could kill for," he licked his lips. The three women stared at him, silently. "Sorry," he muttered.

Liz ate. But she couldn't get over the feeling that it was all unreal. That she was going to wake up any minute and decide the nightmare was due to eating cheese for supper. It was unbelievable that she and Jackson were sitting here with Trish and Polly in Annabel's kitchen eating a late lunch, while Pierre and Annabel sped across to France with the girls, trying to escape with their lives . . . Polly had been pushing the food round her plate but making very little progress. Suddenly she clapped her hand over her mouth and fled.

Liz shoved her chair back and dashed after her into the yard, put her arm round the shaking shoulders while Polly threw up into a patch of weeds in a corner. "Never mind," she said. "You can try to eat later. Meantime we have work to do." She knew she didn't sound very sympathetic, but that would have turned on the tap to another bout of tears.

When they returned to the kitchen, Jackson was holding the phone. "Charles Daley for you."

Liz took it from him. "Charles?"

"The first consignment of equipment is here. Your ration is waiting for you."

"Thanks. Any further developments?"

"Want me to come?" Jackson asked when she'd put down the receiver.

Liz nodded. "We'll have to go on to my surgery after and see what's waiting there for us. Then Charles wants us to visit our farm patients to estimate and list their facilities and requirements." She ran her fingers through her hair. "This is going to be a long day."

His Excellency the Lieutenant Governor followed Willy Watts down past two heavy iron doors into the old German bunker which was built into the hillside. The Nazis, or rather their Todt workers, had constructed extensive concrete fortifications in all the Channel Islands during the war; there had been dozens of gun emplacements, radar and searchlight installations and all manner of other dugouts, intricately linked by tunnels and camouflaged trenches, all over Guernsey. Despite the energetic work of the Civil Defence enthusiasts the big bunker still felt damp and cold but there was no smell of mould . . . only of emulsion paint which had been applied liberally over the years. Sir Mark had been down here before, purely on a visit of interest soon after he had taken up his appointment, but this time it was different. "Amazing how much better it all looks with the addition of phones and computers," he said. "Really alive and functional."

Willy was very proud of the emergency command centre he had created, and smiled into his beard at HE's words of praise. "The cables are permanently *in situ*, of course, and regularly checked, but the high-tech equipment we keep in a more suitable atmosphere. In here," he opened yet another door, "is your private room, sir."

"Good gracious! Complete with bed, desk and all mod. cons!"

"Well, almost, sir. I'm afraid we do have to share the er . . . washroom facilities. I'm sorry your good lady can't be here with you."

"No, she's fine with Sir Hugh's wife," HE said. "Now, has the Bailiff arrived yet?"

"He called to say he's staying at the Police Station for the time being. I think he feels more in control there, and he likes to be visible to the people, as you might say. But there is a direct line to you here, sir. And there are several other people here already, including computer operators and switchboard staff. We have installed good catering facilities, too: could I offer you a cup of tea, perhaps?"

"Later, I think. Let's go to the control room, shall we."

"Yes, yes. Of course." Willy was slightly disappointed. He enjoyed showing off this place, his favorite hobby, especially to such illustrious company. "Through here, sir." He left HE amongst the computer banks and bustled away through each room, checking and double checking the details he had planned for so many years, rooms, high-tech paraphernalia, plans which were in use at long last. His chest expanded, beard bristled and voice deepened. He contrived to maintain a severely serious expression on his face, concealing the fact that he was very elated. This was the moment he had worked for during most of his adult life . . . his zenith.

Sir Hugh was taking a shower. His wife had sent down a change of clothes and his razor – there was no way he could leave the station, so Sue Johns had shown him into this extremely utilitarian shower room. It was cold, standing barefoot on the tiles, adding to his weariness and chill horror of the situation. He had one foot in his underpants when someone knocked on the door. He jumped, nerves on edge, and grabbed the washbasin to keep his balance. "Yes? Hello?"

"Sir Hugh!" It was Sue Johns' voice. "The Dean is on the phone for you. I told him you'd call back, but he says it's urgent."

The Bailiff sighed. "Very well. Tell him I'll be there in ten seconds." It was sixty. "Yes, Mr Allbright, you wanted me?" He panted after the two flights of stairs.

"Sir Hugh! I've been trying to get you for hours. Look here, I feel that throughout this emergency the most important factor has been neglected . . ."

. . . oh no, the Bailiff thought, what have I forgotten?

". . . God."

"Eh?"

"I want to hold a service of supplication at the Town Church this afternoon, but I'm told it's not possible because of this curfew thing."

"I'm afraid that is quite true, Mr Allbright."

"Why?" There was an angry note in the Dean's voice. "You cannot possibly refuse people the solace of prayer at a time like this."

Sir Hugh was still trying to dry his hair on his sodden towel. "I'm afraid . . ."

"Surely you can lift the curfew for an hour or so, purely for those who wish to attend the service."

"I can't see the point. No one will know such a service is going to take place."

"It can be announced over the radio. Everyone has their radio on."

The other members of the Emergency Council, who were currently seated round the table, watched with varying degrees of amusement as the Bailiff tried to control his exasperation. "Mr Allbright, if I give permission to you, I must do likewise for the Catholics, the Presbyterians, the Methodists, the Baptists . . . for everyone in every parish, not just in town. No, no, hear me out," he went on as the Dean tried to interrupt. "We people, here in the Emergency Council Chamber, have hundreds of police and voluntary workers desperately trying to control this horrendous situation. The last thing we need is to have the island population abandoning their homes and preparations to attend various church services. I agree, prayers, in fact, a full service of supplication, should be available to everyone this afternoon . . . on Guernsey Radio. You have my permission to leave your house to go to the broadcasting studio for that purpose. However, I warn you that your service may have to be interrupted at any time. God bless you."

As he replaced the handset, several Council members applauded. Sir Hugh raised his eyes, appropriately to heaven, and said, "Now, gentlemen, back to business."

The well advertised relaxed ambience at the South Winds Hotel had totally vanished under a cloud of gloom, anxiety and agitation. There were one or two determined souls round the swimming pool but only one lonesome child had been allowed into the water . . . to keep it quiet while its parents cogitated. Most of the residents were gathered in the lobby and hallway, some leaning over the reception desk demanding the information no one had. A couple of men were visible through the door of the bar, sitting on high stools and pouring pints of lager into naked, hairy stomachs. When hotelier Paul Pritchard arrived he was instantly surrounded, several voices shouting questions at once. He raised his hands for silence. "Ladies and gentlemen. I am sure some of you will have seen the Bailiff on television, or heard him on radio, making his announcement, so you will know that as visitors to our island, you all will be evacuated on the earliest ships or aircraft as a matter of priority. This hotel is near the top of the list so buses have been ordered to collect you immediately, to take you to the White Rock for embarkation."

"Hey!" called one of the men from the bar. "What's all

this about ships? We came by plane and that's the way we're going!"

"Scheduled flights have all been cancelled. Departures are strictly in accordance . . ."

"Cancelled! What a bloody nerve! I've paid in advance . . ."

"We are here to listen to Mr Pritchard's instructions, not your stupid bleatings! Kindly be quiet." That from a very large lady nursing a very small dog.

"Hear, hear!" An elderly man with a military moustache applauded. "Just give us our orders and we'll get on with it. Will there be room for luggage?"

"There'd better be! I got all my stuff brand new in London before coming," a peroxide blonde claimed. "I'm not leaving any of that behind."

"I'm not leaving till I get my money back. We only arrived Friday night," one of the naked stomachs insisted.

"Splendid," grinned the man with the moustache. "That'll leave room for someone whose life is worth saving."

"Each person may take one suitcase which they will have to carry," Paul continued, ignoring interruptions. "Please will you go to your rooms and pack immediately then reassemble here in fifteen minutes. If you leave any possessions behind in your rooms, please lock your door and return the key to reception. You may reclaim everything when this emergency is over."

There was a sudden commotion near the door as a woman fainted. Her husband dragged her up on to a chair and someone fetched a glass of water. Noise of an argument issued from the bar. The hairy gentlemen wished their wives to do the packing while they carried on drinking. "Sonia!" a woman yelled. "Will you come out of that pool this minute!" The demand was repeated several times. But Sonia carried on swimming.

The afternoon was absolutely still; all wind had dropped. Thus sound carried for miles, and the Cotentin

Peninsular was one huge traffic jam. Every road leading to the south was solid with bumper to bumper traffic. Every car, truck or van was either sounding its horn or gunning its engine, and this had been going on for twenty-four hours now, since the evacuation had been ordered. Although everyone switched off whenever there was a longer than usual hold-up, to preserve fuel, a steady emanation of noise and exhaust fumes rose into the air. Philippe supposed that if they were not already all contaminated with fall-out, they were extremely likely to die of carbon-monoxide poisoning. Or suffocation; they had been warned to keep all the car windows tight shut, and not a lot of oxygen was getting in through the filtration system.

He had no idea where they were. St Mère Église seemed light years away, and since then they had travelled hardly fifty kilometres. Two kilometres an hour . . . He looked down at Monique, watching her eyelids flutter. She had been sleeping deeply, mentally exhausted. Now she looked up at him. "I need to pee."

He grinned. "Well, you can get out and go behind that hedge. I'll still be here when you're done."

She sat up, evaluating the situation. The line of cars was moving, but only about six feet every five minutes. "What's the hold-up now? You'd think it'd get easier as we go south."

"God knows. Go on, get on with it."

She opened the door, got out, and climbed over the hedge. Several other people were doing the same thing. "Can you see what the delay is?" Philippe asked a man who was returning to his car.

"There's a police check-point down the road."

"Police? I thought the police wanted everyone out?"

"They do. But it seems like they're looking for some guy. Must be the one blew up the plant."

Philippe rolled up his window again, turned his head as Monique got in, still pulling up the zip on her jeans. "Did you hear that?"

"So?"

"If they're stopping all the cars, they must be looking for something."

"Yeah. You and me. But as they don't know who we are . . ."

"What makes you think that? If they're looking, they must have something."

She glanced at him. "You're scared. What the shit, man? Like you said yesterday, we're dying anyway."

"There's no reason why we should be. That stuff won't have started to come down yet."

"I'm all in favour of optimism." She lit a cigarette. "Anyway, there's nothing we can do about it, right? If you're that scared you should've kept on going with Georges."

"I stayed because of you."

She blew smoke at him, then took his hand off the wheel and rested it on her knee. "And I'm grateful. When we get out of here I'm going to make it worth your while."

"When! Listen, I'm going to make a break for it."

"Just how the hell do you expect to do that? This heap of iron can't fly."

"Over there, see, there's an opening in the hedge."

"So? That's a field."

"It must have another exit."

"You're crazy," Monique protested. "Look, sit it out."

But Philippe, having reached the gap in the hedge, swung through it into a field yellow with rape and divided every six feet by deep furroughs. The car went forward, and stopped. Behind them people hooted and shouted. Some cheered. Philippe changed down into low gear and the car moved forward again, up and down, up and down, at barely one mile an hour. But it was moving. "Jesus!" Monique gasped, grabbing the wine bottle to stop it smashing. "What's that?"

There was a tearing sound, and the engine noise increased.

"That was the exhaust," Philippe told her.

He had spotted what he wanted, another opening on the far side of the field. It was a long way away, but they were getting there. A huge noise overbehaved above them. They had seen the helicopter earlier, one of several circling over the traffic jams. Now it was clearly coming down. "Get the gun," Philippe said.

"You can't be serious," Monique protested,

"Just do it." He concentrated on the gap. There were cars on the lane in front of him too, but maybe they didn't have a police trap in front of them.

Monique took the automatic pistol out of the carryall, and checked the magazine. She had a peculiar sense of finality, a sort of gathering weight in the pit of her stomach. On the other hand, she had had that just before jabbing François with the hypodermic, and she had survived that. The helicopter settled into the yellow sea, and a man jumped down. He ran towards them waving his arms. Monique rolled down her window. "You must not do this," the man shouted. "There is no point. There is traffic on every road. You must be patient."

"We just got bored," Monique answered, while the Renault bounced and juddered towards the far opening.

The man was running beside them now. "You must go back," he said.

"Fuck off," Philippe told him.

"I have the power to place you under arrest," the man panted. "You must go back." He jogged beside them for another few moments then, as they were obviously not going to stop, waved his arms.

Two more men jumped down from the helicopter, and they were carrying assault rifles. "Oh, shit," Monique said.

"All right," Philippe said. "We surrender."

He braked, hard, and the car came to a halt. But Monique had seen red. She always operated on a short fuse when roused to action, and as the policeman reached for the door and pulled it open, she levelled the pistol and shot him in the stomach. He gave a scream and half turned away from her as he fell to his hands and knees.

"Oh, Jesus!" Philippe shouted, and looked at the two men in front of them. As he did so they opened fire.

Chapter 23

SUNDAY, 24TH JULY – EVENING

The Bailiff sighed, and looked at his watch. It was past nine, and just beginning to grow dark. It was a still, warm evening and the windows of the command room were wide open. Through them drifted an endless cacophony of sound. From the airport, a steady stream of planes landed and took off, punctuated by the tolling of church bells. The Bailiff did not see that this was at all helpful, but he had not the heart to forbid it. But behind these identifiable sounds there was a gigantic *seethe*, of thousands of people in a torment of indecision: to go or not to go. To leave family, business, the accumulated property of a lifetime, abandon pets and livestock . . . or risk slow death from radiation . . . He looked up as Nugent came in. Normally the most tidy of men, the shipping manager's jacket had been discarded and his tie was under his ear. "God," he commented, mopping his face.

"Report?"

Nugent sat down, and Susan Johns hurried forward with a cup of coffee; she was taking a turn at being their charlady.

Nugent opened his folder. "British Airways, Air UK, Jersey-European, British Midland *et al*, plus the charter firms, have committed everything they have, but of course they must share with Jersey, and naturally they can't use their jumbos on our runway. That rules out Virgin, but they are helping Jersey. Anyway, since two o'clock this afternoon we have had forty-two flights out of the airport; that is one roughly every ten minutes. I must say that the staff out there, plus the voluntary workers, have been quite magnificent."

"Numbers out?"

Nugent checked his notes. "Two thousand, five hundred and seventeen. Next, Condor. There are two vessels operating to Weymouth. It's a five hour turn round, what with loading passengers and fuel, so they've only done one trip so far, but we are expecting them back again in the next half hour. That's another four hundred people."

"A drop in the ocean," the Bailiff grunted.

"Every drop helps, sir. As you agreed, I sent *St Pierre* off at eight, and she was back at four. By then *St Helier* had come and gone; they carried three thousand five hundred people between them. That's over and above the fifteen hundred *St Pierre* took out earlier. I sent them to Weymouth as well, because that's closest, and the port has been cleared of other shipping to facilitate movement. Going flat out they were there at six, and started their return at seven. I'm sorry about the delay, but it is simply not possible to get so many passengers off any quicker. They should be here at ten, that is, within the next hour. Unfortunately the freighters are not capable of that kind of speed, and of course they were delayed by the tide; they loaded and went off at seven, carrying a total of seventeen hundred people by making use of their hold space. However, I don't expect them back again before dawn, so for the rest of the night we'll have to make do with the passenger ships, the two Navy destroyers which evacuated Alderney – they should be back by ten as well – and the two Hovercraft from Dover. We have the next lot of passengers waiting down on the dock for embarkation; and more buses are being loaded up by the police and volunteers right now. Hopefully this batch will all be away by midnight at any rate."

"They are making a hell of a racket down there."

"Some of them. A bunch of scruffy-looking individuals

are playing pop music on a weird assortment of instruments, well supported by those who decided to drink what they couldn't carry away. It's pretty good-natured at the moment," Nugent said. "Touch of the Dunkirks, you know. There's the odd hysteric, but the stiff upper lip is holding out."

"Still, the fact is, Nugent, that in the seven hours since ordering the evacuation, we have only embarked just under ten thousand people. Out of an estimated eighty-five. And I presume most who have gone so far have been tourists."

"Plus some critical hospital cases and mothers with small children. But we'll quicken up, sir. The staff in the office are contacting every agent in every port within striking distance, trying to get hold of all available ships and so far they've managed to charter two more ferries. They're not very big, but they'll be a help. We're expecting them about three tomorrow morning. So, we should have another ten thousand people off the island by midnight, and another twelve by dawn."

"Say thirty thousand," the Bailiff muttered.

"Actually more than that. And there's no sign of the wind coming from the east yet, sir. Or coming from anywhere. It's flat calm. If we can hold on till Tuesday . . . that aircraft carrier will be here, and I'm hoping to have at least three more ships available by then. The carrier alone can take several thousand."

"Tuesday," the Bailiff said. He picked up the phone. He had had direct lines connected to both the Meteorological Office and the Civil Defence headquarters in the bunker. "Walter? Give me an update"

"No change in my forecast, sir. I still reckon the wind will come up from the east during the night. Could be stiffish by noon tomorrow."

"Tuesday," the Bailiff said again as he replaced the phone and picked up the other. "Willy? Any readings?"

"Not as yet, sir. Everything is normal."

"Tuesday," the Bailiff said a third time, and listened

to the pealing of the bells. "Do you know, this is the first time in my life I have ever prayed for a hard-working civil servant to be wrong."

"I'm starving. When do we eat?" Jenny was sitting on the windowsill, peering down into Victoria Road through a hole torn in the net curtain. The light was fading and no street lamps had come on, nor had anyone bothered to switch on a light in the room which was illuminated only by the flickering TV screen. Shaun, Carole and Glyn sat on the bare mattress. There wasn't much furniture in the room except the bed, a chair and a table . . . and of course the telly, an old model with a faulty tube. No one was following the distorted action on screen, but they watched nevertheless. A matter of habit.

"When's someone goin' out to get something?" Glyn growled.

"What wiv?" Shaun demanded. "I lent you my last fiver." He looked up at Jenny. "You got anyfink?"

"No."

"What about the cash you got from that feller last night?"

"What d'yer think I paid Boyo with? Buttons?"

"Just fer that little packet? Yer nuts!"

"I earned the bloody money, din' I? And yor the one what popped it all. I just seen the packet. Empty!"

"Yer'll 'ave to earn some more tonight, ven, won' yer!"

"Don' be bloody silly. 'Ow many johns'll be on the street tonight, d'yer reckon?"

"Try lookin', lazy bitch!"

"Shuddup, you two," Glyn groaned. "Next cash we get's fer food, right?"

"No! Let's get some decent stuff. If we're all goin' ter flake it, let's go cheerful." Shaun rolled sideways off the bed and staggered to the window. "Not one bleedin' soul out there. Say, 'spposin' everyone's scapaed, we got the place to ourselves, eh? We kin take what we want."

"Where from?" Jenny asked. "You may not be able to see anyone, but they're all still there, waiting to be called. Fucking sheep."

"Show me a place I can't get inter, luv, even if there is somebody on the inside! The fuzz haven't got the time to answer nine-nine-nine calls: they're too busy shepherding the sheep. You lot comin'?"

"Didn' the Bailiff say the cops'ud be armed?" Carole picked at the remaining red varnish on her thumbnail.

"That's to stop people rushin' the boats." Shaun grinned through his dreadlocks. "C'mon. Let's go."

It wasn't that the others were wildly enthusiastic about the idea, but they had always followed his lead. He was the one who "found" money for food and fixes, even when it meant sending Jenny and Carole out after johns. "We might get a nice Chinese Take-Away," Glyn joked. "But where we gonna find crack?"

"Boyo's. Unless he's gone and taken his whack wiv him."

"If 'e's still around 'e'll carve us up!" Carole complained.

"Shut yer bloody whingein', yer silly cow. He'll 'ave gone off on 'is boat. But there may be a few snorts around still." Shaun gave her a shove and she nearly fell on the stairs. She shut up.

Across the road another curtain moved. Someone else had the same idea and intended to get to Boyo's place before Shaun's lot cleaned it out.

Margaret Ferbrache staggered upstairs with a cat basket in each hand, putting one down on the landing to turn the knob on her bedroom door. The spare room was already over-tenanted with yowling moggies and now she'd have them climbing all over her own bed. She looked at it longingly as she deposited her load, but wrinkled her nose. The room had begun to stink. It was hard to tell if the fear, frustration or pure exhaustion was getting her down, but she had an increasing desire to sit down and howl.

The phone rang downstairs. "How are you coping? Need any help?" Liz asked.

"Hi. Yes. Well I'd be okay but for the transport. I've made four trips and each time I get back to the Shelter there are more animals dumped there than when I left."

"You need Owen Clark. He has a lorry and is delivering loads of pets for us. I'll get him to call you if you like."

"Brilliant. That's a lifesaver . . . if you'll forgive the expression." They both giggled, but neither thought it was funny. "What are you doing about the cattle?" Margaret asked.

"Nothing, yet. All vets are keeping in touch on that score and taking turns in monitoring met, reports on radio."

"Had many calls from pet owners?"

"The phone never stops. Half of them are weeping and the other half seem to blame me, personally, for the situation."

"Really! What a nerve! Well, I'll wait to hear from you or this Owen Whatsisname. I'm going back to the Shelter now for another load. You might phone me there if he can come. Thank goodness the outside kennels all have electric light."

"Long may it last," Liz commented. Then wished she hadn't. At least she had Trish, Jackson and Polly with her: poor Margaret was all alone.

The moment Liz put the phone down it rang again. "Hallo. Is that . . . er the vet lady? Jackson Ridgeway's friend?"

"The same, David. I recognise your voice. Where are you?" The Alderney people had been evacuated to England, as far as she knew, and she wasn't looking forward to coping with his enormous hound for an indefinite period.

"In St James's Church."

"You mean you're in Guernsey?" She couldn't keep the relief out of her voice.

"I got a lift down on a fishing boat. Thought I could be

more use here than in England. I'm sorry about dumping Trouble on you. Is he behaving himself?"

"He is having a ball. We are loaded with animals here. When can you fetch him?" She listened to the ominous pause.

"Not entirely sure, actually. I've nowhere to stay . . . although I reckon most of the hotels must be empty by now. Is your brother helping . . ."

"My brother has taken his family to France. My phone is transferred here, to his place. We have turned it into an overloaded animal refuge," she added as the dogs broke into uproar.

"We?"

"Jackson is helping and so is my aunt . . ."

"They're still here?"

"Yes. When might we see you?" Though Trouble was behaving perfectly, he certainly ate three times as much as any other dog.

"I'm just about to take a busload of kids down to the White Rock. Then another load to the airport. I really can't say . . ."

"Forget it," she capitulated. "Join us when and if you can. You're doing a great job." She couldn't help wishing her job might be that simple.

Jackson came in as she replaced the receiver. "Would it help if I drive up to the surgery to see if there are any more animals?"

"Please. And bring as many as you can . . ."

She was interrupted by the phone again. Jackson kissed her on the forehead before she answered, and picked up his car keys.

Paddy ran down the uncarpeted stairs two at a time, Randy, Jock, Steve and the others close behind. Instead of following Shaun's bunch down Victoria Road, Paddy headed up to the top of the Grange, to cut along Queen's Road and down to the Charroterie. There were policemen on the corner who shouted at them, but they ignored them, and the guns they were carrying; there was no way a Guernsey policeman was going to open fire without the most serious reason. He and his mates were all in sneakers, fast and quiet. They had to get to Boyo's first. But they needn't have worried. Jenny and Carole were hungry and their first stop was the takeaway – much to Shaun's disgust. He was itching for a snort.

Margaret saw the body as soon as she drove in. It was a beautiful Collie bitch laid out carefully beside a tub of geraniums and with a note attached to her collar. "I have had to go with my sick father. Please will you cremate our darling Theo."

Tears filled her eyes. Oh dear God what do I do? Where can I put her? She bit her thumb, hard. She stared around at the various buildings, then blew her nose. Better get on with sheltering the living, she told herself, and headed for the kennels, leaving Theo beside the flowers.

Joe Thompson drove down to the Esplanade as the ships came alongside; the time was nine forty-five. His policemen, stationed across the access road to the White Rock jetties, paced restlessly. Along the Front houses blazed with light, and people were mostly outside their homes, gathered on the pavement, watching the ships, waiting their turn to be summoned. He hadn't the heart to over-react to their anxiety, and they were at least not wandering about or panicking.

The fleet of requisitioned vans, buses and cars had just about emptied all the hotels and guesthouses, Joe knew, and the White Rock was a solid mass of people. As Nugent had reported to the Bailiff, these too were mostly patient and good-humoured. But they knew they were getting away. His car radio bleeped. "Yes?"

"Hankey over in Torteval, skipper. We have some trouble."

"What trouble?"

"Some drunks have just left the pub and now say they're

not hanging about to be last off. They're coming into town."

"Well, stop them."

"Skipper, they have cars. I need more men."

"And I have no more men. Which pub, anyway? The licencee should be booked when this is over: those people should have been in their own houses. If they refuse to go home you must stop them coming into town. You have a gun."

There was a gulp over the airwaves. "You mean . . ."

"Tell them they must stay at home until we send for them. If they won't take any notice of you, shoot out their tyres. They're not likely to walk into town from Torteval."

"Shoot . . .! They'll sue us."

"Why the devil do you think you've been issued with a weapon? This island is under martial law, Hankey. Those people are not supposed to be out of doors, anyway. Send them home. And remember, if any of them come into town before they're sent for, I am going to have your stripes."

He drove down the length of the docks. People, who were now starting to board the ferries as well as the waiting hydrofoils, made way for the police car. Overhead, aircraft continued to drone into the night, both coming and going; they were the most reassuring aspect of the evening. He stopped the car and got out. Darwin was in his office, barking orders into telephones and radios. With him was Glen Mahy, acting as an extra deputy harbourmaster. "How's it going?" Joe asked.

"So far, so good. A few minor problems but we're sorting them out."

"What about the marinas?"

"A few owners jumped the gun. Including Mr Bloody Barrington and that creep Parker. I have their names and the names of their yachts. But most left in an orderly fashion. We're just about out of fuel, of course, and there have been some complaints because I'm not giving any to the yachts. The powerboats have to have priority."

"The yachts can't move without wind," Joe pointed out.

Darwin grinned. "When there is a wind, if it is from the west, they can all return to their moorings and say thank God. If it is from the east, they can clap on all sail and get the hell out of it. This fall-out, as I understand it, can't travel faster than the wind, so as long as they have a couple of hours start and keep going they should be all right."

Joe felt Darwin was being unreal; not even a sailing yacht can keep going forever – it would depend on how much food and water was on board. But he had more important things on his mind. "Any word on those destroyers?"

"Yes. They'll be here in about forty-five minutes."

"Thank God for that."

"They can only take about fifteen hundred apiece, you know," Darwin said. "And that's going to be more than they should."

"Fifteen hundred and fifty," Joe told him, and went back to his car. "I'm going to make room," he added to himself.

All of the inspectors and sergeants were out, having been made responsible for the various parishes. The exception was Bill Collins, who had been left in charge. He was looking haggard. "Problems," he told Joe. "There's been some kind of a brawl over in Torteval . . ."

"I know about that," Joe said.

"Did you know there's been gunfire?"

"I ordered it. Anybody hurt?"

"Well, no report of any casualties. But skipper . . ." the sergeant's voice rose an octave. He was appalled.

Another time, another place and Joe would have been amused by Collins' expression. Here and now he was only irritated. "Do you have any idea what might happen if a few dozen drunks got loose on the White Rock? Right now everything is going very smoothly, but it'd take only some incident like that to spark off a riot." He went upstairs to tell the Bailiff his idea.

"Are you suggesting we might need extra men?" The Bailiff's bushy eyebrows shot up in surprise.

"I'd rather be safe than sorry. I don't think we're going to get through this without some degree of trouble. I'm worried about young thugs like the ones we pick up on Saturday nights, high on drink and drugs. Some are islanders, but a goodly proportion are imported labourers who make trouble wherever they go. I know I wasn't happy when you authorised the arming of my men this morning, sir, but now I agree it was absolutely necessary. I've instructed Hankey to use their weapons out at Torteval if necessary . . ."

"What!" The Bailiff leapt to his feet.

Thompson stepped back. "Only to blow out the car and bike tyres of some drunks if they don't get indoors and stay there. As they've already been told."

Sir Hugh sat down again. "Where did you say you'd get these men?"

Joe breathed a sigh of relief. "From amongst the crew of the destroyers, sir."

The Bailiff wrote rapidly on a sheet of headed notepaper. "Here you are. There is an authorization. You'll have to get it signed by HE as well. Only use the men on the docks, and keep them out of sight, until and unless you have to use them."

"Will do." But Joe had his own ideas about that.

Boyo Wilson ran a guesthouse up the road from Trinity Square. He used this as a cover for bringing in the dope he peddled round the pubs and nightspots. The police knew about it, of course, and from time to time turned him over, without a great deal of success; Boyo was a past master at concealment. They also turned over his couriers at the docks and the airport whenever they could nail them amongst likely looking suspects, and did much better at this. Guernsey had a strict drugs policy, and conviction usually meant several months in gaol followed by deportation for non-islanders. But as Shaun had pointed out, Boyo had cut and run and there was no way he could have collected all his stock to take with him. Too risky: and Boyo never took risks himself. But when they got to the house, still eating the Chinese takeaway handed over by a threatened and terrified Oriental gentleman, they saw lights on. "Who do you reckon?" Shaun asked.

"That fucking Paddy and 'is lot," Glyn suggested.

"Shit! How many, d'you think?"

"I dunno. Maybe we'd better scapa."

"No way. Come on." Shaun's fingers closed on the flick-knife in his pocket as he went quietly up to the door; the lock had been smashed, and although the door was shut it opened to a push.

"Easy now," Glyn murmured over his shoulder to the girls, as he followed. "An' get rid of that mess." They dropped the foil and paper containers on the floor.

Shaun tiptoed along the hall, listening to sounds from the lounge. He peered through the dirty dreadlocks over his face, threw open the door and stood there, arms akimbo. Six heads turned. "For Jesus' sake, look what the cat brought in," Paddy remarked from the sofa.

"Well?" Shaun demanded. "Where is it?" Quite apart from the smell he could see that all the drawers and cupboards in the room had been torn open, and any container which might have held a packet of drugs had been smashed. The whole house had no doubt been thoroughly looted.

Casually Paddy attempted to peer past him, to see how many people he had with him. "You buyin'?"

"Funny joke," Glyn growled.

"Cut the crap . . ." Shaun strode in, still clutching the hidden knife, ". . . an' 'and it over."

"Now who's jokin'?" Paddy sneered as Randy and

Jock appeared from the kitchen, both with hands in their pockets.

It wasn't hard to guess what else was in their pockets: they hadn't ripped open the cushions on the chairs with their fingernails. And heavy feet were coming downstairs. Shaun decided to strike a bargain. "You can't take the stuff with you. So why not split it all round?"

"On the uvva 'and why the 'ell should we?"

The smell was getting to him. "Tell you what, the girls'll give you a trick each for a snort."

"Like hell we will," Carole screamed. "He's got the clap."

"I 'ave not. The doc's cured me. He's give me pills."

Carole pouted. She was keen for a share, too. She swung her hips, at once seductively and sullenly. "Gimme a snort, then."

Paddy had always fancied this bird. "Sure, baby. But you come upstairs with me."

Carole glanced at Glyn. "Snorts all round," Glyn said.

"Okay," Paddy said. "But we'll have her as well." He pointed at Jenny.

"Me first," Jack laughed, and led Jenny up the stairs behind Paddy and Carole.

"Beats me 'ow he can think about sex at a time like this," Randy grumbled, scratching the shaved stubble on his scalp.

"'E finks about sex all the time," Steve pointed out.

"Look 'ere," Glyn said. "What're you guys gonna do?"

Steve giggled. "Get higher an' higher."

"We should get the 'ell out of 'ere," Glyn argued. "This 'ouse ain't sealed."

"The man wants to live forever," Randy commented.

"Listen . . . them fuzz couldn't stop us getting in 'ere, right? They saw us, but they didn't stop us. So they won't stop us getting back out. If we was to do that, and get down on the dock, and mix in with the people there, we'd get away."

Randy looked at Steve. "Could work," Steve said. "We'll talk to Paddy, when he's finished with your Carole."

When the ships had cleared, the dock was strangely quiet. The buildings lining the esplanade were still lit – even if it was past midnight the occupants were not going to sleep – and the second destroyer could still just be seen in the distance, lights glowing eerily in the mist as she steamed out of the north end of the Little Russel.

"Condor One will be the next one back," Darwin said into the telephone. "ETA zero three hundred. Bring out your dead, Joe. Sorry, that wasn't very funny."

"It wasn't," Joe Thompson, now back at the station, agreed. "OK, Bert, listen. Paul Pritchard has reported that all the hotels and guesthouses seem clear. He's having a last check around now, but he reckons all the mothers and children and all the stretcher cases are gone, so we can ship islanders now, beginning with teenagers and then those on the esplanades. Right?"

"We've time. I'm not expecting the ferries back much before dawn," Darwin said. "But according to Nugent, there could be another couple of ships in before then: those other ferries he's chartered."

"Well . . ." Joe looked at his watch, "it's one now. That's only four hours off. My men are rounding up the school kids now. As soon as I get some idea of total numbers, I'm starting on the next area. But those kids will need keeping an eye on."

He hung up, and listened to the report Sergeant Collins was waiting to read to him. Things had quietened down over the past couple of hours: people had got the message that the police meant business. There might be an upsurge of trouble as some of the families were broken up, but there was nothing for it. Women and children first! He supposed that was a bit old-fashioned in these days of liberated women. But Guernsey was an old-fashioned place, for which he thanked God.

"I don't like Banning's report from the back of town," Collins was saying.

"Tell me."

"Well, you know what some of those streets are like. The so-called guest houses round there are really behind God's back, housing illegal tenants who are contravening the housing and labour laws. Half on them are on drugs . . ."

"You mean Boyo Wilson's customers?" Joe said.

"That's it."

"Didn't Wilson leave on his boat, earlier?"

"Yes, sir. But Banning reports there have been people in his house."

"What people? Friends of his?"

"Hardly. They smashed their way in."

"Well, tell Banning to go in and get them out."

"Yes, sir. He feels it may not be as easy as that. There has been a lot of activity in that neighbourhood, people coming and going, ignoring the curfew. Banning didn't want to come down heavy on it, in case he started something too big to handle alone."

"Listen," Joe said. "Tell him I'll send some blokes down to help get those people out. Tell him they'll have to use force if necessary. And if the beggars resist they are to be placed under arrest and brought in."

"Yes, sir. But what if the people are no longer there when he arrives?"

Joe looked up. "Just what are you trying to tell me, sergeant?"

"Banning reckons he has identified some of the ones who were in Wilson's house. He's pretty positive about Shaun Scott and his bunch, and a few of the Paddy Glasgow gang. But now some of them have gone."

Joe gave a grunt of exasperation. Wherever there was trouble on the island, one or other of those two were sure to be involved. Maybe he should have taken them into custody on some pretext, right at the start.

"Where were they heading?"

"He lost them, but he reckons they may have moved down towards the front."

"That's all we need. Right, sergeant. How is the round-up of school kids going?"

"Slowly, sir. You know, anguished farewells and far more luggage than they can carry. That kind of thing."

Joe nodded, and thanked God his daughter and her children lived in England. "Tell Banning if he gets any sight of those bastards, to bring them in. But he's not to leave his area to do it. When his reinforcements arrive he can move in to clean up the rest." Joe went upstairs to report to the Bailiff.

Sir Hugh asked if there were any more trouble spots anywhere, and was irritated to hear about the druggies. "How many are there?"

"A dozen or so, at the moment. But there are plenty more around and they usually have a teams of scrubbers in tow."

"A couple of dozen people are hardly going to disrupt an operation like this."

Joe hoped he was right.

Chapter 24

MONDAY, 25TH JULY – PRE-DAWN

The Condors loaded and surged away into the small hours of the morning. The planes continued to drone overhead. The destroyers, as predicted, were soon back, and the assembling of the under-eighteens commenced. The commanders of the two warships readily agreed to Joe's request for support, and fifty armed seamen from each ship came ashore. Despite the Bailiff's request, Joe had them marched up to the police station in full view of anyone who might be watching. He didn't want anyone to be in any doubt that the authorities meant to maintain control to the bitter end. By now it was just three, and the night seemed to have been going on forever.

The lights of the two chartered passenger vessels appeared at the north end of the Russel, calling for pilotage, as they did not know the waters. The two pilot boats, one from St Sampson's and one from St Peter Port, put out immediately, while Nugent, looking more harassed and weary than ever, but clearly enjoying himself, hurried in to the Bailiff. "We reckon that the entire school-age population can be accommodated on the two warships and one of those reserve ferries, sir" he told the Bailiff. "She'll be alongside in half-an-hour. That means that we can start loading the adults on the other vessel and our two ships as they come in. It's all in hand."

"You really are a hero, Nugent," the Bailiff said. "I'm

going to see you get recognition for this. I just can't believe it's all going so smoothly."

"Well, keep your fingers crossed."

"I am doing just that," the Bailiff said. "I . . ." he gave a gulp as one of the papers on his desk fluttered.

Nugent stared at it, and then at the east-facing window. "Oh, shit," he commented.

A phone jangled. "Just thought you should know, sir, the east wind is here." Walter Marquis sounded almost apologetic.

"Yes," the Bailiff said. "Strength?"

"It's about six knots, right now."

"Four hours from France. Nearly twelve from Barfleur."

"That's right, sir. But . . . I reckon it'll freshen come sun-up."

"I understand that. Right, Walter, you and your team have done a great job. Now you take yourselves home to your families. You'll be evacuated according to the schedule."

"We've been in contact with our families, sir. Our old folks and the kids are away, now. But with respect, sir, we feel we'd like to hang about a while longer. There could be another shift in the weather coming along."

"What do you mean?"

"Well, sir, there's a low out in the Atlantic trying to come in."

"A depression? You mean south-westerly winds?" He knew that while winds circulate round an area of high pressure in a clockwise direction, they circulate round a low in an *anti*-clockwise direction. A low in the Channel would bring south-westerly winds . . . if the high over France allowed it to develop.

"That's right, sir."

"How long have you known this?"

"Well, sir, it was on the charts yesterday. But you see, the normal pattern this time of year is that when a high builds, it holds off the rest of the weather. You have a succession of lows coming in, and being checked, so they sidle off round the top into Scandinavia. This one is different."

"You mean it's a hurricane or something?"

"No, no, sir. It's the high which is the maverick. It's there. The glass was over ten thirty millibars two hours ago. Now it's dropping again, weakening. I dunno if it's anything to do with this stuff in the air over there or what, but I'd say the low has a good chance of pushing the high back a bit."

"How good a chance, Walter? This could be a matter of life and death, quite literally."

"Well, sir, that kind of puts me on the spot. Everything depends on whether or not the high keeps on weakening. Right now, going on the normal pattern, I'd say the chances are maybe twenty-five per cent that the wind could shift back to the west some time during the next twenty-four hours."

"Twenty-five per cent," the Bailiff muttered.

"But the chances could improve, if the high declines."

"Thank you, Walter. But you still reckon there will be an east wind for the next few hours?"

"Well, sir, it's likely."

"Thank you, again, Walter."

"So if it's all right with you, sir, me and the others'll hang on here for a while, just to monitor the situation."

"You do that, Walter, and God bless you." He replaced the phone and looked at Nugent. "You hear that?"

"Yes. What are you going to do?"

"Oh to have a crystal ball. If the east wind is only going to blow for maybe twelve hours, perhaps we'd be better to keep everyone here, in sealed houses."

"That's not on, Sir Hugh. If the east wind blows for twelve hours, Guernsey could be totally contaminated. Everyone would have to move out anyway. So why not get them off while we have the chance? Or as many as we can."

The Bailiff nodded. "Keep them going for the time being, certainly. But I must have more information."

He punched the numbers of the direct line he had been given to the Home Office. There were no delays now; the seriousness of the situation brought an instant response. "I need to know the position of that fall-out, and whether or not radiation is still escaping from Flamanville . . . it's been capped? Oh, thank God for that. Now what about the fall-out? . . . Heavy concentration over the Bay of the Seine, yes . . . Le Havre being evacuated, yes . . . nothing too much west of Barfleur, yes . . . how far west? . . . Ten kilometres . . . right. Thank you very much."

Nugent was already at the huge map of the area which had been pinned to the wall. "Ten K," he muttered. "Just about over Cherbourg Airport. That's . . ." he used the dividers. "Fifty miles from Guernsey."

"Eight hours."

"If the wind doesn't freshen."

The Bailiff nodded. "Keep going with the evacuation."

He called Joe in. "We've got more than thirty thousand people off," he told the Police Chief. "And we should get another fifteen thousand away by dawn, and maybe another four by mid-morning. After that, unless Walter's miracle happens, we'll have to get the remainder under cover . . . rapidly. We're going to be left with around thirty-five thousand people in their sealed homes until we can get them out with protective clothing. I think we should stick to the original embarkation plan, which means a large percentage will be in the centre and over on the west side of the island."

"Most of them," Joe agreed.

"Right. Now those people have got to be put in the picture, but I'll delay broadcasting the information as long as possible, in the hopes that Walter Marquis will be able to give some more positive information on this approaching area of low pressure. However, I don't think we can delay longer than the sailings of Nugent's reserve vessels at five o'clock. By that time Willy Watts and his crew from the Emergency Command Centre will have alerted the next four thousand, and that will have to be the final four thousand, to go down to the dock for embarkation on the big ferries. Has all the protective clothing arrived?"

"We have about half what we need."

"Well, chase it up. For God's sake, those planes are coming in empty. Surely some more gear can be found in England and put on board one of them? All right, Joe. Good luck."

"If you can pass me another length of wire, I think I'll be able to finish off this last one," Jackson said. He was sitting astride the ridge tiles on top of Pierre le Tissier's house, his arms wrapped round a terracotta chimney pipe.

"Just a minute," Liz called back. "I'll have to cut it. Same length as before?"

"Yes. I'm going to turn the torch off until you're ready. It's going on the blink."

A few moments later Liz edged out of the attic window and started to crawl up the lead gully towards the ridge, the vital piece of wire clamped between her teeth. She didn't need torch light: there was no sea mist up here, and the half moon was bright enough to see where she was going.

"You okay?" Jackson asked.

"Mmmmm!" she responded.

"What's that supposed to mean?"

She paused to remove the wire. "That I don't speak too well with a mouthful of metal. Here, can you reach it?"

He flashed the torch in her direction. "Yeah. No problem. Now you can get back inside."

"No. I'll wait and help carry the tools down."

Jackson withdrew two thicknesses of heavy plastic sheeting from inside his shirt, placed them over the top of the last pot and weighted them in place with two lengths of wood. Then he passed the piece of wire round the back of the pipe, over the plastic, and began bending the two ends towards each other, as though tying a cloth over a Christmas pudding. "Thank heavens Pierre had the others sealed up when the central heating was put in. They're not nearly so accessible," Liz remarked.

"You call this accessible?" the American jeered, horribly aware that if he lost his balance he must be sure to fall to his left, into the shallow vee between the front and back roofs . . . to his right was a forty-foot drop.

"Just be glad this isn't a skyscraper!" Liz retorted without sympathy.

"Tell you what, it's suddenly gotten really chill up here." He had been on the roof for over half an hour.

Liz turned her face instinctively towards the soft breeze – and stopped breathing. "Oh my God," she muttered. "Oh God."

"What is it?"

"Wind, just starting up. From the east. It's always chilly when it comes from the east."

"East?" Jackson twisted his head round to face her and almost lost his balance. "East?" he clutched the pot in his arms. "Oh God! Oh my darling!" The torch flickered and went out. "Oh shit!"

"Liz!" Trish yelled from below. "A Charles Daley is on the phone. Says he needs to speak to you, urgently."

"Ask him to give you a message, or I'll call back."

Jackson could no longer see the ends of the wire so he had to keep twisting them by feel. "That's it, I think. Can you take these pieces of wood?"

"Oh, just chuck them down into the yard. I can take the pliers and cutters. You bring the rest." She felt sick. Right up to that moment she had only half believed it could happen. That the dreaded threat could actually reach her world. As long as there had been no wind the earth had stood still . . . along with the radiation. But now . . . Charles was going to summon her out into the fields at dawn, to start the slaughter of fine, healthy beasts.

Jackson closed the window very firmly behind him, and Liz passed him the roll of tape to seal it, in silence. When he had finished and cut off the tape, he put his arms round her. She breathed a long, shuddering gasp and exhaled into his shirt.

Downstairs, Trish relayed the dreaded message from Charles. "But before you go anywhere, you drink this up and go to bed for an hour. I don't expect you'll sleep but at least you'll be resting." She handed them each a cup of hot chocolate.

"What about all the animals here? They'll need . . ." Liz began.

"I'm in charge here and Polly is my second in command," Trish said severely. "You do your job. I'll do mine."

Liz gave her a thin smile and blew a kiss across the table. "You haven't had any sleep yet, either. And where is your lieutenant?"

"In bed, surrounded by cats, and sleeping like a baby."

Trouble lifted his head from the floor to watch Cocoa and Horlicks nudging their heads against Liz's elbow, spilling some of the chocolate on to her jeans, tongues competing to lick it off.

They didn't really need Press badges: virtually everyone in the island who mattered knew who they were. But they wore them nonetheless. Hank and Jane stood at the Weighbridge end of the White Rock, watching busloads of school-children arriving and being checked at the police barrier. "Reckon we have enough footage of this lot, don't you?" Hank said, lowering the heavy camera from his shoulder on to the top of its case on the footpath.

"Yes. You're right. We'd do better up at the far end, getting the ships as they enter." Jane had interviewed Bert Darwin and Chief Inspector Thompson, but still hoped for a chance to speak to some more of the evacuees themselves.

"How the devil can the police work out who's meant to be here and who is actually breaking the curfew?" Hank pondered.

"Either by their official badges or by age and description," Jane suggested.

"Well that lot on the other side of the old wall, opposite the cafe, don't look as though they fit into any likely category."

Jane stared in the direction he indicated. "You are dead right! I recognise those dreadlocks: that's Shaun Scott, one of the druggie bunch. What the devil is he doing down here?"

"Nothing legal, that's for sure. Amazing they haven't been spotted."

"In this crowd?" She stood still for a few minutes to gaze at the traffic, and the people. A fleet of buses were discharging their passengers in the customs enclosure, where police, harbour officials and volunteer workers, all displaying badges, herded the first adults into crocodiles, ready for embarkation. Police cars rushed up and down flashing their blue lights to clear their passage: an ice cream van was dishing out hot drinks and biscuits, and the WRVS Meals-on-Wheels van was parked alongside serving hot soup and rolls. Jane approached a young woman dressed in denims and sweatshirt, with a huge haversack on her back, who was clutching the handle of a pushchair containing a sleeping infant, while trying to hold onto a bawling two-year-old who wanted to "go see boaties". "What are you doing here?" Jane asked. "I thought all mothers with tinies were gone."

"I was down on the beach when the police first came round," the woman said. "Never realised what was happening."

"You've got your hands full," Jane commented into her microphone, as Hank started rolling the tape. "Do you mind if we ask what part of the island you've come from?"

"The Villocq. No, darling," she tugged at the toddler. "Look, this lady is going to put you on telly."

"Presumably your husband is unable to travel with you?"

The harrassed mother nodded. "He's in London on business. He hopes to join us in England at my parents home."

"Oh, good. You do have somewhere to go?"

Even in the weird artificial light her eyes looked sad and tired. "Thank God. But I only pray we can get back here within the next week. This is horrendous."

"Potty!" her daughter demanded.

"Surely not again! Well just a minute." The haversack was unslung and a plastic pot produced from under the pushchair, shoved under the child as she pulled down her pants.

An extraordinarily loud noise heralded a fearful smell. "Bigs!" the performer announced with pride. Hank's bulk shook with laughter . . . so did the camera.

"What the hell am I supposed to do with it?" groaned the child's parent, staring up and down the length of the crocodile.

Jane stared at Hank. He stared back . . . then lowered the camera and said, "Here. I'll take it," and holding the pot at arm's length raced out of the enclosure to the dockside to tip the offensive matter into the water.

Jane was still laughing as they reached the high walkway at the end of the White Rock. "Wonderful to discover you have a natural human streak. You should have been a father. You'd be a great dad."

"Bloody hot work!" He flapped both sides of his jacket to allow access to the cool breeze. "Whew! That's better."

"Is it?" Jane's voice was sombre.

"Ugh?" he stared at her, then swallowed hard. "Oh Jesus!"

They were facing out across the water, northeast towards Herm. Normally brightly lit up, it was only a dark shadow tonight; abandoned, not a single light was visible, only its outline silhouetted against the first lightening of the dawn sky. Hank turned to Jane, watching a wisp of hair drift across her face. "So this is it." He leaned against the granite wall. "Do you plan to leave, if it's possible?"

She shrugged. "Dunno. What about you?"

He opened his mouth . . . then closed it, and shook his head.

Jane touched his arm. "I go where you go, hon."

He looked down at her hand, then patted it and nodded. "If it takes a nuclear disaster to bring you round to my way of thinking, so be it." He grinned and punched her shoulder. "Look! Here comes the next boat. Kid, we got work to do."

The destroyers steamed out of the harbour, and the first of the two chartered ferries, which had been waiting in the roads, began her approach very cautiously, into the restricted area of St Peter Port. The spring tide was out, and there were large areas of uncovered mud and shingle. But the pilot got her safely alongside, and instantly the long queue of school children, mostly wearing uniform so that they could be identified as belonging to which school, began making their way down the sloping ladders.

Behind them, the police and civil defence workers began to call the people out of the houses along the esplanade, and here too patient queues were forming, clearly visible now in the first light. But by now, too, the chill breeze, and its direction, was apparent to all, and there was a good deal of muttering. The officials marshalling the lines were resolutely cheerful. "You'll soon be away," they told the anxious people. "No need to worry, you'll soon be away."

Sergeant Crowe strolled up. "Everything okay?" he asked, then frowned at a face he recognised, and then another. "What the hell . . . where did you come from?"

"Waiting to leave, sergeant," said Glyn Hardy.

Crowe looked over the ten faces. "You don't live on the esplanade?"

"We don't live anywhere, now, sergeant," Carole explained. "We've left home." She giggled.

"Yeah? Well, you come out of there. You go when the Victoria Road lot go. Won't be long now. Out."

He signalled his constables forward.

The waiting people watched, patiently.

"You want us to die?" Paddy shouted. "If we stay, we're gonna die."

"Be quiet, you little punk," Crowe said. "Nobody's going to die. You get back up to Victoria Road and wait your turn."

"You ain't got the right," Jennie shrilled.

"Right!" Crowe said. "If you don't move, now, I'm placing you under arrest. That way you don't get evacuated at all; you sit out the emergency in our cells. Come on!" He stepped up to the nearest of the group, and seized his arm. But this was Shaun, who had snorted more than any one, and who was regarding the morning through an euphoric haze, in which only hatred of men in blue was real. As Crowe seized his arm, Shaun whipped out his flick knife and drove it deep into the sergeant's tunic.

Chapter 25

MONDAY, 25TH JULY – DAWN

"Not a ruddy drop." Pierre sat on the edge of the pontoon and dangled his feet in the water; they were burning. "I'm pretty sure there is some, mind, but they aren't giving any to foreigners. Talk about the Common Market!" It was just light, and the marina at Perros-Guirec was just about empty; most of the French boats had left during the night. Now the tide was out, exposing, beyond the lock, a huge area of sand stretching a mile and more to the sea; no one was going anywhere for several hours.

But they wouldn't be going anywhere anyhow, without fuel.

The Le Tissiers had travelled very fast; the sea had been calm and it had been an exhilarating run. But although Pierre had topped right up before leaving St Peter Port, his tiny tank only held sufficient fuel to reach Perros; he had never doubted he would be able to fill up here – his requirement was so small – and get on down the coast. But Perros was just as agitated as Guernsey had been; the town was already largely evacuated in case the wind shifted.

Ros and Penny also trailed down the pontoon, shoulders drooping. "No bread. The *boulangerie*'s closed."

Annabel had been a tower of strength throughout the night. Now for the first time a note of panic crept into her voice. "What are we going to do? We've no fuel, very little bread, almost no water . . ."

Pierre sighed. He wondered if they should have stayed in Guernsey. If it hadn't been for the girls . . .

"There are a lot of people waiting at the bus stop," Penelope volunteered. "If we joined them, maybe they'd take us as well. I mean, they could hardly leave us behind."

Ros shivered. "Oh, that breeze is cold."

"It's from the east, that's why," her sister pointed out.

"Pierre!" Annabel said.

Pierre sighed again, and nodded. "Let's see if we can get on that bus."

"The satnav has gone off," Janet remarked.

"I know," Peter said. "I switched it off. We need to conserve battery power. That's why the radio is off as well, and the radar. And the auto-pilot." Not that there was any steering to do; there was no wind, and the ketch rolled gently in the swell. By his reckoning, Guernsey was only fifty miles away. Although in this mist it could have been five, and he still wouldn't have seen it.

"But don't you think we could use the engine again, for a little while?" Janet asked.

"Listen, woman," Peter said. "We used the motor for seven hours yesterday. That got us here. Because those damn fools wouldn't let us top up our tanks, we only have another seven hours fuel left. We may need those seven hours."

"But we can't just sit here and drift!" Janet wailed.

"There'll be a breeze at dawn," Barrington said confidently. "There always is. There! I told you so." He pointed to one of the tell-tales – thin bits of ribbon tied to the stays – which were fluttering and suddenly standing out straight. The ensign, which he had neglected to take in during the night, was also fluttering, and a moment later the sails began to fill, and the ketch moved through the water.

"Oh, thank God for that!" Janet said. "But . . . it's from the east!"

"Well, of course it's from the east. Blowing us where we want to go. Ushant and then all points south."

"But . . ." she peered back into the morning mist. "Those poor people in Guernsey."

Peter shrugged. "We just got away in time."

"We'll never be able to go back," she said.

"Well, of course we'll never be able to go back. We won't want to go back. No one will. Guernsey is going to become one large, empty, radioactive rock. Uninhabitable. Even the birds will shun it. Those that survive."

"It's a horrible thought."

"Well, *we'll* survive. Now look here, why don't you get below and make some breakfast? I'm starving." He grasped the wheel as the yacht began to yaw, seated himself behind it, and hummed a little tune. He enjoyed being at sea. And when he thought what he had left behind him . . . of course, he had also left his career behind him. But what career? He was due for retirement in two years anyway. They could not possibly cut off his pension because he had done the sensible thing and left. He'd sue them. In any event, all those who might complain about him leaving would be dead or dying. He knew their sort. They'd stay at their command posts in their roles of stalwart citizens until they dropped. Well, good luck to them; he had the boat, and a modest clutch of investments, and his pension . . . and Eddie Parker's thirty-two thousand pounds in cash, safely tucked away below.

He was still humming when Janet emerged with a plate of steaming bacon sandwiches. By now it was four o'clock and nearly light but the mist was still thick. He was very tempted to put on the motor for five minutes so that he could run the radar. He knew roughly where he was, of course, by dead reckoning, but with the strong tides around the Channel Islands there was always the chance of an error, and it was important that he approach Ushant from the right direction, so as to avoid the rocks which stretched out some distance. Should he use the Chenal du Four, inside the island, or should he stand out to sea? Might be better to keep well out. On the other hand he was still a good sixty miles off Ushant, so there was no great hurry to reach a decision; much would depend on visibility when he got there.

Janet sat on one of the cockpit benches, a cup of coffee held in both hands. "That tastes good. Look! What's that?"

Peter raised his head and peered into the murk. "What's what?"

"Thought I saw a flare."

"Out here?" Peter frowned, and then saw a faint red glow.

"There!" Janet said. "You must have seen that."

"Yes. I think we'll just make an alteration to course and give it a miss."

"Peter! You can't!"

"Look, if someone has got himself into trouble it's his lookout. Not ours. Right now it's every man for himself." He turned the helm, adjusted the sheets.

"Peter!" she snapped angrily. "If you don't go to help those people, I shall never speak to you again."

Peter stared at her in amazement. In their entire married life she had never dared address him like that.

"I mean it! What's more, when we get wherever we're going, I'm going to tell everyone how you ran out on the job in Guernsey. I'll sell my story to a newspaper." There was a wild look in her eye, her face was flushed and she was panting.

Silly bag! "Oh, all right," he snarled. "If you're going to start making a scene. I don't suppose it can do any harm, getting over there to see what's wrong." He turned the helm back again, re-adjusted the sheets.

"You should put the engine on," Janet said. "They could be sinking."

So let them sink, he thought. "They're not sinking. We'll be there in half-an-hour. Fetch up the glasses."

Janet obliged, and he levelled the binoculars, steering

with his knee. "One of those flash motor-cruisers," he commented. "Vaguely familiar."

"A Guernsey boat?"

"I would say so. Hell of a lot of people on board, jumping up and down. Oh, shit! They are very low in the water." He had no idea who they were, except they were flying a Guernsey Yacht Club pennant, and he had an urgent desire to shout at Janet to prepare to repel boarders. But she was already bending on the fenders for them to go alongside.

Katey Martel couldn't stop crying. She wandered round her home from room to room touching things, stroking her precious porcelain *objets d'art* on the drawing-room mantlepiece, wiping – imaginary crumbs off the kitchen counters, adjusting the angle of a heavy, antique carved chair in the lobby. Looking up, she caught sight of her reflection in an ornate gilt mirror . . . and screamed. "Katey! What is it?" Milford rushed to the top of the stairs. "Are you all right?"

"Of course I'm not all right!" she gasped. "Look at me!"

Milford stared down at her, frowning. He was utterly exhausted, having remained in his office throughout Saturday and Sunday, responding to frantic clients' worries and queries, finally arriving home two hours ago to collapse into bed. "I'm sorry but I don't see . . ."

"Are you blind? Look at my face," his wife wailed. "Look at my mascara! Have you ever seen such a mess?"

"Have you woken me up to tell me your mascara is running! Doh! Pull yourself together! Are you packed, yet?" Dumbly she shook her head. "Well for heaven's sake get on with it while I try to get some sleep." He stamped back to the bedroom and slammed the door.

Neither of them slept, of course. Both Liz and Jackson agreed it would be an awful waste of time. Instead they clung to each other, kissing, caressing, occasionally whispering questions, wanting to know every detail of the other, both mental and physical. Pale pink light was sihouetting the curtains when Trish knocked on the door. "Come in!" Liz called, pulling up the sheet.

Trish, in kimono and mules, carried a tray bearing two mugs of tea and two thick slices of toast and marmalade, and placed it on the bedside table. "Four o'clock, my dears. Did you sleep?"

"You darling! The best aunt in the world!" Liz passed a steaming mug to Jackson. "No. I don't think we did. What about you?"

Trish grinned. "Not a lot. But there are some healthy snores coming from behind Polly's door."

"Any more news?"

"I must confess I turned off the radio for a while. But I've had it on for the past half hour and there's been no further announcement, save to say that they're hoping to have all the school-children loaded in the next hour, and to alert the adults along the front that they're next. Pity Pierre never thought of living down there, isn't it?"

"Well," Liz said, ignoring the quip. "I suppose we'll have to get on with it." This was not a day she was looking forward to.

"We'd better take those awful looking suits with us," Jackson said.

They had loaded up the car with the suits, Liz's medical case and extra supplies, and were waving good-bye to Trish, when a very large cyclist wobbled into the yard on a very small bike.

"David!"

The newcomer placed both feet on the ground and allowed his mount to continue without him. "Why in God's name do you have to hide away in the depths of the country?" he asked, grinning. "I've been on that confounded machine for nearly an hour!" He rubbed his sore bottom.

"Ouch!" Trish exclaimed, clinging to the front doorpost

to regain her balance as a huge white form hurtled past her and leapt at David.

The latter collapsed on the paving stones, motionless, while Trouble washed his face several times. "Thought I'd got rid of you for good." He tried to sit up. "Okay, okay. That's enough. Have you been behaving yourself?"

"Perfectly," Liz said. "But we are pleased to see you. When did you last eat or sleep?"

"Some charming ladies have plied me with sausage rolls and cake, from time to time. But I've lost track of days so I can't answer your other query."

"Take him in and look after him, will you Trish?" Liz slammed the car door. "Sorry we can't stay. Trish will explain, but you're welcome to remain if you wish."

Charles Daley was waiting in the driveway outside his surgery with a number of other vets. There were several boxes stacked by a garage door, all stencilled with a skull and crossbones. No need to speculate on the contents of those, Liz thought.

Winifred Potts was last to arrive, gravel flying onto the flower borders and she braked to a sharp stop. "Sorry I'm late, boys. Couldn't leave till I'd fed all my house guests."

"No humans, I imagine," Liz smiled. "How many have you?"

"A horse, two donkeys, a pair of Great Danes and innumerable other canines including a chihuahua. And I've lost count of the cats. How about you?"

"I honestly haven't the faintest idea, but at least I have moved into my brother's old farmhouse and I've folks back there dishing out feed. By the way, this is a good friend of mine, Jackson. He's acting as my assistant today."

"Bully for you. Maybe if I was your age I'd find a friend, too." Then she cocked her head on one side to contemplate Liz's diminutive figure and added, "But on the other hand, maybe not!"

Charles had spread a map of the island on the bonnet

of his estate car. "Would you all gather round, please, hopefully armed with your Perry's Guide Books, and make note of your designated areas of responsibility."

They crowded round the car but not everyone could see at once. There were questions and suggestions and the meeting took over half an hour, by which time Charles's wife had arrived in her Metro, with a boxload of thermos flasks of hot coffee. "Drink up, everyone," she ordered. "Sorry there are no scones and cream. You'll have to put up with biscuits." Like several of the others she was desperately trying to lift people's spirits, without noticeable success. Most of the vets obligingly drank her coffee, but no one had any appetite for mixed fancy biscuits at four-thirty in the morning, especially in view of the task ahead.

Charles disappeared indoors and returned a few minutes later looking grave. "Well that's it I afraid. The met. office has informed the Bailiff, who has just informed me, that with this easterly wind we can anticipate the radioactive fall-out here by noon." There was a groan from the others.

"I don't know about you folk, but this surgery and our home are both stuffed full of animals. We cannot accommodate any more. I suggest that each surgery should have at least one person in attendance, an assistant if possible, while the rest get on the road to the other patients. Remember, they cannot come to us without breaking the curfew. So we, displaying our permit badges, must go to them. I assume you all have made lists. Apart from which, all farms must be visited by whoever is designated for that area. We may be taking on each other's clients, but time is too short for professional niceties."

"What about domestic pets outside our areas?" Winifred asked.

"I suggest you do them as and when you can, according to your route."

"What is this Perry's Guide?" Jackson asked when they were back in Liz's Volvo.

"Just a detailed road map of the island. Jolly useful. Here," she opened it at the appropriate page. "We are here, and our first call will be down this road . . ." she turned the page, ". . . here."

They drove in silence until Liz drew up at a gateway in a narrow lane. A middle-aged man opened the door. "Yes? Oh, it's you, Mrs Cobb. Come in. What can I do for you?"

"I'm on a sad mission, Mr Dorey. I have to ask you if you intend leaving the island and if so, what do you intend to do with your pets and your two cows?"

He wiped his hand over his bald pate. "The wife and I are staying, so we can look after the animals ourselves."

"That's fine for your house pets, but you do understand that you must seal up your house and not open the door till you are told it's safe."

"Yes. We know. We've put tape round all the windows and we'll keep the doors closed all the time, except for doing the milking."

Liz grasped his arm. "No, no. You cannot do that. You cannot open the door otherwise you will be contaminated by radioactive dust. Then you'll bring it into the house and contaminate everything inside, including your wife."

"Haven't I been telling you that, Stan, for the past day?" His wife had appeared and spoke over his shoulder.

"I can't believe it!"

"You must believe it, Mr Dorey. You must get your cats and the dog inside, and keep them here. And keep a big stock of newspapers ready for their toilet facilities."

"That won't help much with the cows!"

She shook her head. "That's why I'm here. They will have to be put down."

"I told you, Stan."

Liz thanked heaven that one of them had some sense. Later, she looked at her watch as Jackson drove the Volvo away up the lane. "That took over half an hour! We won't get anywhere near halfway before midday."

Jackson felt so sad for her. She had devoted herself to

the lives of animals, and having just watched her lead two fine, healthy young cows out into a field, well away from the cottage, kill them both and pour formaldehyde over the corpses, he was near to tears himself.

The next house was sorely in need of paint, and surrounded by the evidence of recent young children. A swing and a climbing frame stood in knee-high grass, a one-time lawn, discarded and broken toys lay everywhere. "Mrs Parry rang up before leaving with her brood, to say the two dogs are in the kitchen. She's left the door unlocked," Liz muttered.

The two chow bitches, mother and daughter, greeted Liz as a long lost friend. Hypodermic in hand Liz led the mother into the utility, leaving Jackson to scratch the ears of the younger one.

Leaving there, Liz doubled up in the passenger seat, her face buried in her hands. Now they were heading for Mr de la Mare's farm.

Eddie Parker was safely in port, enjoying a breakfast of fresh bread and a bottle of wine. Around him the locals were obviously discussing the Flamanville explosion: he couldn't understand the lingo but but didn't need to for words like *radioactivité* and *nucléaire*. A Breton fisherman pointed through the open window at the flag on a yacht mast, flapping in the breeze. Another pointed west to the Atlantic. The patron shrugged. Nobody knew what the wind would do, least of all himself. But having paid several times the normal price to refuel for a quick getaway if necessary, Eddie was quite content to remain here, waiting to see if Guernsey became contaminated – or not. Because if not, he was belting back to the island at full speed: there would be fast bucks waiting for anyone with an eye to business. Barrington's wasn't the only house on which he'd put a low deposit; and he'd picked up a couple of dozen cars at giveaway prices. He'd sold two big cabin cruisers the same day he'd bought them – they had netted a cool twenty-five grand profit each, and his offer for the

Hotel Corbelets had been accepted – with signatures. He rubbed his palms together. If only he could rub a lamp and get some genii to produce a good sou'westerly, he could classify himself in the millionaire bracket overnight!

"It's very damp in here," Molly Brache complained as she filed into the German Underground hospital with her elderly mother-in-law and her two unmarried sons. Like all the other people coming in, they were carrying sunbeds and blankets and boxes of food and drink.

"Like I say, we'd have done better to stay home," the old lady moaned. "I can't sleep on one of them things."

"We told you, Gran, we couldn't seal up the house properly. There was nothing for it, we had to come, eh?" Wayne said. He and his brother Louis had agreed it would be more fun down here, rather than stuck home with Ma and the old lady. So they'd invented the excuse about not being able to fill in all the cracks and gaps round the doors and windows.

"The only thing you're here for is girls," Gran grumbled, "I'm not daft, like some." She stared at her daughter-in-law's back.

Louis giggled, and Wayne turned round to frown at him to shut up. "Here you are, ladies," said a tall man with a moustache and a badge. "Would you like to settle down beside Mrs Tostevin and Mrs Torode." It was an order, not a question. "No, no. Not you, gentlemen, I'm afraid. You will be further on in the next ward with the men."

"You mean my sons cannot stay here with us?" Molly demanded.

"They can visit you during the day, but I'm sure you will agree it is better for the sexes to be segregated at night."

"Hah!" laughed the old lady, grinning at her grandsons. "That'll thwart your little plans, eh?"

"What do you mean, Ma?" their mother demanded. "They're good boys, looking for the best for us all."

"Oh yes? And pigs might fly." Gran sat down on the

end of a sunbed, which tipped, and in the kerfuffle to pick her up and dust her off, the boys were led away to their quarters. There were people lining the walls all the way along. People in an odd assortment of clothes, some in heavy winter gear, sweating, others shivering in tee-shirts and shorts.

"This looks like a flea market," Wayne said to his brother, eyeing the miscellaneous piles of bedding, clothes, suitcases and cardboard boxes.

Louis was looking over his shoulder. "Say, did you see those birds down there?" he asked, and tripped over someone's feet.

"Look where your going, you daft bugger," snarled the owner.

"Daft bugger yourself, sticking your bloody great plates of meat in the middle of the road!" Louis framed up and flexed his muscles.

"Give over, Lou. Let's get this gear dumped, then we can take a walk and size up the talent."

The man with the moustache pretended not to hear. He undid the shirt button under his tie and eased his neck. It was going to be hell down here.

Adele jumped up from her chair when the phone rang. "Yes?"

"Mum, are you three all right?"

"It's Glen, Ma," she said with her hand over the mouthpiece. "Of course, love. We're fine. But what about you? Are you coming home?" Glen had been supposed to leave today, in normal circumstances, to rejoin his ship. But these weren't normal circumstances.

"Not until all the boats are away. You haven't changed your minds about going, then?" He wished they would, but with memories of the German Occupation still in mind, they were reluctant to leave home. Anyway, there might not be time, now.

"No, we're staying. Do you want to speak to your father?" She passed the phone to John.

The two men discussed the latest news, and Glen tried to change his father's mind. But John could see his wife tilt her head towards the old lady, and wave a negative finger. "We'll not seal up the back door till you're in, Glen. So hurry home." He replaced the receiver. "He's a good boy, that one. And to think they made him face that inquiry." He still hadn't got over the anger of that embarrassing event.

"Never mind, John. After today they'll all have egg on their faces, eh?" his mother nodded over her knitting. "Adele, have you got plenty more wool? If this is going to be a long business, I'll have time to make at least one more jumper."

"More than enough, Ma. Now, do you reckon that gache is risen enough to go in the oven, yet? If so, I can start making the Guernsey biscuits."

John grinned. "Doesn't sound as though we're going to starve, whatever else happens."

Glen Mahy had just finished speaking with his father when a sharp exclamation from Darwin had him hurrying to the window to stand beside the harbourmaster. "What the hell . . .?"

To their right, and occupying the outer arms of the White Rock dock, were the long lines of patient school childen, filing on board the first of the small ferries, the *Bristol Queen*. The second, the *Torquay Belle*, waited her turn, unable to get alongside because of the low tide. Behind her, the Little Russel was shrouded in fog, and Herm and Jethou, as well as Sark, were invisible. And empty. To the two seamen's left, the first of the adults had been marshalled at the land end of the dock, waiting to start boarding the very moment there was space. Both Nugent's passenger vessels had reported that they were south of Alderney, only twenty odd miles away, although they had had to reduce speed because of the poor visibility. In front of them the last of the yachts and pleasure cruisers waited to leave the marina, as soon as the tide came in.

So far the evacuation had gone off with exemplary patience and good humour, and discipline, but now they saw the head of the adult line suddenly dissolve, people moving each way, while someone collapsed on to the ground. "That's a policeman!" Glen shouted, and ran for the door.

"Stay put," Darwin commanded. "Our job is here."

"But for God's sake . . ."

Sergeant Crowe uttered a groan and fell to his knees, and then to his face. "You bastard!" shouted WPC Howard, swinging her truncheon at Shaun's head. He jumped backwards, the knife thrust out in front of him.

"You just drop that," yelled PC Nichols.

"Sod off!" Shaun screamed at him, then turned towards the crowd. "Scatter!" He swung the knife in a menacing circle.

Glyn and Jenny ran towards him, shoving the policeman and woman aside. Shaun and Carole ran at the people behind them, followed by Paddy's lot. For a moment the law-abiding citizens hesitated, but the sight of the flick-knives drove them back. Howard had dropped to her knees beside the sergeant. "God, he's badly hurt," she muttered as she saw the blood welling through the tunic. She thumbed the mike on her shoulder radio. "Howard on the dock," she snapped. "There's trouble. We need an ambulance, fast. And support."

"Stop those people!" Nichols was shouting, but the orderly lines of people had now become a milling mass, many bolting in terror. Nichols blew his whistle repeatedly.

That alerted Sergeant Carling down near the White Rock roadway. People flooded past him, away from the ship, shouting and screaming. "A man's been stabbed!"

"A policeman!"

"There's nutters down there, with knives."

The crowd was spreading right across the approach road, leaving the policemen helpless; their orders were to stop people rushing the docks out of turn – they had been given no instructions about what to do if people starting running *away* from the docks, out of control. As for who had started the trouble . . . "You stay here," Carling told his two special constables, and ran along the dock to where Crowe lay.

Howard was sobbing. "He's dead," she said. "I think he's dead!"

"You've called an ambulance?" Nichols asked. She nodded.

"But what *happened*?" Carling demanded.

"That Shaun Scott mob, together with Paddy Glasgow and his lot. They decided to jump the queue. Sergeant Crowe told them to get on out of it, and Scott knifed him."

"You're sure it was Scott?"

"I was right here, sarge."

"And they've run off with the mob, is that it?"

"Most of them," Howard said. "Two others were heading for the car ramp."

"Right. Go get them. They have knives, but you have a gun. Use it if you need to, but get them!"

Howard stood up and looked along the dock to where the last of the school children were still boarding, but now distinctly wavering, their teachers shouting at each other, unsure what had happened in the misty dawn gloom at the other end of the dock road. "If the bastards are mixed in with that lot," Nichols said, grinding his teeth in fury . . .

"Go get them," Carling said again, listening to the wail of the ambulance.

"What the hell has happened?" Joe Thompson demanded of Bill Collins.

"There's been a knifing on the dock, sir," Collins replied. "One of our people is hurt."

"Good God! You mean someone tried to rush the queue?"

"I don't know, sir. They seem to think it was one of the drug mobs."

"Have they rounded them up?"

"Afraid not, sir. But they will."

"They'd better." He went in to the Bailiff.

"What's happened down on the dock?" Sir Hugh wanted to know; the screams had been clearly audible all over town.

Joe told him. "I should've used the emergency powers and locked that scum up," he growled. "*Before* they could start trouble. Now they're loose."

"You'll get them, Joe," the Bailiff said reassuringly. He had worse things on his mind than even a stabbed policeman. "The Home Office has just been on. The French report that radiation levels have fallen over Barfleur and the Bay of the Seine, but have risen rapidly west of Cherbourg. They've capped the reactor, so nothing is escaping from there. That means the wind has reversed the drift and now the cloud is definitely headed our way. London estimates it's already approaching the French coast."

"And we have about six knots of wind," Joe muttered. "Then it's four hours away."

"At the very most, if the wind freshens as the temperature rises. So, we're talking about an hour and a half from Alderney, and two and a half from Sark."

"Well, they're both clear of people, anyway," Joe said. "As far as we know."

"If anyone was foolish enough to stay, there is nothing we can do about them now. Where are Nugent's big ships?"

"Just entering the Russel. But they can't both get in the harbour together at this state of tide, and the reserve ferries are still being loaded."

"I realise that. However, presumably they can both be loaded and away in two hours?"

Thompson stroked his nose. "Make it three. We have a fair amount of panic to sort out down there."

"Right! Three. That will be eight o'clock. That will have to be it. The Home Office asked if we wanted the destroyers back again, and I said no. We just cannot take the risk of having several thousand people exposed on the dock when that cloud gets here. I am going to make an announcement now, that after the two regular passenger ferries sail, that is it. Everyone else must remain indoors until we can assess the level of radiation over the island, and equally until we can obtain sufficient protective clothing to equip them and the crews of the ships which will have to take them off. I am also ordering the cessation of all flights as from eight o'clock. The same goes for Condor."

Joe gulped. "Yes, sir. Am I allowed to bring out those sailors?"

Sir Hugh frowned. "Are you sure it's necessary?"

"Well, sir, as I said, right this minute people are in a very excited state, at least down on the front. And we know we've got a gang making trouble down there as it is."

"But the people on the front are guaranteed to get off."

"Well, sir, not all of them. Nugent's ships can carry maybe two thousand each, at a pinch, but we have about six thousand who were officially resident down near the front, according to our census figures. Added to which we cannot estimate how many have jumped the gun. We suspect that there has been a lot of infiltration done by friends and relations over the past twenty-four hours."

"Put your sailors on stand-by," the Bailiff said. "But we are not going to take any chances of *provoking* trouble. So keep them out of sight. I want that clearly understood, Joe."

"Yes, sir." Joe was clearly unhappy. "If I have to use them . . ."

"You will refer to me first."

"Yes, sir," Joe said.

Blue light flashing, siren screaming, the ambulance sped

down the road from the dock. People who had fled in panic from the flick-knives and were now moving back towards the ships, hurriedly stepped aside to allow it to pass. Before the ranks closed again a cavalcade of cars and motorbikes roared up, horns blaring.

"Oh Jesus!" Carling thumbed his radio. "Tell the Inspector that the Torteval lot have arrived, *en masse*. I'm waiting instructions and assistance." He followed the newcomers at a run, the specials hard on his heels.

Chapter 26

MONDAY, 25TH JULY – MORNING

"God!" Liz muttered. "I don't know how much longer I can go on."

"You have gone on one hell of a lot longer than I could've done," Jackson told her. "When they're handing out medals . . ."

"Hold on." The music on the car radio had stopped suddenly, and now she recognised the Bailiff's voice. She turned up the volume.

". . . there now seems little doubt that the cloud will be over us by noon at the latest. I have therefore taken the decision that the ships about to start loading will be the last, as anyone in the open after nine o'clock will take the risk of being exposed to a lethal dose of radiation. All flights will also be terminated at eight o'clock. Now, I must tell you all, and this applies also to those who are carrying out essential services, that when the sirens sound, which will be when our monitors in Alderney and Sark tell us that the cloud is imminent, you must immediately take shelter. I know many service personnel have been issued with protective clothing, but even so you should take shelter until the exact amount of radiation to which the island is exposed has been ascertained. You will be informed by radio as soon as it is safe to proceed with your duties. I wish you to understand how heavy my heart is today, that such a disaster should have overtaken this island which we all love so well. I can only again ask you to keep the faith and believe that we shall, somehow, surmount even this ordeal. God bless you all." The radio started playing Land of Hope and Glory.

"Well," Jackson said.

"Oh, my darling!" Liz turned into his arms. "What exactly do we die of? First degree burns?"

"No, no, you're thinking of an atomic blast. If you receive a lethal dose of radiation, well . . . I suppose the short answer is acute leukaemia. Your hair drops out and you begin to waste, while your blood is turning to water. No doubt a doctor would put it more technically than that."

"How long?"

"Sometimes several years. Depends on the strength of the dose, I suppose, and how long the exposure to it." He kissed her hair.

"I had imagined it would be much quicker than that."

"It can be. A really heavy exposure can result in serious diarrhoea and vomiting and death in twenty-four hours. A slightly more moderate dose and one might last a month." He released her. "What do you want to do now?"

"It's not yet six. Let's get on with the job." She forced a smile. "After nine, we're going to have a lot of time to spare."

Chief Inspector Thompson's car raced on to the White Rock, blue light flashing, siren screaming, with the police personnel bus and the two white, misnamed, Black Marias in hot pursuit. The chaos in front of them was obvious; legitimate evacuees were cowering behind buildings and walls while a band of drunken louts were fighting and shouting obscenities at the people on the lowered car ramp.

Carling strode up. "Some of that lot have got on board. The ship was already three-quarters loaded, and the captain has radioed the Harbourmaster's office to say that most of the kids are holed up in the lounges. The crew have closed up the bulkheads to keep the drunks confined to the car deck."

Thompson pulled at his nose. "Hm. Hold on a minute. Get me the Bailiff," he said into his radio, and waited. "Hello? Thompson here, sir. Big trouble on the dock. A hundred or so drunks brawling and preventing embarkation. Can we move in with arms?" Carling saw him nod with a grim smile on his face.

It took less than a minute to unload the bus. The men knew what they had to do and stormed down onto the ramp, firing into the air. Within ten minutes the Black Marias and the bus, together with several commandeered cars, were full, their passengers looking down gun barrels as they were driven off to the Police Station to be packed, like sardines, into the limited cell space.

Like the Bailiff, Thompson had been dubious about the public reaction to the use of weaponry . . . but they need not have worried. An elderly woman stepped out from behind a shed, put her suitcase down and began to clap. Others followed and suddenly a great cheer went up. "Nice to be appreciated, isn't it, Carling?" Thompson said, waving to the audience. "Just fancy them responding like that on the worst day of their lives." A lump was developing in his throat.

"What'll you do with the prisoners?" Carling asked.

"When they've been charged, we'll take them out to Torteval, near their homes. Can't just lock 'em up and leave them. Unfortunately."

"Well, that's that, Joe," the Bailiff said, when Thompson returned. He looked out of the window; it was going to be a perfectly beautiful day when the mist cleared, with hardly a cloud in the sky. Save for the invisible cloud of death which was steadily approaching. He had meant what he had said on the radio: he just could not believe that this was happening to the island, where he had been born and bred, and which had been placed in his keeping. "There's not too much time. Sort out the last evacuees, and get everyone else into their houses. Then have your men ready to take shelter." Joe Thompson nodded, sighed, and left the room. The phone buzzed. The Bailiff picked it up. "Yes?"

"Walter Marquis, here, sir."

The Bailiff's head jerked. "Yes, Walter!"

"Pressure is definitely falling, sir. And quite fast. I've had a report from Ushant. Ten zero zero three millibars. Wind south-westerly, Force One, but it's certain to freshen."

"What did you say?"

"It's coming this way, sir."

"How quickly?"

There was hesitation on the other end of the line. Then Walter said, "We're talking in hours, sir."

"How many hours, Walter. We still have a light easterly here, and that cloud is crossing the coast of France right this minute. That means it's four hours away, if the wind doesn't freshen."

"It won't freshen, sir. Not now. Not with this big one coming up."

"But will your low get here before those east winds?"

"Well, sir . . . I can't say. But it'll be here by this afternoon, for sure."

"This afternoon," the Bailiff muttered. "Very good. Thank you, Walter. Keep me informed."

He replaced the telephone. This afternoon! But it was the next four hours that mattered. He dared not reverse his decision. He dared not even make an optimistic announcement, for fear of causing widespread disruption, with people uncertain whether to go or stay, take shelter or not . . .

"That's the last one," said Purser Middleton. The ferry was crammed, young people standing several deep on the decks, every available space below taken, even the cabins filled with youthful humanity. As the huge steel ramp was raised and the inner doors clanged shut a great wail went up from the two hundred still waiting in patient lines. "Don't worry," the purser shouted down to the nearest ones. "Our sister ship is just out there. She'll be in the moment we leave, and you'll all be boarded." He used his radio to the harbour office. "*Bristol Queen* pulling out, Captain Darwin."

"Good luck," Bert replied.

Glen watched through his binoculars as the great vee of her bow was lowered into place over the raised car ramp and the ship moved astern. "God, she's crowded. We're lucky the sea's so calm."

"Can't lose 'em all," Darwin muttered. "*Torquay Belle*, would you prepare to come in please. Sergeant Carling, would you and the dock wardens move six hundred people down to the outer berth, ready for boarding."

"Will do," Carling said. "If I can round them up." The people who had scattered from the gangs of thugs were starting to reassemble, but the confusion was complete; many had dropped their suitcases and carryalls, and now there was some argument as to who had been in front of who in the line. "Come along, now," the sergeant bawled. "Come along." He signal his special constables and the wardens to act like sheepdogs, and get the line under control again.

"What do you reckon?" Jim Nichols asked. "They must've got past us, and back into town." It wasn't until after the Chief had driven away, in the wake of the loaded Black Marias and the bus, that WPC Howard thought she saw Glyn Hardy running into one of the dock sheds. The two police constables had searched through the building, then every nook and cranny at the end of the White Rock, investigating the toilets and the various closed and locked ticket offices.

"No way," Amy Howard objected. "We'd have seen them. They're here somewhere, Jim."

"Well, then, they must be on the levels under the dock," Nichols said. "I'd better go down."

"Be careful," Amy begged.

Nichols drew the revolver with which he had been issued. As with every police officer, he was familiar with weapons and did his turn on the firing range . . . but he had never anticipated ever having to use it on a human being, not in Guernsey.

The tide had been out long enough by now for the steps to the deserted lower levels to be dry, but he still placed his boots very carefully, reassured to hear Amy's heavy shoes behind him. It was broad daylight now, despite the clinging mist, but Nichols nonetheless used his torch, held in his left hand, sending its beam to and fro from one huge square concrete pile to the next. Amy Howard followed, using her flashlight as well, and it was she who exclaimed, "Oh, my God!"

Nichols turned round sharply, gun thrust forward, and saw the foot just protruding from round one of the pillars. Amy had fallen to her knees. One violent death in the island was more than she had ever expected to face . . . and here were two more! Jenny had been stabbed at least twice. The teenage boy lying beside her had been strangled, quickly and expertly . . . and then stripped to his underwear. His body lay in a crumpled heap. "Oh, God," Amy muttered again, and vomited.

Nichols felt like doing the same. But as he had begun his career in Liverpool's notorious Moss Side his stomach was more inured; he had spotted the pile of filthy clothing lying to one side. He thumbed his mike. "Sarge," he gasped, forgetting about code procedures. "There's two more bodies down here. Knifed! Glyn Hardy has killed his girl friend and he's probably got on board one of the ferries . . . wearing school uniform!"

Carling had the next batch of six hundred evacuees – mostly adults – marching down the dock, while Inspector Lucas had arrived to take charge of summoning the following group. People were now flooding out of their houses from along the front and from the small streets behind, clutching their suitcases and their bundles. A line of buses waited to carry the less able down to the docks. "There's one hell of a lot more than four thousand," muttered PC Nolan.

The entire front was jammed with people, a dozen abreast; the line even stretched up St Julian's Avenue, and that certainly was not on the front. "Well, keep counting," Lucas told him, as people filed past him. They had simmered down to a considerable extent after word of the stabbing had been passed around, but there was little humour left now; everyone was grim-faced and anxious . . . only a few noticed that the breeze had dropped again, and it was once more flat calm. No one found any cause for hope in that.

Horns blared and a police car came down the hill. People parted reluctantly, and there was some swearing. Joe Thompson braked beside Lucas. "Hold your people here for five minutes," he said. "There's more trouble down the end of the jetty. Did you hear?"

Lucas shook his head. "I've been kind of busy."

"Right. Well, there have been two more deaths and one of those beggars is still on the loose. We reckon he's got on board one of the ferries wearing a dead kids' clothes. You'd think their friends would have noticed one of their lot being taken off by a bastard like Glyn Hardy."

"They were all in such a state of panic, and it was dark down to a little while back, what with this mist . . ."

"Well, hold these people here while I sort it out." There was much grumbling from those held back, and even more when the two police cars reached the end of the dock and Joe called a halt to any further embarkation. Only some hundred of the waiting adults had got on board as yet. "We won't be long," he explained, and ran up the service gangway, followed by three armed detectives.

"What's the problem?" Purser Jones asked.

"You could have a murderer on board. Disguised as a schoolboy."

"No way," Jones objected. "I'd have spotted that."

"Nevertheless, I must search the ship."

"That'll take you a while," the Purser pointed out. "I thought you were in a hurry to get these people off?"

Joe bit his lip. Then he squared his shoulders. "I must search the ship. You get your crew together. They can help."

"What about the other one, skipper?" asked Collins, who had accompanied him down. "She was still loading when those two were killed."

"Shit, yes," Joe said. He peered into the mist. The *Bristol Queen* was just visible as she turned up the Russel; passing her was the first of Nugent's main line ferries, waiting her turn to get into the harbour. "You have a boat, haven't you, Bill?"

"Yes," Collins agreed, cautiously: he owned a small, shallow draught motor boat.

"Can you get her out?"

Collins nodded in the direction of the St Peter Port pool. "I have a deepwater berth."

"Right. Radio that ship to stop and await a boarding party. Then get out there with two constables. And Bill, make sure you're armed."

Collins nodded, and slapped the holster at his waist.

"Now," Joe told Purser Jones. "Let's get with it."

Radio Officer Lowndes went on to the bridge of the *Bristol Queen*. Unfamiliar with the waters, Captain Roberts and First Officer Beldam were like cats on hot bricks, despite the presence of Guernsey Pilot Lesueur; the islands to either side were already almost lost in the mist, and so were most of the great black rocks which bordered the channel – but those that could be seen were well clear of the water, even if the tide was turning. They watched the bulk of Nugent's first big ferry looming out of the mist, siren blaring. "Starboard a point," Lesueur told the coxswain.

Roberts peered through the screen, and Lowndes

cleared his throat. "Yes?" Roberts asked over his shoulder.

"We have been instructed to stop, and await a boarding party from St Peter Port, sir," Lowndes said, diffidently.

Roberts stared at him. "Are you out of your mind?"

"I asked for confirmation, sir. It seems . . . well . . ." he glanced at the other three men on the bridge, "that we may have a murderer on board."

Roberts gulped, and looked at the pilot. "What?" Lesueur demanded.

"Someone killed a policeman on the dock. Now they think he may be responsible for two more deaths. He could be masquerading as a schoolboy. The police are coming out to search the ship."

"Holy Mother of God!" Roberts said, thinking of the massed ranks beneath him. "If we panic that lot . . .!"

"We must stop," Lesueur insisted. "Prepare to anchor. You had better make an announcement, Captain. Keep them calm."

Roberts hesitated, then squared his shoulders. "Stop engines, Mr Beldam. Drop anchor." He picked up the tannoy microphone. "This is the captain, speaking," he said. "We have been requested to anchor, so that we may be joined by some more passengers from Guernsey. Please do not be alarmed about this. The delay will only be for a few minutes."

"Good work, skipper," Lesueur said, as the anchor splashed into the sea; the engines were already in neutral.

"More people?" muttered Graham le Prevost, standing at the rail to peer into the mist. Graham was Head Boy at the Grammar School, and was obsessed with a sense of responsibility. Despite the presence of various masters and mistresses, all of these kids were really in his care; it had been decided between them that the Head Girl, Sue le Maitre, would be in charge of that smaller group travelling on the second ship. He had had an exhausting time on the dock before embarkation, trying to keep the kids in orderly lines. They had kept wandering off and coming back, in different positions. Then of course there been that tremendous row down the other end of the dock, with the news that a policeman had been hurt, which had just about spooked the lot, especially when someone had shouted that they had seen two people running down the dock minutes later. Then they had really broken up, and he and Sue had had to call upon all their teachers to get them back under control. He still wasn't sure one or two hadn't just wandered off. Well, he thought: blow it. If they wanted to stay that was their business.

Someone elbowed his way into the throng around Graham. "What the fuck is going on?"

"Watch it," Graham snapped. "There are juniors about." He didn't like kids swearing anyway, although he knew they all did. But when they were seniors, and wearing school uniform, and this was undoubtedly a senior, at least as big as himself and . . . Graham frowned. He knew all of his schoolmates, at least in the upper forms, but he had never seen this bloke before in his life. And – his eyes widened – what was more it was very obvious he had never been at the Grammar School. Quite apart from the fact that his blazer and pants were grotesquely ill-fitting, his hair was unkempt, he badly needed a shave, and he clearly hadn't had a wash, much less a bath, in days. His eyes were wild and staring . . . and there was blood on his hand. "Who the heck are you?" Graham demanded.

"What's it to you?" the stranger said aggressively, peering over the side. "Why are we stopped?"

"Some people coming out from St Peter Port," said the boy on Graham's other side.

Glyn stared into the mist, and made out the blue uniforms. "Sodding coppers!"

Graham frowned at his obvious fright. "You . . . you know about this?"

"Out of my way, punk!" Glyn said, and pushed Graham aside.

316

"Listen . . ." said another of the senior boys, and jumped back, as Glyn flashed his blood-stained knife.

"Heck!"

"A knife!" one of the girls screamed. "He's got a knife."

People threw themselves left and right as Glyn ran along the deck. At the foot of the ladder to the bridge a twelve-year-old girl had slipped trying to get out of his way. He seized her arm and pushed her in front of him.

"Let me go!" she screamed, trying to hit him with her satchel.

"Listen," he said, "shut up, or I'll cut your heart out."

She gasped in terror, and was pushed up the stairs to the bridge. "I'm sorry," First Officer Beldam said. "You can't come in here."

"Get out of my way, mate," Glyn said.

Now Beldam too saw the knife, gasped, and stepped backwards. Glyn pushed the girl into the bridge, stared at Lesueur and Roberts and the cox, who stared back at him: Lowndes had returned to the Radio Room. "What the devil do you think you're doing?" Roberts demanded.

"Get your anchor up, and get moving," Glyn said.

Roberts looked at Lesueur. "He's going to kill me," the girl screamed. "He's got a knife."

"You heard," Glyn snarled. "She won't be the first today."

"I know this one," Lesueur muttered. "He's one of our local nutters; brain dead with drug abuse. He could do it."

Robert picked up the phone. "Just what do you think you're doing?" Glyn demanded.

"Instructing the anchor to be raised," Roberts said. "That's what you wanted, isn't it?"

"Well, watch it." Glyn pushed the girl against the bulkhead, one arm round her neck now, while the other held the knife in front of her, against her white shirt. "Anything I don't like, she gets it."

The girl gasped for breath, nearly fainting in terror. "Please . . ."

"Anchor's weighed, sir," Beldam said.

"Slow ahead, cox," Roberts said.

"Fuck that!" Glyn snapped. "Full speed."

"Look here, in these waters . . ."

"Full speed, God damn it, or I cut her throat!"

Bill Collins sat at the helm of his motorboat, eyes screwed up, squinting into the mist. Two constables sat behind him, more scared of the sea than their errand. They saw the big ferry move by to the left, preparing to enter the harbour as soon as the *Torquay Belle* pulled out. Then PC Nichols, pointed: "There!"

At least the *Bristol Queen* had obeyed orders and anchored, Collins reflected. He opened the throttle. As soon as they were spotted he could see the agitation on her decks, with school children screaming and shouting as they pointed. "Put down a ladder!" he bawled, not really expecting to be heard above the din. But there were two crewmen on the afterdeck, and these dropped a rope ladder.

Collins put his engine in neutral to glide up to the ferry's stern, stood up and grabbed at the swaying rope ladder, but as he did so, the propellers began to turn. The sudden upsurge of water took the motorboat away from beneath his feet, and he was left dangling from the ladder, while Nichols gave a shout and reached for the helm. But now the *Bristol Queen* was moving ahead fast, into the mist. Desperately Collins wrapped his arms and legs round the ladder, which was swinging precariously and banging into the steel sides of the hull. From above him there came a fresh chorus of screams, intermingled with shrieks of "Knife!", while from behind him Nichols gave encouraging shouts as he got the motorboat back under control.

But Collins knew he was close to his man, and with gritted teeth climbed the swaying ladder, being bumped and bruised against the hull. At the top several hands were waiting to help him over the rail. "Where is he?" he demanded.

"On the bridge!"

"With Patsy Fuller!"

"He's threatening to kill her!"

"Right! Move aside." He looked down at the motorboat and the two constables, now falling away astern. The ship was moving at some fifteen knots, and the motorboat was only capable of twelve, flat out – even if the men knew how to handle her they hadn't a hope of catching up. Collins looked at the rocks which seemed to be hurtling by, far too close for comfort. Then he ran for the bridge ladder, while children hastily got out of his way.

"Anything we can do to help?" Graham asked, running beside him.

"No. Keep clear. There's only one of them, isn't there?"

"As far as we know. But Patsy . . ."

"I'm not going to take any risks with Patsy," Collins promised, and reached the ladder. "Hardy," he shouted. "This is Sergeant Collins. Throw down the knife and let the girl go."

"Bugger off," Glyn retorted.

"Just be sensible, man," Collins said. "It isn't possible for you to hijack a whole ship. You don't have a hope in hell."

"So what?" Glyn asked. "I'm for the high jump anyway, ain't I?"

Collins slowly edged up the ladder, watched by the now silent school-children. "Don't make it harder on yourself, Glyn," he said.

"Fuck off," Glyn said. "You come on this bridge, Collins, and I'll cut her throat." Collins checked, his head just below deck level.

On the bridge Lesueur was desperately giving the cox

directions, so that the ferry was moving to and fro as she entered the narrows between the reef north of Herm, known as The Humps, and the rocks off Beaucette Yacht Marina at the north of Guernsey. It was at this moment that Patsy Fuller stamped on Glyn's foot. He gave a yell as she twisted free and threw herself across the bridge. Glyn lunged after her, and Captain Roberts attempted to stop him. Glyn threw him aside and he stumbled into the coxswain, with such force that he released the helm. Instantly the ship swung to the fast-running tide. Lesueur gave a shout of alarm and grasped at the wheel, but as he did so, Glyn, still reaching after Patsy, who was on her hands and knees on the far side of the wheel, drove the knife into his back. Lesueur gave a gasp and fell to the deck, and the ferry continued on its way, out of control. A moment latter there was a shattering crash.

"What the hell was that?" Glen Mahy asked, jerking round. He could see nothing through the mist, but almost immediately the radio chattered.

"Mayday, mayday, mayday," Lowndes shouted. "Ferry *Bristol Queen*, on rocks off the Platte Fougère! Mayday, mayday, mayday!"

"Christ!" Darwin shouted. "Get out there. Glen. Take any and everything you can raise; there are damn near a thousand kids on board that boat and they won't have lifeboats for that number."

Glen ran for the stairs, while Darwin thumbed his mike. "*SS St Pierre!*" he shouted. "Did you hear that?"

"Am proceeding to the casualty immediately," replied the ferry captain.

"*SS St Helier* . . ."

The *St Helier* was just entering the harbour. But her engines were already going astern. "We are responding to the call," her captain said.

Joe Thompson raced up the ladders to gain the deck of the *Torquay Belle*, to find himself in the midst of a mob of screaming school-children and equally agitated adults. "What the hell is happening?" he bellowed.

"She's struck!" Purser Jones gasped. "The *Bristol Queen*. She's struck!"

Joe watched the maroon rockets carving into the misty air, summoning the lifeboat crew. But how the hell were they going to get here? "She's sinking!" one of the schoolgirls screamed. "She's sinking, with all of our friends on board."

The wail spread down the dock. "She's sinking!" People burst from their hitherto orderly rows and ran towards the north-facing carpark, to see for themselves what was happening.

"My kids are on board that ship!" one man shrieked. "My kids!" Lucas could only get out of the way; his orders had not envisaged a catastrophe like this. Then someone saw the big ferries disappearing into the mist.

"They're leaving!" he shouted. "They're abandoning us."

"Rubbish! You know they're not!" Lucas bellowed. "They're going to help the casualty. For God's sake . . ."

The mob continued to surge forward.

"I think," Jackson said, "that you need a break."

"I'll take one," Liz said. "When the siren goes. That's going to be the worst break of my life." He wanted to argue, then decided against it. This was her scene. He was nothing more than a hanger-on. Time to come on strong when she really needed him, which he knew would be when she felt her job was done. Then, he expected a collapse, engendered by exhaustion not less than despair, which would be frightening. "So who's next on the list?" she asked.

"Someone named de la Mare. Down that lane . . ." he checked, at the huge upsurge of noise from the harbour and the Russel. With the wind, however light, still somewhat from the east, the blasting of ships sirens and the firing of the maroons could be heard quite clearly. Moments later a rocket glared in the sky before disappearing. "Something's happened," he snapped. "Should we get down there?"

"What for?" she demanded. "We can't help them, whoever they are and whatever has happened."

He had already braked at the turn-off down to the de la Mare Farm, now they looked at each other, his every instinct being to drive towards the immediate crisis, hers being to continue with her dreadful, but necessary, duty. Then he looked along the road, at the four people who stood there. Three were men, and one a woman. They looked untidy, and frightened, even from a distance. "Maybe they know what's happening," he said, and rolled down his window. "Hi, there! What's the racket down at the dock?"

The group came closer. "How the fuck should we know?" Paddy Glasgow snarled.

Jackson blinked. "I just asked, friend."

"Let's get out of here," Liz muttered.

But the man had stepped in front of the car. "You guys should be at home." A heavily booted skinhead leaned through the open window. "Don't you know there's a curfew?"

"We're working," Jackson said, trying to assert a note of authority; but he got bad vibes as he looked at their eyes. He'd seen people high on drugs before.

"Yeah?" Carole asked. "But you got a home?"

"Of course we have a home," Liz snapped. "Now, would you mind moving . . ." She gasped, as Paddy's hand came out of his pocket, together with his knife. She looked to the left and right and saw that one of the other thugs had a knife, too. And the skinhead produced a piece of metal pipe from behind his back.

"You could take us to your home," Carole said, almost wistfully. "I bet we'd be safe there. And you could feed us. I'm starving."

"We have work to do," Jackson snapped.

Paddy joined skinhead Randy, thrusting the knife forward. "Listen, jerk," he said. "Just do it, eh?"

Liz saw Jackson's hands closing on the wheel, realised he was on the point of exploding. But with Paddy at his window, knife drawn, and the other knife aimed at her, it was hardly the moment for heroics. "It's all right," she said. "We'll take them home, Jackson." Jackson glanced at her, seeking some signal. "Home," she said again. Home was the only place they might find some help.

Paddy and the third man, who had dreadlocks, pulled open the back doors and got in, together with Carole. Randy got in the front beside Liz, forcing her to sit half on his knee, the end of the pipe balanced on the dashboard. Liz gulped.

Jackson drove slowly back to Pierre's house. He was trying to think, but his mind had gone numb. "As we're all gonna die," Paddy said, "we may as well die easy."

"And have some fun doing it," Shaun giggled.

Once again Jackson glanced at Liz, and once again she refused to respond. She guessed he was just needing some signal from her to take them on, and she refused to risk that. He drove into the front yard of Pierre's house and braked. Randy got out, pulling Liz behind him. "Just remember, mate," he told Jackson. "Any funny stuff, and she gets it."

"All done?" Trish asked, opening the door. "I bet you feel like a drink . . ." she stared at Liz and her escort, then at a ginger-bearded man and another with filthy dreadlocks, and a young female with spiky hair and a leather pelmet for a skirt.

"They want food," Liz explained.

"I wouldn't say no to a drink," Paddy of the beard remarked, "unless you can offer a snort."

Trish looked at Jackson, reading the seething anger in his eyes, while he tried to send her a message with his gaze. "Then you'd better come in," Trish said.

Paddy stepped up to her, knife in hand. "How many in there?"

"Why, no one at all," Trish said, and gulped, as the lounge door opened and David came into the passageway.

"What the devil . . .?!" he gazed at the knives, then gave a bellow, advancing with hands held in front of him, edges forming blades as he whipped them through the air, while uttering a succession of heavy grunts. Jackson estimated the distance between himself and the beard, tensed ready to spring. Liz shouted, "Look out for the knives." Trish used her opportunity to dive for the kitchen door.

David charged at Paddy, who took a couple of steps back and the actor never reached his man: Randy, who had followed Trish, stuck out his leg and David tripped over it, hitting the ground with a terrible thump, to lie still. "David!" Liz screamed, trying to run forward, and being checked by her captor.

But assistance was on the way. The kitchen door was opened and Trouble emerged, a huge white bundle of angry energy, who took one look at his fallen master and threw back his head to give a baying howl, and charged . . . followed at a respectable distance by Cocoa and Horlicks, the le Tissier's retrievers and a pack of miscellaneous canine refugees. "Holy shit!" Paddy shouted turning to run for the car . . . and instead ran straight into Jackson's swinging fist, which sank through the beard and connected on the very point of his jaw. He went down without a sound.

Randy had elected to join him, but Trouble had him by the seat of the pants. Carole backed against the car, screaming again and again. Shaun dropped his knife and raised his hands. "Get this dog off me!" Randy screamed.

Liz ignored him. "That was a super punch," she said. "Are you all right?"

Jackson was trying to unclench his fist. "A few broken bones, I think," He nudged the motionless Paddy with his toe. "Hopefully he has one too."

"What about you?" Trish asked, kneeling beside David as he sat up and rubbed his head.

"Amazing," he remarked. "I did that in a film once, and knocked out four chaps."

As he spoke, the siren began to wail.

Chapter 27

MONDAY, 25TH JULY – MID-MORNING

The siren's wail rose and fell, surged and receded like waves of nausea, washing through the open doorway to penetrate into each room, each corner of the old farmhouse. It submerged them all in the fearful horror of its warning . . . all except the dogs. Trouble continued to stand guard over his quarry, while his lieutenants, Cocoa and Horlicks stood snarling, teeth bared at the intruders on the floor and the other hounds circled the yard at speed with their discordant chorus.

Jackson had watched the whole episode in slow motion; only the ache in his arm and hand seemed truly real. Time had almost stood still as dogs, feet and arms had hurtled through the air. Now, as the warning filled the minds of all eight of them, fear drew a motionless grey mask over their faces. Even the dogs now slowed to a stop, hackles raised, tails stretched straight with aggression. Jackson stared at Liz. She looked so tiny and vulnerable in her stained jeans and tee-shirt, hair dishevelled and face drained of all colour save for the black circles under her eyes. "Bed," he ordered. "You cannot be of any further use to man nor beast until you've had some rest."

She was finding it hard to breathe normally, lungs snatching short gasps of air. "What about these . . .?" Her hand flicked a brief gesture over the floor.

"I'll deal with them," David said. "Got any box cord?"

Trish nodded. "In the utility. I'll get it."

"I'll give you a hand," Jackson said, leaning over the smelly creature with matted dreadlocks. "How does nature manage to produce this human garbage?" The question was purely rhetorical.

Trish waited, holding the scissors, until the last of the gang was bound up, before taking Liz firmly by the arm and marching her into her bedroom. The men surveyed their handiwork. "What'll we do with them?" David asked. "I suppose we'll have to keep them inside."

"I'll call the police to take them away, as soon as they can. Meanwhile, why don't we just leave them here in the hallway?" Jackson saw that the cords were cutting into the flesh on their wrists and ankles. But what the hell, it was the least they deserved.

"Okay, skipper. Then why don't you go take some kip, too? You can soothe the little lady's troubled mind at the same time."

Carole started to scream and shout. "You bloody effin' bastards! You carn' leave us lying 'ere. We knows our rights!"

The three others joined in, shouting and swearing.

"Has Liz got any tough packing tape?" David asked. "We'll have to gag this lot to get any peace."

The threat silenced them. "Now," Trish said, returning, "let's get Tangle and the goat and the pig in here as well."

The wreck of the *Bristol Queen* was perched on the rocks just south of the Platte Fougère; she had been travelling so fast and struck the rocks so hard that she was firmly held, and thus had been unable to sink. Everywhere there were people. Every available boat which could get out was there. The entrance to the Beaucette Marina was dry when the ferry had stranded, but a few boatowners had managed to drag inflatable dinghies across the rock sill, and relaunch them in deeper water to reach the casualty. Small power boats had swarmed up from St Sampson's and Bordeaux Harbour and St Peter Port, in many cases having to be dragged over rocks and sand to put to sea. Nugent's two big ferries were still standing by in the Russel, having lowered all of their boats, and the *Bristol Queen* had put down her own.

Schoolchildren had been taken on board the other ferries, or landed on the shingle beaches to each side of Beaucette; the entire north-eastern shore of Guernsey seemed to be a mass of green, crimson and navy-blue blazers, and the chatter of voices sent the sea-birds sweeping high into the sky.

The Bailiff had driven out to the north, accompanied by Thompson, and was listening to the reports given him by Collins, who, as the man on the spot, had largely organised the rescue operation. "You mean there were no deaths at all?" The Bailiff was astonished – and relieved.

"Not one, sir. Although Pilot Lesueur is in a critical condition."

"And this fellow Hardy?"

Collins grinned. "He's in custody, sir. I'm afraid he suffered a few minor injuries . . . resisting arrest."

The Bailiff stuck his tongue in his cheek. "I'm glad to hear it. Now what we need are those other thugs."

"Oh, we've got most of them, sir," Joe said. "A report came in just before we left the office. Seems four of them, including Shaun Scott himself – that's the one stabbed Sergeant Crowe – attacked some people out at St Andrew's . . . and got more than they bargained for. They're all in custody."

"Well, thank God that turned out all right." He got into his car, Joe beside him, and they began their drive back to town. "But it's still a God-awful mess. We've got to find berths for those kids . . . what's that?" He pointed at the ship steaming out of St Peter Port Harbour.

"That's the *Torquay Belle*, sir. As she's fully loaded, I told her to move out."

"What's her complement? All school-children?"

"I'm afraid not, sir. Six hundred adults, two hundred

children. I didn't know what was happening when I told her to carry on."

"You did the right thing, at the time," the Bailiff said.

"No man can do more than that. But the fact is . . . those shipwrecked kids will have to be loaded on to one of Nugent's ships, and then . . . I don't know if we have the time to load anyone else. That cloud was over Alderney when I had the siren sounded, and that was an hour ago. It'll be at Sark by now. By the time we get those ships back alongside, it'll be another half hour . . . all those people, lined up on the dock, exposed . . . we'll have to try to get them back under cover, Joe."

Joe did not reply. He knew that that was going to be an almost impossible task. Just re-establishing control was going to be difficult enough. As they drove along the esplanade there were people everywhere, staring out to sea, staring east; some were just standing – mute and dazed, others shouting and arguing . . . Tell this lot they couldn't leave and there would be a riot. They were being forced to drive dead slow; the Bailiff punched one of his preset numbers, "Willy? What's your reading?"

"No increase, Sir Hugh."

"But it'll be here any moment. Damn!" Joe had braked hard to prevent hitting a group of people running across the road, jolting the Bailiff against his seat belt. "Where are all your policemen, man?"

"Helping with the rescue. But, sir . . ." Joe's voice was suddenly choked with excitement. "Look!" The Bailiff raised his head, and gazed at the flag flying above Castle Cornet. It was streaming in the suddenly freshening breeze . . . towards the east! "Walter's westerly weather!" Joe breathed. "Oh, glory be!"

Mrs Lawson put the empty watering can away in the shed and walked back up the garden to the house where sparrows were arguing under the eaves. How peaceful it was since the destroyers had left yesterday; she had had her best night's sleep in years. As for leaving Alderney herself, and abandoning her pets, that was absolute rubbish. Behind her the blackbirds swooped onto the freshly mown lawn and hopped, heads on one side, seeking the next meal. A thrush was breaking a snail out of its shell. She looked at the old oak clock on the kitchen mantlepiece. Ten past twelve! She'd been gardening nearly all morning. Time to start making some lunch, she thought as she put her hands under the tap . . . not that she felt very hungry. Maybe she'd got a touch too much sun.

Her old tabby cat rolled and stretched happily on the concrete step outside the backdoor, and the dogs lay sleeping in the shade of the cherry tree.

Yes, I'll go for a lie down too, after my lunch, she decided.

Eddie had had a good lunch and was sitting in the harbourside cafe with his coffee and cognac when he heard a fisherman shouting to his friends. He looked up, and saw the man pointing at the pennant on a masthead. The offshore wind had had it streaming out towards the Atlantic all morning, then, just as Madame served his *côte d'agneau* he had noticed it flapping idly round in all directions. Now, he smiled to himself, this really does look hopeful. A breeze was building by the minute, inshore from the west.

The Bailiff put down the phone and surveyed the faces in front of him. "It seems certain that the westerlies will continue for the next few days at the least."

Paul Pritchard wiped sweat from his face. "You mean it's over?"

"Something like this can never be over," the Bailiff said. "Radioactivity levels are dropping over the Cotentin Peninsular, and are being recorded over the Channel. The cloud appears to be moving up towards the Straits of Dover, and that means both Kent and the Pas de Calais are at risk. However, it is definitely dissipating into the atmosphere: the recording levels are dropping all the time. There are of course going to be horrendous side effects from all of this, but we have got to manage as best we can, and be thankful for small mercies."

"You mean we can start bringing everyone back?" the Comptroller asked.

"The Home Office feels that would be premature, at least as regards the children. We have to be absolutely sure there is no contamination here. But I think we can stop the evacuation. If there has been any radioactive material deposited on the island, it is certainly not sufficient to affect healthy adults."

"And Alderney?" Joe Thompson asked.

The Bailiff's expression became grave. "Willy has reported a lethal level of fall-out. But whether that was confined to the area near our monitor or actually reflects the count islandwide we won't know until the Home Office sends in their experts complete with equipment and protection. As far as we know at this moment, it looks like the worst possible scenario. Thank God we got everyone off." He looked around the faces. "I suppose we are quite sure of this?"

"I'm afraid I don't know," Joe admitted. "Everyone was supposed to leave, but . . ."

There was a knock on the door, and Sergeant Collins entered. "Sorry to bother you, sir, but Hank Applegate and Jane McAvoy are here, looking for an interview."

"Oh, yes," the Bailiff said. "I think I owe them that."

Hank and Jane both looked very windswept: they had just returned from Beaucette where they had been filming the rescue of the school-children from the wreck of the *Bristol Queen*. "May we ask, sir, for some words on the evacuation?" Jane asked. "It has been halted, hasn't it."

"Yes," the Bailiff said.

"Because of the imminent arrival of the death cloud?"

The Bailiff smiled at Hank's camera. "Because the death cloud is not going to arrive, Jane. Listen."

Outside, the sirens wailed to a continuous crescendo, sounding the all clear.

Chapter 28

AFTERMATH

Janet had always refused to cross the Bay of Biscay, after her first trip south through a vicious storm. Instead, she had flown to Gibraltar each year to join Peter for the more pleasant cruise in the western Mediterranean. And each year he had told her of the perfect weather conditions he had had on the trip down – "such a shame she had missed it". There was no question of flying down this time, and she supposed it was inevitable that the weather should turn foul again in her honour. Which was bad enough in itself, but to make matters infinitely worse, every last one of their eight unwanted passengers was throwing up, everywhere. At first they had taken over the guest head, queueing outside, banging on the door and moaning, she having wisely omitted to mention the other head *en suite* in the master cabin. But now the human cargo were past caring where they deposited their previous meals . . . and the entire yacht was stinking. "Oh God!" a dishevelled female yelled seeing Peter emerging from the after cabin, having shaved. "Are we sinking?"

He screwed up his face at the stench. "What are you on about? Of course we're not sinking!"

"Then who's holding the steering wheel?"

"We're on auto pilot," Janet explained gently. "Look, couldn't you possibly use this bucket?"

Peter stepped over the woman's legs to climb into the cockpit and adjust the sails; what had been a reach last night had suddenly become a beat, and the wind remained strong. Then he went back down to the saloon and the radio. "The wind direction has altered," he said, to no one in particular. "Let's hear what's happening." It took a while for him to pick up reasonable reception on an English speaking channel, cutting into the middle of a forecast which mentioned all areas of the west European seaboard other than their own. "Damn. We've missed the beginning," he said, reaching to switch off . . . then paused, hand in mid air. ". . . that the radioactive cloud over northern France and the English Channel is now drifting towards the North Sea before a strong sou'westerly wind, which is forecast to continue for at least the next twenty-four hours. The Bay of St Malo and the Channel Islands are therefore no longer under threat of radioactive fall-out. The French Government . . ."

A shout went up from the passengers. Peter switched off and headed back to the companionway. "Now we can go back home," someone yelled.

"Ye-es!" chorussed the others, seasickness temporarily forgotten.

"No!" said Peter. "We are maintaining our course for Corunna."

"Not bloody likely, mate. We're going back to Guernsey!" This from a funny little bloke in a trilby.

Peter continued up through the hatch, ignoring him.

"I'm not havin' that!" Trilby told his friends. "I'm bloody well goin' to tell 'im!" and he followed Peter into the cockpit.

Janet wondered which would last up there the longest . . . Peter's temper or the trilby hat.

Liz never took pills: she hated them. But to-day was an exception. Swallowed with a cup of camomile tea, the Panadol suppressed her headache, helping her to relax a little, and by the time Jackson joined her she was dozing off. But it wasn't a peaceful sleep; he watched her twisting about, grimacing, muttering. Twice she raised her head shouting "No!", and then drifted off again. Then he slept for awhile, and when he woke she was snoring softly, so he slid gently out of bed, dressed and crept off to the kitchen.

It took her several minutes to surface through the sleep haze, even longer to register that she was in Pierre and Annabel's bed. Then she sat up with a start, looking round for a clock. Two thirty? Daylight, therefore afternoon. "Oh good Lord! The Ozanne and the de la Mare cows!" she muttered aloud. "I've got to get out to them . . . without letting any radiation into the house."

She staggered into her clothes and found David and Trish, Jackson and Polly in the kitchen, chatting happily with the backdoor open. . . "Are you people mad!" She slammed it shut.

The four of them burst out laughing and Jackson gathered her up into his arms, her feet kicking in mid air. "It's over, my darling. It's all over. The dust never got here, and now it's travelling away at the rate of knots."

Liz frowned at him. "Over? How do you know?"

"The Bailiff was on the box half an hour ago," Polly squealed excitedly. "The All Clear was sounded. Went on for ages."

"Are you sure? I didn't hear anything." Then she glared at Jackson. "Why didn't you wake me?"

"You were so darned tired, honey. You were sleeping like a baby and I hadn't the heart." Jackson sat her on the edge of the table. "Here, sweetheart, have some of your brother's champagne." He tilted the bottle over an empty flute and passed it to her.

She stared at him, aghast. "You can't be serious!" A sob caught in her throat. "Don't you realise what this means? We have spent most of the morning murdering animals unnecessarily . . . and now you want me to celebrate!" She covered her face with her hands and rushed out of the room.

"Oh shit!" David commented.

* * *

It was nearly five o'clock before the buses arrived to take people home from the Underground Hospital, and Clive and Mildred Falla were almost the last to be dropped at their house, so it was nearer six when Clive put the key in the frontdoor. "That's funny," Mildred said, standing in the doorway of the lounge. "Where's the telly?"

Clive looked over her shoulder. "And the video. Lordy! And Mum's clock. It was on the bookcase." They rushed from room to room to see what else had gone. "The portable radio cassette player," Clive called from the bedroom.

"And my new microwave! You'd better call the police."

"I'm trying. But all I get is some blessed recorded message. Tell you what," Clive said as he ran downstairs again. "I'm getting the car out. Quicker to drive down there," and he dashed out of the door. Two minutes later he was back in the kitchen. "It's gone. The car's gone, too!"

In Mrs Lawson's garden in Alderney the birds were no longer singing. She didn't notice it at first: she wasn't feeling very well and had gone to lie on her bed for a nap after lunch. She still wasn't feeling too good, but decided a cup of tea would put her right. In the kitchen one of the dogs was whining at the door so she let him out . . . and then she noticed the silence. Picking up the jar of bird seed, she went out to put some on the birdtable. There was a bluetit on it . . . dead.

Mrs Lawson looked puzzled. Surely the cat couldn't have got up there . . . "Tommy!" she called. Sometimes he slept down by the garden shed, so she walked along the gravel path. A blackbird was there in front of her, flapping its wings in distress, and as she got near it suddenly heeled over. It was still alive, but as she held it in her hands, smoothing its feathers, it went limp. "Tommy," she called again. But she couldn't wait for him. She had to run back inside to the toilet. There was a terrible pain in her stomach.

Tommy had heard her, but he couldn't move. He was lying hidden under a bush, panting. Each breath was more painful than the last.

Owen Clark's truck was much in demand, but Maggie Ferbrache had bagged him first. Together they caught all the cats in her bedroom and shoved them back into their boxes, or someone else's which didn't seem to matter, and loaded them up. Then there were the birds and the dogs and the hamsters. There wasn't half enough accommodation for them all at the Animal Shelter, but by putting two or three to a run wherever possible, she managed to cram them in.

When Owen dropped her at home and she walked into the cottage she reeled back. Damn what a stink! She fetched a plastic pail from under the sink and filled it with a strong solution of hot water, Pine disinfectant and Ajax, wondering if it would ever be possible to scrub away the smell.

The argument was still raging when they berthed in Corunna, two days later. Miraculously, the trilby hat survived the voyage but had certainly developed character on the trip. Right now it was bouncing up and down, along with the little man underneath it, who was making very little progress with Peter Barrington. "You had no business to come on down here with us, when we all wanted to get back to the island."

"Much against my better judgement," Peter told him, "I allowed myself to be talked into saving your life, plus the lives of your family. Now I suggest you take yourself off to the local Tourist Office, or the British Consul, and get yourselves on to planes or trains, anything heading north."

"I'll do no such thing! You brought us here and we are staying on your boat till . . ."

"Till you've scrubbed out the stench of your joint offerings. Good idea. The yacht is unliveable in at the moment."

Trilby opened and shut his mouth making no sound, as the surgeon walked away to join his wife in the restaurant of a rather chic hotel.

A little colour was creeping back into Janet's cheeks as she sipped a medicinal cognac. "I suppose we shouldn't have brought them this far," she began. "Perhaps we should take them back . . . and maybe Parker could be persuaded . . ." she was thinking about the beautiful prestigious home they had left and all the possessions she'd abandoned.

Peter flopped into a chair opposite. He was having similar thoughts; yes, the house was the most impressive amongst all his colleagues' properties; his was one of the largest yachts in the island, though small in comparison with Mediterranean standards; he was one of the senior medics, shown due deference by his juniors and within the wide social circle in which he moved . . . he and Janet, of course. But they could never go back. Not now. Scared out of his wits he had run like a rabbit . . . left his colleagues to get on with it . . . signed a contract to sell his house. It had seemed like the sane and sensible thing to do, at the time . . . but in retrospect . . . Dammit, he should never have allowed Janet to talk him into it.

"Don't be so damn stupid, woman! For a start, you would have to put that silly animal of yours in quarantine." He scowled at the poodle on her lap.

"Where are we going to live if we don't go back?"

It was a question that had been troubling him for most of their journey. France? Spain? Italy? He didn't fancy any of them, chiefly because so few of these confounded foreigners could speak English. And anyway, getting the money out of Parker could take time. "On the boat, of course. Where on earth did you imagine?"

That's it, Janet decided. At the first opportunity I'm going back to England to live with my sister. She has a huge house, with ample room for all my things when I collect them from the island. Peter can find someone else to be beastly to for the rest of his life. But it won't be me!

* * *

Everyone had a story to tell . . . of arriving in England and being herded into warehouses, church halls and even a concert theatre . . . anywhere large enough to accommodate such numbers. Some claimed to have been offered sympathy, generosity and kindness; others swore they had been treated like cattle. One contingent had been subjected to a thorough examination for lice, which caused considerable indignation. Several groups had found themselves stranded in France without money or transport and had had amazing adventures getting back. A number of seasonal workers from the United Kingdom decided not to return.

Several people returned to their homes to find everything of value had been removed. Much was tracked down, the culprits pleading that the homes had been abandoned, giving them the right to take what they pleased. A few non-Guernsey people decided they no longer had any desire to live under the threat of another nuclear cloud and moved – in more than one instance nearer to a nuclear plant than Guernsey had been: but not knowing this they felt much safer.

The Flamanville Nuclear Power Station was closed down . . . and Lynn Battle took the credit.

In September, Pierre and Annabel le Tissier gave another Barbecue Party in their garden. The sun had shone all day, but it was almost dark when the first guests arrived. "Katey, Milford, lovely to see you," Annabel kissed them both, leading them through the house onto the back terrace. "You remember Pierre's aunt, Trish? She's staying with us for the week-end."

Penelope, Ros and Niall were serving jugs of *sangria*, while Pierre was lighting the grill. "Hi, you folk," Pierre called. "Got yourselves straight, yet?"

Katey looked as lovely as ever, in an ankle length skirt printed with tangerine flowers, and a matching tangerine cotton blouse. Her large plastic beads and earrings were green, like her sandals. But there was something different about her face. Liz appeared from the kitchen, drying her hands on her borrowed pinny. "Hi, Katey. How are you?" But as she leaned forward for the customary pecks on the cheek she paused. "You don't look quite your old self. Everything okay?"

Katey grimaced. "I'm not sure I ever want to be my old self . . ." she began.

Liz stared at her, head on one side. "What do you mean? Why on earth not?"

"I'm not very proud of the way I reacted to the emergency, that's why."

"Go on?"

Katey shrugged. "I was awful! All that seemed to matter was my possessions. My home. Poor Milford was working his butt off for so many people, and I was doing nothing for anybody. I just moped and wept and felt sorry for myself. I really am ashamed."

Liz put her arms round her friend. "We all have our strengths and our weaknesses. I suppose in the normal course of events they don't show up, much. But in a time of crisis . . . I went to pieces, afterwards, ranting and weeping alternately, distraught about all the animals we had put down."

"But you had to, there was no choice, was there?"

"Not really. And one has only to read of the suffering of animals left in Alderney, the death of poor Mrs Lawson, to realise the extent of the impending disaster here. But in my mind I contrived to assume responsibility for all the exterminations, myself. Very childish and pompous of me." She shuddered. "I know that, now, but I don't think I'll ever get over it. I still have nightmares."

Suddenly hordes of people were arriving, all at once. Glen Mahy came with his parents, Walter Marquis and his wife, and Bert Darwin. Owen Clark arrived with Maggie Ferbrache. On leaving the office the day before, Pierre had run into Hank Appleyard and Jane MacAvoy and asked them along; they arrived minus cameras. A huge bunch of helium balloons appeared, with Mike Cobb clutching the strings, singing Land of Hope and Glory at the top of his voice. "And what a beautiful, balmy evening it is," he said, giving Annabel a smacking great kiss.

"Somewhat better than our last barbecue, thank goodness," Pierre grinned. "If we all had to eat indoors tonight we'd stifle: thanks to dear Auntie Trish it's impossible to open any of our windows!"

"How long were you away?" Bert Darwin asked.

"Longer than we'd intended. We ran out of fuel in Perros, which still seemed rather too close to Flamanville for comfort, So the four of us got on a bus, going south."

Annabel took up the story. "It was hilarious – in retrospect. The passengers all decided the route, down through Pontivy. Second class roads, up hill and down dale until the poor old bus collapsed trying to make the incline in the Forêt de Camois. Eventually we reached a campsite in Vannes on a trailer towed by an obliging farmer with a tractor . . ."

"And there we stayed for over a week, penniless, until I managed to persuade a French bank to part with sufficient funds to pay our debts and head for home."

Polly arrived and shyly introduced her boyfriend.

Suddenly there were whoops and shouts of greetings and a massive streak of white shot into the crowd to hurl itself at Jackson. "Trouble! What are you doing here you old devil?"

Fortunately Cocoa and Horlicks had come to the party and, together with Annabel's golden retrievers, they collected their friend and bounced away into the garden. Liz threw her arms round David's neck. "Am I pleased to see you, you old reprobate! When did you get back from England?"

"Last week. As soon as I had persuaded Forsythe to come back and look after me."

"How long are you staying?" She knew that no one

could return to Alderney, where the radiation count remained dangerously high.

"For keeps. I've just bought a house over here."

"What? Where?" Liz was genuinely pleased. David was one of the people for whom she had developed enormous respect during the emergency.

"Not far from here. Bought it off a chap called Eddie Parker."

Milford's head jerked up. "Eddie Parker, you say? You'd better be careful of any dealings with him."

David grinned. "You mean because he's on the list of people to be investigated for profiteering out of the emergency? Yes," he nodded, "I know all about him. But this is a straight transaction. I had a pal of yours in Court Row look into it. But I agree, he is a right little shyster."

Milford laughed. "You can say that again! But not to worry, he's already met his come-uppance. Seems half the cars in his yard are without registration books, and while he was out of the island a bunch of felons did the lot over, radios, batteries and tyres gone, and anything else moveable. And it would appear that the police have not been very sympathetic."

Glen's father, John Mahy, hooted. "I'm glad to hear it! Mum has often told me how the people who made money on the black market during the occupation lost the lot when they were investigated after the war."

Milford nodded. "Eddie thought he was going to make a million out of the Guernsey Donkeys. What he doesn't realise is that we've got one hell of a kick. He'll never be able to sell a button over here, after this."

"Right, everyone," Pierre called. "Your meat will soon be cooked. So will you help yourselves to starters, please."

"Just one moment," Jackson held up his hand. "While we are all gathered around I would like to announce that Liz and I are to be married next month."

There was a chorus of cheers and congratulations, a trifle subdued in the cases of Glen and Mike. Then Jane

MacAvoy stepped up onto the terrace. "I don't want to steal anyone's thunder," she said, "But I would like to take this opportunity to announce that Hank and I have decided to get hitched, too."

More cheers and back slapping. Then Ros and Niall appeared beside her, looking embarrassed. "Er . . ." Ros began, then dried up.

Niall cleared his throat. "We're going to be married soon, too."

"What?" Pierre demanded. "Who says?"

"Darlings!" Annabel laughed. "You're both far too young. There is plenty time . . ."

Her elder daughter swallowed hard. "Mummy, we must."

"Must? But why, my darling?"

"Because we're going to have a baby!"

There was a moment's deathly hush, then David shouted "Well done! Congratulations!"

And everyone joined in. And the kissing started all over again.

EPILOGUE

The Bailiff sat in the Governor's office sipping a whisky and soda. It was November, but the wind and rain lashing the windows scarcely registered on the two men. "Do you think, Hugh, that your island will ever be the same again?" HE asked.

There was a long silence before Sir Hugh replied. "One cannot answer that with a firm Yes or No. Yes the people, the spirit of the islanders will always survive, no matter what. If one reads the island's history over the past two millenia, you will see that. On the other hand, No. There are some aspects of our lives which will be forever changed. The island economy has been severely damaged. As you know, the States are claiming enormous sums of compensation from the French Government, but it will be years, probably, before the matter is cleared up. Then there are all the private, individual claims as well."

His Excellency nodded gravely. "What a terrible task you have had to face. My wife and I think you coped marvellously. There were so many diverse problems to be dealt with in such a short space of time."

Sir Hugh sighed. "True. But we had a tremendous committee sharing the responsibility. And voluntary helpers."

"Tell me, in retrospect, what would you say was the single, worst problem you had to face?"

The Bailiff didn't hesitate. "The fear factor," he said. "Undoubtedly the fear factor."